To Make You Feel My Love

MAGGIE WELLS

To Make You Feel My Love

Copyright © 2020, Margaret Ethridge

Cover Art Design by Margaret Ethridge

Editorial by Lopt & Cropt Editing Services

ISBN: 978-0-9963586-6-8

First Edition, May 2020

DEDICATION

For Bill – Thanks for letting me be me.

ACKNOWLEDGMENTS

This book would never have been created without the support of Julie Doner, my critique partner in crime, and my Super Cool Party People. Special thanks to the Super Sara(h)s: Sarah Pesce of Lopt & Cropt editing for her skill, patience, and care with my characters, and Sara Megibow, and her unwavering enthusiasm for my writing.

And you, dear readers. Thank you for reading!

1

Pulse pounding. Feet stamping. Whistles. Howls.

A tidal wave of applause washed over her as she took one final bow. A sea of glow sticks and cell screens undulated in front of her. The noise was as warm and welcome as a lover's embrace.

This was what Brittany Owens was born to do.

She thrust both hands high in the air. The red-sequined microphone she clutched caught the stage lights as she waved both arms in wide arcs, shooting dazzling sparkles of love right back at the audience. She did love them, nearly as much as she loved being on stage. Every grueling minute of it. The B.S. she had to deal with offstage drove her nuts, but this…this was everything.

If she didn't go, they'd keep screaming for more. She didn't want the set to end, but it wasn't her show. She was one of a slew of performers slated to play the Pieces for Peace concert. Brit certainly wasn't the biggest name on the ticket, but the gig marked the last stop on an extensive North American tour. Her latest single had been getting tons of airplay on both the country and pop stations. Her previous release was covered on a national singing competition. Download numbers were through the roof, and judging from the crowd's reaction, she was gaining momentum. Her public relations and social media teams were running at full tilt. The video they'd uploaded of the entire team breaking down into giddy shenanigans over a minor wardrobe malfunction during one never-ending rehearsal session had gone viral.

Her momager was ecstatic.

After another full body wave, she blew kisses to the sold-out crowd then dashed for the wings. Sweat rolled down her face and back. The skintight jumpsuit she wore was spangled and fringed, but had enough stretch to allow her to keep up with her back-up dancers. Unfortunately, it didn't contain one iota of natural fiber. Thank God she wouldn't have to wear this particular costume again. The next album would unveil another phase of Brittany Owens's metamorphosis.

She was leaving this stage a former child-star-turned-pop-star, but when she came back, she'd be a chart-topping phenomenon.

Her mother would settle for nothing less. Neither would she.

Though Brit was completely on board with the whole plan for world domination, at the moment she was tired of touring and anxious to get into the studio. And escape her mother's micromanaging for a few days.

Merle Owens's star power might have skipped a generation, but it had landed squarely on Brit's shoulders. Her mother, Wydetta, intended to make the most of the family legacy. Being Merle's only grandchild had given her advantages in terms of money and opportunity. People thought Merle was God's gift to country music. Brittany yearned for the same kind of adulation, but she wanted to earn every accolade on her own.

Every bit of her hair, makeup, stage attire, and offstage styling were all a part of the master plan she and her mother had so meticulously dreamed up, but the talent and drive were hers. God's gift to Brit. And it was one she had no intention of squandering.

Wydetta appeared at her side as if conjured. "Hydrate."

The microphone was plucked from her hand and a bottle of water shoved into her clutching fingers. The roadies were shifting equipment and resetting for the next performer. Brit looked up to find her mother scowling fiercely at one of the backing musicians hustling onto the stage. Teams of veteran studio players had been tapped to back up performers not traveling with their own bands, but the music industry was like a small town. It wouldn't be a stretch to find a number of people they knew on the stage. Brit followed Wydetta's gaze and found the object of her mother's annoyance was busy fiddling with his guitar strap. Her heart did a slow flip.

She didn't need to see the man's face to know who he was. The muscular slope of his shoulders, the line of his back, the tight ass covered in perfectly worn-in blue jeans. Scuffed western-style boots replaced the flashier pairs she remembered him favoring, but stylistic changes didn't fool her. She'd memorized every bit of him long ago. Been fantasizing about the one single kiss they'd shared since she'd last seen him, five years ago. Dreamed about him falling in love with her for even longer.

Like a deer scenting danger in the air, he lifted his head, and for Brit, the commotion surrounding them fell away.

Thankfully, the intensity of Wydetta's glare hadn't generated one of those red dots at the center of his forehead, though if looks could kill, her mother would have tagged and bagged Cash Dorsett years ago. But Brit couldn't help but stare at him, transfixed. This wasn't the Cash she knew. Back in the day, he'd been all swagger and bravado. Tonight, he simply looked... resigned.

And possibly regretful.

Their eyes met and her mouth ran dry.

As if reading her mind, her mother nudged her. "Drink your water."

Like an automaton, Brit uncapped the bottle and raised it to her lips. Holding his gaze, she downed half the contents. He didn't blink. Nor did he look away when she wiped her mouth with the back of her hand, accidentally smearing the thick red gloss she'd worn on stage. She cringed when his mouth twitched into a half-smile. Before she could wipe the streak of gluey gloss from her cheek, he shifted his weight, allowing the spotlight to shine on his instrument and leaving his face in shadow.

She stared at the shadowed silhouette of him. He looked different, but the same. Older, but not worn. More like he'd finally fit into his skin. Confident. Centered. Not words she would have ever ascribed to the man he'd been. No matter how cocky he'd acted in his heyday, Cash Dorsett had chosen flight over fight. Not literally. He'd simply dropped out of the music scene, but Nashville wasn't New York City. Their paths were bound to cross here and there, but they hadn't. He hadn't left town, he'd simply disappeared from her life.

He'd hidden himself from her, just as he'd stepped out of the spotlight moments before. But she still saw him. She saw him more clearly than he could ever imagine.

When she caught him looking at her again, she raised one

eyebrow in unspoken challenge, beamed a saucy grin at him, then turned away. The frown lines between her mother's brows cut deeper.

"You're showing your elevens, Wydetta," she said with a pointed nod at her mother's forehead. "Smooth 'em out and hoist the girls up a couple inches," she advised, letting her gaze drop. "Here comes Sir James Paulson."

Wydetta threw back her shoulders and thrust out her assets. Her mother might not have inherited her father's musical abilities, but she certainly inherited her mother's famous figure. It used to make Brit giggle when someone referred to her MeeMaw as the Bayou Bombshell. Of course, she'd seen the old photographs. She knew exactly why PawPaw had picked her out of a crowd. Brit made a point of not thinking about her grandparents' relationship beyond in anything but a grandparently way.

"Thanks for riling them up a bit for me, love."

As susceptible to a husky British accent as any woman with breath in her body, Brit turned and found herself gazing into the crinkling brown eyes of Sir James Paulson. The man was only a decade younger than her grandfather, but an accumulation of years didn't dampen the effect he had on females in the vicinity. Sir James was a legend for many, many reasons, and not all of them were musical. Tales of his early romantic conquests were as ubiquitous as his four-decade songbook. The story of his love affair with his late wife, the stuff of romantic legend.

"My pleasure." She whipped out the sexy-sassy smirk she'd been perfecting since her days as the feisty songstress on the hit television show, *TeenScreen*, then she added the word, "Sir," with a playful wink.

His mouth curved in appreciation. "Does your mother know about you?"

She tipped her head toward Wydetta. "Ask her yourself."

The older man turned in surprise and gave Wydetta a once-over so thorough, Brit felt the need to avert her eyes. Of course, when she did, they landed smack on Cash. The lighting tech had captured him again, and for a heart-stopping moment, he stood in a pool of blue-white light. She swallowed with a painful gulp when she realized he was subjecting her to the same sort of all-consuming inspection her mother had just undergone. But Cash's interest in her didn't feel as playful as Sir James's inspection of her mother.

He snatched a black cowboy hat from atop a set of amps and settled it low on his brow. Tearing her gaze from him, she tuned in to hear Sir James was saying to Wydetta, "Meeting your father was one of the most inspirational experiences of my life. I'm a big fan."

Her mother poured on the Southern charm like she was drenching a short stack with maple syrup. "I'll be sure to remember you to him. I'm sure Daddy will be pleased as punch to hear how much you enjoyed shootin' the breeze with him."

Disconcerted by seeing Cash, and too tired to try to keep up with her mother's verbal volleys, Brit closed her eyes and practiced some meditative breathing. Her stubborn heart refused to slow. Beyond the curtain, pockets of fans continued to chant her name. She let her eyes drift shut as she drank it in, letting their energy feed hers.

Big things were about to happen for her. Wow things. Huge things. She could feel it. So could the sharks who circled her every day. She needed to stay centered. Focused on the music and what she wanted her career to be. She may have been born a country music princess, then fashioned into a television star, but Brit was determined not to stop until she ruled the pop charts as well.

There were strategies. Massive campaigns drawn up like battle plans. Some she liked, others she didn't, but she could sort the details out later. She already had fame and fortune, but this next step would give her something different. Something few people managed to gain, much less sustain.

Superstardom.

It would be hers. Not because her record label, publicity team, or her mama wanted it, but because *she* did. And she'd have it on her own terms.

An electrifying riff jolted her from her inner thoughts. When she opened her eyes, she found Cash watching her, his hand wrapped tight around the neck of his guitar. The chord hung in the air as he stepped up to the nearest mic and murmured, "Check. Check. Check," never taking his eyes off her.

Brit jumped when Sir James stepped up beside her. "Good to go, fellas?" he called to the assembled musicians.

"We're ready."

The rest of the backstage crew likely assumed Cash was answering the rock legend's question, but she knew better. He was speaking to her, whether he wanted to admit it or not. And she was ready too. For everything.

Particularly for him.

"I'm heading back to the hotel," Brit announced. She shot Sir James a pointed glance, then turned to her mother. "Are you coming?"

Wydetta paused for a moment, then turned back to Brittany. "You run along. I want to stay for this last set, then I'll meet you back at the hotel. Remember, we're leaving at the crack of dawn."

Brit snorted softly, dividing a look between her mother and the rock legend standing in the wings. "Looks like I'm not the one who needs to be reminded about our early morning. See you on the bus."

With a wave, her daughter was gone. Wydetta moved to the side as introductions were made and Sir James took the stage. He raised one arm over his head and waved to the roaring crowd. He took his spot behind the mic stand, but the noise did not abate. Grinning like a boy, he acknowledged the adulation coming at him by making two swooping bows, his hands pressed together at his chest in prayer position.

When the crowd showed no sign of giving up, he laughed, shook his head, and plucked the mic off the stand. "We're going to have to calm down a little bit otherwise you won't be able to hear the lads," he said, hooking a thumb at the band behind him.

Wydetta's gaze clicked to the far side of the stage, where Cash Dorsett stood at the ready, his guitar slung low across his hips and his fingers working the fretboard in anticipation. He struck a chord, and Sir James Paulson was off and running.

As they settled into the short set, Wydetta allowed her mind to run through the vast field of worries she navigated each day. Today, a new one had sprung up. It was inevitable they'd run into Cash at some time. For five years, Wydetta had done her best to keep her daughter's days and nights so jam-packed Brit had little time to moon over the guitarist, and Cash... Thankfully, the man had sense and scruples enough to stay out of Brittany's ever-expanding orbit. Wydetta supposed she should feel grateful to him for that, but the naked longing on Brittany's face when she saw him told her time hadn't mattered one bit. Even after so long, her daughter's fascination with the man clearly hadn't faded to a fond memory.

Leaning against a stack of unused amplifiers, Wydetta crossed her arms over her chest and surveyed the man who had wreaked so much havoc in her little girl's life. He looked good, she could admit as much. He looked a damn sight better than he had the last time she saw him. She'd heard he'd mended his wild ways, and it showed.

And while getting clean was good for Cash, Wydetta wasn't entirely sure his rejuvenation was good for her daughter. Biting her lip, she glanced backstage, hoping she wouldn't catch a glimpse of Brit lurking about. She exhaled when she failed to spot her daughter's shining platinum mane of hair. Brit tended to stand out wherever she went.

Puppy love. That's what Brittany's feelings for Cash had been. And wasn't it good that she hadn't allowed her daughter to wallow in those feelings? Brit had a bright future shining on the horizon, and Wydetta wasn't about to let the stray her father had adopted all those years ago to distract her.

She snapped out of her reverie when she heard James introducing the musicians who'd provided him backup for the performance. She braced herself for gasps of recognition and cheers of delight when the rock legend worked his way from one instrument to another. But when he gestured to Cash, the guitarist pivoted in such a way his hat hid his face from the light.

Wydetta's brows rose in surprise. Then her whole body jerked with shock when James gestured to the man she and Brittany had once knew so well and introduced him to the crowd as "Johnny Smith."

She was still blinking away her shock when the band brought the song to a feverish crescendo. The final crash of the cymbals still rang in the air as Sir James took the microphone in hand and spoke directly to speak to the howling crowd.

"For our last song tonight…" He paused, waiting for the roar to abate ever so slightly. "For our last song tonight," he began again, "I'm going to play a little tune I wrote for a girl."

He paused, glanced over at the wings where she stood, and Wydetta's breath caught. She pressed a hand to her chest, confusion chasing all thoughts of her daughter, the man who'd broken her heart, and his fake name from her head. Sir James couldn't have written a song for her. They had only just met. Why was he looking at her like he was talking about writing a song for her?

He blew her a cheeky kiss, then turned back to the screaming crowd. "You all knew her too. She was a good girl, that one." He waited for a beat, then struck the opening chord of one of his most enduring ballads. "I'm of the opinion every guy should fall for a good girl, at least once in their life." He grabbed the mic stand, adjusted his guitar, and glanced over at Wydetta once more. "But I'm also partial to the bad girls as well."

As the band launched into the opening chords, Wydetta leaned against the travel trunks parked in the wings and cocked her head as she listened. Sir James Paulson was one of those men every girl daydreamed about at one time or another. Handsome, charming, wildly successful, and endearingly open about his love for his late wife. He was exactly the kind of man every girl wanted to snag.

But Wydetta had never been every girl. She'd never had visions of marriage or white picket fences. Sure, she had a child, but Brit had been a teenage accident. A happy one, as it turned out, but an accident. And though she was officially a woman of a certain age, she'd never heard the telltale ticking of a biological clock.

She'd always had a thing for musicians, though. Particularly the British ones, and there was no reason in the world she couldn't indulge her weakness, if only for one night. She straightened up as the song ended, and James jogged off the stage to chug a bottle of water. He had mere seconds to catch his breath. The crowd called for an encore, but he spent a few of those seconds smiling at her.

"Good. You're still here." He handed the bottle of water to an assistant, then beamed at her. "Stay put, love. I'll only be a moment."

She opened her mouth to respond, but he dashed back onto stage to the roaring approval of his adoring fans. Wydetta found her feet glued to the spot.

Cash Dorsett glanced over at her, and their eyes held. At last, she tipped her chin up and mouthed the words "Johnny Smith?" with such exaggerated enunciation he couldn't possibly miss her meaning.

But Cash's only response was a shrug before he faded back into the shadows at the edge of the spotlight. Wydetta's lips thinned into a determined line and her eyes narrowed. Now she remembered why she tempered her taste for musicians. They were a pain in the ass.

If Cash Dorsett knew what was good for him, he'd stay in those shadows where he belonged.

Turning on her heel, she shoved all thoughts of washed-up guitarists and flirtatious rock legends aside. She didn't have time for such complications. Her daughter stood poised on the brink of everything they'd worked for. There was no way she would let a man—any man—push them off course.

A harried festival coordinator wearing a headset and clutching a tablet ushered people in and out of a seemingly endless stream of shiny black sedans. When Wydetta approached, the young man looked up, his eyes wary. "Yes, Ms. Owens?"

"Has my daughter left?" Wydetta asked without preamble.

"Yes, ma'am." He glanced down at the tablet. "Miss Brittany took car number fifty-three to the Fairmont Hotel."

Wydetta chanced a glance back at the stage. The crashing of cymbals and a volley of dissonant chords signaled the end of the encore. Soon, Sir James Paulson would come jogging off the stage, his long, lean body drenched in sweat, his smile wide with exultation. He wanted her. She knew that from the moment their eyes met. And Wydetta knew from experience that a man was never more potent than in those moments he felt on top of the world. She needed to get out before she got caught in his gravitational pull.

But Cash Dorsett, apparently also known as Johnny Smith, would be trailing right behind him. She needed to get to the Fairmont and intercept her daughter before she did something foolish—like chasing after a man who couldn't come up with a more original stage name than Johnny Smith.

"I need a car, please," she said to the young man. "Now."

"Yes, Ms. Owens," he replied, simultaneously toggling the mic on his headset.

2

Brittany somehow escaped the festival with a minimum of fuss and only a couple dozen autographs, but she didn't hang around the Fairmont for long. Worried she'd be cornered by her mother, she showered and changed as quickly as possible. Her security detail had gone on to their own rooms, assuming she was done for the night. Usually, they'd be right. But she wasn't done this night.

She wasn't even close.

After slipping out of her room, she holed up in the last place anyone—including her mother—would look for her, a deserted conference room on the first floor. Perched on a straight-backed chair, she scrolled through the browser on her phone, while a tinny musical rendition of Bob Dylan's "To Make You Feel My Love" playing through the speakers embedded in the ceiling tiles.

Brit smirked as she hummed along, admiring the symmetry. Her recording of the very same song helped her leap the chasm from teen star to pop sensation. Now, it played while she prepared to go searching for the man who'd dashed the last of her childish daydreams.

Narrowing her eyes as she scanned the list of local hotels, she winnowed her choices down to a few likely suspects. Cash wasn't at the Fairmont. She'd asked the moment she'd arrived back at the hotel. No surprise, as he never did like being railroaded into doing what everyone else did. So she browsed through the area's various hotel options, hoping to narrow them down. Cash wasn't the chain type, and he certainly didn't go for modern boutique or made-over mansions. In the end, she forced herself to choose no more than five potentials. If she couldn't find him in one of those, she wasn't meant to find him at all.

The venerable old Driskill was her first choice. Cash always did like places with a good backstory. She dialed, not expecting to strike gold on her first attempt, which was why she had to laugh in surprise when she called, asked for him by name, and was immediately connected to a guest room.

She hung up the second the call rang through, even though she knew there was no way he as back from the show yet. Clutching her phone, she took a few deep breaths to center herself. So it was true. Cash Dorsett's days of fake names were well and truly over. She knew he'd stopped recording his own music, but she had no idea he was playing the festival circuit. Catching a quick glimpse of him, holding his gaze for one moment, well, that had been enough to pique her curiosity.

Tapping into the live stream, she waited until the festival had moved into the final acts to make her move. With a little time to kill, she recorded a couple quick messages to her fans and forwarded them to her social media team. Wydetta didn't want her posting anything to her accounts without it running the public relations gauntlet. Given how tired and punchy she'd been by the end of the tour, Brit had to admit the edict had merit.

But she wasn't tired. Seeing Cash had given her a jolt of energy she hadn't felt in a long time. And now he was within striking distance.

Fifteen minutes later, she stood in the Driskill's marble lobby. Anywhere else in this college town, her ponytail, ball cap, and hooded sweatshirt would have helped her blend in. But she'd miscalculated. The people crowding the cowhide and club seating in the bar were elegantly clad. The opulent lobby was teaming with music fans of all ages heading out or breezing in. Twenty feet from the reception desk, a young man in a slim-cut suit and name tag stopped dead in his tracks.

"Brittany Owens."

He stated her name in the flat tones of one in the first grip of shock. She scanned the tag pinned to his suit coat and resolved to make this guy her new best friend.

"Hey, Jason," she said, flashing a megawatt smile. Holding a finger to her lips, she signaled for his silence as his eyes widened with shock and awe. "Hush, don't give me away."

"No. No," he breathed, waving his hand frantically as if to fend off any doubts she might have had about his discretion. "Of course. Hello. How may I help you?"

In a move she'd perfected at countless *TeenScreen* fan appreciation days, she touched his arm briefly, cementing the connection between the two of them. "I need some help locating an old friend. I think he's staying here. Cash Dorsett?"

Though she wouldn't have guessed it was possible, Jason's eyes grew rounder. "Mr. Dorsett? Uh, yes, he, uh—"

"He played on my first album. I passed him at the festival tonight and wanted to say hi, but we didn't get a chance to catch up." She glanced over her shoulder as if she were worried bad guys were hot on her tail. "I was hoping you could tell me what room he's in, and I could run up there and say hello." She nodded to the grand staircase dominating the lobby. "But we have to be quick. I can't hang around down here, can I? I mean, if *you* recognized me…"

She let the thought trail off then dropped a conspiratorial wink on him. Wrinkling her nose, she whispered, "I don't want to make a fuss. Can you help me?"

Jason sprang into action. "Give me one moment."

Brit swallowed a triumphant whoop as he scurried toward the front desk. She wasn't a huge fan of using her fame to get what she wanted, but there were times, and this was a desperate one. Five years. It had been five years since she'd last seen Cash. Since he'd kissed her, then given her the "go away, little girl" brush off. Well, she wasn't an over-eager teenager anymore, and she didn't believe Cash Dorsett was immune to her.

There were some things a woman knew right down to her bones.

She started when Jason popped up at her elbow once more. "He's in one of our historic balcony rooms," he murmured, pressing a slip of paper into her hand. "But, please, you didn't get the room number from me."

Brit looked down at the hastily scrawled numeral, then up into Jason's eager but anxious face. "Of course not," she said, widening her eyes as if she was Little Bo Peep looking high and low for her lost sheep. "I was never here, right?"

"Right." Jason bobbed his head like a bird pecking for worms.

"If I could—"

He didn't need to finish the request. She took the notepad and pen from him and murmured along as she wrote in big looping script, "For Jason, You're the best." After adding both a winking face and a heart, she scribbled her signature. The guy's ears turned bright pink the second he glanced at the paper. She didn't wait around to see if the blush reached his cheeks.

Ignoring the signs pointing her toward the elevators, she set her sights on the grand staircase. She'd been trapped in elevators often enough to know she couldn't risk them on this mission. She took the stairs in twos, silently thanking her grandfather for passing on the length of her stride. The hours spent rehearsing intricately choreographed dance sequences paid off. Brit was barely winded when she reached the fourth floor. But her heart was hammering.

Double-checking the number on the paper, she squinted at the directional signs. Naturally, his was the very last room on the corridor. A corner room. Judging from the faint swatches of music floating up, she guessed it was the side of the hotel overlooking Sixth Street.

Rolling her shoulders back the way her mama had taught her, Brit took a breath outside the door. The music was slightly louder. She'd bet anything he had the balcony doors open. He might have been a cocky sonofabitch when he was at the top, but Cash was never too cool when it came to indulging his love for music. All types. It didn't matter to him if it was rock, pop, blues, or bluegrass. If there was a melody nearby, Cash wanted to ride it.

Brit had never been able to outrun her love for Cash. The two of them were a pair. Should be a pair. They both knew it then. In her gut, she was every bit as sure of it now. It was high time one of them to press the issue.

Lifting her hand, she gave the door three sharp raps. Once, it had been a joke. An old song her granddad liked to sing to her grandmother. Something about three knocks if she wanted him, but only two if not. Once upon a time, she'd told Cash about the song because he liked hearing stories about Merle Owens. He claimed to know the tune, and three knocks had become a sort of signal between them. She'd also become smitten. The problem was, in all the weeks they'd spent in the studio working on her first album, Cash treated her like she was his little sister. At least, he had until the night he'd kissed her, and all hell broke loose.

The door swung open, and Cash stood there dressed in nothing but his faded jeans and a snug-fitting T-shirt. The heathered cotton was the exact same shade as his eyes. Storm-cloud gray. His gaze was cool. Appraising. At least it was tonight. The night of her eighteenth birthday, he'd all but smoldered when he stared at her with those gunmetal-gray eyes chock-full of unspoken secrets and deep-seated desires.

"Hello, Cash."

The corner of his mouth kicked up. "Why, hello, Miss Brittany. Fancy seeing you here."

It was all she could do not to nip at the bait. "I didn't expect to see you in Austin this weekend."

"Tom Sorra fell and broke his wrist." He raised one shoulder and let it drop. "I got a call."

"I'm sorry to hear about Tom. I'll make sure we send some flowers."

Cash snorted. "Better flowers than Jack Daniels. His old buddy Jack's the one who tripped him up in the first place." He stepped back, wordlessly inviting her into the room. "You gonna stand out there until someone happens by and snaps a good picture?"

Brit bit back the urge to make a smart retort. Instead, she took him up on the offer. It didn't escape her notice he was making her mission easier than anticipated. Too easy. After the fuss and show he'd put on all those years ago, she expected more resistance. Cash seemed to have been expecting her. So much for the element of surprise.

"I can offer you water…or water," he said, nodding to the case of plastic bottles on the counter above the room's small refrigerator. "There might be a Coke or something in the minibar, but I didn't let them give me a key."

He wasn't drinking. Good for him. Possibly bad for her. Seducing him would be a helluva lot simpler if at least one of them had a hit of courage in them. "I'm fine with the water."

"I notice you didn't have your boy band backing you up," Cash said as he moved to the dresser.

Brittany chose to ignore the jibe and took the bottle of water he extended to her. He'd kept up with who was backing her these days. The admission spoke volumes. "No, we go into the studio in a couple weeks. After recording, we have rehearsals and right out on the European leg of the tour. I needed to make sure everybody had some time off."

Cash uncapped his own bottle and took a sip. "Very thoughtful of you."

Brit rolled her eyes. "You'd be amazed how much I think."

"You've got a thing going with one of your boy musketeers, don't ya?" he asked laconically. "He won't like that you're here."

Brit would've been angry by the jibe had she not caught the tiny jut of his chin. He was uncomfortable. She remembered the little tick. When Cash was uncomfortable, he went on the offensive. Gripping her water bottle between two fingers, she let it dangle as she strolled around the room, trailing her fingers over random surfaces, tilting a lampshade, and repositioning the alarm clock. They both knew the list of people who wouldn't like that she was there was long and distinguished.

"We weren't musketeers, we were 'sceners,' remember?" She glanced back over her shoulder. "The teens who made every place they went seem like *the* scene." Repeating the now-defunct television show's cheesy tag line still made her cringe inside, but she'd be damned if she'd let it show. "And contrary to popular belief, Dylan and I are *not* a thing." She looked up and met his gaze directly. "At least, not any more than you and I ever were."

"Oh, but the rumors—"

She raised her hand stop him. "There were rumors about me and you too, and those were more… salacious."

She enunciated the last word, carefully lingering on every syllable to let him know she knew exactly what she was saying. The days when he could tease her about being a set-tutored showbiz kid were gone. She had a bachelor's degree in her back pocket—people would be shocked to discover—and had started working on some graduate-level courses when her schedule allowed. Most people didn't realize the star of the show had a lot of downtime. Brit had decided to put hers to good use. No man, woman, or record executive would ever dare to talk down to her again.

Cash tipped his head to the side and gave her a long, hard perusal. "Maybe you have grown up."

"No maybe about it," she said saucily. "I've had to. Things are moving fast, and if there's one thing I've learned, it's that I don't like being at other people's mercy."

An odd expression flickered over Cash's face, but he quickly replaced it with a smirk. Crossing his arms over his chest, he rested the bottle of water in the crook of his elbow and leaned back against the bar set-up. "How is Wydetta?"

The false joviality in his tone made it clear his lack of segue was intentional. In his mind—and in hers, she could admit—the leap from discussions of control to her mother was not a stretch.

"Mama is fine," she said, using the title they both knew Wydetta loathed. "Doing well for a woman who's getting up there in years," she drawled, casting a sly glance in his direction.

Right on cue, Cash snorted. "Getting up there in years," he muttered disparagingly. "There's not much more of an age difference between me and your mama. Certainly less than the gap between you and me."

Brit snorted. "I see your math skills are still sharp." She raised the bottle of water. "Do you always drink your water at room temperature?"

Again, he shrugged. "A habit I picked up from some girl I once knew."

Her. He'd gotten it from her. She'd never been able to drink refrigerated water. The cold made her pant and gasp, so she'd conjured some cock-and-bull story about it being bad for her vocal cords. He'd teased her about it then. Tonight, he was admitting she'd left a mark on him.

"I'd ask why you're here, but I think the answer is obvious."

His tone was mild, but the implication stung enough to make her cheeks burn. He wasn't wrong, and if Cash wasn't going to beat around the bush, she wouldn't, either. After all, asking for what she wanted straight out was part of being a grown woman, wasn't it? Striving for a cool opposite from everything she was feeling inside, she cocked an eyebrow.

"You game?"

Apparently, she'd hit the right note. Cash laughed and gave his head a slow shake. "You always did have a pair of big brass ones, kid."

"Don't call me kid. I'm not a child anymore, and I won't let you treat me like one."

His expression shifted, the curve of his lips a tad more bitter than sweet. "No, you're not." He gave the scruff covering his cheeks and chin a thoughtful rub. "How old are you these days?"

"Twenty-three." She hated the overeager puppy yip in her tone. Vowing to slow things down and take control, she drew a deep breath.

"Twenty-three." He gave a low, soft whistle. "I guess that makes me..."

He paused a beat too long and her resolve crumbled. "Thirty-four," she volunteered.

"Thirty-five," he corrected with a swiftness of someone springing a trap. "I had a birthday last month."

Pissed he still had the power to play her so easily, she tapped into her infamous stubborn streak and redoubled her efforts. He wasn't going to turn her away. As far as she was concerned, he'd surrendered the moment he'd stepped aside and let her into his room. She needed to hold onto the rush of power she'd felt crossing the threshold. Feed off it. Exploit this one moment of weakness to get what she'd wanted since she met him.

"Happy birthday."

Making sure to keep her movements slow and controlled, she removed her ball cap, then pulled the elastic from her hair. She didn't need a mirror. They'd used the exact move in a music video. Why men found it so enticing, she never understood, but it worked. If the flare of Cash's nostrils was any indication, it was working on him, too. Pitching her voice low and husky, she finger-combed the ends of her platinum blonde waves. "I should give you a present."

"Twelve years." He hurled the words like they might conjure some kind of force field between them. "I'm twelve years older than you."

"I find one doesn't need math once you master the one-plus-one-equals-two bit." She closed the remaining distance between them.

His chest rose and fell. "Brittany—"

She reached out and placed her hand on his chest. "It's okay. You do math your way, I'll do it mine."

"Nothing about us adds up, Brit. I've told you this. I'm too old for you. Plus, I'm done chasing the spotlight, and you've got a thousand of them trained on you."

"I'm aiming for ten thousand of them." She shot him a glare, daring him to tell her she wasn't going to get exactly what she was planning for.

Instead, he rubbed the back of his neck, something he used to do when he was feeling pushed or cornered. "One plus one," he grumbled. "You're not one woman. You come with hundreds, hell, thousands of people. I can't deal with your circus. I don't want to. Not when I've finally stopped screwing up everything in my life."

"I'm only asking for one night, Cash."

She let her hand slide up to the warm skin of his neck, traced his fingers with the tips of hers, then caressed his throat. His singing voice was somehow gravelly and smooth all at once. Catching one of his old songs on the radio was enough to send her pulse into hyperdrive. Her thumb grazed his Adam's apple, and it bobbed obligingly. The pad of her middle finger pressed against his pulse. His heart rate had hit warp speed, and Brit knew she had him. At last.

"One may not be enough."

"But it will be something. Something for both of us." She leaned in, but instead of kissing him on the mouth, she ducked her head. Her lips found the throbbing spot she'd caressed. "Surely you can give me one night."

He groaned low and rumbly.

One night.

He'd had a moderately successful track by the same title way back when. A song about a man and a woman and a need so inescapable, they plum wore themselves out trying to deny it. Lyrics she'd let herself believe he'd written for her. Until the day he made her stop believing.

Her smile faded, but she didn't have the willpower to lift her lips from his skin. His throat was rough and stubbled. He smelled like night air. Cash wasn't going to push her away, and they both knew it. Like they both knew the bit about needing a single night was complete bull.

But they could deal with the fallout when they were back in Nashville. She'd pretend what happened in Austin, stayed in Austin. Whatever it took to get herself into his big, fluffy king-size bed.

"This is a mistake," he grumbled. But mistake or not, he wrapped her up in his taut, muscular arms and pressed her body flush against his. "A big mistake."

Brit kissed her way along his scruffy jaw, savoring the taste of his much-anticipated capitulation. "Good. Let's make it the best mistake we've ever made."

3

Her mouth was ripe and sweet. And soft. Unspeakably soft. She tasted exactly as he remembered and like every damn thing he'd tried to forget.

Brittany moved closer, and for once, Cash didn't inch away. Why bother? This thing between them. All this pent-up want. He'd known all along it had to come to a head sometime. And, apparently, that sometime was now.

His grandma used to make iced tea so dark it looked like Coca-Cola. Said if you wanted something strong, you had to let it steep. And this kiss, and what they were about to do to each other, had been brewing for longer than he cared to admit.

Her lips slid against his. Soft. Supple. But there was nothing tentative about it. No, the innocent girl she'd been once upon a time was gone. He'd crushed her teenage crush and nearly destroyed himself in the process. A single kiss stuck through five years of hard living, barely surviving, and not-so-memorable loving. Was it any wonder he'd run from her?

He'd seen Brittany's star power the moment he'd clapped eyes on her. Hell, he wouldn't have been at all surprised to hear she eclipsed the sun one day. He'd known from the start she'd be trouble. A teenager full of sass. A cable-ready television celebrity on the verge of realizing her power as a woman and as a performer. She'd been primed and prepared to put the pedal to the metal.

He simply wasn't willing to let her leave tread marks on his hide.

Cash angled his head and pushed his hand into her hair. Cradling the back of her head, he tipped her chin up and kissed her harder. But instead of retreating, she parted her lips and launched an all-out attack on his senses. Lips. Teeth. Tongue. Those crazy noises she kept making. Like he was the most delicious fucking cupcake she'd ever tasted and she was determined to devour him. In big, sexy bites.

They'd been on a collision course since the day she walked into Sunshine Studios all those years ago. At twenty-eight, he'd already penned and performed on nearly a dozen chart-toppers. He'd also recorded three albums for three different labels with only middling success. But he'd been a hotshot. Three songs he'd written for other artists were parked firmly at the top of the country charts. Another dominated both country and pop. And he'd had a single of his own chart at last. "One Night."

Christ, the song would haunt him forever.

He didn't need to chase stardom anymore. Not for the money, anyway. He had enough income from royalties and residuals to keep him comfortable, if not rich, for decades to come. His session work paid his mortgage. He had a knack for spotting talent, too, and usually finagled a piece of the gross profits in exchange for writing guitar tracks for songs. Some went on to become hits, and he was making it just fine.

But he'd wanted it all back then. The money, the fame, the power that came with them. The next song would be his breakout, he was sure. The career-defining moment when he'd become a household name. All he'd had to do was get some extra exposure on Miss Teen Queen's country-pop album and he'd be out of there. What a fool he'd been to think he'd been in control of anything then.

Brit's hand swept down his back. Her palm came to rest on his ass. He nearly yelped into her mouth when she gave one cheek a hard squeeze. He covered it with a growling snarl sort of thing, then dipped his head to gain better access to her neck and throat. "You manhandling me?"

"Well, you are a man, aren't you?"

"Damn straight I am." He breathed the boast into her ear, a rush of gratification warming him when she shivered. "And you're a woman."

She slid her hand down so her fingernails trailed along the seam between his legs. "I'm a grown-ass woman."

He chuckled, then caught her earlobe between his teeth and gave it a tug. "Grown-ass women don't call themselves 'grown-ass women.'"

Brit plowed both hands into his hair and yanked his head back. "Shut up."

He growled. The woman was trying to snatch him bald. Tightening his hold on her, he hauled her up onto her toes. "You wanna play rough?"

"Dear God, yes," she answered in a husky rush.

"Well, then, you got it, Princess."

He scooped her up and carried her over to the bed. The covers were rumpled from where he'd stretched out, but he hadn't pulled them back yet. He didn't see the need in bothering with such niceties.

She wanted to finish this? Fine, they'd finish it. And then it would be over and done.

An itch scratched. At last.

But instead of staying put, Brit rolled up onto her knees and began to unzip her sweatshirt, her face alight with arousal and an eagerness so earnest it hit him like a punch to the throat. Five years gone or not, she was still so damn young. And he was nothing more than a guy with a hot hand on the fret, a fickle way with words, and a handful of fake poker chips proclaiming him clean and sober.

"Cash."

He jumped. The command in her voice cut through the mental confetti he'd manufactured with his pity party. Her pointed stare and sharp tone made it clear this wasn't the first time she'd called to him. Her tank top was bunched halfway up her torso. His inattention had been noted and not appreciated.

"Sorry."

She lowered her hands, and he wanted to kick himself for losing those precious few inches of taut, creamy skin.

He turned away. "I just..."

He trailed off, and damn if her perfect nose didn't wrinkle like it had in the days when she was charming America's adolescents. "It's a lot, isn't it?" she asked, guileless. She tilted her head, and her wattage seemed to increase. "I about fell over when I saw you on stage."

"I'm surprised your mother didn't come after me with a mic stand."

The smile morphed into a sort of grimace. "Yeah, well, Wydetta was distracted tonight." She lifted a bare wrist and mimicked her mother's habit of checking her diamond-studded watch. "If I'm not mistaken, she's likely blowing the rust off some rock-and-roll royalty."

He didn't bother trying to hide his surprise. "Sir James?"

Her expression turned wicked. "She's always had a weakness for the Brits…" She whipped off the tank top and tossed it at him. "Like I've always had one for you."

Of course she wasn't wearing a stitch underneath. He froze, but Brit was completely unabashed. She'd been stripping down for costume changes since her pre-teen days. She'd never had the chance to become a normal, self-conscious kid.

"Com'ere."

She didn't have to say anything more. His gaze locked on the peachy-pink tips of her upturned breasts, he planted a knee on the bed and lunged, catching the finger she crooked at him between his teeth and holding it there for a protracted moment. Then he sucked the digit deep into his mouth. Brit threw her head back and unleashed a throaty moan. The husky timbre of it sent a zing straight to his dick.

He released her finger with a loud pop. "Please tell me you're not a virgin anymore," he said gruffly.

She laughed at him. Looked him dead in the eye and laughed. "Cash, I wasn't a virgin when you kissed me."

He blinked, taken aback by the cavalier way she tossed such personal information out there. "You weren't?"

Her laughter softened to a fond chuckle as she reached for the hem of his T-shirt. "I lost it when I was sixteen, like any normal teenager. You were the only one who thought I was some kind of vestal."

Stymied, he lifted his arms when commanded. He had nothing better to do while he waited for his brain to catch up and start processing again. Sixteen. She had a point, but he still wanted to shove a boot up the ass of the guy who'd been lucky enough to pop her cherry. He'd been fifteen when he'd lost his. One of his mama's bridge ladies offered to pay him double if he trimmed her hedges as well as mowed the lawn, and he had his eye on the red Fender Stratocaster on display at Mercer's Music.

Brit smoothed her hands up his chest with a low purr. Before he could zero in on the task at hand, she leaned in and buried her nose in the hair between his pecs. "Okay there, old man?"

Old man. What was once a jibe stuck as a nickname, and he never tried to shake it off. Compared to her, he *was* an old man. At least, too old for her. He'd clung to the idea of Brit the Virgin. It was safer to control himself with the misconception firmly in place. Without the barrier, real or imagined, in place, he was as susceptible as any other guy. "Who was he?"

The question slipped out of its own volition. But Brit didn't seem to mind. Actually, she looked downright amused. "Who'd I lose my virginity to?"

"Yes."

He nearly missed the slight upturn of her lips. "Who'd you lose *yours* to?"

"Mrs. Parker," he answered immediately.

"Ooh! A wicked older woman. A wicked, older, *married* woman." She stared at him, goggle-eyed. "You didn't even call her by her first name? Even after she seduced you?"

He shook his head. "Never. Unlike some people, I don't disrespect my elders."

"Justin didn't seem to mind me calling him by his name." She wrinkled his nose. "Would have been weird, calling him Mr. Timberlake."

"Bullshit."

She somehow kept a straight face, though she was clearly delighted to get a rise out of him. "Okay, his name was Justin, but it wasn't *that* Justin."

He narrowed his eyes. "I'm not gonna bite on Bieber, either."

Her brow puckered, and for a moment, she actually looked wounded. "You don't think I can get the Biebs?"

"I have no doubt you could. I have every doubt about him, though. You would have scared the crap out of him. Even at sixteen."

The frown cleared and her face brightened. "I was pretty fierce."

Not willing to be diverted, he pushed the conversation back up onto the tracks. "Just a regular Justin?"

"A regular Justin," she confirmed. "He was older than me, but not at risk of jail time."

"Unlike me."

"Unlike you."

"No reason for me to hunt him down and hurt him?"

She shook her head. "He wasn't a very good kisser, but at the time I didn't have much to compare him to, so I couldn't complain."

He was a fool for asking, but he did it anyway. "And these days? You leavin' them strewn all over the place?"

Her warm, soft hand slid down his belly. Limber fingers curled around the buckle on his belt and she pulled him closer. "These days, I know better than to answer loaded questions. Why don't you shut up and kiss me again?"

So he did. He kissed her the way he'd wanted to back in the days when she'd been forbidden fruit. He swept his tongue over hers, around it, demanding she follow his lead on this long-awaited descent into madness. She moaned into his mouth. Each breathless mewl or pant set his blood on fire, and Cash didn't feel any need to think cold thoughts. Tonight, he wouldn't require an icy shower. There'd be no reason to go out looking for a willing woman. He had one right here in his arms. On his bed. Half-naked. And, for the life of him, he didn't understand why she had the other half covered.

Breaking away, he took a moment to drag in a gulp of oxygen. Then he laid siege to the creamy column of her throat with fevered open-mouthed kisses. He wasn't the only one charged up by the electricity flowing between them. She fumbled with the buckle on his belt, even though she talked as though she popped a different guy's fly every night. Her knuckles grazed the outline of his dick as she went to work on the zipper. A groan filled the air. His. Hers. It didn't matter. He was going to have her at last.

Thank Christ there'd be no need for the soft-focus, sensual deflowering he used to dread botching. Judging by the clumsiness of her normally graceful hands, she wanted him as badly as he wanted her. He could fuck her the way he'd dreamed of fucking her for years. Hard, fast, and dirty.

"Hard." He spoke the word into her skin as if saying it out loud could make it so.

Brit plunged her hand into the opening of his jeans and grabbed a handful of cock. "Yes, you are."

He wanted to chuckle, but need had him in a choke hold. "Fast," he managed to gasp.

Brit took the promise as a command, and the next thing he knew, she'd wrapped those talented fingers tight around him and was jerking him off. He reached down and stopped her. If she kept going, things would go fast, but not in the right way. "Not so fast."

She laughed and put up a token fight, but he was stronger. In the end, he pried her hand away. He watched her fingers curl toward her palm. Pianist hands. She could have played fancy pieces in fancy halls with all the talent she carried in those digits, but she didn't. Wydetta had intentionally set her prodigy of a daughter on a very different path. Bach didn't pay the big bucks like pop.

Lifting her hand to his mouth, he pressed a reverent kiss to her palm. Over the years, despite his excesses, he'd managed to do pretty damn well for himself. What he'd give to have half her gift. Not because he had hopes of being a star. Those were gone. Drowned in the bottom of a bottle. But to have music flowing through him and out of him as easily as she did...

"Lose your nerve, cowboy?"

Cash jerked back to reality and found her stroking his cheek like he was some kind of kitten. The barely-there curve of her full lips made his chest tighten. Not the teasing grin of the girl she'd been when he'd high-tailed it out of her life. This was a woman's smile. One that said she might understand more about him than he was comfortable with her knowing.

He pushed her back, laying her out on the bed and stretching over her, but keeping enough space between them to rouse a growl of disappointment from her. It was his turn to call the shots. "I never lose my nerve."

He sat back on his heels. She lay splayed across the bed, her arms flung high over her head, her legs spread for him. Curling his fingers into the waistband of her stretchy pants, he yanked them down over her hips. A flash of pink told him she'd been wearing lacy panties he hadn't taken even a moment to appreciate, but some collateral damage was to be expected in situations like this. Seconds later, he'd shucked his jeans and briefs and rejoined her on the bed.

"There's a condom in the pocket of my hoodie." She gestured lazily to the jacket she'd left tangled at the foot of the bed.

"A lady who comes prepared."

Brit cocked a saucy eyebrow at him. "I expect to come real soon, so let's get a move on, buster."

26

He groped in the pocket of her sweater. One packet. She'd only brought one. Relief and disappointment waged war inside him as he tossed the hoodie to the floor. One should be enough. He'd fuck her, she'd get a few smart-assed remarks in as she dressed and made a star-worthy exit from his life, and the dance they'd started all those years ago would come to an end. This was exactly as it should be. He had no place for Brit and her traveling circus in his life.

He didn't respond to her taunt. With steady-handed efficiency, he rolled the condom into place. Then, he hooked an arm under her knee and pressed it up as far as it would go, opening her wide. She was ready.

Christ, he could see how wet she was. Pink folds glistened. She was fashionably bare, which wasn't his preference. Not that anyone had asked him, but he loved the magical thatch of hair that hid a woman's most private places. The first time he'd ever touched a woman between the legs, feeling the moisture trapped in those coarse curls nearly made him come in his pants. There was something earthy about it. Primal. He couldn't understand why they wanted to strip everything natural and sexy away.

He trailed a finger through her folds, parting them, but not enough, judging by the way Brit writhed and squirmed. His lips curved as she pressed up, literally trying to force his hand. "You want something, sugar?"

"Touch me," she ordered through gritted teeth.

Her back bowed when he made another feather-light pass. She pressed her head into the pillow, exposing the delicate line of her throat, and he ached to bite. But he couldn't. Wouldn't. She'd walk out of here tonight satisfied, but unmarked. The world would never know five years of painful foreplay had finally come to an end. They had to be a one-and-done. It would take a man stronger than him to survive her.

Shifting his weight, he fell forward. Her knee caught in the crook of his elbow, he thrust into her.

Brit squawked, her eyes popping open wide and her hands balling into fists. She pressed them into his shoulder blades, holding him there and pushing him away all at once. He froze, waiting for the outcome of the battle raging inside her. She'd been the one who came here loaded with swagger and swish. He was only giving her what she'd asked for. Still, if she pushed him away, he'd go. Even if it killed him to pull out.

She dug her heels into the mattress in what might have been a half-hearted attempt to escape, but the movement merely tilted her hips up, giving him the chance to sink deeper into her. They moaned in perfect unison. Sliding his arm down, he lowered her knee and took hold of her ass. Heat. So much heat. In him. Around him. Surely his blood was boiling. He closed his eyes and thought cool thoughts. Icebergs. Snow drifts. Avalanches.

Beneath him, Brit chuckled. Was she aware every muscle in her body tightened when she laughed? Was she doing it on purpose? Was this a ploy to drive him out of his ever-lovin' mind?

"Baseball?" she asked in a husky whisper.

He shook his head. "Cold."

She ran her hands up his back, her fingertips flying over every vertebra as if she were running scales. "You don't feel cold to me."

Ducking his head, he inhaled the scent of her shampoo and attempted to put individual words into a sentence. "I think of cold things."

"Like sno-cones?"

He rewarded her with a weak laugh. "Good one."

"Ice cubes?"

The mere mention of ice had him picturing the tight peaks of her nipples. He squeezed his eyes shut and shook his head with a tad too much violence. "No."

As if she'd followed the breadcrumbs in his head, her mouth stretched wide. He felt the movement of her cheek against his temple. Part of him wanted to stay where he was, his face hidden in the curve of her neck and his dick buried deep inside her, but he couldn't. Resisting the lure of her smile was as impossible as controlling the urge to move inside her. He pushed up, and sure enough, she beamed at him, lighting up like a spotlight. His hand contracted, and he kneaded the soft curve of her ass as he began to glide in and out of her.

She was mind-bogglingly wet. So wet and slick it was hard to control the urge to pound into her. He looked down and soon found himself mesmerized by the vision of his cock sliding into her over and over again.

"Hey," she called to him.

Her nails bit into his back, and his head snapped up. She touched his cheek, forcing him to look her straight in the eye.

"Hard and fast, cowboy. My bus leaves in four hours and I'd like to be asleep when we hit the road."

Then it struck him. She wasn't the same vulnerable young woman he'd kissed and left behind. She was more than older. She was colder. And knowing he'd played at least a minor part in lowering her core temperature chilled him to the bone.

He slowed. Brit grunted, then shoved at his shoulder. Feeling defeated, if not deflated, he gave way. Pulling out, he flipped onto his back beside her. His dick remained embarrassingly hard, proving he didn't have an ounce of pride left in him. He'd drank it all away not long after he'd turned the sweetest girl he knew sour.

Arching an eyebrow at her, he gestured to his erection. "Have at it."

He flung an arm over his head as she climbed aboard. He wanted to pretend it didn't feel fucking incredible. He wished he wasn't as keyed up as a teenager watching his first porn, but a man would have to be dead to not appreciate the view. Her small breasts jiggled and bounced as she rose and fell. She rode him like he was a thoroughbred and there was a blanket of roses waiting for them at the finish. She threw her head back, each moan a testament to pleasure taken as much as an admission of frustration. He groaned when she slid a hand down to stroke herself, glad he wasn't the only one dealing with a case of unmet expectations.

"Maybe we should have done this back then," he admitted, his voice hoarse. "Mighta been better if we'd gotten it out when it was all so pent-up."

She cried out, but he wasn't exactly sure what prompted it. Frustration? Agreement? Coming? Either way, the chatter seemed to be doing something for her. It was definitely doing it for him.

"I wanted to fuck you on the piano. The night we reworked the arrangement on 'Love You So.'" Her moan was every bit as ragged as his voice. "I wanted to set you up there, push up your skirt and pull down your panties." He felt her muscles contract and clench around him. "They were purple. I saw them when you climbed onto the stool. I wanted you. Wanted you so bad, but..."

He paused, unable to catch his breath or his scattered thoughts as she came and came hard, squeezing the life right out of him. He filled the condom, all the while cursing the need for it. He wanted to fill her. Had since the days when thinking about it could have landed him in a jail cell. Would have, if her mother had any say about it. There had been something between him and Brit since the moment they met. Something neither of them could outrun.

He growled, pushing his hips up into her even as their breathing slowed. "Wanted you so bad I couldn't run far enough, fast enough."

Brit gasped, but it sounded like a sob. He opened his eyes to see her clamp a hand to her mouth. The next thing he knew, she'd pushed up out of his reach and swung a leg over. Had he said too much? Not enough? She'd known how he felt about her back then. Was she messing with his mind now?

He jackknifed, bending his body in two in an attempt to catch her. But she had youth and speed on her side. By the time he rolled onto his side, she was shrugging into her hoodie without bothering with the tank top.

"So, there." She smiled brightly, but it didn't reach her eyes. "That's done."

"Brittany—"

She found her pants and shook them with enough violence to silence him. "I should take a picture of you in bed and post it. Bucket list," she sang in a cheery falsetto. "Check!"

"Please don't." He watched as she shoved her legs into the pants and yanked them into place. "Listen, we—"

"There's no we," she said abruptly. "Let's not pretend there is." She shoved her toes into her flip-flops and searched for the discarded ball cap. With it on her head, she could blend right in with the thousands of students in Austin. Patting her pockets, she glanced around, snatched her top from the floor, and shoved it into one of the pockets of her hoodie. "Phone, money, hotel key...I'm good."

He'd barely managed to get his legs over the edge of the bed when she closed the distance between them in two strides. Her lips landed on his cheek. The kiss was a spectacularly disappointing encore for what had happened, but it shouldn't have surprised him. She'd proved her point, gotten a bit of her own back, and it was his turn to be brushed off. After all, fair was fair.

"See ya, Cash." She gave his shoulder a squeeze as she straightened. "Take care of yourself."

He was still searching for his voice when the door slammed between them. "See ya, Brit," he murmured to the empty room. "Be well."

Cash stared at the ceiling for a long time after she left. Unmoving. Almost unblinking.

Music wafted through the open windows, carried on a warm breeze. It tickled his bare skin. Still, he lay there a good while, letting his heart rate return to normal, concentrating on the prickle of sweat cooling on his skin, and trying to think about anything but what just happened, or how badly he wanted a drink.

The first issue was too new, too fresh, to parse apart. And the second? Well, he'd been battling that urge nearly every hour of every day for years now. Though he was fairly certain he wouldn't give in to the temptation, one could never be sure.

Look at poor Tom Sorra.

If his old buddy hadn't toppled off the wagon and into a bottle of whiskey, none of them would be in this mess. But he had. After years of hard working and clean living, Tom had slipped. And that slip had not only cost him the chance to play with Sir James Paulson, but also threatened his ability to make a living in their chosen profession.

Closing his eyes, Cash sent up a silent prayer to whichever guitar gods might be listening that Tom regained full range of motion in his fret hand.

Rousing himself at last, he snagged his boxer briefs from the wad of clothing on the floor and shook them out as he prowled the room. Pausing in front of the locked minibar, he slowly and deliberately stepped into his briefs as if donning body armor. The waistband snapped into place and an involuntary chuckle escaped him. The underwear hadn't done much to protect him from Brittany Owens, and the good Lord knew all the potions and poisons in that locked bar posed more of a threat to him than sweet Brit.

Brit.

The girl he'd never been able to forget. How could he? Every time he walked into a grocery store, he saw her beaming at him from the cover of one magazine or another. Beautiful. Talented beyond reason. Headstrong. Sexy.

He caught himself up short at the last one. More out of habit than any hope of denying his unquenched thirst for her. He'd been forcing himself to stop thinking about Brit in any way other than strictly platonic for so long, it was almost incomprehensible to believe he'd actually been buried deep inside of her just a short time before.

He stared hard at the cabinet, wondering exactly how long it would take for one of the Driskill's hyper-helpful staff members to deliver the magic key to his room. He could almost taste smell the smoky finish of a good glass of bourbon.

His back ached. So did his heart.

He could still smell Brittany on his skin. Raising one hand to his sternum, and the other to the small of his back, he closed his eyes as tight as he could and inhaled deeply. She'd smelled like shampoo and some kind of fruity soap. Sweet. Heady.

Intoxicating.

Brittany was the lemon-yellow sunshine on a spring day. The lilacs that used to bloom beside his grandma's porch. She was too good for him in every way. He knew it, she knew it, the whole damn world knew it. But he'd known the moment he'd laid eyes on her that this would happen eventually.

He'd known, and this time, he hadn't done a thing to stop it.

If sleeping with Brit didn't prove him to be a man and not a saint, he had no idea what would. But having a drink would make him less of the man he wanted to be. And for that reason, he'd allow himself one weakness, but not the other.

Moving to the desk, he bypassed the hotel phone he could use to summon the key to the minibar, and picked up his cell instead. Despite the late hour, his friend and sponsor answered on the second ring.

"Jace? Hey, it's me. Listen, do you think your friend with the jet is still here? I need to bail. Think I can hitch a ride?"

Brit should not have been surprised to find Wydetta in her suite when she made it back to the Fairmont. Still, she gave a guilty jump when she spotted her mother lounging on the couch, scrolling through her phone.

"Well, that didn't take long," Wydetta commented without looking up from the screen. "I figured I had at least another hour before you sneaked back in."

Pressing her hand to her hammering heart, Brit forced herself to act calm. She was no longer a teenager. She wasn't sneaking anywhere. She was a grown woman, entitled to come and go as she pleased. And, until just a minute before, she'd been mightily pleased. Not only by the sex itself, but with the fact that she'd initiated it. And she'd controlled her exit, as well. All in all, she'd been feeling pretty smug, up until this moment.

"I'm not sneaking. As far as I know, I don't have a curfew," she said, placing her keycard on a marble-topped table with a deliberate snap.

"No, but you do have a security detail. A detail naïve enough to believe you were safe and snug as a bug in your room." Wydetta pressed the button to close the screen, then looked up at last. "Then again, they don't know you as well as I do."

The sing-song tone in her mother's voice told Brittany someone was in trouble. And since, technically, she was the boss, she was fairly certain it wouldn't be her. Either Andy or Tess, the two security guards assigned to travel with her to the festival, would pay the price for her adventure. Her stomach twisted into a knot. An almost crushing wave of exhaustion of washed over her.

With privilege comes responsibility.

One of her grandmother's favorite reminders flitted through her head. Sighing, she moved to the sofa and dropped down beside her mother. Her head bounced off the cushion and she winced as she turned to look at Wydetta.

"Don't start—"

"I have to start, it's my job."

The lines between her mother's brows were back. A year or even a few months ago, Brit would have playfully rubbed them away with her thumb. But the North American leg of her tour had been grueling for both of them. Stakes were high, and so were tensions. And every day the line between mother and manager blurred a little more.

Brit sighed and held up a hand in a staying gesture. One would think the unprecedented success of playing one sold-out arena after another would have supercharged them. But, in truth, the rapid escalation of expectations and the pressure to deliver on everything people were predicting for her were overwhelming.

Brittany was all too aware that Wydetta was feeling it too. After all, she was the one charged with making promises and maintaining the hype. All Brit had to do was show up for fourteen-hour days, dance until her muscles screamed, sing until her voice gave out, and smile as if she couldn't imagine doing anything more delightful than meeting a roomful of strangers after leaving her body and soul on the stage.

But there was no use in complaining. She had it all. The dream she'd chased all her life was ripening into reality. She was getting everything she'd ever wanted. A small laugh escaped her as she realized that she'd even added Cash Dorsett to the list. Her mother's frown deepened, and Brit blew out a breath.

"Don't fire Andy and Tess. I've never ditched before, and they had no reason to believe I would tonight."

Wydetta studied her for a long moment, then inclined her head. "I won't fire them, but they can't lead your detail. I'll talk to Hank when we get back, and we'll discuss a redistribution of duties."

Brit snorted. "Redistribution of duties."

Her mother cocked a single brow. "Or I could fire them."

"Stop," Brit groaned, too tired to spar with her mother. "Redistribute. Sheesh."

"You cannot—"

"I know," Brit said, heading off the first lecture.

"And for God's sake, Brittany, you can't honestly still...after all this time—"

"I can, I do, and I did," she interrupted.

"It's ridiculous—"

She threw up a hand to halt any other attempt to find an avenue of attack. "I am not going to discuss this with you."

Wydetta blinked, then sank back into the sofa, her eyes fixed on Brit's staying hand. "So that's how it's going to be?" she asked, her voice pitched lower and about three times softer than her usual no-nonsense tone.

Brit cringed and looked at her own hand. This was how Wydetta used to put an end to discussions. Apparently, the apple had barely cleared the trunk of this particular tree. She'd even delivered the line with the exact same inflection Brit's grandmother used to quell minor insurrections. Curling her fingers into her palm, she wet parched, kiss-swollen lips as she lowered her hand to her lap. Drawing a steadying breath, she nodded at last. "I don't see the point. I did it, you disapprove. Noted. Let's move on."

Wydetta gave a jerky nod, then catapulted herself from the sofa.

"The bus leaves at six. Don't be late."

Brit simply nodded and stared straight ahead as the darkened television screen as she waited for the door to close. The moment the latch caught, she exhaled as if she'd been underwater for hours.

In a way she had.

The encounter with Cash had been a reckless impulse, it was true. Her hastily planned escape from her security detail had been selfish. But it had also been liberating. For once, she'd taken what she wanted and made no apologies for it. Redistribution of duties or not, she couldn't regret it. That scant hour spent with Cash was the culmination of years of daydreams.

Now, all she wanted to do was climb into her bed and invite him into her dreams once more.

4

Nashville was a very small town. At least, it was if you ran in the circles that Wydetta Owens ran in. And that tight circle revolved around the music industry, and tourism generated by that industry. Like many of the natives, the members of the Owens family tended to frequent local establishments that may not appear trendy or chic to the untrained eye, but were well known among those who were in the know. This bit of insider exclusivity provided a modicum of privacy in a world where far too many things were made public.

Seated under a dryer at Foils, the seemingly unassuming salon she'd been patronizing for the last twenty years, Wydetta flipped the page of the magazine she'd been gazing at with unseeing eyes. There was a flurry of activity near the entrance followed by a hush so thick and heavy, it seemed all the oxygen had been sucked up into the driers. She glanced up and saw Nicole Kidman sashaying through the reception area wearing a loosely crocheted sweater over a pair of faded leggings and scuffed ballet flats.

The two women exchanged nods and polite smiles that conveyed the prescribed amount of vague recognition, but neither spoke. After all, this was just another Wednesday afternoon at the hair salon. No reason for anyone to get excited.

Abandoning the pretense of the magazine, Wydetta took a moment to scan the room. As usual, the space was packed with customers in varying stages of their beautification processes. The third wife of a local philanthropist sat in the tall pedicure chair having both her hands and feet attended to at once. Now that Nicole was seated, both shampoo bowls were occupied, as were two of the four stations the owner, Trina Michelson, leased to only the most rigorously vetted stylists.

Foils offered no private rooms or complimentary flutes of champagne. The owner took perverse pride in calling the establishment a beauty parlor rather than a salon. The old-fashioned feel of the moniker suited the atmosphere and allowed her clientele to feel as if they all shared a smug little secret. Wydetta had to admit it was a brilliant angle. She was a woman who admired a solid strategy.

Housed in a tiny house in an old Victorian in the trendy downtown area, Trina had hit the nail on the head. The interior was cozy. Conducive to hushed conversation punctuated only the occasional burst of laughter. Rolling her shoulders back, Wydetta tried to loosen the knots in them as she squirmed beneath the hood of the dryer, but it did no good. She checked the time on her watch, then huffed loud enough to make the woman seated across from her start.

She mouthed an apology, then nudged the hood of the old-fashioned dryer up a centimeter to allow a smidgen of cool air to waft and cool her forehead. Annoyed at being trapped beneath the hood, she turned a piercing glare on an advertisement in the glossy magazine on her lap. The second the words 'anti-aging cream' registered, she smoothed her consternation from her features. She didn't want to have to invest in the advertised product one moment sooner than necessary. But it seemed like all she did these days was worry.

She fretted over everything. The new album her daughter was recording. The upcoming tour. The unbearable silence that filled the space between them any time they weren't in the recording booth. Brittany and Cash.

The two of them were a train wreck everyone saw coming from miles away. Wydetta had hoped time and circumstance would derail her daughter's devotion to the man, but she knew Brit was a goner the moment she clapped eyes on him again in Austin. Worse, she wasn't the only one who knew it.

The letter had come the day before. Unsigned, and with no return address.

And though its contents weren't an outright threat, the fact that the author knew Brittany had seen Cash in Austin was disturbing. Usually, she felt a surge of disdain for the cowards who wouldn't even sign their names, but this one was different. It felt different. Something about it seemed vaguely familiar. And the sender came across as earnest in their determination to warn Wydetta of the of the grave mistake her daughter was making in 'taking up with' someone like Cash.

As if she didn't already know.

Wydetta kept the letter to herself. Brit made it clear she wouldn't welcome any questions about cash, and really, there wasn't much she could do. Her daughter was an adult who needed her less and less with every passing day.

Her phone vibrated in her lap. She glanced down and saw an incoming call from the phone number she had labeled 'Cocky Cockney Bastard' appear on screen. A laugh of disbelief escaped her as she stared at the phone in baffled wonderment. Then, she declined the call without hesitation. How James Paulson had procured her phone number was anyone's guess, but the fact that he could didn't surprise her. This town was full of star-fuckers, and there were few stars bigger or brighter than legendary rock star Sir James Paulson.

But he'd been calling every day, and, to be honest, she wasn't quite sure what she'd done to attract his notice other than ditch out on their backstage flirtation. Maybe he was simply one of those men who loved the hunt. She stared at the dark screen, willing the voicemail alert to chime. Seconds later, it obeyed.

Lifting the dryer hood enough to press the phone to her ear, Wydetta allowed herself a small, smug smile as he left yet another rambling, but charmingly self-effacing message for her. Message number nine, to be exact.

"You're still not taking my calls? Is it because I didn't wait three days as all articles say one is supposed to do? I hate to come off overeager, but I also hate wasting time. Are you planning to avoid me forever? I'm everywhere, you know. Ask anyone." There was a pause, then he blew out a long breath. "All right. Seriously, love, if you truly don't wish to see me, then give me a simple no. Silence doesn't work in my world. It leaves me to wonder, and wondering allows me a chance to hope... You can even send your answer in one of those annoying text messages. Do you want to see me? Yes or no."

Another gusty breath followed. "Christ, now I sound like a schoolboy," he muttered the last as he ended the call.

Wydetta listened to the message twice through, then allowed herself the indulgence of listening to the previous day's appeal. Maybe it was time to put him out of his misery. After all, he wasn't just some peon label executive she could jerk around indefinitely. But even though she found his insistence on telephoning rather than texting charming, she wanted to keep at least a little of her edge. A smug smile curved her lips as she dropped the phone back into her bag. He could wait a little longer.

Every time Wydetta Owens refused to answer his calls, James Paulson tamped down his impatience, left yet another voice message, and dug his heels in a little deeper. He walked back into the recording studio where he's been consulting on a friend's album, and slumped onto the sofa. After a minute, he propped his booted foot on the edge of the narrow coffee table in front of him, then gave it a little shove.

"Girl trouble?"

James glared at the man seated in a leather desk chair rolled up to the console. Once upon a time, he and Richard Starling had once been members of one of the most successful rock 'n' roll bands of all time. Since they split up, Rich had stepped out of the spotlight and become one of rock's most coveted producers. But James had kept grinding away, unable to escape his addiction to brightly lit stages and cheers of adulation.

James could tell by the smirk curving his old friend's cheek that his former bandmate thought he was making some sort of uproariously funny joke. Because, of course it couldn't be girl trouble. James Paulson, one of the most famous musicians— possibly persons—in the world, could have any woman he wanted. Except the one he'd loved and lost. Now, it seemed everyone wanted to cast up as some kind of martyr to love.

But he wasn't a martyr, he was a man. A man who found himself inexplicably intrigued by a woman. Perhaps it was nothing more than her easy dismissal of his attentions that attracted him to Wydetta Owens, but he thought not.

There's been something there. Something in her eyes that struck a spark inside him. A spark he thought died with his wife, Lydia. Lunging from the couch, he prowled the cramped studio space. "So what if it is?" he asked, almost to himself.

Rich nudged a switch on the mixing board and the volume on the playback they'd been analyzing dropped to a whisper. He swiveled in his seat to face him straight on, blinking as if he were still trying to process what James had said.

James couldn't help noticing that with his thinning grey-brown hair and wide-set eyes, Rich was actually starting to resemble an owl.

"Is it?"

Growling with frustration, he snatched up the guitar he'd propped against the mixing board. It was a battered acoustic he'd had for years and kept specifically for these sort of kicking-it-around days. Ducking his head, he fiddled with the tuning pegs, even though he knew the guitar was perfectly in tune.

"Perhaps."

The single word answer snared his friend's full attention. Rich leaned forward, resting his elbows on his splayed knees. "Who is she?"

For a split second, James considered confiding in his old friend. After all, there were few people left who knew him as well as Rich did. Knew what the loss of Lydia had done to him. And had an inkling of how lonely he'd been in the years since. Still, it wouldn't take his friend more than a minute to draw the lines between Wydetta Owens, Merle Owens, and the pop star poised to go supernova, Brittany Owens.

This was Nashville, and the mere mention of the Owens name was enough to send people into a tizzy. Merle was country music royalty, and Brittany's name seemed to be the one on everyone's lips these days. Still, he wasn't thinking about Merle or Brittany day and night. He'd been thinking about Wydetta. And he's be damned if he knew the why and what of it all.

He swallowed the temptation to pour it all out for his old mate. Better to keep it simple. Keep it quiet. After all, who knew if Wydetta would ever actually give him a shot.

Both amused and amazed by how giddy it made him feel to be practically ignored, he pushed a hand through his hair, shook it back into place, then tossed off a shrug. "Just someone I ran into in

Austin."

Rick eyed him carefully, and James made a mental note to start coming up with owlish nicknames for the man.

"Someone we know?"

James's lips twisted into a wry smile. Their world was a small world. Nothing proved that more than the fact that two men who'd been inducted into the Rock and Roll Hall of Fame the moment the thing came into existence were now sitting in a studio in Nashville, mixing an album of what the studio wags were all calling "Americana." And, no, the irony of the trendy genre's name applied to an album produced by two men knighted by Queen Elizabeth II wasn't lost on them.

But he wasn't really ready to talk about the woman presently jerking his strings. So, he answered as honestly as he could. "I don't think you know her. May turn out to be nothing to speak of anyway," he added dismissively. Rich fell silent for a moment, then turned back to his control panel. "Been a long time."

"Mmm."

A long pause hummed between them, then Rich broke the tension with his good-natured laugh. "Glad we had this talk. What do you say we wrap this up for the day? I'm ready to get home."

With the mention of the word home, James's head popped up. Of course. He himself might be holed up in a suite at the Newcomb, but Rich lived here full-time these days. He knew everyone who was anyone. And it wasn't like James was trying to hunt down some unknown woman whose name he barely caught.

Wydetta was well-known in Nashville. She'd grown up in and knew her way around the industry. He'd scored her phone number from one of the journeyman musicians easily enough. He'd bet his estate in Wilshire his old friend Rich could dig up some scoop on where he might "accidentally" run into the elusive Ms. Owens.

Once.

He'd allow himself to play the creepy, demanding superstar just this once. And if she still rebuffed his advances…well, he'd escape to the estate he hadn't slept in since the day Lydia died, and bury his heart along with the last women who'd wanted it.

"Hey, Dickie?" he murmured, knowing the affectionate old nickname would grab his chum's attention. When Rich looked up, he plunged ahead with his cockamamie plan to flush Wydetta

Owens out into the open. "D'you remember when we met Merle Owens?"

Brit sat on a banquette at the back of the production booth listening with closed eyes to the playback of her upcoming album. Everyone around her seemed convinced this album would make her a superstar. Brit wasn't so sure. Something felt off.

She swallowed the lump of apprehension lodged in her throat and tried to concentrate on listening with a critical ear. She'd authored only one of the songs on this album. The rest were songs written for their crossover potential, cranked out by the Nashville machine. Tailor-made for stars like Brittany Owens. Maybe that was why it felt off, she mused.

But if this album did as well as expected, her next would be a completely different story. She'd have leverage. Creative control. If this album failed to meet expectations, then she'd have a built-in excuse for why listeners failed to connect with the tracks. Either way, she would come out the winner. Still, the last thing she wanted was to blow anyone's expectations. Particularly her own.

As the last track queued up, Brit opened her eyes and glanced about the cramped control room. Her producer, a man known only as Leelo, nodded along with the peppy techno backbeat. To his right, her mother leaned her hip against the console, scrolling through the messages on her oversized phone. A grizzled old engineer by the name of Heywood nudged a lever here and there, even though he knew damn good and well most of the mixing was being taking care of by the sophisticated software system. Brit didn't blame Heywood for his need to push and pull the knobs. She felt helpless too.

Something wasn't right with the album as a whole, and she couldn't quite put her finger on what it might be.

A short harrumph snagged her attention. She glanced over and spotted Wydetta absorbed in reading something on her phone. Without looking up, her mother made a couple of quick notations in one of her ever-present notebooks. Brit couldn't suppress a sad smile. Their shared notebook habit had once been one of many inside jokes they shared. Nowadays, they barely spoke.

The days since the Austin gig were some of the loneliest Brittany had ever known. Focused as ever, Wydetta was oblivious to everything around her—the music, the something missing, her daughter. Brit blinked rapidly and swallowed the lump in her throat. She refused to feel sorry for herself. Not when everything in her world was so obviously going well.

But, like the album, something was off between her and Wydetta. Oh, her mother was on top of everything in terms of Brit's career, but that seemed to be all she was to Wydetta these days. As much as she resented Wydetta watching and commenting on her every move, she did miss the forced proximity of being on the road.

The sprawling estate purchased in Brit's name back in her *TeenScreen* days was too big. And though their cousin Martine lived with them as housekeeper and domestic dictator, three women were too few to fill all the echoing corners of the mansion.

Her trainer and the other household staff came in daily, and though they were friendly, they weren't exactly friends. Then again, Brit had never had much time for friends. Sure, she'd stayed in touch with some of her former co-stars, but they all had busy professional lives of their own. Others had drifted off into the normal world, and eventually they'd lost touch. Her lead guitarist, Dylan, was the only of the TeenScreenn cast who'd stuck close, and Brit had few delusions as to why.

Dylan had aspirations of his own. He saw himself as the next Brad Paisley, and his dreams weren't coming to fruition fast enough for his liking. So, he stayed put right by her side, always on the perimeter of the spotlight trained on her. Brit didn't begrudge him any reflected glory. For the most part. She and Dylan shared a bond most other people would never understand. Certainly not people who had normal childhoods. Those lucky kids who hadn't been educated by a revolving door of tutors and weren't constantly shepherded around by various levels of handlers.

But Dylan wasn't in the mixing room. He was down the hall laying down tracks of his own. Songs he'd written on his own. An album destined to fly or die on its own merit. A project no one could say succeeded because Brittany Owens helped him.

The final strains of the final song faded away, and no one spoke for a moment. Thick, cloying silence filled the tiny room. They were waiting for her to say something. She resisted the urge to glance at Wydetta for guidance. This was what she wanted—control.

With four pair of eyes boring into her, Brittany shook her head and whispered only, "Something's missing."

Leelo immediately jumped into the fray. "The mix is great. You've got single potential on tracks two, three, and seven, but I don't think you can go wrong with any of them." When she didn't rush to agree with him, he plunged ahead as if he were selling her a used car. "They're going to play awesomely on stage. Think of the choreography."

Heywood nodded mutely, but the tight line of his lips said he agreed with her about the missing ingredient.

"It's perfect," Wydetta announced, without looking up. "Smack on brand. Exactly what we planned." She chucked her phone into her massive handbag, then locked eyes on Brittany. "You have costume fittings this afternoon, then we start shooting the videos on Thursday. It's perfect."

"Hmm." A low, skeptical hum came from behind her.

All eyes swung to the studio door. There stood Sir James Paulson, his lanky body propped against the doorframe.

"Excuse me," Wydetta said, her voice high with indignation. "This is a private... you can't just... they can't allow just anyone..."

She trailed off, and Brit's cheeks burned with embarrassment for her mother. This man wasn't "just" anything. He could do about anything he wanted in the music world. A fact that was driven home back the fact that he didn't move a single muscle in the face of Wydetta's escalating outrage.

"Hello, Sir James," Brittany said, cutting through the awkward moment.

He inclined his head. "Hello, Miss Owens."

Brittany looked into his eyes and knew instinctively that he got it. The thing they were missing. "It's Brit." She gestured to Wydetta. "But you should probably feel free to call my mama Miss Owens."

"Thank you," he replied in a grave tone. "I believe I will."

But he didn't spare a glance for Wydetta. A move Brit admired for its sheer audacity. Sir James appeared to be a man of great wisdom. Latching onto that thought, she waved a hand at a studio monitor. "You know what I'm saying, don't you?"

The music legend simply shrugged, then nodded. "There is no love song. I've always thought a person needs at least one love song on an album. Something people can latch onto and hug to their hearts." He folded his hands over his chest, as if they needed a roadmap to know exactly where the organ in question might reside.

"You're young and beautiful, even if you do dress like a street urchin most of the time. Don'tcha have a nice ballad layin' about? Something soulful and achy. The kind of song meant to make a bloke squirm a little?"

"A ballad," she repeated, latching onto the glimmering gold key Sir James had conjured out of thin air. She stared at him. "Yes. We need something slow. Something soft."

"Achy, but not squishy," Sir James corrected. "You have a lovely break in your voice. Go for something you can get your hooks into."

Brittany stared at the older man. Like most people her age, she'd forgotten he was more than some rock 'n' roll relic they trotted out at award show time. "My hooks?"

He nodded emphatically. "You've got all the pop and rock anyone could want there, but by the end of the album, one song blends into the next, you know? If you mix the bippity-boppity with something achy, you'll catch the listener off-guard. It's what keeps them coming back to an album."

"Nobody sits down and listens to a whole album anymore," Wydetta snapped. "These days, people download singles. No one uses a turntable."

James cocked one stylishly arched brow. "You don't say? Poor sods."

His tone was cool and droll enough to freeze a normal person in their tracks, but her mother was no normal person. Wydetta simply glared back at him, daring him to come at her.

Brittany watched the exchange, riveted.

A beat passed, then he grinned, his face creasing into well-worn folds and his eyes crinkling into slits. "Well, I suppose that's what I get for feeling relevant," he said to Brittany as an aside.

She smiled, feeling a fresh surge of affinity for the older man, even if he was staring at her mother like she was the last piece of chocolate cake trapped under a glass dome.

"I listen to albums all the way through," Brit said, pleased to share a connection with him. "I like to get the feel for what the artist was thinking when they put it together."

James met her eyes, his gaze probing. "And what did it made you feel while you were listening? What were you feeling when you put these tracks together?"

It was a loaded question. They both knew she had very little input in the song selection other than to say whether she liked a song or not. And while she did actually like all twelve of the tracks on the album, the only song that spoke to her soul was the one she had written. Brit listened to the advice of the experts around her, which wasn't necessarily a bad thing, but it was simply advice. She could take it or leave it or change it as she saw fit, as long as she could get her producer to agree.

Shifting her gaze to Leelo, she cocked her head and asked, "Why don't we give it a try? One track. Roll it into the mix to see what the change does to the album as a whole. It can be track number thirteen, or we can lose the track and keep it as an even dozen."

Before Leelo could respond, Sir James jumped in with another suggestion. "Don't trash any track, love. These days there are all sorts of ways you can use a tune. How about a teaser on ViewTube or one of the other online sites? Or even a satellite radio exclusive." He shrugged. "Something along those lines."

Directing his attention to Wydetta, he lifted one corner of his mouth into a smirk. "Maybe we could go get all those shoppers rushing out to buy new turntables specifically for your album. You are pressing on vinyl, aren't you? I hear it's all the rage again."

Brit watched as her mother narrowed her eyes at Sir James.

"Okay, enough. Don't you have someone's phone to blow up or something?" Wydetta snapped her fingers as if Sir James Paulson were a mischievous dog she wanted to bring to heel. "I'll walk out with you."

Brittany watched in amazement as one of the most revered musicians of all time gave her mother a docile nod of acquiescence, lifted a hand in farewell, then followed her from the studio as if she had a string tied to his belt buckle.

"What the hell are you doing here?"

Brit heard Wydetta demand before the door had fully closed.

"You won't return my calls," Sir James Paulson replied, unruffled.

Brit exchanged glances with Leelo and Heywood. "Kind of hate to miss that conversation."

"Probably for the best," Heywood said, turning back to his precious console.

"Listen, we can't just go adding songs—" Leelo began.

"We're ahead of schedule, and it won't hurt us to give it some consideration," Heywood grumbled.

The producer glared at the engineer, his expression mulish.

Heywood nodded as if the matter were settled, then went back to fussing with his levers. "I think Paulson has a point. There's some heart missing."

"Yes," Brit agreed quietly. "It can't hurt to try something else."

Leelo sighed, then shrugged off his defeat. "I guess we're two against one. See what you can come up with, and we'll listen."

Rising from the banquette, Brit walked over and placed her hand on the famed producer's broad shoulder. "Only a fool ignores unbiased opinions," she reminded him. "Weren't you the one who told me to be open to suggestion? I think it was on the first song we did together."

Leelo rolled his eyes. "Don't toss my words back at me, kid. In this business, it's better to have bad short-term memory."

She gave his shoulder a friendly squeeze. "I'll kick some things around, and we'll meet back here tomorrow or the next day. If I don't have something by then, we'll go ahead as we are. But I really do think we should give it a shot. Something isn't sitting right."

Leelo shrugged, then gave her a lopsided smile. "It's your name on the cover."

Brittany couldn't muster even the slightest curve of her lips. "A fact I think other people forget sometimes."

Heywood nodded, his attention riveted to the task of backing up the master to an encrypted file storage service. "As long as you don't."

She shoved her hands into the pockets of her jeans and averted her face away so they couldn't see her blush. "If it's okay with you guys, I think I'll go in there"—she nodded toward the empty studio space on the other side of the glass—"and...commune with Patsy."

Leelo snorted, shaking his head as he rose from his chair. "We are not doing a cover of 'Crazy,'" he warned her. "This ain't no karaoke bar."

Backing toward the door, she pitched her husky contralto toward the low end of her natural range and beamed her best center-stage smile at the grumbling producer. "I'm crazy...crazy for workin' with you," she crooned.

The last note cracked on a laugh, and she darted from the room when the two men shooed her away. Brit walked back into the recording studio and straight up to the microphone. Gripping the clasp of the stand with one hand, she tilted it towards her.

Closing her eyes, she took three deep, meditative breaths. Then, on the fourth, she opened her mouth and let the queen of country music speak to her from beyond.

"Sweet dreams of you," she wailed into the microphone.

She opened her eyes to belt out the next line and found the two men at the mixing desk sitting upright in their chairs, staring at her with their mouths open like guppies. Rolling her eyes, she shook her head. "What? You've been listening to me sing for weeks."

Leelo leaned over and toggled the switch to open his mic. "Not like that."

Heat rose in her cheeks. Pointing a finger at the glass like a pistol, she ordered, "Mic off, please, fellas."

Heywood opened up the switch long enough to let her hear their combined groans of pain, but she remained adamant. "I'll wait until y'all are gone," she threatened, speaking into the hot mic.

Leelo held up his hands in a gesture of surrender and started for the door. Brit tapped her foot as Heywood fiddled with a few more dials and switches.

He looked up and gave a sheepish shrug. Speaking into the control mic, he said, "I'm leaving it on. Grab a headset. You need to hear how you sound." Without giving her a chance to respond, he waved and disappeared through the door.

Rolling her shoulders back, Brit stepped up to the mic again and closed her eyes. This was her home. When she was a little girl, her granddad told her stories about a beautiful songbird named Patsy. A woman whose voice made people weep for its pure beauty, he said. Whenever she asked him what to sing, Merle Owens always asked her to sing something pretty like Patsy. He wasn't a big fan of the path her career was taking, but he was her biggest fan. And when she needed a boost of confidence, she always consulted the exalted Ms. Cline.

Holding fast to the mic, she hit the first line of the song again, then let the melody carry her off. For the next fifteen minutes she sang to an audience of none, hoping the angels above would hear her and help make her most fervent wishes come true.

Cash Dorsett wasn't one of those fools who inhaled all the money he'd made straight up his nose. He might've been a mess once upon a time, but he was a frugal mess. He'd preferred booze and pills. Cheap highs. And why pay for drinks and drugs when people would give them to you for free?

No, he hadn't let his addictions bankrupt him. His grandmother would have been pleased to know he'd managed to hang onto some money. She'd never been overly impressed with his brush with stardom, but Granny Fannie appreciated a person who knew the value of a dollar. Hell, she was the one who'd suggested his name to his mama. She liked to say she'd known it was the only chance his parents would get at holding onto any cash for the next eighteen years.

When he'd come out of rehab, he'd hidden away from the music world for a good two years, afraid he'd slide down a slippery slope again if he ever walked back into a studio. Through some of his AA connections, he found work as a carpenter—something to keep his hands busy and steady and his days full. Then, one night he'd been invited to a jam session at his mentor and sponsor, Jace Allen's, house. It was weeks before Cash finally felt strong enough to take his guitar out, but he was glad to keep coming back to Jace's. To know he could find his way back to music.

Some of the men in the group had been old-fashioned pickers. The kind of guys who could make a banjo, mandolin, or even a dulcimer cry like a baby aching for its mama's touch. The rest of them were the fools who came to Nashville looking for the bright lights and found themselves blinded by the lifestyle. But the one thing they all had in common was every man drank nothing stronger than a glass of sweet tea.

In time, Cash found himself getting pulled back into the music scene little by little. But this was a different scene. He was no longer on the fast track to stardom. For a while, he was the same as any another working musician schlepping his guitar from gig to gig, and he loved it.

He was clean, sober, and business-minded. The guys he hung out with were straight arrows and a bit insular, but their steadiness worked out well for him. He'd come to appreciate their almost corporate regard for the almighty dollar, and the evangelical way they guarded their sobriety. Jace was the one who had pulled Cash in on the deal to take over StarRise Studios.

Once the home away from home for some of Nashville's biggest names, StarRise had been the birthplace of dozens of multi-platinum albums and boasted nearly as much gold as they held in Fort Knox. Sadly, the previous owners had about run it into the ground. The moment they heard whispers of bankruptcy, their sober little consortium of investors had it together enough to make an offer to buy the place outright.

Knowing they were heading into direct competition with hotter, newer setups, they took their time renovating the famed A and B studios, making sure they had nothing but the best to offer. Then, they set up low-cost, low-overhead facilities designed to cater to the constant stream of up-and-comers who flowed into the city like the Cumberland River. Since every one of the guys in their group had been there and done everything they could to wreck themselves, they were all keen on the idea of helping some of those starry-eyed dreamers reach for the stars without getting burned.

He had just finished a session sitting in with a young male vocalist with a set of pipes capable of blowing the music industry out of the water, but only a thimbleful of self-confidence. Cash had spent the better portion of the kid's not-exactly-dirt-cheap studio time amping him up. He'd also thrown in another hour of free studio time to work out the kinks in a song Cash thought might have real potential. An hour he'd have to pay out of his own pocket because, though his partners had agreed they wouldn't fleece anyone, they also liked to remind him they weren't running a charitable institution.

But all in all, StarRise was on the rise again. They'd produced their first Grammy winner the previous year, thanks to a trio of female singers reunited after a lengthy separation. They'd hung four new gold albums on the walls, and one platinum. And when Cash returned from Austin, he learned they'd landed their biggest client yet for Studio A—lightning-hot crossover star…Brittany Owens.

Of all the partners, only Jace thought anything about the connection between Cash and the Owens family. His friend and partner had taken him aside the moment he got back from Texas and told Cash he'd have veto power over the booking if he wished to exert it. But Cash was no fool. His Granny Fannie would've been proud of him when he told their managing partner to sign that contract on its very lucrative dotted line.

Having a producer as hot as Leelo working the desk in one of their studios was enough of a boon. Leelo combined with Brittany packed enough star power to light up an entire constellation. The producer had deep connections in every sub-genre of the music industry, but Brit… Brit was about to break big, and the whole town knew it.

He'd have been a fool to let old feelings and new complications screw this up for StarRise, and Cash's days of playing the fool were over. Carrying his battered guitar case loose in his grip, he walked the halls from the small warren of studios in the back to the larger state-of-the-art showpiece studios.

As part of their continued recovery, every one of the partners had put in physical labor in rebuilding the space and bringing the studios up to acoustical snuff. Cash himself had cut what seemed like hundreds of thousands of tiny pieces of wood to create a single wall meant to diffuse sound but preserve the music's natural tone.

It was the focal point of Studio A, the studio Brit was using to record her make-or-break album. And though he knew he was better off keeping a safe distance between them, a part of him itched to know what she thought about his handiwork. He paused outside the studio door and checked his watch. Brittany and her crew had likely knocked off for the day. Reports said they weren't far from being done. From here on out, they would be tweaking, mixing, and overdubbing.

Curious, he twisted the handle on the door leading to the control room and opened it a crack. The seats in front of the desk were empty, but the studio was still lit bright as day. He was about to close the door when he heard someone singing in the studio beyond.

The voice was gut-wrenchingly recognizable.

A scratchy version of "Walking After Midnight" filled every inch of the space. It floated out of the studio monitors and settled over him like a hot summer night. If he didn't know better, he'd think his precious studio was being haunted by a super-sultry version of Patsy Cline's ghost.

He froze, his fingers clamped around the door handle. He knew the voice, but the woman it belonged to was nowhere in sight. Cash propped his guitar against the wall and used the door as an anchor. He craned his neck to peer into the studio, but still, he couldn't find her. Cautiously relinquishing his hold on the handle, he stepped into the booth and leaned over the desk.

Brittany Owens lay flat on her back, sprawled across the thick rug, her feet bare and a microphone clutched in one hand. Her eyes were squeezed shut, as if belting out a song to an empty room was tearing her to shreds inside.

It sure as hell wasn't doing him any favors.

He stared transfixed. How could he do anything but stare? She was beautiful. Her face was scrubbed clean of makeup except for some eyeliner and a truly outlandish set of false eyelashes, and her white-blond hair was tied in a messy knot atop her head. The whole effect was deceptively angelic. Her skin glowed with exertion. And youth. Sweet, intoxicating youth. And a sort of innocence. Which was ridiculous, considering she'd practically been birthed on stage. But she had the kind of shiny newness he'd lost long ago.

Her cheeks were flushed and her chest heaved as if she was on pace to win a marathon. Other than the finger wrapped tight around the mic, she lay loose, her other limbs splayed akimbo as if she'd forgotten she had them. The cumulative effect was that of a woman who'd experienced a pleasure so intense she couldn't move.

He should know. He'd taken her there.

Cash stared at the tableau openmouthed. He finally regained his senses and clamped his jaw shut, but then he found himself wishing he could work up enough spit to swallow.

Would she ever loosen her grip on him?

He figured it wasn't likely. Five years hadn't made a difference. A month had passed since she'd walked into his hotel room, and his yearning for her proved to be every bit as strong as it had ever been. Stronger. Because this version of Brittany was a thousand times more potent than the young woman he'd walked away from one balmy summer night.

Seconds ticked past. The last note of the song lingered in the air. He needed to make his choice now. Stay and make his presence known? Or go and preserve his sanity?

A derisive laugh rolled up from his chest as he took a step toward the console. He'd spent many months learning to be honest with himself. There was no point in trying to slip out. He'd always gravitate right back to her. Flipping a switch, he leaned into the desk mic.

"Are you taking requests?"

5

The thud of the microphone hitting carpet reverberated through the booth. Indignant feedback screeched from the studio monitors. Brit reflexively covered her ears as she sat up. She caught sight of a pair of broad shoulders covered in gray plaid. Seconds later, a headful of tousled dirty blond hair popped up, and unforgettable blue eyes locked on her.

Cash.

She swiped at her hair, even though it was secure in its bun. Catching herself mid-futile-gesture, she grabbed for the microphone she'd dropped, then scrambled to her feet. Tugging the band of her sweatshirt down as she straightened, she narrowed her eyes at the man smirking at her through the glass. "What are *you* doing here?"

She hated the way she practically spat the words at him. They made her sound defensive and childish, the last thing she wanted him to think of her. He lifted one golden-brown eyebrow and made her feel like she'd been caught doing something she wasn't supposed to be doing, rather than doing her job—which was singing—in a studio space she'd paid for. She stopped fidgeting with her clothes, shoved Patsy down deep, and channeled her inner Wydetta.

"Does this place let people wander in off the streets? First it's Paulson, now it's you. I'm going to have to talk to the owner about security."

"I'll pass your concerns along on my way out," Cash said, his drawl thick with unconcern. Then he blinked. "Paulson? As in James

Paulson?"

When she nodded, he took two steps to the side and lifted a guitar case so beat up she was amazed it hadn't disintegrated. Her heart squeezed with recognition. Same case. Same man. She'd bet her every last rhinestone he carried the same Taylor mahogany guitar he'd bought years ago. But judging by the state of its case, the guitar had seen as many rough days as its player.

"I had a studio gig," he explained, jerking his head toward the back of the building. Then his gaze landed on her again, and she nearly forgot how to breathe. "I'd forgotten you could sing like that," he said, his voice gruff.

A shiver of pleasure ran up her spine, but she held strong. She wouldn't let him bait her into the old argument about the type of music she should be making. She'd been following her instincts since the day he'd walked away from her, and look where they'd gotten her.

"I can sing any number of ways," she replied with an ingratiating smile.

Lifting the microphone, she rolled out a few words of painstakingly memorized Italian building into a crescendo meant to leave one feeling like they were dangling from a cliff by their fingernails. Cash's jaw dropped again, and she sweetened her smile with a few more drops of honey.

"I sang a few songs with Andrea Bocelli at the World Cup a couple years ago. Those Europeans sure like their soccer."

"They do."

"Here's the difference between you and me, Cash," she said, speaking into the microphone so he was sure to catch every word. "I've learned 'can' doesn't always mean 'should.'"

He flinched as if he'd been struck, but she refused to feel bad about speaking the truth. Her truth.

"I can sing like that," she asserted. "I can also sing like this."

Inserting the mic into the clip, she clutched the stand and pulled it into her like a lover. Pitching her voice low, she treated him to a few blatantly seductive lines of Chris Isaak's "Wicked Game." When he held up a hand to stop her, she closed her eyes and segued into a gender-flipped rendition of Bruce Springsteen's "I'm On Fire." When he raised his other hand, completing his surrender with a slight bow, she let the last note hang in the air, her eyes locked with his.

Feeling more confident, Brit stepped out from behind the microphone and walked to the door to the booth. The moment she opened it, he spoke. "You're incredible."

"I'm blessed," she countered without an ounce of irony or false humility. There was no point in using either. God had given her a voice people loved. She owed it to Him to use it well.

"You are," Cash agreed with a solemn nod. "I can't compete."

"Oh, I don't know. It's all about the song selection." She stepped closer to him, challenging his claim on the space he'd invaded. "You've got the whole scruffy acoustic guy thing going here. Some Neil Diamond might work wonders for you. Why don't you try countering with a little 'Girl, You'll Be a Woman Soon' or 'Play Me'?"

"You know the difference between can and should, but I know better than to play with fire."

She smirked, then tugged gently on the rumpled T-shirt he wore. "Maybe that's our problem. We're both too smart for our own good."

She watched as his Adam's apple dipped and rose. "Never been accused of being too smart."

"First time for everything. I've never sung Springsteen into anything other than my steering wheel," she said with an amused laugh. "It wasn't bad. I may need to let the song simmer on the back burner for a while."

"It was incredible. You ought to scribble it on a set list." He gestured to the abandoned booth. "How's the recording coming?"

"It's fine," she answered a beat too quickly. Catching herself, she offered him a sheepish smile. If anyone would understand, it would be Cash. "It's pretty much done, but there's something missing."

He frowned. "Missing?"

She raised one shoulder and let it fall. "Heywood says heart. Sir James thinks I need something achy."

Her comment had both of his brows reaching for the sky. "He was really here?"

"Just showed up out of the blue. I think he was looking for Wydetta," she reported. "This place really is a bit lax on security, now that I think about it."

"I don't think there's a studio in existence that would bar Sir

James Paulson."

"True. He seems to have taken a cotton to Mama for some reason." She shrugged. "I don't get the attraction, but I probably won't think too hard about it." Unable to hold his gaze, she moved past him to take a seat at the console. "Maybe they had a fling back in Austin. You know, some people aren't as good at one-night stands as we are."

To her surprise, Cash dropped into the other chair and scrubbed at his face. "Listen, about that night—"

"Don't even," she said, stopping him hard shake of her head. "You weren't my first."

"You made that clear," he replied grimly.

Brit chuckled. "I mean first one-nighter." She cast him a sidelong glance. "Sometimes, it's easier to scratch the itch, you know?"

"Oh, I know," he muttered. "But I did mean to call."

"You didn't have my number," she pointed out.

"I think I could have gotten it. We still know people in common."

Boy, did they. Like half the town. Including her grandfather.

Brit watched as he powered down the control desk with a few practiced flicks of his fingers. His utter competence was fascinating. And new.

The Cash she'd known had been cocky. As slick and shiny as the expensive boots he'd loved so much. She glanced down at his feet. He wore the same well-worn pair he'd had on in Austin. Watching him move with such confidence and command now made her wonder what else had changed about him. Did the tender heart he tried to keep hidden under all that varnish still beat inside this much humbler man? Could he still weave together words and melodies that made her heart ache? Once, they'd known each other as well as two people not physically involved could. Now, they'd broken the barrier to bits, but he remained a near stranger.

"So, how have you been?" she asked, hating the nervous quaver in her voice. If he noticed it, she could always claim strain from the interlude with Patsy.

Cash's hands stilled on the controls. He looked over at her. "I've been fine. How about you?"

"Fine. Fine," she added as if repeating it would make it more believable. She gestured to the control panel. "Busy."

"Do *you* think it's missing something?"

She nodded, then shrugged again. "Maybe it's only me. I like all the songs on the album. I think we've made smart choices. There are a couple surefire hits on there."

"I have no doubt."

"But there's something…I don't know what..."

"Yeah, it's a tough thing to balance." He pulled his hands back from the controls and laced them together atop the desk. "It's like, with each album you want your sound to change a little. *You* have changed," he said meaningfully. "No one stays the same, and neither does the music. I think stubbornly clinging to the same beat is where people get into trouble. They don't let the music change with them."

"You look the same to me."

The words popped out of her mouth. She wished she could take them back. It was a ridiculous sentiment given all he'd been through over the past few years, but it was true. When she looked at Cash, she saw the same guy she'd fallen for the minute he walked into her life.

She shook her head. "I mean, you're the same person."

Cash shook his head. "Not even by a long shot, sweetheart."

"I mean down inside. You're the same guy, just without all the"—she paused, searching for the word—"crapola."

Her word choice startled a bark of laughter from him. Her lungs ceased to function when she saw the corners of his eyes crinkle. Yeah, he was a little bit older, but he was still every bit as beautiful as he'd been in his twenties. A little scruffier around the edges, maybe. It also made him even more devastating, her subconscious reminded her. Star or not, he still could have any woman he wanted by crooking his finger. Not for the first time, she wondered how he'd managed to remain unattached for so long.

"How come you haven't gotten married?"

If he was fazed by the non-sequitur, he didn't bother showing it. Their conversations had been like this for as long as she could remember. Like rocks skipping across a placid pond. Some topics created ripples, but they somehow always managed to sink into the comfort and companionship of the sandy bottom. Mutual respect. And love. They did love one another, even if it hadn't been the kind of love she'd imagined once upon a time.

This time, it was Cash's turn to shrug. "Been busy trying to keep myself straight. Figured it wouldn't fair to bring someone else into the mess I'd made." He sneaked a glance at her, and she caught him. The sheepish up tilt of his lips made her heart rate speed up. "I think we both know I have some unresolved issues in the relationship department."

Brittany stared at him, stunned he'd admitted so much. Wetting her lips, she tried to play it cool. "And here I thought we'd worked all this out in the hotel room in Austin."

"It was never about the sex, Brittany," he replied, holding her gaze.

"Wasn't it?"

"You know it wasn't. If it had only been about sex, I might have taken the chance," he confessed, not breaking eye contact.

Every bit of oxygen she owned tangled up into a hard knot in the center of her chest. Unable to free enough for a full exhalation, she whispered, "Then what was it?"

At last, Cash looked away, a bitter huff echoing through the otherwise silent room. "Hell, sugar, it was everything. Sex, money, fame, power," he listed. "Everything soap operas are made of."

"We were a soap opera?"

"We were daytime programming heading for nighttime drama." He shook his head and rose from the chair. Tapping his fingers on the console, he took a step back. "Then I became tabloid fodder, and everything went to shit."

She was about to speak, but he forged ahead.

"My grandma saw it all too," he said softly. "She died knowing I'd made a mess of my life. Knowing I'd blown every chance I ever had because my ego was out of control, and I wouldn't listen to anyone or anything." He stared down at her. "The only thing I can be proud of is she didn't know how hard I lusted for a girl who was far too young for me."

He started for the door and she spun in the chair. "Cash, wait—"

Pausing at the door, he hefted this guitar case but didn't look at her.

At a loss for anything else to say, Brittany fell back on good old-fashioned Southern manners. "I was sorry to hear about your Granny Fannie. Merle told me she passed. I hope you got the flowers."

His back still to her, he nodded. She heard the smile in his voice when he spoke. "Your grandmama sent a veritable buffet to the house. She was always really nice to me." He turned back, his expression grave as he studied her for a long moment. "So, yeah, if I have one thing to be proud of in my life, it's I didn't disappoint either of our grandmas by doing something bad with you."

"I don't think us wanting each other was bad," she stated frankly. "I don't think sex is bad, or dirty, or wrong, or any of those other things people who don't want to admit they don't like it want you to believe. I believe sex is good, and healthy, and it can't possibly be wrong when two people care about each other."

"Would you have said the same thing five years ago? I mean, I know you're Janet Jackson now, all grown up and in control, but would you have been able to say the same to me back when you were eighteen?"

"The only thing I wanted to say to you when I was eighteen was 'I love you.'"

"And I was trying to tell you I wasn't good enough for you or deserving of your love."

"You were. Otherwise, my heart wouldn't have let me love you. I see the good in people, remember? That's what you always used to tell me. I see the good."

"It wasn't supposed to be a compliment," he grumbled.

"But I choose to take it as one," she countered. "It was my choice to see what was good in you. It was my choice to give you my heart."

"I've been wanting to say something about your questionable choices," he muttered. "But it's not my place."

Juggling the case slightly, he twisted the handle on the door. "Good luck with finding your something, Brittany. Think about you, and how you've changed, and what the music means to you as you are now. I have every faith you'll find the missing piece."

When Brittany walked into her enormous estate in the Brentwood area near Nashville, she found herself wishing, not for the first time, she had a normal sort of family. Or maybe not normal, but more like a television family. The kind she fantasized about having from time to time. But hers was anything but normal, and she knew from the moment her grandfather first put her in front of a microphone on the stage at the Grand Ol' Opry what she wanted to be when she grew up. She might've been four, or maybe five.

But other than the expectations of stardom she'd been born to fulfill, Brit knew overall, she had a good family life. Her grandparents were awesome. Not many kids could tote both a legend and a famous beauty to Grandparents' Day at school—even in Nashville. And though she had never met her father, and her mother was about as ambitious a stage mother who ever lived, she knew Wydetta still loved her in her own way.

Of course, her own way actually meant on her own terms. And those terms were usually laid out in bullet points.

"I love you, honey, but—" were the words she'd been hearing her whole life. Frankly, Brit wasn't convinced Wydetta truly knew how to love anyone. Not without a codicil, anyway. It was boggling. Wydetta's own parents were generous and loving people who'd never forgotten their homespun values of God, country music, and family. At least, they were good at the family bit when it came to loving Brit. She could see now that it wasn't always the case with their own daughter.

Her grandparents still lived on Old Hickory Lane in Hendersonville, not far from Johnny Cash's old place. Her granddad liked to say he was 'Old Nashville,' which was a polite put-down to anyone not conversant in Southern speak. When she and Wydetta had settled on this estate in the Brentwood area, he said she'd moved to the wrong side of the river. But the house was beautiful. Spacious enough for people to live totally separate lives under the same roof.

"Hello?"

Her voice echoed back at her in the sound chamber created by the three-story high entry. She winced at the rough edges. She'd need warm water and honey. And she needed a little quiet if she wanted any chance at getting a hook into the melody circling around in her head. The growl in her voice made it unique and instantly recognizable, but it also meant she was susceptible to strain and had to treat her instrument with the care a violinist would show a Stradivarius.

She'd reached the third tread on the stairs, but stopped when she caught the click of heels on tile. Leaning over the bannister, she saw Martine hurrying from the back of the house, wiping her hands on the dishcloth.

Martine was a cousin on her grandmother's side. A somewhat distant relation, but close enough in age with Wydetta for them to form an odd-couple sort of bond when they were growing up. She was tall, and slender, and of mixed race. Brit, ever vigilant about her own nearly translucent complexion, openly envied Martine her smooth, tawny skin. She also basked in her cousin's warm and generous nature.

Smiling with relief, she greeted the woman who'd moved into her house and taken over her life. "Hey, Marti," she called, backing down the stairs again. "I wasn't sure if you were here."

"I'm always here," Martine replied.

A faint Cajun accent made the simple phrase almost musical. It was one of the reasons Brit loved talking to her cousin–slash–housekeeper. Marti could read off a recipe and make it sound like a love song. Never one to blow a chance at blurring the line between family and employer, Brit leaned in to kiss the older woman's cheek. "Are you implying I never give you a day off?"

Both women laughed because they knew the opposite to be true. Brittany had to practically pry Martine from the house and ship her bodily back to Louisiana to visit her family twice a year.

"Oh, *cher*." Martine waved her away, a flush darkening her cheeks. "I simply mean I'm always here for you."

Brit tormented her with an impromptu hug.

Laughing, Martine wriggled from her grasp, "Enough. Enough. You love me, I know."

"Is my mother home?"

Martine wrinkled her nose as she shook her head. "I assume she's at some meeting. I swear, the only time I see her is when she drops off her dry cleaning." She sniffed disapprovingly. "She needs to be around more. She has a daughter to raise."

Brittany laughed. "A twenty-three-year-old daughter to raise," she repeated with a scoff.

Martine waved her off. "Doesn't matter how old you get, a woman always needs her mother to be her mother."

Brit caught the other woman's wrist and gave it a squeeze. "Who needs a mother when I have you?" When Martine opened her mouth to make the same old argument about salaried employees, Brit cut her off with a brusque gesture. "It isn't like I don't pay Wydetta as well. Don't forget she's taking her cut off the top."

"Now don't be getting on your mama's case," Martine chastised, always quick to jump to Wydetta's defense. "You know she earns every penny."

"Yes, and she wrings every bit of sweat out of me she can,"

Brittany replied.

"Now that's not fair."

Exhaling loudly, Brit gripped the newel post at the bottom of the curved staircase. "Okay, fine. Not fair. But you were getting on her case too," she concluded, not even caring that she sounded like a child. "I don't know why I'm getting huffy. Tired, I guess. These long days are killer."

Martine beamed a hopeful smile at Brit. "I know, *cher*. What are your plans for the evening? Anything fun?"

It was a reasonable question. She was a twenty-three-year-old woman with the world at her feet. She ought to have some sort of plan for an evening, any evening. But, as usual, she didn't. If the tabloids only knew how very boring her life actually was, they'd...leave her alone.

"I plan on taking a hot bath, then eating whatever is in the kitchen. I have vocal early tomorrow, then Mark and I are going to be working on the new choreography. I'll probably just crawl into bed with one of my Chrises."

"Which one will it be tonight?"

Brit pondered her options for a moment, then shrugged. "I think Pine. I'm not in the mood for any man who takes himself too seriously."

"Good call," Martine said with an approving nod.

"What are your plans?"

The older woman's lips curved into an enigmatic smile. "I have a date."

"Oooh. Wild thing," Brit teased.

"You know it, *cher*. I have salad fixings in the fridge. And some grilled chicken. I know you're not big on the meat thing right now, but I really think you need some protein to build up strength before the tour begins."

Brit smiled at her. Who needed an actual mother when she had Martine? The woman was a mother and a sister all rolled into one. "I'll chop up a little chicken and throw it in the salad, if it'll make you happy."

Martine rolled her dark eyes, flinging the dishtowel she'd been holding over her shoulder, then spun on her heel. "Oh, my goodness, you have no idea how ecstatic it will make me to know you have eaten the chicken I have prepared for you with my two humble hands—"

Laughing, Brit wagged her head. "Okay, okay."

"—And then, when I return from my dinner date, I hope to be able to wash the plate from which you have consumed the salad I made for you with my two humble hands and the chicken I so lovingly throttled and plu—"

"Don't take that one word further if you want me to eat your chicken," Brittany warned.

"Good night, Brit the Brat."

"Good night, Smarty Marti," Brit called back, leaning over the banister. "Have some fun for me."

From the depths of the house, Martine called back to her, "Oh, you know I will."

As she trudged up the stairs, Brit tried not to think too hard about the fact that both her mother and their cousin had far more active social lives than she did. Sure, she went to all the usual industry functions and award shows and all the places where people were photographed to make this business look more glamorous than it actually was from the inside. But she couldn't remember the last time she'd gone out and done something for the fun of it.

She walked into the sumptuously appointed sitting room that adjoined her bedroom and stopped dead in her tracks, giving herself a full body shake.

"No. You won't do this. No poor little rich girl."

She closed her eyes, inhaled, then exhaled—centering herself and taking the time to choose a particular path of thought. Gratitude. She needed to find her attitude of gratitude.

And she was grateful. Brittany was all too aware of how blessed her life was. Her grandfather's fame and fortune were substantial. Neither she nor Wydetta had ever wanted for anything. She'd been born under a lucky star. Born to *be* a star, her mother said. And now she was one. Wydetta never missed a chance to remind her there were thousands of young women in this very town alone who would give anything to switch places with her.

Opening her eyes, she toed off her half-boots and took a look around the room, willing herself to take it all in with fresh eyes. The comfortable overstuffed sofa upholstered in the softest velvet. Plump throw pillows. A television the size of a movie screen. A sound system elaborate enough to make any audiophile weep.

And that was only the sitting room.

The house her mother had found for them was an oasis. Had been their oasis since Brittany first became a teen sensation. Living here took them out of Merle Owens's country-oriented orbit and opened her up to a world of possibilities. She would never turn her back on her family's country origins. Country music was in her blood. But she wanted something more than to be an extension of her grandfather's legacy. She loved him with all her heart, but there was only room for one King of Country Music in the Owens family.

With Wydetta's guidance, Brittany had carved out a space for herself. First, in television, then in the music world. She shone brightly, all the while enhancing Merle's star power and burnishing the family name with a fresh coat of gloss. And Nashville would always be home, even if she hadn't chosen country music. Though he would never admit it out loud, Brit was fairly sure her grandfather was relieved she hadn't followed directly in his footsteps. Merle was many wonderful things, but he wasn't keen on sharing the spotlight.

But there was no time for self-pity or intense family analytics. She had serious business to attend to. The business of injecting some heart into her art.

She usually hated it when people called making music "their art" but had to admit there was some artistry involved in coaxing music to life. To Brit, music was indeed a living entity. The backbeat provided a pulse, the melody was carried on each breath. It reached out to people when they needed it most. And people like her—the singers, musicians, and other talented people who helped bring it to life? They were merely temporary caregivers to the art. She believed people couldn't own music outright, because once it escaped into the world at large, it belonged to everyone.

A belief she was careful never to share with her legal team.

Chuckling at the thought, she moved through the sitting room to the bedroom, where she went to the tall dresser in the corner. There, in the top drawer where one might expect to find underwear and socks, or maybe some star-quality lingerie, lay a treasure trove of notebooks. Simple, single-subject, wire-bound notebooks. The kind every kid used in school.

Each of those notebooks was filled with page after page of hopes, schemes, and, most importantly, song lyrics. Not songs she'd written to become hits, but songs flowed from her heart. If Sir James wanted some ache, she had plenty to share.

Perching on the edge of the bed, she sorted through the books. Red, green, blue, red again, and then she spotted it. The unicorn in the pack. A sparkly pink foil-printed cover she remembered with startlingly clarity. Because *he* had given it to her.

She wasn't a fool. She'd known even then the gift was meant to remind her of the difference in their ages. But Brit hadn't cared. All that mattered was Cash had picked something out for her. This notebook special.

Over the years, friends and family had given her fancier journals. Leather bound with lined pages. She had countless blinged-out binders and a handful of hipster Moleskines in her nightstand drawer in case of paper emergency, but she hadn't had to bust into them yet. She knew most other girls her age would record their thoughts and ideas on their phone or some other device, but Brit had always been a pen-to-paper girl. Once she wrote something out, she never forgot it.

She'd been a teenager with a massive crush on an older man. The lyric haunting her had to be in there. Where else could it be but tucked inside the gift he'd chosen for her?

6

Cash sank back into the worn leather of his sofa and propped a bottle of root beer on his knee. It wasn't the type of beer he wanted, but it would have to do. Jace had been the one to teach him this little trick. There was something about holding a glass bottle the relative size and shape of the real thing made him feel slightly less deprived and exponentially more in control.

Grabbing the remote control from the crease of the couch cushion, he pressed the power button and waited as the massive flat screen flashed to life. Oh, good, a football game. It didn't matter what teams were playing, he'd watch it. Watching sports while holding an ice-cold bottle made him feel almost like a regular guy. Tipping his head back, he took a long pull on the foamy soda and let out an exaggerated "Ahhh" as he lowered the bottle.

He was practiced at the art of self-deception.

Seeing Brit sprawled out on the rug in his recording studio had been a punch to the gut. He hadn't wanted to drink so badly in months. Maybe years. Driving home that evening, it was all he could do to bypass the bars and nightclubs lining the city's streets. Only sheer force of will made him dial Jace's number instead of one of the half-dozen other guys he knew would be more than happy to lead him back to the dark side.

His friend was calm and understanding. Their talk had been honest. Jace knew about his feelings for Brittany. But the knowledge was also a double-edged sword. When they were about to hang up, Jace hesitated for a moment, then echoed the very thought running around in Cash's own head.

"She's not a kid anymore, you know. And you would hardly be the first guy to fall for a younger woman. Hell, look at me."

But Jace's girlfriend was only five years younger than him. Not more than a decade. There was a difference. Or so he told himself. Plus, Jace and Aubry had only been dating a few months. The new had yet to wear off.

When he returned from Austin, Cash had spilled his guts to Jace. His friend made some crack about not being a priest, but to Cash, Jace was the closest thing. No one else understood where he was coming from and what he was struggling against. And even if his friend couldn't offer him absolution, he had been able to lend an understanding ear. But lately, their conversations had been going a little differently. Now, Jace spent most of them playing devil's advocate, striking down Cash's every objection like a Wimbledon champion swatting down lobs.

Truthfully, Cash wasn't as on the fence about Brittany as he wished he were. About eighty percent of him was ready to go after her. The twenty percent holding him back was reinforced by an internal chorus of "What would people say?"

A question he'd stopped asking himself in most other areas of his life years ago.

The fact of the matter was, it didn't matter what anyone said. She was a grown woman by every standard. And he needed to remember he no longer gave a crap if the rest of the world approved of his lifestyle choices. He was determined to live the way he wanted to live whether they liked it or not.

He sat through about half of the football game, abandoned the root beer for a sandwich and a bottle of room temperature water, and was sprawled across the couch half asleep when his phone buzzed in his pocket.

Frowning, he pried it from the denim confines and swiped his thumb across the screen without checking to see who the caller was. He had a very small circle of friends these days, which made simple things like answering his phone so much easier.

"Hello?"

A husky female laugh tickled his ear and rippled down his spine. "Hi. It's me."

The distinctive rasp rippled down his spine, and Cash sat up like a shot. Brittany. When being upright didn't seem to be enough of a defense, he sprang to his feet. Scrubbing his face with his hand, he clutched the phone so tightly it buzzed again. Panic gripped him as he thought maybe he'd accidentally dropped the call. "Brit? Are you still there?"

She laughed again, and this time the noise traveled due south. "Yeah, I'm still here. Do you have a minute?"

He ran his fingers through his hair and rolled his shoulders back, bracing himself to do some conversational sparring with her. Suddenly his T-shirt seemed woefully inadequate. What he really needed was some full body armor. With a chest plate. Or at least a shield he could use to cover his heart.

Shaking himself out of his reverie, he realized he hadn't answered her. "Um, yeah. Actually I do." He glanced around his own living room as if seeing it for the first time. "I'm just hanging out here at the house."

"You have a house? Gave up the swinging bachelor pad, huh?"

Cash grimaced thinking about his old condominium. It'd been an open-floorplan loft done in cheesy bachelor style. "Oh, yeah. I sold it years ago."

"Where are you living these days?" she asked.

Wanting to keep things vague, he answered only, "I'm still here in the city. Not far from downtown."

"With the hipsters? I'm surprised you haven't grown a beard."

"I look like crap with a beard." He refrained from commenting on the patches of gray stubble creeping in when he tried to grow one.

"I doubt it."

He waited a beat, then asked the question nagging at him. "How did you get my number?"

She laughed out loud this time. Then, clearing her throat, she spoke in a deep, menacing rasp. "Made a phone call."

He rolled his eyes at his own naïveté. "Right. Because you're Brittany Owens."

"You're the one who reminded me we have friends in common," she reminded him. "It wasn't like I had to pull strings."

He heard the icy edge of hurt in her tone and it made him wince. He was being an ass, and he didn't even have to try. "I'm sorry. I didn't mean—"

"It *was* what you meant," she said, her voice suddenly breezy and too lighthearted to be believed. "But that's okay, because I'm gonna pull a little star power on you, anyway."

"You are?"

"Yeah, if you don't mind."

"Stars don't ask if people mind. They assume everyone wants to give them everything."

She snickered. "Never could get the hang of the making demands thing." Clearing her throat again, she carried on. "Anyway, I could use an opinion on something, and since you were there today but aren't directly involved with the album, I'd like it to be your opinion."

Sinking back down onto the couch, Cash ran a suddenly slick palm down the front of his jeans. "Okay. What can I help you with?"

"I want to read you some lyrics, and I want your honest opinion as to what you think about them."

He blinked twice, then swallowed hard. Nobody understood what lyrics could mean to a musician better than another musician. This wasn't a simple request to listen to some words she'd thrown together. She was asking him to listen to something she'd written from her heart. Her soul. It wasn't a request he was about to take lightly.

"I'd love to. Thank you."

He leaned back against the couch cushions and smiled as he heard the sound of flimsy pages being flipped. She was working up to it. He knew what this was like. Psyching oneself up to share their innermost thoughts with another person wasn't an easy task. He tried to put her at ease. "Still using the spiral notebooks?"

"They're the best," she retorted.

Cash closed his eyes and settled in. "Hit me."

He listened to her speak the words. Some of the phrasing and word choices were a bit adolescent, but the sentiment was one hundred percent relatable. Love. Impossible love. Innocent. Pure. Heartbreaking love. The song was about him.

And her.

If he had a chance, he'd leap in there and answer every one of her tender pleas with one of his own. But this was her song. Her story. And he had to keep his feelings to himself. As usual.

Sinking deeper into the cushion, he forced himself to concentrate on the melody starting to unfurl in his head. He almost had a grasp on the riff when she stopped speaking. Desperate to hold on to it, he ordered, "Read it again."

Brit complied without question, and a truckload of memories slammed into him. This wasn't the first time the two of them had written a song together. The first one was a bubbly little pop-country tune they'd included in her first solo release. The label hadn't slated it to be one of the singles, but someone—he suspected Brittany herself—had released a studio video of the two of them running the song through together.

Of course, the clip went viral. And though it was perfectly innocent, the chemistry between them fueled rumors about up-and-coming country star Cash Dorsett hanging around with a girl barely old enough to go to prom.

Not long after, he ducked out of her life entirely.

Their age difference hadn't mattered in terms of the connection the two of them shared. But he also knew the rest of the world wouldn't have understood their soul-deep affinity for one another. All they'd have seen was a reckless young star messing with a girl he had no business messing with. And they'd have been right.

By the time she finished reading the lyrics again, he had a grasp on the tune flitting around the edges of his mind, but he wasn't sure. Humming, he hoisted himself from the sofa and grabbed an acoustic guitar from the stand near the television.

"Again," he whispered as he plopped back down with it.

Brit gave him another read-through without hesitation. As she sang-spoke the words, he plinked and plucked his way around the notes he wanted to use. When she was done, he pressed his fingers to the guitar strings to silence their echo.

"How did you envision the song?" The question came out a tad too strident, but he was excited and he couldn't help himself.

"I—" Brit stammered. "I'm not sure."

He waited patiently, knowing her brain and her gut would fill in the blanks when they could.

"Slow," she said at last. "I think it could be a ballad."

"Hang on." Pick between his teeth, he strummed until the instrument was perfectly in tune. "I think it's a fucking heartbreaker," he muttered around the triangle of plastic. "Give me a sec."

She did. Brittany remained absolutely silent as he tuned up and fiddled a little with the notes he was trying to put together in his head. Only a musician would understand the importance of silence the way Brittany did. Songs were elusive, cruel creatures. Sometimes, they stalked like a lion, sneaking up behind him, then batting him about with big paws, doing their best to elude capture until the melody was good and ready to be taken in.

At last, Cash got hold of the meat of it and began to play a melodic line in a loop. "Start reading again," he whispered, unwilling to break his concentration.

Brittany naturally waited for the beginning of the loop, then began speaking the words she'd written. She seemed to gain confidence with every word spoken. By the time they were halfway through, she was singing them full voice. Singing them straight from her heart to his.

At the start it was easy,
You were you and I was me,
But they told us over and over,
We were never meant to be,
We could never be we.

Each syllable burrowed into him. The feelings behind the words nestled under his skin. They throbbed, begging for a soothing touch. But he couldn't rub them away. Only she could make this hurt feel better. When she finished, and the last note died away, they were both breathless.

A full measure of silence passed between them. At last she whispered, "It's perfect."

Cash harrumphed. "It's not perfect. It needs a bridge and some transitions, but it's pretty good."

"Yeah, pretty damn good." Her voice was soft and swollen with emotion. "Can you… Will you…" she trailed off without finishing the thought.

Cash didn't need her to finish. He owed her at least this much. "Meet me at StarRise tomorrow. Studio F. The tiny one in the very back. We're going to get you your achy, gut-churning song, Brit, if it's the last thing I do. I'm gonna help you sing a song from your heart."

And then he ended the call.

She was right on time. Cash almost stopped dead in his tracks when he saw her leaning up against the door to Studio F, but somehow, he willed his feet to keep moving. His guitar case nudged her denim-clad knee when he came to a halt in front of her. "You know, no one's ever going to treat you like a star if you show up on time."

"I don't need to be treated like a star to be a star," she replied evenly. "My time is valuable, and I assume other people's time is valuable as well."

"A very un-rock 'n' roll attitude you have there, Miss Brit," he said as he slid the key into the lock on the door.

Brittany hung back as he strode into the studio and began setting up. When he glanced over his shoulder to see she hadn't followed him, he raised both eyebrows and asked, "You change your mind?"

"Do you like doing this?" she asked, gesturing to the small studio space.

The doubt in her tone raised his hackles. "I make a good living doing this." He refused to explain himself to her any further than they absolutely had to. The more she knew, the more ammunition she'd have, and the more dangerous she could be in the long run. Hell, having her around was already like having an unarmed nuclear warhead in his studio.

Never in a million years would he have pegged himself as a guy he got turned on by girls wearing ripped up jeans and baggy sweatshirts, but he was. Maybe because he knew what lay beneath her camouflage. Or maybe because he didn't give a good goddamn what she wore—he just wanted her near. And if his selfish desire for her didn't condemn what was left of his soul to hellfire for eternity, he didn't know what would.

"I don't miss the spotlight, if that's what you're asking." Opening his guitar case with a jerky motion, he paused to look up at her. "Is that what you're asking?"

"I guess so." She shrugged and stepped into the room. "Sometimes I wonder, you know? Would I miss it? Could I walk away from it all?"

Cash snickered. "No, you couldn't."

"You did."

He heard the note of stubborn defiance in her tone and sighed. "I didn't walk away. I was shoved out, remember? And don't forget, I lit a match and tossed it over my shoulder as I was going. Absolutely nobody missed me."

"I did."

Biting his tongue to keep from saying anything, he lifted his guitar from its case and slung the strap over his shoulder. There was no better shield than his precious Taylor acoustic. It worked with most people. Strap it on and park in a far corner. Once a minute or two, most singers forgot there was an actual human making notes come out of the thing. But he knew the guitar would be no match for Brit.

"You were the only one."

Tuning the instrument, he told himself being here was a test of will. Like pressing on a bruise to see how much pain you could tolerate. But it was bullshit. He'd wanted to see her. Be near her. Hear her sing those words she'd written about him back in the day. He'd lain awake most of the night wondering if he might be more deserving of them now than he was when she wrote them. He hoped so. He wouldn't allow himself to go there. He wanted to believe he was a better man. Had to believe it. Otherwise, all his hard work would be for nothing.

He glanced up at her and found her unzipping the hoodie. His mouth dried up as she shrugged out of it to reveal a plain white ribbed tank top. The kind drunk old men wore on TV. Her arms were smooth, sleekly muscled, and tan. She moved with the grace of a woman who'd been dancing since she could walk. She began to hum softly, warming up her vocal chords gradually. Cash stared as she unconsciously stroked the long column of her throat.

Perhaps he wasn't as mentally tough as he thought he was.

"You're right, I don't think I could leave it."

Cash scrambled to pick up the thread of the conversation they'd been having, but he was too distracted. Brit walked over to the single microphone stand parked on the three-by-five square of thick carpet. She lifted the mic from the clip, and he smiled as she squinted to read the lettering on the side. She didn't need to know he'd come down here at the ass-crack of dawn to get her set up the way she liked it.

The mic wasn't one of the garishly sparkly versions she used on the stage, but it was the same model. She held it loose and easy, facing him with a smile the opposite of sheepish.

"I think I'd miss performing in front of people. I'm not sure I could hide back here where no one could see me. Even if they heard me, I'd never know if they were with me." She cocked her head. "Do I sound egotistical?"

Cash shook his head slowly, drinking her in from his perch behind the stand. "No, ma'am. You sound honest." He shrugged, then bent his head to fiddle with his instrument, even though he knew it was already in tune. "Some people are meant to be up front, and some people do better tucked away in the back."

She gave her head a rueful shake. "I look at you and I think there's no way in hell this man was meant to be anything other than a star. You're the whole package, Cash."

He smirked at her. "I might have all the ingredients, but I'm like lasagna. You can get lasagna about anywhere and it's always going to be good, but you're not really going to remember one slab over another." He tugged the strap on his guitar and fingered the frets. "You ready to knock out some music?"

A laugh burbled from her lips. "Lasagna." She took a step closer to him, all loose limbs and tanned skin. "I love lasagna."

"Brit," he said in a low, warning tone. He strummed the opening notes of the tune he'd noodled around with the previous night. It had played on a constant loop in his head as he replayed every second of their encounter in Austin. "We're here to work," he said, as much to remind himself as her.

She stared right at him as she lifted the mic and hit her mark without a second of hesitation. "Try as I might, I could never see," she sang in a voice so low it rumbled like distant thunder.

Trouble. She was trouble. This song was too much. They would destroy each other. The warnings scrolled through his brain even as his fingers moved over the strings.

"How you can be you, and I can be me. How come we can never be we?" Her voice sweetened with every syllable.

He closed his eyes and bent his head over his instrument, unable to maintain the intense connection. One of the greatest lessons a man can ever learn is to recognize his own frailties. His weakness stood square in front of him. A temptation more potent than pills. An urge stronger than his most powerful thirst nearly choked him.

Danger. Danger.

His brain screamed the words, but every molecule in his body reached for her. His music twined around her words. Sometimes, they stumbled a bit, but overall, the fit was almost surreal in its perfection. How often did a connection like this happen? Johnny and June. Faith and Tim. Working with Brit felt more like communion than collaboration. And it wouldn't be wrong.

The song built, slow and heartbreakingly sincere. He opened his eyes to find she'd closed hers. She often sang with her eyes closed when recording. He loved the way she'd retreat into her own head in the studio. Like the music coming from her lips was for her alone. On stage, she was all excitement and expression, drawing the crowd in and feeding off their adoration. But here in the privacy of an acoustically paneled room, she was as contained as she'd ever be.

She wasn't a kid anymore. She was a woman. A headstrong woman on the brink.

The brink of what? Superstardom? World domination? Exploding like a supernova? If he flew too close to this star blazing bright, would he fall again?

He could name dozens of other musical collaborators who ended up nearly destroying one another. Shifting on his stool, he leaned into the bridge, urging her to let loose with her magical voice. The crackle of the plastic-wrapped package he'd shoved into his front pocket taunted him.

A condom. He'd showed up to a practice session with nothing but his guitar and a condom. He'd told himself it was a talisman. Protection against the need for protection. No one actually had one when they needed one. Except for Brit. She'd showed up at his hotel hellbent on having him. Well, today, if she was as willing as he hoped she was, he was going to have her again.

Because he'd said he was done lying to himself. And the biggest lie of all would be pretending he didn't want her with every molecule of oxygen in his body.

"Because if you are you, and I am me, we were meant to be," she crooned, letting the last note trail away into the thrumming silence.

Brit opened her eyes, and, without a word, he lifted the guitar strap from his shoulder and rose from his seat. "You are you, and I am me," he said hoarsely, holding her gaze.

"We were meant to be," she whispered back.

"I want you."

"I know you do," she answered. Fact, not flirtation.

"You want me too," he asserted, slipping an arm around her waist and letting his fingertips graze her hip.

"I've never been a denier."

Her sharp retort didn't quite cut it for him. If they were going to do this—again—then he needed to know they were both heading into it with eyes wide open.

"I don't think it's only sex."

"No, but the sex is nice," she said, letting a shoulder rise and fall with studied nonchalance.

"We are an unholy mess waiting to happen." His voice creaked under the pressure of not snatching her up and kissing her smart mouth. Hard.

Brit slipped her arms around his neck and pressed up against him. He groaned low and ragged.

"Creative differences already," she murmured, tipping her head so her lips hovered dangerously close to his. "You think we're a mess, I think we're blessed."

She teased him in a breathy sing-song tone. He might have laughed if he weren't so damn hard up. Cash adjusted his grip, gathering her to him and pressing the length of his dick to the seam of her worn jeans. "I'm not feeling very holy at the moment."

"I think it feels like heaven." She wriggled against him, letting her impatience show.

"There's no going back, Brit," he rasped. "No pretending it was a one-time thing. An itch to be scratched. An old score to be settled. We go here now, and we're in it. Thick."

"God, I hope so," she answered her voice wispy and hoarse.

"I'm serious."

"I know." She drew back enough to lock eyes with him and held steady. "You are you, and I am me, and we are meant to be."

"God help us both," he muttered, then crushed his mouth to hers.

8

Wydetta wasn't happy, and when Wydetta Owens wasn't happy, nobody was happy. She'd finally given and agreed to have dinner with James Paulson when she received the text from Brittany.

We've got the song, meet us at the studio in the morning and we'll play through for you.

She'd looped Leelo and Heywood into the conversation as well, as if that was going to stop Wydetta from demanding to know who the magical 'we' included. She had a sinking feeling she already knew.

"Trouble?" James asked, taking a sip of his water.

Wydetta attempted to physically shake off the heavy sense of foreboding. But when she looked up into his concerned brown eyes, she was assailed by another wave of trepidation. The man was mesmerizing. She'd been avoiding him for that very reason. Yet, here she was, seated at a corner table at the Palm, mentally listing all the reasons not to fall into bed with him.

He's too old for me.

Too famous.

Too… too…

"Wydetta?" He enunciated each syllable of her name in an officious tone, adding his little British "er" on the end. "Perhaps there's something wrong with the wine?" he asked, gesturing to her untouched glass.

She shook her head, and he lounged in his chair. Wydetta moved her feet aside as his shoe brushed hers. It seemed absurd for such a lean man to take up so much room, but sitting across from him at the table for two was overwhelming. But the warmth of his gaze was oddly comforting. The moment was short-lived. From the second she slid into the back seat of his car, he'd been chipping away at her like a miner with a pickaxe.

"The wine is fine. Thank you." To prove her point, she took a hasty sip.

"You have an unusual name. How did your parents come by Wydetta?"

She stared at him, nonplussed by the conversational gambit.

"I mean, it's not a common name here in the States, is it?" he persisted.

Her brow puckered in puzzlement, she gave her head a cautious shake. "No. It's not."

"How'd they come up with it? Is Wydetta a family name or something along those lines?"

She gaped at him. She knew the Brits had a ridiculous respect for tradition, but he was too much. What kind of family would pass down a name as utterly ridiculous as Wydetta?

"No. I was supposed to be named Loretta." She unearthed the bit of family lore and doled it out with caution. For some reason, his asking about her name felt like he was laying the groundwork for a trap. "Why do you ask?"

He shrugged, looking far more charming and boyish than a man his age should. "Just curious. I like it. Wydetta." he drawled, his lovely accent adding the bizarre British twist on the pronunciation again. "Actually, I like it more than Loretta. Loretta sounds like someone slinging hash in a coffee shop. Wydetta sounds more like a gun slinger. Like Wyatt Earp." He cocked his head to the side. "Tell me, do you happen to carry a pair of six-shooters?"

She gave an unladylike snort. "I usually do, but they wouldn't fit in my bag."

Before she could process what was happening, he reached across the table, took her hand, and brushed a fleeting kiss to her knuckles. "How did Loretta become Wydetta?"

Shaking her head in disbelief, she couldn't help but admire his speed and confidence. But rather than jerking back, she retracted her hand as if she were a monarch accustomed to such gestures of deference.

"Why are you so curious about my name?"

He jerked his head up to look at her, clearly startled from other thoughts. "Hmm?"

"My name," she repeated. She brushed a strand of hair from her face and forced herself to assume a more relaxed posture. "What's with the questions?"

He held up both hands in surrender. "I'm only trying to get to know you better. Isn't that the point of a dinner date?"

Her heart lurched. It was a reasonable gambit, given that she had agreed to dinner to get him out of the studio, but she still hadn't figured out how to handle his candor. The music business wasn't known for its straight shooters. But he seemed like a genuinely nice man. A nice, lonely man—rock legend or not. She offered him a wan smile. "I was supposed to be Loretta because my daddy always said he never would have amounted to a hill of beans if Miss Loretta Lynn hadn't let him open for her on his first tour."

James nodded. "Ah, yes, makes sense." He gazed at her, and the frank admiration in his eyes made her stomach do the flip-flop thing again. "Did I get the 'Wy' part right at least? Is it from Wyatt Earp?" he asked hopefully.

A laugh escaped her before she could temper it. "More like Wynonna Judd. My mama and Naomi Judd became good friends when she was carrying me, and she loved the name Wynonna. She decided to combine the two, but Wynetta would have sounded too much like Wynette, and my mama never liked Tammy Wynette overmuch because she flirted with my daddy all the time, so it became Wydetta with a D. The end."

But James wasn't satisfied with getting the condensed version of the story of her name. He wanted more from her. She could see the hunger in his eyes, and she had to admit she liked the way they gleamed.

"What brings you to Nashville?"

He smiled and tossed off another one of those boyish shrugs. "Oh, I visit once or twice a year, actually. I have a couple of tunes I'm working out with some friends, so we're meeting up here. I like to skulk around a few of the clubs in different cities, hear what's new and happening, get the lay of the land." He waved a dismissive hand.

The conversation lagged momentarily. She almost let out a whoosh of relief when their waiter appeared bearing their salad plates. "Oh, good. I'm famished," she said, flashing a smile at her jacket-clad savior.

James smirked as the man served them, then faded quietly away. "I've never seen anyone so happy to see a salad."

"I like salad," she retorted primly, picking up her fork.

"I'm a vegetarian, and even I don't like salad that much," he murmured. "You don't talk about yourself. Why is that? Don't you think you're interesting?"

She blinked, once again taken aback by his direct manner. "It isn't that," she began, but the words trailed away. Before she could come up with a palatable reason, the truth slipped out. "It's just that most of my attention is focused on Brittany."

"She's wonderfully talented. That voice." He shook his head in admiration. "And now, the world is practically panting at her feet. You've done well by her."

Offended by the easy way he managed to boil her life's work down to a few paltry compliments, she dropped her fork with a clatter. "Brittany is a very ambitious young woman. She knows what she wants. No one is forcing her to do anything she doesn't want to do."

"Except sing songs that mean nothing to her."

He tossed the accusation out so casually, she almost blew right past it. But when their gazes met, she saw the challenge in his eyes and rose to meet it.

"Yes, well, apparently she has one she wants to sing." She gestured to the phone she'd placed face-down on the table. "We're supposed to meet at the studio tomorrow to listen to it."

He clapped his hands together, and the people seat at the next table jumped. Then they tried not to stare look directly at him. The town might be chock full of country music's brightest stars, but he was still Sir James Paulson.

"Excellent." He picked up his glass of sparkling water and held it up in a salute. "I can't wait to hear it."

"You weren't invited," she snapped, hating herself for the waspish tone, but disconcerted by the ease with which he inserted himself into her life.

One corner of his mouth lifted. "Invite me, Wydetta. I'm British. It goes against the grain to simply show up unannounced."

"You did yesterday," she reminded him.

"Ah, yes, but you'd left me no choice."

To say Wydetta was flattered to have outshone her gorgeous young daughter when it came to catching Sir James Paulson's discerning eye would be oversimplifying the matter. She didn't compete with her daughter. To do so would only make her look like a fool. Brit was special. A star from the moment she was born. The total opposite of her mother. Wydetta had learned to survive and thrive in the shadows.

Sure, she'd discovered how to accentuate her good features with the artful application of cosmetics. She had the very best colorist in Nashville on speed dial. But there was no point in pretending she was anything other than what she was—an attractive, confident woman who dressed well and might pass for pretty at a glance, but nothing more. She told herself it was only natural she became instantly suspicious when a man like James Paulson made it clear he was into her, and not her twenty-three-year-old daughter.

All her life, people had feigned interest in her in order to gain access to the great Merle Owens. Her father's fame was both a boon and a bane. As Merle's only child, she had automatic entry into the most exclusive circles in the music industry. It also meant she'd spent a lifetime watching the people closest to her and wondering what their motives might be.

"What do you want?"

"I told you. I want to know you better."

The simple statement did little to allay her suspicion. It also made her want to bolt. Because as soon as he did get to know her better, he'd see what everyone else saw: Wydetta Owens was a disappointment.

Her first mistake was being born not-beautiful—a fact that stunned the world as much as it did her parents. How could Merle Owens, the golden god of country music, and Marie Boudreaux Owens, a woman once known as the Bayou Bombshell, have possibly produced such a plain girl? But they had. It didn't matter how many fancy party frocks Marie bought for her daughter, someone was bound to use the words 'silk purse' and 'sow's ear' whenever Wydetta left a room.

And her lack of beauty was only the starter.

To get the full picture of what a disappointment Wydetta truly was, one would have to add in a complete lack of musical talent, an attitude her mother described as 'unattractive' when she was feeling generous, top it up with a teenage pregnancy, and stir.

Thankfully, her unplanned, untimely pregnancy provided Wydetta with a sort of 'get out of jail free' card. Brittany was everything her mother had never been, and so much more. Wydetta had known Brit was one of the chosen ones the moment they placed the squalling newborn in her arms.

"Listen, I'm flattered—" she began.

"Good. Because I'm determined," he said, fixing her with an unblinking stare.

"James—"

"Wydetta."

Wydett-er. The sing-song tone of his teasing tugged at her heart. Her cheeks warmed, and when she dared to meet his steady gaze again, he smiled. "Enjoy your salad. Tonight, we'll have dinner, and tomorrow we'll listen to your daughter's new music. No grand scheme. No nefarious plots. I swear it."

When she arrived at the studio, she wasn't at all pleased to see Cash Dorsett sitting in the studio with a guitar perched on his knee. In the few seconds she managed to corral her daughter, she hissed, "Where did he come from?"

Brit stared back at her, blue eyes guileless. "I do believe his people hail from West Virginia originally, don't they?"

They did hail from West Virginia, and Brittany knew damn well that she knew they did. Wydetta knew everything about Cash Dorsett's background. Merle had all but adopted the boy when he first landed in Nashville. She once suspected her father had designs on pairing her up with his young protégé, but Cash had been no match for the willful daughter of country music royalty. Just as he was no match for a mother determined to see her daughter achieve her fondest dreams.

Brittany had somehow inherited the magical amalgamation of looks, charm, talent, and ambition that skipped Wydetta. Her daughter was the Rolls Royce of star vehicles, and no one was going to stand in their way.

Gripping her daughter's arm, she pulled Brittany aside. "You know what I mean."

This time Brittany rolled her eyes in a way she hadn't since she'd been fifteen years old, and Wydetta found herself distressed by this bit of rebellious regressing.

"Brittany Marie—" she began, but the producer and engineer had walked in, followed by Sir James Paulson.

"And where did *he* come from?" Brittany asked, sotto voce. "Is that where you were last night?"

Wydetta's cheeks blazed as she watched James exchange pleasantries with the other two men. She wanted to reassure her daughter that she hadn't slept with the man, but had the sinking feeling that by even mentioning the possibility, she'd betray her desire to do exactly that.

When she failed to answer, Brittany seized the opportunity to take center stage. Clapping her hands together, she called over her shoulder, "Okay, yeah, we've got something for you to hear. We think it's pretty good, but we could use some input."

Wydetta sat sulking in the back of the booth, pretending not to listen as her daughter leaned in close to Cash and sang a song of yearning and heartbreak. The lyrics were so simple and raw, she knew it could only have been written about the man sitting beside her daughter, holding his battered acoustic guitar. Brittany had not allowed her heart to become involved with any man since the day Cash Dorsett walked out of her life.

An exit Wydetta did her best to help hasten. Still, she didn't have time to worry over this minor inconvenience. Cash Dorsett was washed up, and Brittany, for all her impulsiveness, had as much ambition of her own as Wydetta did for her. There was no way Brit would let this man slow down her meteoric rise, and they both knew it. So, she squashed down her protective mama feelings and donned her steely-eyed manager mask.

They sounded good together, as much as it grieved her to admit it. Each had deep, rasping voices more at home at the lower end of the register than the top, but the ability to fake it when they made it to the top notes. Brit's was sweeter, but the husky timbre of Cash's harmonies gave her voice a fullness Wydetta hadn't heard before. It sent shivers down her spine. She'd forgotten how magical they were together. Forgotten how Cash had helped round out Brittany's sound in those early days.

Riffling through her handbag for her notebook, Wydetta chose not to dwell too long on any part she might've played in hastening Cash Dorsett's downfall. The man had been trouble since the moment he walked into her daughter's recording studio, and here he was again getting her baby all riled up. The problem was, there wasn't much she could do to protect Brittany these days. Her daughter was grown and feeling more and more confident in her decisions every day. The development filled Wydetta with pride and terror.

The duo ran through the song once, then waited. The men in the booth murmured amongst themselves. Then they asked for another listen.

Brittany's voice broke then soared, raising chill bumps on Wydetta's arms as she hit big notes as well as the soft, heartbreaking ones.

Was there anything more painful to a parent than to know they'd played a part in their child's suffering?

Wydetta was a realist. She realized Brittany had a lot of living to do, and a dozen or more big mistakes to make. She figured, in the grand scheme of things, Brit's teenage crush on Cash Dorsett would barely register. Her own obsession with Bobby Durrant, the British pop sensation who fathered Brittany, had faded as quickly as it flared. She'd figured it would be the same for her daughter. But she's been wrong.

Brittany's crush on Cash had never waned. By the time her daughter's eighteenth birthday rolled around, it looked like there was a good possibility they would take their friendship to another level. Wydetta couldn't let nature take its course.

She hadn't.

Sitting back on the banquette, she eyed the couple in the studio as they ran through the song one more time. The lyrics were simple and sweet. Maybe a little too simplistic, but Wydetta knew they were exactly what they needed to be. If Brittany was going to include a love song on her album, it had to be one that spoke to young girls in their most tragic times. She had absolutely no doubt this one had been penned in those horrible months following Cash's disappearance from Brit's life.

"There's still something missing."

Wydetta looked at James. "What?"

"There's something missing in the song," he said waving a dismissive hand. "She's singing beautifully, and the lyrics are something any young person might relate to," he mused, "but there's still something missing."

"You thought the song was the something missing," she pointed out. "Now you want more?"

He scoffed in his haughty British way and shot her a scornful glance. "More of something missing? Is that what we're going for here?"

Not impressed by his tone, Wydetta raised an imperious eyebrow. "Why are you even here?"

"I'm trying to help, love."

"I'm not your love, and we didn't ask for your help."

She had the pleasure of watching genuine shock register on his face. She couldn't help but wonder when the last time James Paulson's input had been rejected outright.

And then, he did something truly shocking. He threw his head back and laughed at her. The flowing locks of salt-and-pepper hair fell away from his face like strands of silk as he let it go. He laughed long and loud enough to garner everyone's attention.

Brittany spoke into the microphone. "What's so funny in there?"

Launching himself from the banquette, James bent close to the microphone on the console. "Not laughing at you, darling. You sound lovely. But I have to tell you, your mother is an absolute hoot." He glanced over his shoulder at Wydetta. "Did I get that right? A hoot?"

"Oh, sit down and shut up," she said, speaking low and deliberately enunciating each word.

James winked at Heywood and then nudged Leelo as he moved to reclaim his seat on the bench. "I guess she told me, right, boys?"

"What the hell is going on here?"

Four sets of eyes swung to the studio door as Dylan Carson burst through, his face red with indignation. Leelo and Heywood swiveled in their chairs and began busily spinning knobs and toggling levers, keeping their eyes averted from both the angry young man in the doorway and the couple huddled together beyond the glass.

"Why don't you tell us, mate?" James demanded, the first to recover.

Dylan stepped into the booth and grabbed Wydetta by the elbow. "What the hell? I'm Brit's guitarist."

She yanked her arm from his grasp, "And you still are. This is just a...demo."

Dylan didn't let up. "A demo? I got a call this morning. They said Brittany was in here recording a song with fucking Cash Dorsett," he cried, incredulous. "Cash Dorsett! I thought the guy overdosed or something."

James stepped in and nudged the younger man back until he stumbled a few inches away from Wydetta. "You need to step back."

Dylan snarled as he turned to face the interloper. "Who the hell are you to tell me to—" His eyes went wide as the mental cards fell into place. "Shit. You're James Paulson." His gaze darted to Wydetta then back to the older man. "I heard rumors he was hanging around, but I didn't think they were true."

James frowned at Wydetta. "Who is this bloke?"

Wydetta rolled her eyes and then inserted herself between the two men for safety's sake. "Sir James Paulson, meet Dylan Carson. Dylan, this is Sir James Paulson." She paused, then added, "It's an honor for you to meet him."

To his credit, Dylan blinked, then thrust out his hand. "It *is* an honor...Sir. Awesome to meet you," he stammered.

Sir James looked down his long, thin, very British nose at the younger man, gave him a perfunctory handshake, then let it go with undisguised distaste.

Shifting his attention back to Leelo, he said, "She needs a little wistfulness in her tone, something to make the listener glom on and say 'Yeah, man. I feel it too.' I keep thinking 'Superstar.'"

Heywood raised his bushy gray eyebrows. "As in Jesus Christ?"

Leelo shook his head. "Luther Vandross?"

James pursed his lips as he gave the suggestion some thought. "Right, but more along the lines of Karen Carpenter." He sang a few bars of the song about a backstage affair gone cold.

Leelo's bobbed his head as the idea took hold. "Yeah," he said slowly. "Something along those lines."

"Not the same thing, obviously," James concurred. "But the same kind of...open longing."

"Yeah, I get you." Leelo flipped a switch and leaned forward to speak into the microphone attached to the console. "Hey Brit, we were talking in here and we want you to try to put a little Karen Carpenter into it."

Brittany stared back at him through the glass, her face blank.

"Hang on." Leelo groped around on the desk, then looked up. "Where's my phone?"

There was a general commotion in the booth as everyone wrestled to get their phones out. It became a race to see who could pull up the version of the old Carpenters song first. Surprisingly enough, Heywood won.

Holding a phone at least four models out of date up to the microphone, he allowed the song to play through the speakers. In the studio, Brit and Cash set perched on matching stools, listening with their eyes closed, absorbing each note.

"Well, they're obviously sleeping together," James said glibly.

Everyone in the booth stared at him openmouthed. Wydetta was the only one who got a single word out. "What?"

Gesturing to Brit and Cash like some kind of overblown game show host, he nodded. "They're sleeping together. There's your problem."

Once the song ended, Brit slid off her stool, strode over, and stuck her head into the booth. "Okay, I get where you want to go with this, but it sounded good to me. What's the trouble?"

Everyone spoke at once.

James wagged his head. "It's not working, love."

"Are you sleeping with him?" Wydetta demanded.

"What the hell, Brittany?" Dylan asked, his tone sharp. "Cash Dorsett?"

"You know, I think you might be right," Heywood murmured.

Leelo swiveled in his chair as if he were a spectator at a tennis match. He sat calmly, absorbing each demand like the crevices in acoustic tile. He didn't say a word, but his speculative gaze settled on Cash in the end.

Then, as suddenly as the furor started, it stopped. A moment of charged silence rang in the air. Just when it became unbearable, Cash spoke.

"I think you've got enough of the track recorded," he murmured. "I'm going to go now."

Brit stared, her lips parted in disbelief as he carried his guitar to its battered case. "Wait, Cash, no. What do you mean?"

Wydetta watched, gritting her teeth as the handsome man who so captivated her daughter closed the lid on the case and secured the latches. As far as she was concerned, they couldn't get rid of him fast enough. He stood, the guitar rested comfortably at his side as he gifted her daughter with the most dazzling smile.

Wydetta stared, unblinking, as he leaned in and kissed Brit full on the mouth. A soft, tender kiss promising more to come, but sealed this particular decision without question.

"You've got enough recorded for Dylan to be able to pick it up." He nodded toward the younger man in the booth, and there was no irony in his tone. "No one knows your sound better than he does." When she opened her mouth to protest, he silenced her with a gentle finger on her lips. "Not even me."

The tender moment was interrupted when James screeched like a broken guitar string. "Yes! Perfection!"

Pushing his way through the small crowd of people in the booth, he burst into the studio. Pointing to Brit, he said, "You sing and let the young bloke play." He spun to face Cash. "We need you in the booth."

"In the booth? What for?"

"You're the one she needs to be singing the song to. She can't get the feeling right if you're sitting right next to her." He swept an all-encompassing arm around the studio, then pointed to the glass separating the room from the booth. "She needs to be calling for you. Go in there on the other side of the glass. Make her work the song." He paused, then cocked his head to the side. "Hey, aren't you the bloke that played with me in Austin?"

Brit's eyes narrowed dangerously. Hoping to intercept her daughter and possibly save James's life, Wydetta followed him into the studio. Speaking in her calmest, most rational manager tone, she shoved her mama bear protectiveness aside and focused all of her energy on her daughter. Her client.

"He's crazy, but he might be right," she informed the duo. She shot James a dirty look, but he simply raised one shoulder and let it fall. "There is something missing in the way you're delivering. It's not something you can sing to someone when they're next to you." Her words came out cool and clipped, but she managed to keep control. "Cash, you head on into the booth, and Dylan, you come on in here and play the song," she ordered.

Brit immediately began to protest. "No, this is Cash's song."

James frowned, he murmured. "I don't remember his name being Cash."

"Never mind," Wydetta hissed.

"It's not my song," Cash immediately responded. "It's your song. I'm only playing along."

She whirled on Cash. "This is your song. The music is yours. I want you to play on this song."

Recognizing the mulish set of her daughter's jaw, Wydetta stepped between them, her hands raised in the peacemaking gesture. "Hang on, hang on." She touched James's arm and he backed off a step. She tried to make eye contact with Cash, but he avoided her gaze. "Why don't we play the track back without the vocal. Everyone but Brittany in the other room."

"But, Wydetta," Brit began, "I don't want—"

Wydetta held up both hands to stave off her daughter's frontal assault, for once missing the days when she would slip up and accidentally call her Mama. "Honey, I'm only saying let's try it this way and see if we get a different result."

Wydetta pointed to the booth, then to Cash's guitar case. "Take it in there." She began ushering the men back into the engineering booth. Glancing over her shoulder, she saw the steely gleam in Brittany's eyes and heaved a sigh. "Try. If you don't like it, we'll talk about it after." Wydetta closed the studio door firmly, then exhaled long and loud.

The interior of the booth was mayhem. James spoke excitedly to Leelo and Heywood, offering suggestions, making random exclamations, his accent growing more indecipherable as he spoke faster and faster.

Dylan complained loudly and in a belligerent tone Wydetta didn't particularly appreciate. She held a hand up in front of his face. "You hush for a minute. You've been off doing your own thing. We need to get this right."

He obeyed, which seemed to surprise him as much as anyone else. The only person who didn't speak a word was Cash.

Sighing again, Wydetta moved to stand next to him but didn't try to catch his eye. "I don't know how you made this all come about, but I don't see any good coming out of it." She kept her eyes fixed on Brittany as her daughter resumed her position at the microphone.

"If you think you can use her as your road to a comeback, you are sorely mistaken, mister."

"Who said I wanted to make a comeback?"

Wydetta snorted her disbelief but refrained from saying anything more when Leelo signaled the start of playback.

Brittany stared at Cash through the soundproof pane of glass, a look of such undisguised adoration lighting her face it made Wydetta's heart ache. Then her baby opened her mouth…and magic came out.

"I'd hoped you'd gotten him out of your system," Wydetta said the moment the men left the recording studio and she and her daughter were alone. Brit looked up, startled. Wydetta hid a smile and pretended to be scrolling through messages on her phone. "After Austin?" she clarified helpfully.

Brittany's expression was wary, but she didn't back down. Mother-daughter bonding moments might not have been the norm for the two of them, but they weren't unheard of. Wydetta experienced one of those occasional pangs she felt when she wondered if she hadn't made a mistake in keeping a little distance between herself and her daughter.

Wydetta and her own mother had never been close, but when she'd told her mother she was pregnant at sixteen, a wall as thin and impenetrable as bulletproof glass rose between them. Wydetta never wanted her daughter to know the pain of having her mother emotionally abandon her in her time of need.

This was why she didn't let herself become overly invested in Brit's romantic choices. Her daughter was an adult, and her love life was none of her mother's business. But it didn't mean a mother couldn't worry. No one knew better than Wydetta what adolescence did to a girl. Once past the age of thirteen, there was no telling any child anything. Even if you were right, they'd never believe you. These days, Wydetta contented herself with keeping Brit on a tight leash as far as business was concerned. As long as her choices in her personal life didn't adversely affect her career, everything between them was copacetic. But this was worrisome.

Wydetta shook her head. "I don't know why I thought so. I should have known the moment you laid eyes on him you were going to chase after him."

"Like I knew you were going to go for Sir Jimmy?" Brit asked snidely.

Wydetta chose to ignore both the comment and its tone. "But like I said, I'd hoped you'd got it out of your system."

"You don't seem to be getting your errant knight out of your system," Brittany observed.

"He hasn't gotten *into* my system," Wydetta snapped.

"Ah, but he wants to."

"Perhaps." Heat flared in Wydetta's cheeks. "He is a persistent man."

Brit didn't miss her cue.

"And the Lord loves a persistent man," the two of them crooned one of Marie Owens's favorite phrases in unison. Surprised and delighted by the unexpected show of solidarity, the two of them dissolved into laughter.

"I guess we both ought to listen to Grandma more," Brit commented as she tried to straighten.

"Well, her influence is kind of hard to escape," Wydetta said with a chortle. "I'm surprised one of her girlfriends hasn't cross-stitched the sentiment onto a pillow for her."

An awkward silence filled the air between them. Rolling back her shoulders, Wydetta charged into the breach. "But he's not out your system, is he?"

"I'm not going to discuss this with you."

"I think we ought to. This could impact things for you, and we need to be on top of any potential—"

Yanking the zipper on her hoodie up to her chin, Brit shook her head. "I said I'm not going to discuss this with you, Mama."

Wydetta did her best not to flinch at the use of the word "Mama" spoken with *tone*. If Brittany was going to pull out the big guns, then she could too. "There are things you don't know about Cash—"

"Oh, I know," Brit interjected.

"I mean about when you were younger. About Cash and me," Wydetta persisted, letting the implication dangle like sparkly bait in murky water.

Brit looked her mother straight in the eye. "You mean about how you rubbed up on him like a cat in heat?" Brit asked. "About how you told him he shouldn't bother with an inexperienced girl like me when he could have you?"

Wydetta narrowed her eyes as she tried to stem the surge of shame filled her gut. "He told you?"

"No, he didn't tell me," Brit said, her voice dripping with scorn. "But you can bet at least four other people told me. They also told me what you said when he walked away from you."

Wydetta blinked. She'd always believed she'd gotten Cash alone. She didn't know anyone else might have overheard their awkward conversation. "Who?"

Brittany rolled her eyes and pivoted on her heel. "Why, Mama?" she asked, emphasizing the title. "So you can ruin them the same as you helped ruin Cash?"

"I didn't ruin Cash," Wydetta shot back. "I didn't have to. He destroyed his career all on his own."

Brit paused in the doorway to cast a smirk over her shoulder. "Imagine someone able to achieve something without you telling them exactly how to go about it."

"If you call ruining a promising career an achievement," Wydetta said with a sneer.

"At least he was able to beat you to the punch." Brit opened the studio door. "I'm keeping this cut on the album, Cash's take. He's getting songwriting credit, and I want him to perform the song with me at the HitMakers Awards."

"Now, Brittany," Wydetta began, taking a step toward her.

"Make it happen, Wydetta," Brit ordered. "Prove to me you're worth more than the extra five percent I pay you over any other manager I could hire."

And with her parting shot launched, the child Wydetta had sacrificed her entire life to protect and promote walked out on her.

9

Cash was able to slip out of the booth after the first take. He didn't even know why they would bother with a second. The damn thing was so perfect the way she sang it. To him. Turns out, Sir James wasn't simply an eccentric rock god at loose ends. He was a man whose unerring ear had earned him decades of success and an enduring legacy.

But he couldn't hang around, not with her eyes fixed on him and with everybody else's swiveling between them, checking their temperature, watching their every reaction. He tried to play it cool, keep his face impassive, act like it was just another song being sung by another singer. After all, this was what he did now. He hung out in the booths and backstage behind the spotlight, not in it, and it was safer there.

But it wasn't just another song, and Brit was way more than any other singer to him. They had a connection. A history. And what he'd dared to let himself believe was a chance for a future.

Proof he was a complete and utter moron.

Because their history wasn't all good, and their future was murky at best. Cash couldn't really say it was a pleasure seeing Wydetta again. The last time he'd spoken to Brit's viper of a mother had been the night of the infamous party. He'd been drunk and hopped up, and Wydetta had seized the opportunity.

He'd never forget the feel of her hands on him, touching him, stroking him, tempting him in a lurid shot at drawing him away from her own daughter. She wanted him out of Brittany's life. What

Wydetta didn't understand was, he didn't want to be in the Owenses' orbit anymore.

While he'd always be thankful to Merle for giving him a leg up, there was only so far he was willing to go for gratitude. Sure, Brit's grandfather had yanked him out of the flea-bit honky-tonk he'd been playing and introduced him to everybody who was anybody in the Nashville music scene, but Cash didn't figure he owed the man his soul in exchange.

He opened the door to the nondescript brick building and slipped inside. The old rectory adjoining St. Michael's Episcopal was no longer in use as a residence, but the parish made the space available to worthy causes. Shoulders tense, Cash trudged down the stairs leading to the gloomy basement.

It was sort of an unspoken secret Merle wanted him for Wydetta, but they were a no-go from the start. And, to be fair, Wydetta never had any interest in him, either. She was no more likely to go for a man her father had chosen for her than she was to wear an outfit her mama had picked out for her at a local department store. As it was, he spent years hoping and praying his friend and mentor had never copped to the fact Cash had fallen in love with Merle's beautiful but far-too-young granddaughter instead.

Watching the Owens women in action was like watching two mules pulling in opposite directions. The last thing he wanted to be was the fool trussed up and tied to both saddles.

The heel of Cash's boot hit the slate tile floor of the meeting room, and he slid a couple inches. His body seized in the split second before he could force himself to relax and go with slide. The low murmur of discussion coming from the small group of people sitting in a circle at the far end of the meeting room stopped abruptly. Cash scowled down at the piddling splatter of spilled coffee on the floor and raised a hand to indicate all was well on his end.

The conversation began again, but he needed a moment to collect himself. Parking his guitar case near two others by the door, he snatched his hat from his head and kept his steps light as he crossed the room so as not to cause further interruption. Seated in one of the cold, hard metal folding chairs, he fingered the brim of the plain felt hat before settling it in his lap.

It had taken him a long time to find comfort in the small rituals associated with the meetings. Now, he mentally equated the stench of burnt coffee with salvation.

He listened intently as they worked their way around the circle. Every person began speaking with the same litany, but their stories were as varied as paint colors. Each had taken their own highly personal tumble into the depths, and all of them struggled daily to climb out.

More than once, Cash had thanked God for the word "anonymous" in the group title. He wasn't proud of the things he had done in those low months before he'd come to embrace the scent of burnt coffee. Occasionally, he spotted a familiar face, but most of the people he knew in recovery made a point of attending meetings far from one another. It was hard enough to speak in the small, intimate circle of chairs, but meeting another addict's gaze in a not-so-anonymous setting was even more mortifying.

When they came around him, he dried sweaty palms on the sides of his jeans, looked up, his expression as sober as he was.

"My name is Cash, and I'm an alcoholic and an addict." He waited for the customary response and nodded his thanks for the welcome, then went on. "It's been twenty-three months since my last drink, and thirty-two since my last pill."

He bowed his head as they murmured their admiration for these accomplishments. It didn't matter if his sobriety was accounted for in days, weeks, months, or years. They were precious to him. And every one of these people knew they were monumental achievements.

"I ran into an old friend not long ago," he said, rubbing his palms together. The group released a collective groan, and Cash had to laugh. Shaking his head, he gave a dismissive wave. "No, this friend was a good friend. Not the bad kind."

He waited until they murmured their acceptance before going on. The last thing he'd ever do was let anyone think Brittany had one bit of blame when it came to his poor decision-making.

"Anyway, I ran into this old friend again this week, and…something happened."

A couple of the women in the group oohed knowingly, and he felt the prickle of heat creeping up the back of his neck. But he couldn't deny it. Wouldn't deny her. It seemed almost as wrong as playing with her had felt right. But he knew Brittany. Knew her right down to the purple glitter polish on her toes. She wasn't going to leave this at a couple of hours spent noodling around in a studio any more than he could pretend the hours they'd spent in his bed were simply some casual fun. There was nothing casual happening between them on any level. He was certain of it. And he had to talk about it.

"Anyway, we're…involved now. Personally. And I also made the mistake of getting involved professionally, and I…I have a pretty good idea we're going to be heading for a crossroads of some kind."

"Why do you think so?" John, the group leader, asked.

"Because she's fierce and strong and ready to take on the world, and I'm—" He opened his hands in a gesture of futility. "All I want to do is hunker down and make it through another day."

Cash didn't know if he could meet her needs. And while he might take a songwriting credit and the royalties, and he might be amenable to letting her using his track on the recording, there was no way in hell he was stepping back into the spotlight. He'd been there, done that, and almost died in the process. He wasn't going to expose himself like that ever again. Even with her.

Oh, but she wanted it all. The spotlight. Him.

And he had no doubt she would want him to stand by her side and say to the world, "Hey, look at us. We're together whether you like it or not."

But Cash wasn't the sort of man who courted attention. Not anymore. He didn't get up in people's faces and demand they accept who he was. He was only trying to live his life. A simple life. The kind of life easily obliterated by a falling star.

Brit spewed a litany of complaints about the songs she'd been given to record, the costumes Wydetta had approved for her upcoming tour, and the relentless training and choreography schedule Mark was enforcing to her driver, Roger. She'd hardly looked out the window once before he pulled to a stop at the curb. Frowning, she took in the neat craftsman-style house. "Roger, are you sure this is the right place?"

She gazed at the slate-gray house with white trim around the windows and blindingly cheerful white shutters wide-eyed. When Cash had brought her here before, they'd pulled into a garage off an alley and entered through the back door. Brit was embarrassed to admit she hadn't paid much attention to where he lived; she was too anxious to get into his bed.

Roger nodded. "This is the address you gave me." When she didn't move to get out of the car, he glanced over at her. "Want me to take you on home?"

Brittany gnawed the corner of her lip, then shook her head. "No." She studied the house with laser-like intensity. As if she could see inside if she squinted hard enough. "It's not what I expected."

The older man in the front seat frowned. When he was younger, he'd been a roadie for her grandpa, but he too had known some hard times with the faster side of the country music life. When he finally got himself straight, he'd burned about every bridge he'd ever built at least twice. Merle Owens had been one of the few people who even took his call. He eventually hired Roger as his own driver and then, as Brittany's star rose, he assigned Roger the task of taking care of his most precious cargo. His granddaughter.

He gave the house a good once-over, then shrugged again. "It's only a house."

"I never thought of Cash as the type to have wicker porch furniture."

"Guys grow up." He chortled to himself. "Well, some guys do, and when they get tired of living out of bags, they generally buy a house. And porch stuff."

Brit smiled at the older man's philosophical musings. Most likely he wasn't far off in nailing down Cash's reasoning. It sounded exactly like something Cash would say himself. "Yeah, I suppose so," she conceded as she tipped her head to the side. "Doesn't look like anyone's home. Cash left the studio a couple hours ago. I figured he'd be here by now."

Roger smirked. "Maybe he had grocery shopping to do."

Brit laughed. Not because it was such an outrageous idea, but because it was entirely possible. When they showed up at his house the previous day, she'd commented on how she'd never seen a man with such a well-stocked refrigerator and pantry. He even had fresh fruit and vegetables. It was so unlike any man she'd ever known, she felt compelled to comment on it. Cash simply grumbled something about paying more attention to what he put in his body.

Brit reached for the door handle, her eyes locked on one of the white wicker chairs situated in the corner of the wide front porch. "You go on, Rog. I'm going to wait here for a while."

Roger's hand tightened on the steering wheel as he shifted to look at her. "Are you sure this is a good idea?"

Brittany raised an eyebrow. "It's the middle of the day. No one is around. I'm going to sit in this chair right here and wait. If it makes you feel better, you can go get a hamburger and come cruising back by see if I'm sitting here."

"I might."

Brittany was well aware of the threats celebrities faced. She generally didn't mess around with security issues. She signed off on having bodyguards and drivers and alarm systems and a sweep team sent ahead of her to check out any public venue she might be using. These were all part of the reality of being in the public eye these days, and she accepted them as such. But she could certainly sit by herself on a porch for thirty minutes and wait for her guy to show up. She had a cell phone and a can of mace attached to the fluffy puffball keychain clipped to her bag.

She could read the worry etched into the other man's expression. "Give me thirty minutes. If he shows up before then, I'll call you and tell you to head home. If not, you can swing back around and pick me up."

"Or I could sit here at the curb, and you can wait for him in the car," Rog suggested, a note of stubbornness creeping into his voice.

Brittany rolled her eyes and pushed against the door forcing it to swing open. "This isn't a Mafia movie, Rog. We're not waiting here to put a hit on the guy." She giggled. "Okay, well, I might be waiting to hit on the guy, but you don't need to bear witness."

"Hell no, I don't," he grumbled.

Brit had been treated to more than one of Roger's cautionary tales over the years, so she bailed before he could warm up to reciting another. "Thirty minutes," she called as she climbed out of the backseat of the dark sedan. "Get a cup of coffee or something."

She slammed the door on any further grumblings. Hunching so the hoodie shielded most of her face, she quickstepped it up to Cash's front porch. She snuggled deep into the cushion on the wicker chair, determined to wait him out, even if it took more than thirty minutes.

She lasted less than four before she pulled out her phone.

Where are you? I'm on ur frnt porch

She waited and waited, but no dots indicating an imminent reply appeared, so she tucked the phone back in the pocket of her sweatshirt. The moment she withdrew her hand, the damn thing buzzed. Huffing, she dug it out again, but her impatience melted away when she saw his reply.

Ru nuts? Get inside.

Smirking, she replied: *Should I break a window?*

This time, the dots appeared immediately. *Look under wicker chair. Key stashed in broken spot.*

Brit blinked, then rose from the creaking chair. Moving slowly, as if scared she might accidentally detonate a bomb, she squatted down and tipped the chair back to peek underneath. Sure enough, there was a break in the weave barely large enough for three of her fingers. The tip of her middle finger grazed cold metal. She gasped in awed surprise when she extracted a single house key.

"Well, what do you know?" she murmured as she rose.

Thumbing her phone, she texted: *Got it. Alarm code?*

A second later his reply appeared. *No alarm. Home in 15.*

Brittany stared at the message. No alarm? She'd never lived in a house without an alarm system. Didn't think anyone did anymore.

She slipped the key into the top lock on the door, and relief curved her lips as the heavy bolt slid back with a clunk. Then she fitted the key into the lock on the doorknob. Surely this wasn't all the security he had. People didn't rely solely on locks anymore, did they? She'd seen commercials. Weren't alarm systems pretty standard? Why didn't Cash at least have one of those ones she saw advertised on TV?

The knob twisted and Brit let the door swing inward, listening intently for the bleeps and blips that signaled the impending screech of an alarm. The house was silent.

"Huh."

Shaking her head in wonder, she stepped across the threshold and closed the door after her. Nothing. No flashing lights or wall-mounted control panel to be seen. At a loss for what to do next, she locked herself in. Security in place, she hit the speed dial for Roger's phone. He answered on the first ring, and she hurried to put him at ease.

"Hey, Rog. Cash had a key stashed so I'm inside the house. He says he'll be home in a few minutes."

"Uh-huh."

She supposed the low grumble was his way of confirming message receipt and plowed on. "You can head home. Cash can drive me later," she added in an attempt to offer him some reassurance, but she really had no intention of going back to the Brentwood estate. Not if she could help it.

"You know your granddaddy has gotten an earful already," Rog warned ominously.

"From you?"

"No, not from me," he growled, contempt dripping from each word. "I'm not a snitch."

"I didn't think you were."

"Yes, you did," he retorted, his injured feelings evident. "You forget what a small town this is, missy. Your grandad has friends tucked away in every nook and cranny."

"Friends who will happen to know you dropped me off at Cash's house?" she asked pointedly.

"Friends who have told him you're hanging out with that Dorsett fella, and it's looking pretty cozy. He called me just a bit ago. It's like he senses it."

"And what did you say?"

"I said I dropped you at a friend's house, but I never said the friend's name." He paused for a second. "But I will, if he doesn't treat you right."

"I love you, Rog," she sang into the phone.

"Don't think you're gonna get past old Merle as easy as you get past me," Roger warned.

"You let me worry about Merle." She strolled over to the enormous leather sofa and dropped into the very corner of the puffy cushions. "Thank you, Rog. I'll call you in the morning."

"Night, Miss Brit," he said gruffly.

Brit ended the call and tossed her phone onto the couch cushion with an exhausted sigh. Word was getting out. Nashville was a damn small town. Particularly her corner of it. And, if she was being truthful with herself, she'd never tried too hard to break free of her family constraints. Though their relationships weren't exactly the stuff sitcoms were made of, she loved them and loved being near them. She needed their support and worked to earn their approval more than she wanted to admit.

Her grandfather wouldn't be pleased.

But maybe he wouldn't be as prickly about Cash as Wydetta was. After all, Merle had been the one to give Cash a hand up once upon a time. Maybe he still had a soft spot for him.

Restless, she heaved herself from the sofa and made in a slow circle, taking in the room she'd barely noticed the night before. The living room was large and decorated in bachelor style. If she wasn't mistaken, the sectional sofa she'd been sitting on moments before had come directly from Cash's old loft apartment. The flat screen TV was new and sleek, a jarringly modern blank space floating on the exposed brick wall. Curious, she pressed her cheek to the wall and peered up at the back of the screen. Some kind of mounting brace had been screwed directly into the brick and mortar. She gaped at it, trying to envision Cash wearing one of those tool belts slung low on his hips and wielding a drill. The vision fit beautifully but didn't jibe with the Cash she'd known before.

The differences between clean and sober Cash and reckless shooting star Cash ran far deeper than she'd initially imagined. Fresh fruit on the kitchen counter, wall-mounted televisions, doors without alarms. Brit made a slow circuit of the room, letting her fingers trail over the strings of a guitar resting in a stand—not his beloved Taylor, but a decent high-end Gibson—as she scanned the spines of the books and DVDs crammed into a black lacquered bookcase.

She knew she wasn't the naive young woman she'd been five years before, but for some reason she hadn't expected Cash to change much. He was older. Fully formed. Weren't people supposed to get more set in their ways when they hit thirty and beyond?

Pausing in the doorway to what she imagined was supposed to be a dining room but was now filled with exercise equipment, she gaped at the well-used weights and massive treadmill. She had a similar, albeit more attractive, set up at her own house, but for security reasons. She imagined other people—people who had locks with hidden keys and no security systems—went to gyms to work out. She'd always sort of envied those people. The ones who got to complain about someone not wiping down a machine, or another person hogging the elliptical machine. Brit never had to stand in line at her gym. No, she had a dedicated trainer who showed up every day like clockwork—

Gasping, she whipped out her phone again and pressed the icon to call her cousin Martine.

"Hello, stranger," Martine purred. "Do I need to ask where you've been?"

"No, you don't," Brit answered, her response clipped. There was nothing her cousin loved more than teasing until it hurt. Brit didn't want to play. She wanted to take care of business and figure out a way to convince Cash her idea of debuting their song at the HitMakers Awards was a good one. "Listen, I forgot to call Mark and let him know I'm not home."

"Yes, we had a lovely breakfast together this morning," Martine purred.

The temptation to ask if her trainer had spent the night at her estate was strong, but Brit resisted. Martine was a man magnet, and she really didn't want to be thinking about her trainer giving her cousin a workout while she was in the middle of another one of his endless sets of burpees.

"I'll call if I'm not going to be home tonight."

"I'll let him know you'll be getting a more organic workout," Marti promised.

The sound of an engine drew Brittany toward the kitchen. A bank of windows let light from the backyard spill into the already cheerful room. She cast a rueful glance at the wooden bowl filled with apples, pears, and bananas, then pressed her cheek to a window. Seconds later, Cash stepped out of the garage.

"Don't let him make you do too many squats," Martine advised.

Cash glanced up at the window, and their eyes met and held for a second until he continued on his way. "I'm afraid I'm going to do whatever he asks me to do," she confessed, unable to peel her gaze from the spot where he'd stood moments before.

"Oh my…"

"Gotta go," Brit said when she heard him slide his key into the lock.

"Please, for once in your life, do absolutely everything I would do," Martine said in a rush.

Brit was laughing when the door swung open. Cash lifted an enquiring eyebrow, but she was already sliding her thumb across the screen as she said, "I will, Marti. I will."

10

Damn, but she looked good standing in his kitchen, Cash thought as he came through the back door. But, being a somewhat wise man, he clamped his mouth shut so the words couldn't accidentally escape. The thought was sure to come out far more sexist than he intended.

He'd have to scramble to explain how refreshing it was to see her there after so many years of coming home to an empty place. It was nice to find someone waiting for him. Doubly nice when the somebody waiting was Brittany Owens. But he wouldn't attempt to say so. Any sentiment about coming home to her was sure to come across as Neanderthal, and she'd be sure to blast him with both barrels.

He settled for a simple "Hey."

Brittany shoved her phone into the pocket of her hoodie and gave him a weak wave. "Hey," she returned. "I was…" She fidgeted, and for the first time, Cash realized she was nervous to be standing in his house. "I was calling Martine to tell her to reschedule the session with my personal trainer," she finally blurted out.

"I see." Cash tossed his keys into a tray on the kitchen counter, then yanked his wallet and cell phone from his pocket and dumped them there too. He felt her eyes on him, absorbing his every move as if he were the one going through some intricately choreographed steps. "I guess I should have known you'd come over when you guys were done. Sorry I wasn't here."

Brit shoved her hands into the back pockets of her jeans and bobbed a nod. "Yeah, I guess you should have."

He smiled at her reply, but the effort felt forced, even to himself. The last hour had been a rough one, but she might turn out to be a balm to his wounds. Closing the distance between them, he slid her hand around her waist and pulled her close. But instead of kissing her, he buried his nose in her hair and let the scent of his own shampoo mixed with the unmistakable scent of Brittany wash away the lingering dregs of burnt coffee.

"I went to a meeting," he said gruffly. He felt her stiffen but didn't look up to see if her expression showed surprise or disapproval. Meetings were his reality, and if she wanted to be here in his kitchen, in his life, she needed to understand.

She frowned, clearly confused. "What meeting?"

"Alcoholics Anonymous," he responded without hesitation.

She didn't back away. Instead of running, as she should have, Brittany ran her hands up his back and over his shoulders, winding herself around him. "Did it help?"

To the pop world, the trademark gravel in her voice screamed Brittany Owens, but to him, she sounded emotional. Vulnerable. He made her feel vulnerable, and the realization was humbling.

He'd forgotten how much she invested in every song she sang. Today's session had involved not only the emotion of the two of them together, but also some family and band drama thrown into the mix. Gathering her closer to him, he pressed his lips to her temple. "God, you sounded spectacular today."

And it wasn't bullshit. She had sung beautifully. And her voice and his guitar together… they'd sounded incredible. So well matched. Perfect together. The realization was one had sent him scurrying from the studio. He wanted to keep the memory of the two of them together precious and pristine. He didn't want to hear another man playing his notes back to her.

Dylan Carson playing his song was an inevitability, but it wasn't one he felt he needed to stick around to hear live and in person. As far was he was concerned, Cash had the take he wanted. He would talk to Heywood later about getting a copy. His investment in StarRise had to have some perks, didn't it?

"It helped," he assured her, finally answering her question about the meeting. Lifting his head, he waited until she met his eyes. "Today was a bit… much."

She dipped her head in acknowledgment. "You can say that again."

He added a dose of smartassery to his attitude and mimicked himself. "Today was a bit much."

She gave him a playful punch on the arm. "Toughen up, buttercup."

He laughed, then Brit nuzzled into his neck. Cash nearly forgot all about the qualms he had when he left the studio. Almost, but not quite. He set her back and dipped his head to peer into her eyes. "How did it go with Dylan?"

Brit shrugged noncommittally. "It was fine." She trailed a finger along his cheek, then grinned up at him as she crooned "He's not you," with an exaggerated twang.

The lazy drawl combined with her natural rasp sent a shiver down his spine. "Your voice has matured."

He winced when he saw the teasing light brighten in her eyes. "Well, you know, everything else has too, so I guess it was kind of inevitable."

"I mean, you've learned to use it better," he stammered. "Master it." Jesus, the compliment sounded dirty. "You've learned to…"—he fumbled his third attempt but refused to be deterred—"nurture it."

He knew she was letting him off the hook easy. This time.

"Yeah, I had some trouble a couple years ago with some nodules," she explained. "We saw a few specialists and switched vocal coaches, and it's really made a big improvement. I think," she added the last with a thoughtful frown.

"I agree." He stroked her hair, marveling as the slippery strands slid through his fingers. "It's richer."

She flashed him a cheeky grin. "So am I." She smirked and twirled out of his embrace. "Judging by this place, location, the decor, I'd say you didn't end up too bad off. This isn't exactly skid row."

Cash chuckled at her bold assessment. Brit never was one to mince words. "I didn't blow it all, no. By the time I got my head on straight, I had enough left to recover some. Once I had my priorities in line." He gestured to the kitchen. "I had to learn to live more like normal folks, not that you would know what I mean."

She grinned at him unabashed. "I can't believe you don't have an alarm system."

"Believe it or not, most people manage without one," he shot back.

"Yeah, but you're not most people. You *are* fairly well-known."

He shook his head. "Here in Nashville, maybe, but the rest of the world has forgotten about me, and I'm okay with being invisible."

Brit wagged her head in undisguised disbelief. "For a while, your only thought in the world was to become the king of country music."

"Things change. Sometimes, people have a wake-up call. I had mine." He reached out to tug on the string of her pink hoodie. "But I hope you never have one. I like you sassy, brassy, and oblivious to the ways of the real world."

She snorted. "Oblivious to the ways of the real world," she mocked. "I'm not oblivious. I know exactly how rarefied my air is. I can even admit to liking it, but it doesn't make me blind to how other people live." She crossed one arm over her chest and gripped the other. The defensive posture made him want to kick his own ass. "I do a lot of good work."

"I know you do. It was a joke. A bad one," he added in a rush.

Honest to God, he wasn't trying to chastise her. She worked hard all of her life, and she deserved to revel in the fruits of her labor. He'd been teasing. And he meant what he said. He liked her exactly the way she was, privileged and unapologetic.

She watched him warily. So cautiously it made his heart hurt. Pressing his lips to her forehead, Cash pulled her close. "I think you're an amazing woman."

"Not a spoiled girl?"

"You should know better than to listen to anything I say. Half the time, I'm talking straight out of my ass. Except when it comes to complimenting you. Those come from right here," he added, tapping his chest.

"I'm honored you finally copped to liking me."

He laughed, as always, tickled by her audacity. "I'm glad we can see each other clearly now."

"I spoke to Wydetta about the song," Brit said, looking him in the eye. "You'll be getting a songwriting credit."

It was on the tip of his tongue to demur. He didn't want to earn any royalties off Brit or their relationship, but he'd been kicking around this town long enough to know there wasn't a single song about longing or heartbreak without two bodies lying prone in its wake. He'd be an idiot to refuse. Any song Brittany put on her album was bound to be a hit, and since he was no longer recording hits on his own, he had to take his income where he found it.

Cash nodded. "I appreciate it. The royalties from 'Oh No No No' paid for that leather couch a few times over," he said with a wry grin. "Oh No No No" had been a big hit for Brittany. The first song to inch her away from teen idol and closer to pop icon. It'd been a throwaway for him, and throwing away his big chances was how he'd rolled at the time.

He was no longer interested in tossing away his talent. These days, he capitalized on every opportunity he could—the recording studio, session work, the occasional back-up gig, and, yes, songwriting. As long as an opportunity didn't thrust him into the spotlight, Cash was willing to take whatever work he could get.

Brittany wrinkled her nose. "Maybe with the money from this one, you can get something less 2010."

He cocked his head, a smile playing at the corner of his mouth. "Sounds like there was supposed to be an insult in there, but I'll be damned if I know what it was."

"Because you've lost your edge, old man." She shook her head in dismay. "Soon you'll be wearing plaid pants and Velcro tennis shoes."

"Hey, I thought Velcro tennis shoes were coming back," he said defensively. "I saw guys wearing them on the Billboard Awards. Bright white ones, too."

Brittany wagged her head and slid her hands down his arm until her fingers tangled with his. "There is no way on earth you're ever going to pass for a hip-hop kind of guy."

"Damn," he said with a straight face.

A laugh burbled out of her, and Brittany jerked on his hand, pulling him out of the kitchen and down the corridor to his bedroom. For a moment, Cash found himself wishing he had the strength or desire to withstand a frontal assault. The meeting had done him a world of good, but he was intent on playing with fire.

He followed her. They were going to end up naked again. And before he could stop it, he'd be in even deeper than he already was. Then again, if he didn't follow her, he'd surely turn to stone on this very spot and eventually crumble away to nothing.

"I want to use our track on the album," Brittany informed him, talking over her shoulder as she led him down the hallway. "Dylan picked it up okay, and he'll be fine on the road, but I—" She paused in his open bedroom doorway to look back at him. "I want to have this bit of us out there for the whole world to see."

"Hear," he corrected.

"Whatever."

Cash tried to work up a laugh at her dismissiveness, but what Brittany wanted was diametrically opposed to what he needed. What they needed, if there was going to be a "them" long-term. He wasn't up for waving their feelings for each other around like a red flag, taunting the world to come and try to take them down. He didn't want to be tabloid fodder again. Couldn't be. The last thing he needed was for his relationship with Brit to be dissected in headlines too ridiculous to be believed. If there was one thing the public loved more than building a celebrity up, it was tearing them down piece by piece.

He shook his head. "I don't think having me on the album would be very fair to Dylan. It's as much his call as it is yours." It was a lame excuse but the only one he could come up with on the fly.

Brittany snorted. "Don't you worry about Dylan. He's got his own thing going on, and my mama is going to make sure he gets every bit of what he deserves."

"Wydetta is managing Dylan too?"

"You didn't think she'd let an easy fifteen percent slip out of her grasp, did you?"

"You don't need to be so harsh with your mother," he chastised. "She works hard, and she does earn her money."

"Since when did you become Wydetta's champion?"

Cash grasped her waist in both hands and steered her into the bedroom. "I think we both know your mom and I aren't going to be starting any fan clubs for each other, but I respect her abilities. She's always been focused on what's best for you."

Brit spun on her heel, catching both of his hands in hers and pulling him along as if he were the reluctant one. "Oh, yes. Wydetta has always known exactly what she wanted for both of us."

"Don't try to make out like you don't want it too," he cautioned. "It makes you sound petulant and ungrateful."

"Well, there's the kind of sweet talk every woman wants to hear before she lets a guy strip her naked." She lifted her eyebrows. "Hey, why don't you also tell me I'm bad in bed?"

He guffawed. "Why would I do that?"

"Since you walked through the door, you've implied I'm spoiled, out of touch, ungrateful, and petulant. Any other compliments you wanna heap on me?"

Cash opened his mouth to protest, then snapped it shut again. He blinked once, twice, and then finally gave in and admitted to himself she was right. Scrubbing a hand over his face, he shook his head. "Boy, I sure suck at the seduction business, don't I?"

"I wouldn't say it's your strong suit."

Cash couldn't resist smirking. "Then what are you doing here?"

She smoothed her hands over the front of his shirt, then gripped enough of it to twist into her fist. "I like the way you play guitar." She yanked him to her and tilted her face up, her lips parted in invitation. "And I like the way you kiss."

"At least I got a couple of things going for me."

Brit released his shirt then yanked on the tab of his belt. "Why don't you show me what else you've got?"

He plunged his hand into her hair and tugged her head back. She looked up at him through heavy-lidded eyes. "You like the way I kiss?"

"Yes," she whispered.

"You want me to kiss you now?"

"Yes."

He ducked his head, his lips curving in gratification as a note of impatience crept into her voice. "Now? You want me to kiss you now?"

"Either kiss me, or I'm gonna punch you in the nose."

He nuzzled her with the tip of his threatened nose, skimming a kiss across the corner of her mouth, then pulling back before she could draw him in. "Well, now, I'm not at all sure assault is the way go about trying to seduce a guy. Maybe we're both bad at this game."

Brit looked him straight in the eye. "I'm not playing any games." Angling her mouth a fraction of an inch so it aligned with his, she whispered, "Kiss me, or else."

"I tell you, Miss Owens," he drawled, "you sure do know how to get a fellow riled."

"Oh, you ain't seen nothing yet," she boasted. She drew down the zipper on her sweatshirt, revealing the lace edging on her bra. Quirking an eyebrow at him, she shrugged out of the hoodie and let it fall to the floor. "You know, eventually I'm going to have to go home and get a change of clothes."

He closed the gap between them again. "I don't really see the point. I don't plan on letting you wear any."

She barked a husky laugh. "Letting me? You're the one who gets all prudish about going to the kitchen in your birthday suit."

"I only said I wasn't cooking naked." He lowered his head and swiped a hot, fast kiss. "No man in his right mind waves the important stuff around near an open flame."

"And you're claiming to be in your right mind?"

He smirked. "I didn't say I was. I only said I wasn't gonna cook."

11

Brit wasn't a fool. She waited until they lay tangled and sated before even thinking about hinting at a live performance at an awards show. But Cash broke the silence first.

"You know, he didn't recognize me at first," Cash said, his voice gruff and quiet. "Sir James," he clarified when she shot him a puzzled look.

The observation came out of nowhere conversationally, which meant Cash was reviewing the day's events in his mind. Which could be good, Brit realized. Or it could be really bad. Playing it casual until she figured out which side of the cool/not cool spectrum his comment fell on, she snuggled closer, letting her nose brush his as she asked, "Recognize you?"

"From Austin," Cash added. "I think I was…scenery. Well, and that and the stage name probably didn't help connect the dots."

She blinked at him. "Stage name?"

He nodded. "I need to remember to tell Wydetta that if she does anything with the publishing rights, we'll need to put the song under Johnny Smith."

"Johnny Smith?"

He ducked his head and frowned at her. "Yes. I use a stage name for my performances and songwriting credits. Didn't you know that?"

She gazed up at him in blank amazement. "How would I?"

Her head moved up and down when he shrugged. "Yeah, well, I figure, with a name like Cash Dorsett on my birth certificate, no one in country music would ever suspect me to go by something as plain as Johnny Smith."

"But why?"

"Why what?"

Pushing up onto her elbow, she peered down at him. "Why keep it a secret?"

"Because I like my life the way it is. It's cool he didn't put it together."

Alarm bells clanged in her head. Cool. He thought it was cool one of the most famous musicians in the world hadn't remembered them playing a gig together less than a month before. She would have been livid.

Needing a moment to process, Brit ducked her head and buried her face into the crook of his neck. He smelled like soap, sex, and— she had to be imagining this one—coffee. But Cash didn't drink coffee. He didn't take any caffeine at all, which was as foreign a concept to her as quantum physics. As unthinkable as not wanting to be recognized.

"Do you not want him to know who you are?" she asked cautiously.

"No. I mean, yes." He lifted his arm over his head, an open invitation for her to snuggle in closer, and she did. "It's...nice."

"Nice not to be noticed?" She'd tried to keep her skepticism out of the question, but Cash's chuckle told her she wasn't entirely successful.

"Yes, believe it or not, superstar."

He pressed a kiss to the top of her head and she almost melted into his chest. "Not," she said with a sigh. "I absolutely cannot believe you don't miss the spotlight." She was hoping he did. If not, her chances of convincing him to do the HitMakers show were next to nil.

"Okay, there may be some aspects I miss," he conceded. The second she moved, he pulled back to look down at her. "But not many."

"But you don't miss being recognized by other musicians."

"I miss being a part of the circle," he answered after a thoughtful pause.

Brit settled in again. She had her opening. All she had to do now was figure out the right angle on her shot.

"But you don't want to be part of a circle that includes musicians like Sir James?" she prompted, hoping to wriggle some more true confessions out of him. "Because he's so…I don't know… huge? Influential? Legendary?"

"Yes."

She'd been acting the wise-ass, so the sober, one-word response startled her. It might possibly have been the speed with which he answered was the stunner. Either way, the impact of it struck her like a jolt of electricity. Craning her neck, she peered up at him. "Seriously?"

"Seriously."

"Why?"

"Because he's James friggin' Paulson," he answered with a laugh. "No musician in his right mind would ever say no to James Paulson."

"And you don't—" She stopped herself. Unsure of how to phrase the question.

Thankfully, Cash beat her to it. "I don't want to be the jerkoff who said no to James Paulson."

"Would you?"

He rubbed his chin. "Depends. If he wanted studio work, no problem. A one-off like the gig like Austin? No problem. And face it, anyone would sell their left nut to co-write a song with him—"

"I know I would," Brit interrupted dryly.

"But if he asked me to play with him, you know, regular? Under my own name?" he continued, unperturbed. "I might." A beat of silence passed. She heard his hair scratch against the pillowcase and felt the movement of his nod. "I might say no."

She rolled away and crooked her elbow to prop her head on her hand. "Really? Why?" His mouth tightened at the corners, but she rushed in anyway. "I mean, you played with him in Austin," she hastened to remind him.

"That was different. I was helping a friend. It was for charity. No one was paying any attention to me."

Brit cast her mind back to the night she'd run into him again. She hadn't hung around to hear any of the band introductions. Had he really given one of the most powerful and influential musicians of all time a fake name?

"But why?" she murmured aloud, clearly bewildered.

"Why?" His laugh was short and bitter. "Haven't you been listening to anything I've said? I don't want fame, Brit. I don't want to be the 'Oh, I remember him' guy. I'm done chasing after the spotlight." He rolled onto his side. "I'm too old for all that nonsense." Reaching out, he flipped a lock of her hair loose from the rest of the mess and wrapped it around his finger. "I have a good life. I make a good living. And if I'm lucky enough, sometimes those old dreams come tapping at my hotel room door."

She stared at him, mesmerized by both his words and the unwavering confidence behind them. "I never gave up on wanting you."

"Of course not," he replied mildly. A smirk twisted his lips, but his eyes were warm and caressing. "You're strong and determined and on top of the fucking world. Why should you have anything less than everything you want?"

"I want you to play 'We'll Be We' with me live on the HitMakers Awards."

He barked a laugh. "No way."

"I'm serious," she insisted. "I think it would be awesome. People would gobble it up."

His expression sobered. "No chance in hell."

"I'm asking you. Please."

He blinked as if she'd hauled back and slapped him hard across the face. "Brittany, no—"

"Don't say no yet."

"I will never say yes," he shot back.

She tumbled back when he pushed up into a sitting position. Eyes wide, she watched as he shoved first one hand, then the other through his hair. "Cash, I—"

"I can't believe you're asking me to do this." Incredulity dripped from his every word. He stared at her as if she were a complete stranger. "Have you not been listening? I can't get drawn back into that world. There's too much temptation. Too many expectations."

"I've been listening." She sat up too, clutching the sheet to her chest. "But come on, you can't tell me it didn't feel good, us making music together."

"It felt fucking fantastic," he spat. "Doesn't mean I want to be paraded around like a pet monkey."

"I'm not... I don't want to parade—"

He cut her off with a wave of his hand. "No. Just no. Always no." Before she could recover, he swung his legs off the bed and shot to his feet. "No. Never."

She stared up at him, shocked into immobility by the vehemence of his rejection. "So you're saying no," she said snidely.

"Listen, I love being with you. I love playing with you. I might flat-out love you, but I can't go there. I won't."

Brit gazed up at him, her heart thudding against her breastbone so hard she was afraid she looked like one of those silly GIFs people post on social media. "You *might* love me?" she managed to rasp at last. But his declaration brought her no joy. No pleasure. Only the pain of an uncertain kind of feeling. As if she didn't have enough insecurity all on her own. "Oh, well, thanks."

He ignored her sarcasm in favor of collecting their discarded clothing from the floor. "Listen, we're both...on edge today."

She glared at him. "I *might* be."

Cash had the good grace to wince, but he didn't apologize. "I'm going to take you home. We'll cool off, then we'll talk tomorrow or the next day."

"I have rehearsals tomorrow. I have another tour coming up, remember?" she responded, slinging the words at him like rocks.

"Then whenever." He straightened, a wad of rumpled and crumpled clothing clutched in his talented hands. "I'm going to take you home," he repeated, the words soft as a down pillow. "You need underwear, remember?"

"Don't tell me what I need."

His chin came up as if he were preparing to take a punch. "I won't if you won't." Blowing out a breath, he dropped down onto the mattress and began to sort his clothes from hers. "Listen, it's been an emotional day." When she opened her mouth to protest, he shoved her bra into her hands. "Fine. It's been an emotional day for *me*, okay? I have... stuff I'm trying to work through."

Brit felt a sharp pang of guilt when she remembered where Cash had been before he'd come home to find her in his house. "I get that."

"Then get this. I want to write with you. Play with you. Be with you. But I don't want to get drawn back into the game, Brit." He held her gaze. "I don't know if I can survive it, and I won't let you take me down because I don't want to say no to you."

"I'm not trying to take you down, I'm trying to be with you. I choose to be with you," she argued.

"If you want to be with me, help me. Make it so I don't have to say no to you. I don't want to say no to you, but I will. I'm not one of your entourage, Brit. I've gotten really good at using single-syllable words."

And damn, if his stubborn pride didn't make her love him even more. He was right. She was getting to the place where people don't dare tell her no. Where no one would pass up the chance at basing in her reflected glory. True, she was nowhere near Sir James's league, but she was certainly more in the moment. Of the moment. And Cash was rejecting the opportunity to share this moment with her, not because of ego, but because he believed it to be essential to his survival.

She slipped into her bra without argument. He placed her hoodie next to her on the bed as she untangled the legs of her jeans. He was right. Their emotions were running high. So were the stakes. For both of them. She hadn't worn clean clothes in two days and her skin smelled like bar soap—a good scent for him, but she preferred something less…soapy.

By the time she wriggled her feet into her shoes, he had his keys in hand. She was gratified to hear him jingle them. Cash only fidgeted when he was nervous, and damn it, she wanted him to be every bit as jittery as she was.

The ride back to Brentwood was tense, the silence filled with things unsaid for fear they could not be taken back. As they neared the area where she lived, Brittany gave directions in a quiet monotone voice. When they made the last turn onto her street, Cash glanced over at her. "If this singing thing doesn't work out, you can always get a gig giving GPS directions."

She smirked. "Thanks. It's always good to have a backup in mind."

Another stretch of silence followed, but this time, Cash reached across the console and took her hand in his. He gestured to the gates leading to her house and let out a low, appreciative whistle. "Very nice."

"You've been here before," she reminded him. "For my birthday party."

He pulled up to the gate and wordlessly punched in the code she gave him. As the intricately scrolled wrought iron slid open, he shook his head in quiet regret. "Sugar, I hate to admit this to anyone, particularly you, but I wasn't exactly sober." He crept up the drive through the open gate. "Not that I don't remember the kiss. I do remember. Vividly. But if you think I was looking at your house or being impressed by your guest list, you're wrong. Most likely I was concerned with what kind of booze you were stocking on your bar, or if Wydetta had anything good in her medicine cabinet."

"I see."

Cash dismissed her attempted empathy with a shake of his head. "No, you really don't. And I don't ever want you to," he hastened to add. "Getting sober is the hardest thing I've ever done."

She tried to wrap her head around what Cash saying to her about his battle with pills and alcohol. He was watching her closely. Waiting for something. She could only surmise he wanted her to respond to what he said about his hopes for her.

"I'm not much of a drinker," she admitted. "A total lightweight. I've seen too much of what it does to people."

He nodded. "And I want you to remember what it does. Because once you've battled the demon, there's nothing more important to you than staying on top of it." He looked her straight in the eye. "Nothing."

"Okay."

"I love the way you say okay. Like it's simple."

Brittany tipped her head to the side. "Isn't it? If a person wants to stay sober, their true friends will help them."

He reached over and caressed her face with the backs of his knuckles. She leaned into the caress, but he pulled away before she'd had her fill. "It's more than avoiding bars, Brit. It's more than not hanging out with the wrong people."

"I get what you're saying."

"I don't think you really do, but that's okay, how could you?" he hastened to add. "It's about opting not to do things that may make you want to drink again, or pop another pill. For me, those things include having someone shine a spotlight on me." He paused to draw a deep breath. "I won't do the show, Brit. No matter how bad you want me to. You can try your hardest and use every one of your *very* potent feminine charms to try to convince me." She opened her mouth to speak, but he pressed a fingertip to her lips to stop her. "I'll still say no." He shook his head. "If you were your mother, you'd threaten to destroy the piddling little life I've made for myself—"

"It isn't piddling—"

"But you're not your mother and I won't let you," he concluded. "I'm not the same man I was, but I like who I am now a helluva lot more than I liked the guy I was. It doesn't matter what you say, you won't change my mind. My days of reaching for the stars are over. I like it in the shadows."

"I understand."

He smirked at her. "No, you don't, but you don't have to understand. You only have to respect it."

A lump rose in her throat. She reached for his hand and clutched it tightly. "I do. I will," she amended. "I'll try," she concluded. "It's hard for me to forget when I know how good you are and how good you could have been."

"I don't let myself think about it anymore." Cash raised her hand to his lips and kissed it.

"You never do?"

"I didn't say never. I meant, I try not to let myself." He fixed her with a pointed look. "That way lay danger."

"I only want to be with you."

"You don't really know me. Not who I am now."

One side of her mouth curved up. "You aren't mysterious, Cash. I know enough to be sure I want you around more. I was trying to convince you to perform because I want to be with you. I've got this massive tour starting. I was thinking maybe once in a while you could pop up—"

"Never going to happen," he stated, cutting her off with his quiet conviction.

"I know. I only… I think you're so wonderful. I want the whole world to know how wonderful you are."

He rested their clasped hands in his lap. "They don't need to see me on stage to know I'm not a complete loser. They can see you. Hear you. They have to know if a superstar like you can maybe love a man like me, I can't be a complete loser. But you know the tabloids are going to eat us up. I need to stay out of that mess as much as possible."

"There's no maybe on my side." Brit gave a rueful hum. "My granddad says people aren't particularly smart. They would rather be spoon-fed a heaping helping of lies than figure out the truth for themselves."

"Merle always was a clever man." He stared out through the windshield, unblinking, unseeing. "I hate like hell that I disappointed him."

"I'm sure he hates it more you disappointed yourself," she countered. "Why don't you come to supper with me on Sunday?"

The invitation caught his attention. He stared at her, his lips parting in surprise. "You all still have Sunday supper at their house?"

Brit nodded. "Every week. Well, when I'm in town," she amended.

"Wow. I'm surprised your mom kept it up after you turned eighteen. She never seemed to like those suppers very much."

She shrugged. "She doesn't like them, but she goes every week. They made some kind of deal when I was a baby. Something to do with keeping the family together." She glanced toward the front door. "Wydetta doesn't know I know. I overheard her talking with Grandma one time."

"Wydetta hated going there. She never made it much of a secret."

Brittany faced him again. "You know what? I don't think she does."

"You don't?"

She shook her head. "Cash, I'm twenty-three years old. I'm not a baby anymore. Whatever their deal was has to have been fulfilled by now."

He mulled her theory for a moment, then nodded thoughtfully. "Maybe. Or maybe Wydetta sold her soul to make you a star. It would explain so much," he added in a murmur.

Brit looked at him for a moment. He was only saying the same things she'd thought a thousand times growing up. But she couldn't let the comment pass without defending herself and her talent. "What? You don't think I could become a star on my own? You don't think I have the talent? The drive? You don't think I'm the whole package?" She raised a challenging brow.

Cash laughed, obviously tickled by her diatribe. "Oh, hell yes, I do. Ma'am," he said with a devilish gleam in his eyes. "I was waiting for you to say it."

"Ass." She swatted him on the arm.

Cash didn't flinch or draw back, he only stared at her, his expression growing solemn. "You are a superstar, and you know it." He leaned across and kissed her tenderly, his lips clinging to hers as he drew back. "Go in. Get some rest and pack your panties or whatever. I'll pick you up on Friday, and we'll spend the weekend at my place."

"Friday? You're going to make me wait until Friday?" she asked, incensed.

"I'm going to make me wait until Friday too," he pointed out. Before she could come up with an argument, he kissed her again. "If there's one thing we know better than most people, it's time won't change things," he said. "We keep coming at each other like charging bulls, but we don't have to. There's no rush."

She hated his calm. Hated his reason. And loved him more than she ever had. This was no teenage crush gone wild. He was everything she wanted, and likely exactly the man she needed. An oasis in the clamor and clangor of her life.

"Friday," she repeated, unable to suppress the pout in her voice entirely.

Cash chuckled. "And no sexting. I'm too old to get my rocks off typing into a phone."

Brit snorted, then reached for the door handle. "Fine. Regular old phone sex it is." She paused when she felt his hand tighten on her arm, ready to defend her constitutional right to talk as dirty as she liked.

"Let me get the door for you," he ordered, his voice gruff.

Her forehead puckered as she tried to puzzle out the abrupt shift in topics. "What?"

"Hang tight."

Before she could stop him, Cash bailed from his seat and was jogging around the front of the truck to get to the passenger side. Her hand fell away from the handle and she gaped at him in astonishment. Her grandpa always did this—insisted on opening doors for her grandma. Brit found the gesture useless, old-fashioned, and somewhat sexist, but she knew Merle well enough to know her opinions on what he considered plain old good manners were not welcome. Sure, she'd had drivers open doors for her, but they were being paid, and those were usually red carpet occasions where a star's arrival was very much a part of the show.

She never thought she'd feel a tingle at having a man open a door for her. It was ludicrous. She had two working hands and was perfectly capable—

The door swung open, and Cash stepped into the void, blocking her in. She wanted to tell him exactly what she'd been thinking, but his mouth closed over hers and every shred of indignation she might have known floated away on the gentle caress of his lips. He kissed her slow and sweet. A kiss filled with longing, and promise, and I'm-gonna-miss-you-but-I-know-I'll-see-you-soon.

The kind of kiss people wrote songs about.

The exact kiss Faith Hill had proclaimed to be subliminal and possibly criminal.

The type of kiss that allowed a man to get away with old-fashioned bullcrap like opening a woman's car door so he could steal one.

She wound her arms around his neck and held fast when he tried to break away. "Not yet, you rotten bastard. Kiss me some more."

His laughter ghosted across damp lips and sent a shiver down her spine, but he complied without complaint. Brit melted into him, savoring his heat and his taste, literally turning to putty when he slid his hands into her hair. When they parted, she ducked her head and whispered, "Take me with you."

Cash gathered her into his arms and held firm. "You have work to do. I have work to do. I'll see you on the weekend. We can pretend we're normal people dating."

"I never wanted to be normal," she insisted.

"I know." Framing her face in his hands, he bent his knees to look her dead in the eye. "Good thing, because I don't think you can pull it off."

She started to retort, but he slid both hands down to her waist, grasped firmly, and plucked her off the seat like she was no more than a rag doll. Once she got her feet under her, she gave him a mighty shove. The man barely moved. "I hate you," she hissed without any real venom behind the words.

Cash smirked, then made a show of running the back of his hand over his kiss-dampened mouth. "Yeah, I got the message loud and clear." He backed away. "I'll pick you up at seven on Friday. Bring your clothes for Sunday, and we'll spend the weekend together, then leave for Merle's from my place," he ordered as he made his way back to the driver's side of the cab.

"You're disinvited."

He paused, his hand on the door handle. "You really want to make me call your grandma and finagle an invitation?"

She scowled and flipped him the bird, but Cash only threw his head back and laughed as he yanked the door open.

"Goodnight, superstar. Sweet dreams."

Brit hugged herself as he climbed behind the wheel of his truck. Cash lifted a hand in farewell, but didn't look back as he drove away from her. Rousing herself from her stupor, she made her way up the steps to the porch, then paused to watch as his taillights disappeared into the night. She let herself into the disturbingly quiet house, punched her code into the alarm console, and keyed a few digits into her phone to let security know she was on the premises and to secure the property. Dragging her feet, she made her way to the curving staircase leading to the west wing of the house.

As she grasped the balustrade, she muttered to the echoing foyer, "Another glamorous and exciting night in the cradle of country music, folks," and softly hummed a few bars of that old Carpenters song as she began to climb.

12

She'd fallen into bed with him. Wydetta had known she would. How long could any woman resist?

Therefore, she shouldn't be surprised to find herself panting and staring wide-eyed at the hand-painted shoji screen, decorative bowls, and vases that littered the room. But they couldn't possibly be part of the hotel standard decor. Only someone like James Paulson would try to dress up an already beautifully appointed hotel suite with personal touches.

Sweat cooled on her skin, causing her hyper-sensitive nipples to pucker painfully, but she hadn't the energy to cover herself. Mustering all the strength she had in reserve, she turned her head to look at the bedside clock. No, she hadn't read the time wrong. They'd been having sex for over two hours.

Had she ever had sex for two full hours? She mentally flipped through her Rolodex of former lovers, but none stood out. Her current one flipped over onto his side and fluffed the pillow beside hers with astonishing enthusiasm. "I'm famished," he said conversationally. "Shall I order us a bite from room service?"

Despite the difference in their ages, James was obviously not feeling like a wrung-out washcloth. Good for him. He deserved a knighthood for that alone. Not to mention the orgasms. Those never-ending, one-on-top-of-the-next orgasms.

Had she ever come like that? Not hard and hot—she'd had those. This was something different. Slower, softer, but somehow more intense than anything she'd ever experienced. Truthfully, she couldn't wait to get back to her own space so she could relive them in her head. Dissect them. Figure out exactly what button he'd pushed so she could be sure to point it out to her next lover.

James nudged her with his knee. She looked over and found him peering down at her, his head propped on his hand, and his elbow digging hard into the poor pillow he'd abused. She blinked to clear the fuzz from her mind. He was astonishingly bright-eyed.

She scrambled from the bed and began collecting her clothes.

"Where are you going?"

"I have to get home." Forgoing the crumpled pantyhose pooled on the floor, she shrugged into her bra. "I have a full day tomorrow."

He propped himself up with both hands, his forehead puckered. "A full day?"

"Meetings, calls," she mumbled as she shook out her dress and stepped into it. With the fabric gaping at her shoulders, she approached the bed, pulled her hair over her shoulder as she turned, and presented him with the zipper at the back. "Would you mind?"

"I mind very much," James replied without missing a beat, but he dutifully zipped the dress for her. "I'd like you to stay."

Heaving a sigh, she forced herself to walk away from the bed and the tempting man on it. She wriggled her feet into her discarded shoes, then gathered the sheet she'd draped over a chair in her quest to dress. "I'm afraid I can't. Thank you, though." She gentled her tone as she offered gratitude in exchange for the easy out they both so desperately needed. "As I'm sure you have a lot to do as well. But I had a real good time tonight. I certainly enjoyed your…" She paused, placing the wadded sheet on the corner of the bed and drinking in the destruction they'd left in their wake. "Mindfulness," she finished with a sly wink. "Thank you."

When she glanced back, she saw James scribbling something in the small notebook he kept on the nightstand, oblivious to his own nudity. She marveled at his agile attention span, as well as his astonishing self-confidence. He had the long, lean frame of a man half his age, and the prowess of a guy half again.

If this were the eighties or nineties, she might suspect he used cocaine or some other drug to help him maintain this air of elegant dissipation. But those days were long gone…if they'd ever been part of his reality and not another bit of rock lore. Besides, she'd spent enough time with him since their tryst began in Austin to know the man was practically a zealot about what went into his body. He was a vegetarian, for Christ's sake. And he did yoga for more than an hour each morning without fail.

Grabbing her handbag, she asked the question that had niggled at her since their first dinner together. "So...we slept together. Are we done now?"

"Not by a long shot, love," he replied without looking up from his notes. "Come back to bed."

She hoped he wasn't drawing one of those abstract nudes he'd talked about collecting. Or worse, an anatomically correct portrait of her. She kept in pretty good shape herself, but when a woman was staring down the barrel of forty, there was no denying the impact of gravity.

"No, not tonight. I'm going home to my own bed," she proclaimed.

James looked up then. "Marvelous!" Snapping the journal shut, his eyes lit with anticipation. "I've been waiting for an invitation."

She placed her hand on her hip. "You think I was inviting you to come home with me?"

"This is the closest I've come to an invitation, so I'll take it."

Wydetta's jaw dropped when he swung his long legs over the edge of the bed and tossed the notebook into the nest of discarded bedding at the foot of the bed. He rose with the lithe grace of a cat stretching in a patch of morning sunlight.

She gnawed her bottom lip as she watched, hating him a teensy bit.

The problem was, she liked him too. A lot.

It was damn disconcerting.

He gave her a playful swat on the bottom before nudging her toward the bathroom. "You go freshen up. I want to stretch." He cocked his head at an exaggerated angle, then leered at her. "I think I may have pulled something on our last go."

He was bossy and demanding. Two things she usually resented in a man. But on him...

Their post-coital turnabout disoriented her. James seemed more than happy to let her lead the charge to the bed. But once they got there, Wydetta couldn't shake the feeling she'd somehow played right into his hands.

Unnerved but unaccountably thrilled by the prospect of James wanting to see more of her, she grabbed her handbag, looped the leather straps over her arm, and sashayed to the oversized bathroom with as much dignity as she could muster. Setting her bag aside, she splashed water on her face, then patted her skin dry with the corner of a washcloth. Her makeup was fairly intact. A touch up here and there, and she'd be ready to face the prospect of James nudging his way deeper into her life. Maybe.

Lowering the towel, she studied her reflection with shrewd eyes. Her attraction to him hadn't yet begun to wane. The fact worried her. Wydetta prided herself on her ability to avoid entanglements and attachments. And, at the moment, she was tangled up tighter than a wad of gum in a first-grader's hair.

"I'm not sure it's a good idea for you to come home with me." She tried for casual nonchalance, but her voice came out pitchy and uneven. "Brittany may be home, and we need to talk."

She jumped when James appeared in the mirror behind her. He'd pulled on a pair of gunmetal-gray boxer briefs, but he looked freshly fucked. Wydetta sighed and checked her makeup again. Who was she trying to kid? She totally looked like the woman who'd done it.

He gave her a lazy smirk as he reached for the hairbrush on the counter. The bristles slipped effortlessly through his silky hair. In three easy swipes, every one of his well-trained locks fell into their proper place. If the studied disarray he'd perfected years before could be called proper.

"Brittany's not home, love," he said, a note of gentleness buffering the words. "She and the guitar player bloke are burning off whatever was left after their session." He rested his hands on her shoulders and his chin atop her hair. Their eyes met in the mirror's reflection. "I'm only sad I don't have the stamina I did when I was his age. We could give them a run for their money."

"You don't need an ounce more stamina than you've already got, mister," she admonished. Reaching up, she wrapped tentative fingers around his forearm and squeezed.

He chuckled appreciatively, then kissed the top of her head. "Ah, you are good for the ego."

"If your ego gets any healthier, it's going to start doing one-handed push-ups."

"I can do those," he boasted, then trailed another kiss along her temple. "Anyhow, Brittany is likely at her lad's house. Heaven forbid her mama hear her screaming his name the way you were screaming mine."

"James!"

"Or vice versa," he added quickly. "I'm only saying she's not going to do him under your nose. Particularly since you dislike him," he pointed out as he stepped back.

Wydetta gasped. More at the loss of his warmth than the accusation, but she could play it either way. "Who said I—"

He ducked his head and pressed a kiss to the side of her neck before nibbling his way up to capture her earlobe. "Pfft. Subtlety is not your strong suit, darling."

She whirled, locked and loaded and ready to give him a piece of her mind, but he silenced her with a smacking kiss on her parted lips.

"It's true. And one of the things I like most about you."

He gave her rump another pat, but he was too fast for her to swat his hand away. The man was out of the bathroom before she could even react.

"Shake a leg," he called from another room. "We'll go to your place. I'm thinking tomorrow we should try that new Cuban restaurant the concierge was spouting off about."

Wydetta scowled at her reflection, hating how much she liked hearing someone give her orders for a change. Having someone else come up with a plan. She refused to give in to him without a fight, though. Even if it was a token one.

"I'm not sure I'll be available tomorrow night," she said, strolling from the bathroom as if she hadn't a care in the world.

"Then we'll go the next night," he said, swatting away her roadblocks like gnats.

James had his pants on. A blue silk shirt hung from his lean shoulders unbuttoned. She marveled at the way the expertly tailored fabric clung to his body even in his current state of disarray. Wydetta felt like his shirt. Undone, untucked, and completely at the mercy of those around her.

A part of her, the tender, insecure part she kept buried beneath layers of armor, couldn't help but wonder if Brittany's affair with Cash Dorsett somehow marked the beginning of the end. Not for her daughter's career, but for Wydetta's job as a mother. And her manager.

Brit's choice was a flat-out rebellion. Wydetta and Cash had never kept their animosity for one another a secret. She resented the affection her father had once lavished on the guy. Cash was the son Merle had never had, and he had made no attempt at keeping his regard for the interloper a secret.

And she couldn't fault Brit for indulging in a few minor uprisings. Once upon a time, Wydetta was the crowned princess of rebellion. Still was in some ways, though she'd honed and perfected her skills over the years. To this day, she very rarely did whatever it was her parents wanted her to. She'd learned to be subtle with her insurrections so no one could accuse her of being childish or adolescent.

But she felt like a teenager striking out on her own for the first time when she met James's level gaze. "Fine. Come home with me."

He unerringly aligned the bottom button on his shirt. His eyes narrowed as he studied her. "Okay."

She fought the urge to squirm. It was bad enough feeling as if he could feel her inner turmoil. But he didn't say anything more. She found herself watching him dress, mesmerized by the way his talented fingers flew up the placket, feeding button after button through each expertly crafted hole. He stopped at the third from the top, of course, leaving his throat exposed.

She eyed the braided gold chain he wore every moment of every day. The thin strands lay flat against his chest, weighted down by the smooth circlet of gold he'd worn for decades.

They hadn't talked about his late wife. Or, rather, she never asked about his wife. Doing so would have been too intimate in the beginning, and now too awkward. They were sleeping together, yes, but his marriage was the stuff of legend.

As if he could read her thoughts, he headed for the oversized walnut bureau against the wall. "I guess I'll pack my knickers, then." Before she could protest, he started pulling clothes from the drawers. He glanced back and smirked when he saw she hadn't moved. "Get dressed. We can battle for boundaries in the car."

But something in the way he offered the possibility of a fight made her think she'd already lost whatever skirmish she might cook up.

Wydetta had forgotten all about Martine.

Okay, so she didn't forget about her cousin, she simply hadn't factored in her cousin greeting them when she brought James home with her. She also hadn't considered the possibility of her cousin turning into a complete fangirl the minute she spotted him.

"Would you like some tea, Sir James?" she asked, all sweetness and light.

James held up his hand like a king greeting one of his subjects. Which, she supposed, in a way he was. But his high-handed tactics set Wydetta's nerves on fire.

"Oh, no. And it's James, love. And don't trouble yourself."

"It's no trouble at all," Martine cooed. "I was about to make some for myself."

What a fresh load of crap. Wydetta had never seen her cousin drink a cup of hot tea in her entire life, and they'd been best friends since they were toddlers.

"Oh, well, if that's the case, I wouldn't mind a cuppa," James said with a congenial wink. "If you're sure it's no trouble."

"No trouble at all," Marti assured him, triumph lighting her midnight eyes. "I'll be right back."

But when she headed toward the back of the house, James released his hold on Wydetta's waist, pecked an absent kiss to her cheek, then hurried after her. "Oh, I'll come on through. No need to act like I'm company."

Reeling from the way the events of the day had unfolded, Wydetta follow James and Martine back to the spacious chef's kitchen, where her cousin reigned supreme. There, her mischievous lover dropped himself in the chair at the large farmhouse table they hardly ever used and grinned up at her like a boy who'd landed the prime spot at the soda fountain.

"I don't suppose you ladies keep any biscuits about in case you have gentleman callers," he asked hopefully. "I'm starving."

Unable to contain herself, Wydetta rolled her eyes. "We might keep some about if we knew any gentlemen to come calling, but all we know are a bunch of rascals and scoundrels."

James beamed at her as if she'd handed him a shiny new Grammy award. "Really, now?" He rubbed his chin thoughtfully, as if the tidbit of information needed mulling. When he looked up at her, he wore an expression so deceptively boyish and innocent Wydetta felt an almost irrepressible urge to applaud his performance. "Which of those categories do I fall into? I have to admit, I quite fancy the thought of being a scoundrel."

Martine's tinkling laughter rang out like a bell. Wydetta shot her cousin a death glare, but Marti remained oblivious, her attention focused only on the kettle she was setting to boil and their guest.

"Don't let Etta push you around, and don't let her try to trick you with her tough-girl act," Martine warned.

James moved the chair next to him away from the table with his foot, then planted his chin in his palm. "Oh. This is a tough-girl act, is it, Etta?"

Rolling her eyes, Wydetta dropped into the seat and kept her gaze fixed on him rather than her traitorous cousin. But she did have to suppress a little shiver when his accent turned the nickname into "Ett-er."

Shaking her head slightly, she reminded herself that he was the intruder here. She couldn't believe she let him waltz his way into her home. She never brought men home to stay. Never. And if he thought he was something special…well, he could waltz his way right back out the front door.

Drumming her fingernails on the tabletop, Wydetta fixed him with what she liked to think of as her serious negotiation stare. "So, now you've seen where I live," she began, her tone deceptively calm. "And once you've had your nice *cuppa*," she mocked, "you can feel free to skitter along back home to your hotel room. Pip-pip," she added with a smirk, "and tally-ho."

She rose from the chair and exited the kitchen with her head held high, ignoring his peal of masculine laughter as she hurried from the room.

The suite of rooms she kept on the second floor was on the opposite end of the house from Brittany's, separated by the grand two-story entranceway. It wasn't unheard of for the two of them to be in residence and not see one another through the course of the day.

Seeing her daughter at the studio today made Wydetta realize exactly how much distance had grown between them since the benefit in Texas. It made her nervous. Not because she was afraid of getting fired. She knew Brit knew she was the best manager she could ever hope to have. No, it was more than business. It was…everything.

The more independent Brit became, the more independent *she'd* be forced to become. The more choices she'd have to make. For herself. Wydetta had never been responsible only for herself, and frankly, the prospect terrified her.

Dropping her bag onto the antique settee in her sitting room, she wrung her hands as she walked to the bank of windows looking out over the carefully cultivated jungle of their backyard. The aqua blue lights of the free-form swimming pool beckoned from below. Wydetta couldn't remember the last time she'd dipped a toe into the cool water.

Strategically placed spotlights highlighted the terraced gardens surrounding the pool and its environs. The yard was one of the reasons she'd wanted the house. She'd fallen in love with the gardens the moment she saw them. Back then, she thought her daughter needed some disarray in her life. A place where things grew wild and free. Which was ridiculous. It wasn't as if they'd lived in a tenement apartment before moving to Brentwood. Her parents' luxurious, but comfortable, home was set on acres of lush grounds with terraced formal gardens and open pasture for the horses her mother loved so much.

The truth was, Wydetta had wanted a very different sort of yard for her daughter because she wanted a very different sort of life for her. She didn't admit to Brittany how relieved she was when her daughter passed her sixteenth, eighteenth, and then twenty-first birthday without making any of the tragic mistakes she herself had made in those danger-fraught years.

She probably didn't need to tell her. Brit knew the last thing Wydetta wanted was for her to miss out on all the things she'd never had from her own mother.. Like understanding. The kind of mother who didn't judge, and didn't try to clip her wings. So, she positioned herself in whatever role would keep her most relevant to Brittany. Mother. Friend. Manager. Champion.

She'd given up everything she might have built in her own life to be sure her daughter had choices. Wydetta was all too aware she didn't have half the talent her father or daughter had. And though she was more than passably attractive, she hadn't inherited her breathtaking mother's beauty-queen looks. Rather than shapely and svelte, she was long and raw-boned like her father. She had Merle's dishwater blonde hair and striking blue eyes, but that was as far as the resemblance to her famous father went. No matter how much she spent on highlights, makeup, or her designer wardrobe, when she was standing with her parents and daughter, Wydetta couldn't help but feel like the least flamboyant member of a family of peacocks.

And now, her lover was downstairs flirting with her cousin. Martine the man-killer. The woman who everybody proclaimed to be the spitting image of Marie Boudreaux Owens—the one-time Bayou Bombshell. And she'd left him there. Like he was a sweater she'd grown tired of and wouldn't bother to retrieve.

But she wasn't tired of him. Her feelings were quite the opposite. Whatever this thing he made her feel was, it scared her witless.

"So this is your boudoir."

She looked up to find James lounging against the doorframe. He held a delicately patterned china teacup and saucer Wydetta didn't even know they owned. It should have looked ridiculous clasped in his big paw, but it didn't. He looked as natural holding it as he had lounging naked in the hotel bed a short time before. She marveled at what a gift that must be, to feel so comfortable in one's own skin one fits in anywhere and everywhere.

Quirking a brow she asked, "Not what you expected?"

He chuckled as he took his time looking the sitting room over. Leaning back, she draped an arm over the carved wood at the back of the settee and tried to see the room through his eyes. The fabrics were subtly patterned whites and creams with some hints of platinum thrown in to provide the antiques they graced a more updated feel. The room was comfortably furnished, but not overly busy. The art, soothing and restive.

Wydetta had decorated it herself, though she'd withhold that information until after he'd given his verdict. The last thing her ego needed was a living legend telling her all her taste was in her mouth.

"It's lovely." James stepped into the room and stopped at the threshold to make a more thorough perusal. "Not at all what I expected."

Torn between pleasure and offense, Wydetta asked, "What did you expect?"

He waved a hand and began to prowl the sitting room. The tea in his cup barely quivered as he moved. She envied his innate grace. "I suppose I expected red silk and harem pillows," he said with a dismissive sniff. "Something obvious and flashy." Turning back to her, he smirked. "No matter what I expected, I certainly didn't anticipate walking into this"—he paused, searching for the words—"understated elegance."

Wydetta bristled. "Because there's nothing understated or elegant about me."

"Gad, no," he scoffed. "Not at all the adjectives I would choose for you."

She yearned to ask what adjectives he would pick, but she refused to give him the satisfaction. Instead, she relaxed back against the settee and examined her fingernails. "Red never was my color of choice."

James moved about the room, picking up trinkets and examining them as if they held the key to unlocking all her secrets. "No? I think you'd be smashing in red."

A blush crept up her neck, but she forced herself to ignore the warm rush of pleasure his words brought. He was an uninvited guest. A man who seemed to have forgotten how flings were properly flung. She couldn't blame him. He'd had a long-standing love. She'd have to be the one to toss him aside because he'd obviously forgotten how to end an affair once it had run its course.

Ignoring the twist of regret in her gut, she plunged in. "James, I—"

He held up a hand to stop her. Stalking across the room, he set the cup and saucer neatly on the table beside her perch, then squeezed past her to claim the cushion next to her. "Don't go there." Taking her hand in his, he gave it a pat. "Not yet."

To her surprise, he threaded his fingers through hers and leaned back as if taking in the big picture of her life.

When the silence stretched too long to bear, she cracked. "What? What are you thinking?"

"I'm thinking this room suits you after all," he replied. "I didn't think so at first, but now I see it."

When he glanced at her, she raised an eyebrow. It was an unspoken challenge for him to proceed, but James didn't pick up on unspoken things. He liked to make her say them out loud. She huffed. "Okay, fine. Tell me what you see."

He tipped his head back as if the answer was written on the ceiling, then picked up one of the throw cushions he'd pushed aside to get to her. Tracing his long fingers over the subtle stripe of platinum woven into the fabric, he said, "I see you. Cool and calculated, but with a surprising amount of flash. Not the kind to dazzle on first impression, but the type to niggle at the senses."

"I niggle you?" she asked, incensed at the implication she was annoying.

He rolled his eyes. "I did not say you niggled. I said something in your style teases the senses. Tickles them until you realize it's this bit of… pizzazz underneath it all the carefully chosen neutrals."

Wydetta stared at him, her jaw dropping open slightly. She was unspeakably flattered but unsure she should admit it. "Pizzazz? That's the word that comes to mind?"

He grinned. "Many words come to mind when I think of you."

"Oh my, you are good."

The words came out in an admiring purr. One James accepted as his due.

"I've had plenty of practice," he said with a comically seductive leer.

Narrowing her eyes, Wydetta clenched her teeth to gain strength enough to resist his charm. "I thought you were playing the 'I'm out of practice' card these days."

"I may be a bit rusty when it comes to seducing women, but I did have a wife for a number of years. A smart man never gets out of practice when it comes to issuing compliments."

She tossed her head back and laughed. "Good gravy, you *are* a scoundrel."

"So I'm told by your cousin," he said with a nonchalant gesture. She swatted at him and he threw his head back with a laugh. "Haven't you read all the music mags? Apparently, all these years later, me and my old mates are still the *bomb diggity*."

He enunciated the consonants of the last bit with such overstated dignity she burst out laughing. Tears gathered in her eyes, but she knuckled them away before they could make a mess of her. This was his secret weapon. His superpower was flagrant, unabashed charm, and it was clearly her Kryptonite. She hadn't laughed so much with any man in longer than she cared to admit. Maybe ever. And though at times she was laughing at him—or, at the two of them together— either way, she was laughing. A phenomenon with enough novelty to capture her interest.

She moved closer to him, swiveling her knees so she grazed his leg. "You know, you drive me straight up the wall."

He nodded as if digesting the information. "This may come as a shock to you, but it's not the first time I've heard someone say so."

"What are we doing here, James?"

Pausing to make an exaggerated survey of the room, he shrugged. "You mentioned a wall," he murmured. "My back isn't what it used to be, but I'm game."

"I'm serious."

He brushed a lock of hair from her face with the backs of his fingers. "I know. You always are. It's part of what makes you so damn irresistible."

"I'm irresistible?"

He gestured grandly to the room. "So much so I shamelessly invited myself into your home. I wanted to see your inner sanctum. I needed to see where you come to recharge the spark of star quality you try so hard to cover up with efficiency."

Wydetta blinked at him. No one had ever accused her of having star quality. No one had ever told her she was anything special. When one was the product of a living legend and a legendary beauty, it was hard not to feel like an ugly duckling. When a woman's only child outstripped her professionally by the age of fourteen, it was too easy to believe she'd garner few accomplishments in her own right. Yet, this man, this incredible once-in-a-lifetime genius of a man, thought she was something special.

Who was she to debase him of the notion? Rising from the sofa, she offered him her hand.

He glanced up warily. "Where are we going?"

"Come with me. I'll show you my inner sanctum." She crooked a coy finger at him. "We'll see if we can't strike a few of those sparks you were looking for."

"Darling, you could stand stark naked in a rainstorm and they'd come popping off you like fireworks," he assured her. He studied her for a long moment, then rose, taking her hand in his much larger one. "But I always have been a sucker for an impressive light show. Come on," he said, giving her hand a gentle squeeze. "Take me to your bed, and I'll coax noises out of you that will scandalize even your incorrigible flirt of a cousin."

13

A high-pitched squeal rent the air. Brittany's eyes popped open, but she didn't sit up. Instead, she clutched the sheets in an effort to resist the urge. She'd actually been trained for these occasions.

She blinked once, twice, then relaxed her grip as she waited for her brain to catch up with her galloping heart. The security alarm was going off. There'd been a breach. Either the gate, or the house. She lay listening for sounds beneath the ear-piercing screech. No thumps. No clomps. No shadowy figures fumbling around in the dark in her room.

Drawing a shallow breath, she scanned the outline of her furnishings. Nothing shifted. Nothing seemed out of place. Then, and only then, did she dare to move.

Lessons like this one had been drilled into her since the time she was a toddler. Once, her grandparents' estate had been broken into, and her grandmother had been held at knifepoint while some burglars rifled through her jewelry. Even Merle's public and outspoken love of exercising his Second Amendment rights couldn't change what happened.

The men who had broken in had the knife pointed at her grandmother's throat before either of her grandparents had even awakened. Merle had no chance at reaching for the handgun he kept in his nightstand. The robbery went off without injury, but when Wydetta realized her father kept a loaded pistol in the same house as her daughter, she had packed up their belongings and moved out.

Wydetta's stance on gun control wasn't unyielding, but more she was scared to keep a curious toddler in close proximity to a loaded gun. They moved back in after a couple weeks—mainly because Wydetta's man of the moment wasn't quite prepared to deal with an insta-family situation—but only after Merle had made the purchase of a very expensive gun safe with separate ammunition storage.

Fairly certain her own rooms were secured, Brit snaked a hand out to her nightstand and snagged her phone. Like many celebrities, she carried panic buttons on her when she was out and about. They were usually stashed in various disguises—a ladybug on her keychain or a gold fob she switched from the handle of one handbag to another. A few were set in pendants or earrings, but the one she used most often was an app on her phone.

Tapping the icon, she waited until the green and red circles appeared on the screen and pressed her thumb firmly to the green dot, signaling to all on the system she was not in distress. Once her thumbprint registered, she swung her legs from the bed, shoved her feet into a pair of ridiculously fluffy slippers, then scuffed her way to the bedroom door. A quick check down the hall showed no movement in the west wing of the building.

The soft, disembodied voice of her Head of Security came from the speaker of her phone. "Brit, darlin', are you on the move?"

She raised the speaker to her lips and murmured, "Yes, Hank, I'm on my way to the foyer."

"Ten-four."

Moving slowly but sure-footed down the hallway, Brit scanned her surroundings with every step. She used only the light from her cell phone. In this case, darkness was to her advantage. They were on her turf, whoever they were, and she knew her way through this entire house blindfolded. Hank had made sure of it. He'd worked for her grandpa for years, but now that Merle had cut back on his public appearances, he'd come to work for Brit.

She reached the stairwell in time to hear a cacophony of voices coming from different directions and winced at the sound of a deep male voice spewing British invectives. She hadn't realized Wydetta and James were on the premises.

"Brittany? Wydetta?" Martine called up the stairs, her worry echoing through the empty foyer.

"Coming," Brit responded automatically.

"Bloody hell," James blustered.

Brit looked up in time to catch her mother's gaze. They stared at one another from opposite staircases, then Wydetta broke the slender thread connecting them.

"We're on our way down," she assured Martine without taking her eyes off Brittany.

James followed on Wydetta's heels, one hand pressed to his right ear, the other holding the lapels of a floral print silk dressing gown closed. "Can't they turn the blasted thing off?"

The moment the sole of Brit's slipper touched the foyer floor, the alarm stopped. Her ears rang, but merciful silence closed in around them. She spotted her trainer-slash-choreographer, Mark, hunkering in the shadows behind Martine. Rolling her eyes, Brit stepped to the center of the foyer and held her hands out wide in a grandiose gesture. "Your wish is our command, Sir James."

"Now, Brittany—" Wydetta began.

"Aw, she's only having me on a bit," James said as joined the party in the foyer.

Brit ignored her mother in favor of eying the rock legend currently wearing posies of peonies as confidently as he did his handmade Turnbull and Asser shirts.

"I was only saying how good it was to have him here," she said with an ingratiating smile. "You must really have some pull. Last time, it took them twenty minutes to shut the stupid thing off."

"Damn raccoons," Martine muttered. "I couldn't hear for days." She glanced over her shoulder. "Mark, *cher*, you aren't invisible. Come out. They all know you're here."

"Raccoons?" James asked, knotting the sash of the dressing gown securely at his waist. He chuckled as Brit watched Mark step out of the shadows. "Are we being invaded by vermin?"

Brit split a glance between the two men in her foyer and then shrugged. "It appears so."

"Now, now," Martine chastised. "No need to let the green-eyed monster out. No one made you come home alone."

Wydetta latched onto the information, craning her neck to peer up the staircase Brit had descended. "Cash isn't with you?"

"No, I left him up there to do some hand-to-hand combat with the wombats or whatever it is that set the damn system off this time."

"Wombats are marsupials and only found in Australia," Martine said authoritatively. "I doubt they flew in specifically to trip our sensors."

"No, but this did," came a gruff voice from behind them.

As a group, they startled. Brit let out the breath she'd caught with a whoosh when she spotted Hank coming from the direction of the kitchen. "Lordy, you scared the bejesus out of us," she admonished him.

"Good, because it's not raccoons this time," the former cop announced darkly.

Brit looked down to see him holding the handles of a plastic shopping bag. "A fan dropping off snacks?" she asked, a quaver in her voice.

"Not quite as good." He shifted his gaze to Wydetta. "I've called the police. The security company is doing a sweep of the grounds."

"What's that?" Brit asked, lifting a weak hand to point at the bag.

"It's a rock," Hank answered succinctly.

"Why a rock?" The question came out before she could form the thought and put it in proper sentence structure. Thankfully, Hank also spoke gibberish.

He darted a glance at Wydetta, then directed his gaze to the front door beyond Brit's shoulder. Guilt and discomfiture painted her hulking blond head of security's cheeks a deep pink. "Someone threw it through one of the sunroom windows."

Martine gasped, her hand flying to her mouth. James let loose with a few more colorful phrases while Mark released a low *oof* of breath. Only Wydetta seemed unfazed by the revelation. Brit watched as her mother's lips thinned into a tight line.

"Someone got onto the grounds," Wydetta concluded, her voice taut.

"What's going on here?" Brit asked, her gaze darting from Wydetta to Hank and back again.

"We're clear," someone called from the back of the house. Moments later, her driver, Roger, appeared, huffing as if he'd run the perimeter of the property himself.

"Rog?" Brit called to him, bewildered.

"You okay, Miss Priss?" he asked, falling back on the nickname he'd bestowed on her when she was a small girl.

But the endearment brought no comfort this time. In fact, it only served to emphasize how very little she knew about what was happening in her own household. "I'm fine. What the hell is happening?"

"I saw a guy running across the lawn," Rog explained as if he thought she had any clue as to the context of his statement.

"Saw what? Who?"

"One guy?" Hank demanded, ignoring her questions.

Roger nodded. "Yeah, one. Young. Skinny. An inch or two taller than me." He paused long enough to give Brittany a look so filled with regret it hurt her heart to see it. "A lot faster than me. Sorry, Priss."

"Don't be sorry," Brit said quickly. "And don't go chasing after people. Are you nuts? What if he had a gun or something?"

Hank stepped between them. "I don't think he wanted to hurt you. I think he wanted to get something to you."

"To me?" Brit asked, jabbing a finger into her chest hard, as if it might stop her mind from whirling. "Why do you say it's for me?"

"There's a piece of paper wrapped around the rock," Hank explained.

"A note?"

When she stepped forward, he held up a hand to stop her. "We're not touching it. We're waiting for the police," he said sternly.

"But if it's a threat, don't you think I should know?"

"No," Hank, Wydetta, James, and Martine all answered in unison.

Only Mark looked as stunned as she was. Brit glanced at each of them in turn, trying to give herself time to process. "No?"

"Honey, stars get dozens of crackpots trying to get close to them," Martine said, dismissing this invasion of their home with a flick of her hand.

"There have been notes now and then," Wydetta said dismissively. "We let the security team follow up on them."

"How am I just finding out about this?" Brit demanded.

"It's best not to read them," James piped in helpfully. "You're just hearing about them now because it's best to leave it to the professionals," he advised, nodding to Hank, then uncertainly at Rog. "They'll know what to do." She opened her mouth to protest, but he stepped out from behind Wydetta, tall and authoritative in spite of his floral splendor. "You can't let them get into your head, love. If you go down the rabbit hole, you might never come out. Trust me on this."

Brit gaped at him. Here was one of the most famous musicians of all time standing in her foyer, wearing the silk Robe Brit had given her mother for Christmas, telling her not to worry about what might be in threatening notes some crackpots were sending to her. How was it she had no clue any of this was going on?

As if her mother could read her thought, Wydetta spoke quietly. "We have a team of people in place."

Brit shifted her focus to her mother. "Oh? *We* do?"

"Yes," Wydetta replied, unperturbed by her sarcasm. "Why don't we let Hank handle the discussion with the police, and we all go back to our rooms?"

Brittany gaped at her mother. "Are you crazy?"

"No, I am not," Wydetta assured her. "And I am not about to stand around in my robe talking to the police about something I did not witness and have no evidence to support. Let Hank do his job, and Roger give his statement." She hooked a hand through Brit's arm and steered her toward the steps. "I'll get a full report from them in the morning, and if there are any changes to be made in the security protocol, we will do so tomorrow."

The urge to dig her heels in was great. But Wydetta had a point. She had nothing of value to contribute, and her presence would only be a distraction. Frowning at her mother, she asked, "You'd tell me anything I need to know, wouldn't you?"

"Withholding vital information would only put you in jeopardy," Wydetta said quietly. "You know I would never do anything to risk your safety."

And Brit did know. Because for all her faults and foibles, Wydetta had always put her safety first. She had no doubt. "I don't think I'll get back to sleep." She faced her mother at the foot of the stairs. "Will you be able to sleep?"

"No, probably not," Wydetta admitted. "But I think we should try. We have a jam-packed schedule for the next few weeks. Rest is the best thing for all of us."

Wydetta gave her arm a gentle squeeze of reassurance, but Brit really wanted a hug. She gave a moment's thought to throwing her arms around her mother to see how Wydetta might respond, but her hesitation lasted a moment too long. Before she could say another word, Wydetta was shooing Martine and Mark back to Martine's room, and James toward the opposite stairs. Resigned to returning to her empty room, Brit trudged up each step without looking back.

Brittany awoke early after a restless night. She rolled out of bed, twisted her hair up into a knot, and stepped into the shower for a quick wake-me-up rinse before her workout. Dressed in the shapeless T-shirt and baggy shorts she wore as gym gear, she padded down the stairs to the kitchen.

If Martine wasn't yet awake, she needed to be. After all, the woman was holding Brit's trainer captive in her bedroom. A wave of relief washed over her when she spotted her cousin standing at the kitchen island manning the controls of the blender.

"Good morning," she said, her trademark rasp more pronounced after hours of disuse.

Martine reached for a tall glass and poured a noxious-looking green concoction into it. "Good morning." She spoke the greeting in a stage whisper.

Brit clamped her lips shut and opened her eyes wide, telegraphing her understanding of the message received. The silent treatment wasn't anything new or related to recent events in any way. Brittany's voice was a delicate instrument, and Marti was reminding her to treat it with care. It was a task Brit took seriously. They all counted on her voice for their livelihood to some degree, and all three women in the house were keenly aware of the care to be taken in maintaining her precious gift.

Wrinkling her nose, Brit squinted dubiously and dutifully began to gulp down the juice drink. Thankfully, it didn't taste nearly as bad as it looked. Licking her lips, she raised the glass again and downed the rest of the contents in a series of long, slurping gulps. She understood the value of juicing in terms of health and energy, but she didn't have to like it.

The kettle sang out as she set the glass on the counter, and she opened her eyes to find Martine smirking at her. "What?" she croaked.

"*Tante* Marie would be very upset if she heard you making such an unladylike noise."

"Don't talk to me about unladylike noises," Brit said with a raised eyebrow. "This house was full of them last night."

Martine scoffed as she poured hot water into a mug. "As if you heard a thing. You were most likely up there playing your emo music and writing in your journal about how mean everybody is to poor Brittany." She delivered the tease with a twinkle in her eye. "Dear diary, today I picked a fight with a grown man and came home in a huff. Why won't he bend to my will? Hasn't he seen how pretty I am?"

Brittany took no offense to the mockery. She and Martine shared a bond so tight it might have made Wydetta jealous, if her mother took her eye off the prize long enough to care about her daughter's affections.

She blew a kiss as she took the mug from Martine, squeezed a generous amount of honey and lemon into the steaming water, then topped it with a splash of cold water once it was all mixed together. She sipped slowly. No sense in burning her tongue. Especially since she was the only woman in the house with no one around to kiss it.

"Have you released Mark from your dungeon?" she asked, leaning against the counter. "Did he escape unscathed?"

Martine rolled her eyes as she wiped up splatters of honey and lemon Brit hadn't even noticed she'd left behind. "He is downstairs waiting for you, your Majesty." She paused. "Intact, but I'm not sure I can say unscathed."

Brit smirked and took another sip of the warm water. "I'm surprised there's anything left of him."

"I imagine he'll have stamina enough to put you through your paces." She tipped her head to the side and eyed Brit speculatively. "He tells me this is going to be a rough tour."

"None of them are a cakewalk."

"True. I know," Marti retorted dryly. "But this one is bigger. More countries, more dates, more songs, more dancing."

"Higher heels." Brit hoisted her mug in a toast. "More everything."

"Are you ready for more everything?"

"And more," Brit answered with the training of a true professional. She never missed her cues. "I wanted to do some flippy Cirque du Soleil things, but Mama says Pink has the acrobatics all sewn up. As if there's not enough air space for the two of us," she added with a playful pout.

"I doubt there is." Martine's reply was wry and dry, but her gaze remained watchful. "Are you sure you want to do this?"

Brit avoided her cousin's probing gaze by pouring the remainder of the lemon water down the drain. "You know, you're one of the few people who ever asks me what I want," she observed.

"Brittany—"

"Ever," she added with emphasis. She rinsed the mug, then set it on the counter. "It's funny how these things are planned without anyone ever really asking me what I want to do."

"And by "funny," I take it you don't mean funny ha-ha," Martine concluded.

"I mean, they ask me if I'm ready to take things up a notch, but no one asks me if I have songs I want to put on my albums, or about video concepts. Hell, not even what I want my costumes or sets to look like." She shrugged. "Everything in my life is decided by committee."

"Well, only one person can change your path."

Brit sent Martine a sharp look. "Thanks for the pep talk."

"The reason why you pay people to do these things is so you won't have every decision on your shoulders," Martine explained evenly. "Do you really want all those questions coming at you? Do you want complete and total control?"

"No." Brit shook her head. "Besides, it's not a possibility."

"Of course it is," Martine argued.

"You want me to fire my mother?"

"I want you to decide what you want and what you don't want and stop letting life blow you around like a..." She paused, searching for a metaphor. "...A leaf! Or like dandelion fluff."

"Well, this conversation is really making me feel good about myself," Brit muttered. "Why does everyone think they have the right to explain me to me?"

"Because you let them." The triumphant gleam in Marti's eyes said she clearly thought she'd won this round. Lifting her chin, she asked again, "Do you want all the decisions to come to you?"

"Only a masochist would want to make every decision."

"Then stop complaining."

"I wasn't complaining so much as observing," Brit said, instantly defensive.

"Sounded like complaining."

"I get...frustrated."

Martine nodded. "I know, *cher*. And I understand why. But you can't have it both ways."

"I *can* insist on more creative control," Brittany said. "Over the music, I mean."

"Yes, you can. And I think you should." Reaching out, Martine caressed Brit's cheek with the tenderness Wydetta had never quite been able to show. "Your songs are good. Every bit as good, if not better, than the things they're giving you to sing." Her smile faltered slightly. "So, use this time wisely. Sing your song for the world, then go on the road and sing their songs. Make this album everything everyone thinks it should be and knock this tour out of the ballpark." She shrugged. "Then you can make the albums you want to make, with the music you want to make, and the decisions you decide to make."

Brit covered Martine's hand with hers, prolonging the caress. Their eyes met, and Brittany sighed. "You know, a part of me wants to stomp my feet and scream it's not fair."

Martine laughed, but there was no humor in it. "Not fair? You've got the world on a string. What could you possibly think is unfair?"

"Okay, no, I shouldn't have said my life wasn't fair," Brit admitted. "It was a stupid thing to say. I know how good I have it, Marti. I know I'm spoiled, but I'm not an idiot." She held up both hands to stop the harangue before another person laid into her about being spoiled or selfish. "I have it all. It's, you know, there are times when my filter slips, and I forget even the people closest to me can't always see me the way I see me."

A small furrow appeared between Martine's brows. "What exactly are you trying to say, *cher*?"

Brit shook her head, a blush rising in her cheeks. "Oh, no, I'm not going to fall for your tricks. You won't trap me into feeling sorry for myself again."

Martine snorted. "No one can make you feel bad but you. Now go dance your ass off, you selfish, spoiled brat," she teased. "I did my best to wear Mark out so he couldn't work you too terribly hard."

Brittany heaved a sigh as she pushed away from the counter. "I appreciate the effort, but it won't do any good. He doesn't do any of the work, anyway. He makes me do it over and over again."

Martine smirked. "Oh, yes, *bebe*, I know the feeling."

Likely as punishment for missing the day before, Mark put Brit through a grueling workout. And, to add insult to injury, he seemed more exuberant than usual. She blamed the sex. Everybody in her own house seemed to be having sex except her. Sure, she'd had sex the day before, but this was her house. If anyone should be doing the dirty in her house, it should be her.

She'd received a text message from Wydetta requesting a meeting while she was in the midst of a set of burpees. Brit honestly couldn't think which she'd rather do less—have this conversation with her mother, or do another set of burpees. As it was, she got to do both. Petulant, but showered and dressed, Brit made her way downstairs to the east wing of the house where Wydetta kept an office off the foyer.

She wrapped her knuckles against the doorframe perfunctorily early. "Knock-knock. Anyone home?"

It was a lame joke, but it was the best she could manage. She peered around the corner and found Wydetta sitting behind the massive antique desk that served as the room's focal point and, lounging in the chair across from her, Dylan Carson.

"Come in," Wydetta beckoned. "We were talking about the HitMakers show."

Brittany nodded but bit her tongue to keep from blurting out the whole story of Cash's rejection and her night of confusion. She and Wydetta didn't have the kind of relationship that led to girlie confidences, and there was something a bit weird about talking to Dylan about another guitarist.

Sure, they were friends and he was her lead guitarist, but other than one ill-advised kiss in their *TeenScreen* days, she and Dylan had been careful to maintain their own personal space. Chemistry on stage was one thing, but it didn't always translate to chemistry in real life.

Brit took the seat next to his, then turned to Dylan and asked, "Did you have some thoughts?"

The question was genuine. She respected Dylan personally and professionally. She didn't want her doing a song with Cash playing on the track to make their professional relationship uncomfortable. After all, Dylan was the one who'd have to play the song from here on out.

"I did," he said carefully, "but Wydetta says you want Cash to do the song with you on the show."

Brit could see by the tightness in his jaw he wasn't happy about this revelation, but he didn't seem inclined to throw a fit over it. She darted a glance at her mother. Wydetta must've done some managerial tap dancing to smooth any ruffled feathers. Her mother stared back, her expression inscrutable. Brit couldn't help but wonder what carrot Wydetta had dangled in front of Dylan to get him to accept this decision without question.

"Well, it isn't sewn up yet," Brit replied with a breezy laugh and a wave of her hand. "I was all caught up in the rush of the song coming together and juiced from the recording session yesterday."

Something flared in her mother's eyes, but she kept the mask of cool indifference carefully in place. "Yes, I was about to ask you for his management information," Wydetta said, pulling a notepad closer to her. "I couldn't find anything online about who to call."

Brittany had no idea how to answer. She hadn't the first clue about Cash's business dealings other than the fact that he used a stage name for performances. "Johnny Smith," she murmured.

"What?" Wydetta asked, her forehead creased.

"That's his stage name," Brit corrected, a blush rising under her skin. "He doesn't perform under his own name anymore."

"I think Jace down at StarRise handles a lot of their bookings," Dylan chimed in. "I don't know if he does only the internal stuff, for the studio space itself, or if he does some managerial stuff for them, but I've always heard people say to talk to Jace."

Wydetta made a note on her pad. "Jace Allen?"

He nodded. "Yes, he's one of the co-owners along with Cash and a couple of other guys."

"Co-owners of what?" Brit blurted before she could think the better of it.

Dylan gave her a quizzical look. "StarRise Studios. It's owned by a bunch of former musicians. Cash is one of them."

Brittany darted a glance at Wydetta and caught the flash of befuddlement flitting across mother-slash-manager's features. Brit would have bet her last dollar if Wydetta had known Cash was part-owner in Nashville's hottest studio, she would have booked recording space on the other side of the earth.

After the alarm fiasco, she'd lain awake half the night dissecting everything Cash had said and done since they'd reconnected, looking for a way past his defenses. But it wasn't until this moment that Brit realized she knew even less about the man she loved than she believed.

14

The first thing Wydetta did when Brit left her office was call StarRise Studios and book a small studio space for one of her up-and-coming artists. She made a particular point of requesting Cash Dorsett as guitar accompaniment for the session. Jace Allen fell all over himself. Not only was there space open, but he would make sure Cash was available to play. At three on the dot, Wydetta was seated on the tall wooden stool in the middle of the studio, her hands folded neatly in her lap and her expression calm as the door swung inward.

"I'm sorry I'm late," Cash said, his back partially to her as he wrestled his guitar case through the door. "We had sort of a breakthrough on the previous session, but we'll be happy to comp some time—" His jaw snapped shut when he looked up and saw who was seated on the stool. He frowned, then look down at the sheet of paper in his hand. "I thought this room was booked for a Nikki Evans. You're not Nikki Evans," he stated, looking up at her, his voice flat and his expression grim.

Stretching her lips into a thin smile, Wydetta slid off the stool and stood in front of her daughter's lover. "Nikki is a bright, promising young artist. I have great hopes for her."

Cash's expression darkened even further. "But she isn't coming today."

Wydetta shook her head. "No, not today, but maybe sometime in the future."

She gestured to the small room like a game show hostess, then clasped her hands together again.

"So, StarRise… Mr. Smith, was it?" she began, her voice deceptively cool. She'd been simmering beneath the surface ever since Dylan dropped the bomb in their meeting. Brit had been surprised too. She'd seen the questions in her daughter's eyes. And the hurt. This guy had hurt her baby again. And this time, Wydetta hadn't the tiniest thing to feel guilty about. This time, she could go full-on mama bear without being called a hypocrite.

But she wouldn't. She needed to tread carefully. Cash wasn't the washed-up has-been she wanted him to be. He was part owner of the hottest studio in Nashville, and, according to the research she'd done after her meeting with Brit and Dylan, a steadily working musician with a list of glowing accolades from some of the music industry's brightest luminaries. Including her own lover. A fact Wydetta chose not to dwell on too long.

And she'd delivered her daughter right into his hands. "I had no idea you were involved with the studio."

Cash propped his guitar case against the wall, closed the door, and crossed his arms over his chest. "Obviously, otherwise you never would've stepped foot in here."

"No, I wouldn't have. And I certainly never would've brought Brittany here."

"She's not a toddler you accidentally dropped off at a sketchy playground." He scoffed. "Stop talking about her like she's some kind of precious heirloom you tote around and show off. She's a woman."

Not for the first time, Wydetta wished she actually could shoot daggers from her eyes. Yes, Brit was a woman, but she was also precious. If Cash didn't see how precious she was, then he was a bigger fool than she'd believed him to be.

She flung out a dismissive hand. "I had hoped the thing in Texas was a one-and-done."

Cash studied his nails but didn't hesitate in his response. "I bet if you ask Brit, she'd say the same thing about whatever's going on with you and James Paulson." When she whirled on him, he held up his hands as if surrendering. "Maybe what the T-shirts say is true. Maybe it's not just Virginia. Maybe Texas is for lovers too."

Incensed, Wydetta advanced on him. "Was this some kind of set up?" She jabbed a pointy fingernail into his chest. "Was this all part of your plan to get in good with her again? The fake name, the studio—"

He tipped his head back and looked down his nose at her. "Careful, Wydetta, your paranoia is showing."

Frustrated, she threw up her arms and pivoted on her heel. "This can't all be coincidence."

Cash laughed. "Exactly my thought, but it appears it is. My investment in StarRise is no secret. My name was listed in all the trade publications along with everybody else's name. If you'd done your homework—"

Wydetta curled her lip in disdain. "I don't have time to keep track of has-beens."

"And I'm hardly the first artist to work under a stage name. Another not-so-well-kept secret."

"But, why?"

"Why do you care what my reasons are?"

"Because you're chasing after my daughter," she retorted hotly. "You're using the studio to get in good with her—"

"You booked the studio, Wydetta," he cried, incredulous. Edgy laughter bounced off the studio walls. "I didn't chase after you or your daughter. Call it coincidence, call it karma, call it some bad friggin' luck, but I did not plan any of this." He took a step forward. "We both know Brit was the one who came knocking on my hotel room door," he reminded her. "I never would have come after her."

"Bull—"

But he didn't let her finish before delivering the harshest blow to her ego. "You booked the gig in Austin, you booked the studio time. If anyone's the blame, it's you."

"I didn't know it was your studio."

"It's not my fault if you don't keep up with trade news."

"So, Brittany is a convenient coincidence for you?" she accused, narrowing her eyes at him. "She came on to you. That's all it takes?"

"Don't twist this around to make it what you want it to be. You know good and well Brittany and I had feelings for each other years ago. I let you get in the way then because I knew I was in a bad place. I couldn't offer her anything more than a rough go."

"And you're in a better place now?"

"Undoubtedly."

When he didn't offer any more of an explanation, Wydetta changed tactics. "I'm not going to let you manipulate your way back into the spotlight by using my daughter."

"I don't want any part of her spotlight."

She scoffed. "Like I believe that."

"What I can't believe is how you only remember she's your daughter when it suits you," Cash observed.

"What do you mean?" Wydetta wanted to bite her tongue. She'd left herself wide open for attack, and it was her own fault. She knew better than to give people the opportunity to judge her, and this man knew too much.

"I'm not even going to start," Cash murmured.

Stunned by his refusal to attack when she expected, Wydetta cocked her head and asked, "What?"

Before she could leap to her own defense, he held up a hand. "You're a hell of a manager, Wydetta. You've got her poised on the brink of… everything. Everything," he reiterated. "And I want her to have everything, because it's what she wants."

Not one to let an opening pass, Wydetta pounced. "You won't get in her way?"

"Never."

"She has things to do. Great things to do," she emphasized. "She doesn't need anyone or anything weighing her down now."

"What she doesn't need is anyone making decisions about what she does and does not need. I don't know if you've noticed, but I have. Your daughter is a bright, capable, and disarmingly savvy woman. She's more than capable of making her own decisions." He held his hands out at his sides, surrendering the remainder of the argument. "If she wants me, I'm hers, but on our terms. Not yours."

Wydetta squinted at him. "Exactly what are those terms?"

"Those are between me and Brittany," he retorted. "But I imagine you'll be apprised of them as they arise." He smirked. "You two have the most bizarre relationship I've ever seen, but it seems to work for you."

Something in his simple observation struck Wydetta hard. "I don't know," she confessed without meaning to. When Cash quirked an eyebrow at her, she tried to shrug it off, but his piercing gaze invited confidence. "We're not communicating well these days."

"Could it be because you're trying to communicate with her the way you did when she was a kid?"

The question hit too close to home. Wydetta flinched, then hiked her handbag into the crook of her arm. "What goes on between me and my daughter is none of your business."

"Agreed." He stepped aside and gestured to the studio door. "And what goes on between me and your daughter is none of *your* business."

Hitching her chin a notch higher, she resisted the urge to snarl when she brushed past him. "Seems as long as we can both mind our own business, we'll both be happy."

She sailed out of the StarRise Studios on the same tailwind of fury on which she had arrived. Her indignation flared hot, possibly hotter than it had when she'd arrived. She wanted—no, needed—someone to light on fire. The problem was, she was most angry with herself. She let him get to her. Now her own doubts were sinking their hooks in, and she didn't know what to do.

The heels of her stilettos clicked against the asphalt parking lot. Her car chirped to welcome her as she pressed the remote, but once behind the wheel, she felt anything but in control. Tossing her handbag onto the passenger seat, she dug her fingertips into her eye sockets, creating a cage she hoped would ward off angry tears while preserving her carefully applied makeup.

Throwing a proper hissy fit without ruining one's mascara was an art form Wydetta had mastered at a very young age. But tears threatened, and though everything she wore was waterproof, there'd be no hiding the ravages even the tiniest cry would leave in its wake. So, she sucked them up. Tossing her head back, she swallowed hard several times in an effort to stave them off. It might've worked, if someone hadn't come tapping at her passenger side window.

Her head jerked up and swiveled to peer through the slightly tinted glass. The mirror image of her own wide-set blue eyes stared back at her. She lowered the glass, and Brittany stuck her head in.

"Mama? What are you doing here?"

All her reasons for storming into StarRise filtered through her head as if on a digital billboard crawl. Not one of them would be acceptable to her daughter. But instinct told her Cash wouldn't give her up. He had some explaining to do as well.

Forcing a self-deprecating smile, Wydetta mustered enough chutzpah to meet her daughter's probing gaze, then gave her head a shake. "Apparently, I forgot to sign some paperwork." She shrugged. "I can't believe it. You know I'm usually so careful with legal stuff."

It was the understatement of the year, and Brit gave an appreciative laugh acknowledging it as such. "Careful? You're usually relentless about paperwork."

Wydetta held up her thumb and forefinger about a centimeter apart. "There was one teensy-weensy place I forgot to initial." Deciding her best defense would be a good offense, she pivoted. "I don't suppose I have to ask what you're doing here."

"I'm meeting Cash. He had a last-minute session with some new artist booked in," Brit explained. Crossing her arms over the open windowsill, she leaned into the car. "I wonder why he never told me was part-owner of StarRise."

Wydetta ticked off a half-dozen possible reasons from the top of her head, and any one of them might have fit, but she didn't know why. According to tidbits Brit had dropped here and there, Cash seemed to be fairly open with Brit about his struggles. Why hadn't he shared the information with her daughter? Why wouldn't he brag about his success?

"I have no idea."

But she was curious. So curious. And it hadn't escaped her notice the vaguely threatening messages from Brit's stalker had seemed to escalate after the concert in Austin. Was Brit's "biggest fan" jealous? Dangerous? The event the night before certainly had some terrifying implications. How had he gotten so close? Why hadn't the perimeter alarms gone off?

"You haven't given the gate code to Cash, have you?" she asked.

Brit flinched. She actually flinched as if Wydetta had struck her. "What?"

"I'm only wondering," she said in a rush. "Thinking about the stuff Hank and the police were asking this morning." She brushed the thought aside. "Never mind."

"What makes you automatically think it was Cash? Didn't you have to give James's driver the code to get in?"

"I did. I did," Wydetta admitted, holding her hands up in surrender. "I'm…thinking out loud. It was stupid."

"Yeah."

But, in truth, her suspicions weren't too far out in left field. Sure, Cash may have cleaned up his act, but he might have some unsavory friends hanging around. Wydetta pondered the possibility, then dismissed it. Cash Dorsett was many things, but she never had cause to doubt his genuine feelings for her daughter.

She heaved a sigh. "I'm tired. Didn't get enough sleep." A fact, but something Cash said stuck in her craw. She and Brittany did have a bizarre relationship, and it was changing faster than Wydetta was prepared to admit.

And change scared her.

Because her daughter was no longer a girl, and her client was no longer a malleable young teenager. She was a woman now, and not the type of woman to be easily managed. Wydetta would have to navigate this new stretch with caution.

She shook herself out of her thoughts in the midst of a long, awkward pause. Wydetta wondered exactly when and how these excruciating pauses had become the punctuation of their relationship. Brit was her only child. Her everything. She certainly hadn't intended for them to have such a distant relationship. In all honesty, she had hoped for the opposite. But it seemed whenever she opened her mouth, shades of Marie come pouring out.

Encouragement with a side of criticism. Confidence in tones a shade more strident than she intended.

When Brit was a baby, she'd struggled so hard to be sure no one placed any unrealistic expectations on her beautiful blonde head. Now, she was the one who was heaping them on.

Something James has said about wanting her relationship with her daughter to be different echoed in her memory. A light slap on the doorframe indicated the end of Brittany's patience with the stalled-out conversation.

"Well, okay then," Brit said, sounding brusque and dismissive.

"Would you like to have lunch?"

The invitation was out of her mouth before her brain could catch up, but she didn't regret it. Those six simple words were the embodiment of her dearest wish. She wanted something easier with her daughter. Some time, some uncomplicated company, maybe a few laughs and some girl talk. Would it be too much to ask?

"Lunch?" Brit made a point of looking at the fashionably oversized watch strapped to her slender wrist. "It's nearly four o'clock."

"I didn't mean today," Wydetta blurted. "Just…sometime."

Her daughter leaned into the car, her smooth brow puckering with concern. "Do I want to have lunch sometime?" she repeated, her frown deepening. "Mama, is everything okay?"

Frustration welled up inside of her. Wydetta caught herself gripping the steering wheel so hard her knuckles glowed white, but she couldn't force her fingers to relax. She almost felt the wall snapping into place. The stupid wall James insinuated she'd built between her true feelings and the rest of the world. Damn him and his transcendental manure. She *could* feel herself pulling back, shutting down, rebuilding the barrier to keep her sharp-tongued daughter at arm's length.

Brick by brick. Inch by inch. If she let another minute go by, she'd have enough of a wall built up to duck behind with a sarcastic comment and a breezy wave. It was now or never.

"Yes." She forced the word out. "Everything is fine." She darted a glance at her daughter and said in a voice shaky with nerves, "I'm only asking if you would like to have lunch with me sometime."

Brit frowned. "Lunch," she said again, an edge of sarcastic disbelief sharpening the word.

Wydetta stifled the urge to snap back. As James had pointed out, she was the grown-up. Brit might be her child, but she was no longer a *child*. Wydetta needed to treat her accordingly. And not like a client. Mustering every ounce of patience she owned, she forced an over-bright smile. "I think it would be fun. Maybe after, we could look for a dress for the award show."

Brittany's mouth opened and closed, but for once her daughter seemed to be at a loss for words. "I, uh—"

Wydetta didn't blame her. She was at a loss herself. Fear gripped her throat. What if she said no? What if her only child rejected something as uncomplicated as lunch with her mother out of hand? Worse, what if she said yes, but dreaded it with the same ferocity she dreaded going to Sunday supper at her mother's house?

Wydetta couldn't stand the thought.

"Or we could just go shopping. Like normal people."

Brit gaped at her, and Wydetta held up a hand to ward off the forthcoming rejection.

"Never mind. It was a silly idea. I'll call around and have some dresses sent to the house for you to try." She pressed the button to start the car's engine, but Brittany made no move to extract herself from the window.

"I want to have lunch and go shopping." Her daughter spoke in a slow, bewildered tone.

Wydetta cringed. They hadn't actually walked into a store together and shopped for a dress or shoes or anything in two or three years. Not since Brit's solo fame had begun to eclipse her *TeenScreen* fame. She didn't know why she'd even suggested such a thing.

"No. It's a silly idea," she repeated. "We'd never get in and out of a store without making a scene, anyway."

"Maybe not, but I'd like to try," Brit said in a rush. Wydetta looked up at her in surprise, and the younger woman simply shrugged. "It's been forever since we've been shopping. I miss shopping."

"Yes." Wydetta looked directly into her daughter's bright blue eyes. "I miss shopping too."

"It's a plan, then. But shopping might be a little...crazy." Brit wrinkled her nose. "Lunch and maybe meet with Teresa about dresses?"

Wydetta nodded, and made a mental note to call the stylist as soon as her daughter walked away. "I'll set it up."

Brit gave a nod, then straightened. This time, when she tapped on the doorframe, she smiled. "Good." She adjusted the strap of her messenger bag, then lifted a hand in a shaky little wave. "See you later, Mama."

Still thrown off-balance by the bizarre conversation with her mother, Brit wandered through the halls of StarRise Studios until she came to Studio F, the space Jace Allen told her he'd booked out for Cash.

She never considered herself the jealous type, but she'd be a liar if she said she didn't want to catch a glimpse of this Nikki Evans chick Cash was working with this afternoon. She was feeling tired and vulnerable. Between the alarm in the wee small hours of the morning, and the discovery of multiple threats made against her that she had been unaware of, she was feeling exposed.

Dylan blurting out the information about Cash's interest in the very recording studio where they'd reunited made her feel even more off-kilter. Like she'd been tossed a medicine ball and caught it reflexively. A game of "Think Fast" was one of Mark's favorite training tricks, and Brit hated it. She hated being unprepared.

She didn't know what to think about Wydetta. Why did her mother suddenly want to have lunch and go shopping of all things? They saw each other most days. Lived in the same house. Why the need for an outing?

But Brit wasn't about to reject the offer. She hadn't been lying when she said she missed her mother. Deep down, she knew she was partially to blame for the distance between them over the past couple years, but it didn't have to go on this way. She needed to speak up and let Wydetta know what she did want and what she didn't.

Sounded easy, but it wouldn't be. Negotiating with Wydetta never was. But if she had learned anything from hanging out with Cash, it was to own her mistakes. And letting Wydetta call the shots, then resenting her for doing so landed squarely on Brit's shoulders.

Cash was right. She had to stop looking at things on the surface and dig deeper. To use her voice and be clear about her goals. There were three things she knew for certain: she wanted Cash, she wanted a real relationship with her mother again, and she wanted to be a star.

And all three of those things were within her reach.

When she neared the studio, she automatically checked the old-fashioned lights above the door to see if a recording was in progress. They weren't lit. A trickle of unease crept into her belly, but Brit didn't back away.

Instead, she bent at the knees and peered through the narrow rectangular window in the door. The unease morphed to disbelief. She shifted her weight from foot to foot, staring through the glass to be sure she wasn't imagining things. There should have been some petite dynamo of a singer tucked away in a corner. But there wasn't.

Cash was alone, seated on the stool in the center of the studio, his hands knitted together and resting loose in his lap. His expression of sober resignation constricted his handsome features. Twisting the handle, she opened the door a crack and poked her face in.

"Hello?" she whispered into the empty studio.

Cash's head jerked up, but the smile stretching across his face was warm and welcoming. "Hey," he called back. "What are you doing here?"

Emboldened by the beaconing light in his eyes, she opened the door wider and stepped into the studio. "Where's your songbird?"

Cash raised one hand and made a fluttering motion. "Flew away."

"No good?"

"No-show," he corrected. Tipping his head to the side, he eyed her warily. "I don't suppose you knew I own a stake in this studio," he said, a note of resignation in his tone.

Brit let the door close behind her, then crossed the small space until his bent knees brushed the tops of her thighs. She shook her head. "I had no clue," she admitted.

Cash gave a short nod. "I figured you didn't. My missing songbird was Wydetta, and she came in here to tear me a new one."

Understanding dawned. "Oh." A slow smile spread across Brit's face. "Things are making a lot more sense now."

Cash gave a short laugh. "Are they? Could you explain them to me, maybe?"

Grinning, Brit nodded, then framed his face with her hands as she leaned in to press a smacking kiss to his lips.

"Sure I can. Come with me, my boy. I got a driver outside, and a hankering for barbecue."

"Barbecue?" he asked, but rose from the stool and followed her, unresisting.

"Yes. There's a place not too far from here. Sometimes Rog and I sneak in for a sandwich." She checked her watch again. "We're in time to beat the dinner crowd."

"And to get the senior citizens' discount?" he asked, snagging his guitar case as she hauled him out of the studio.

"Now you know why I make Roger pay," she said with a cheeky grin.

"Nothing cheaper than a rich person," he muttered.

"The best way to make money is to save money." She slowed her steps and slid her hand up his arm to lace hers through his. "So my granddad says."

"Your granddad is so tight he squeaks."

"Yep." She gave his arm a gleeful squeeze. "We're having chicken and dumplings on Sunday," she reported. "I'm delighted, and Wydetta is disgusted." They raised a hand and waved to Jace as they passed the glass wall of Studio B. "I've been dancing my ass off all week, and all Martine will feed me is grilled chicken and salads."

"Poor baby."

"I know." She affected a pout as they stepped out into the afternoon sunlight. "But Rog keeps me going. He's anti-low-carb."

15

Dressed only her panties, and a washed soft flannel shirt she'd appropriated from his closet, Brit stretched out across the sectional sofa and put her head on Cash's thigh. She smiled as the muscles tensed beneath her cheek. He wasn't the squishiest pillow she ever had, but he was the most delicious. He wore a pair of track pants and a plain white T-shirt. With his bed-mussed hair, he looked like a slightly weathered version of the oh-so-cool guitar god he'd once been.

Plucking at the fabric of his sweatpants, she smiled. "There was a time when you would have paid a stylist thousands of dollars to get something like this look," she commented.

He chuckled. "Saving myself a lot of money these days. Good thing I picked up a few tips and tricks along the way, huh?"

Brittany laughed. He'd done absolutely nothing to achieve this look, so whatever tips and tricks he might be claiming to employ must have sunk in deep. She snuggled her cheek against warm, taut muscle. "What are we gonna watch?"

"It's a surprise." He stroked her hair with one hand and wielded the remote with the other. "You warm enough?"

If she hadn't already been, the care and concern in his voice would've warmed her straight through to her core. She hummed a couple bars of "I'm On Fire," then ended on a sly, "Mmm-hmm."

Cash chuckled as he cued up the streaming service, and she squirmed, nuzzling his taut thigh.

"Stop it," he warned. But there was no steel behind the order.

Brittany settled back into her comfortable spot again. Running away to his house for the weekend had been the best idea ever. Apparently, James had given up his suite of hotel rooms and was now squatting in the east wing of her house. Brit tried not to give too much thought to how Martine was putting Mark through his paces each night. All she knew was her trainer showed up every morning with a bright smile and dark circles under his eyes.

Marti had made some comment about how it must be the season for May/December romances at breakfast. But before Brittany could think of a way to extract her relationship with Cash from the same equation as the others, Martine twisted it to refer to her own relationship with Mark. Labeling herself Miss December, she accused Brit and Wydetta of being cliché.

As she watched Cash scroll through the movie selections, she asked, "Does the age difference really bother you?"

"What?"

He acted like he didn't understand or hear her, but his finger stalled on the remote control and the screen was frozen on the kids' cartoon featuring a pig dressed as a doctor.

"Our ages," she repeated. "It's truly a problem for you?"

Cash snorted, but his scrolling resumed. "Well, yeah. I'd be a pretty selfish bastard if it wasn't."

She raised a single eyebrow. "How do you figure?"

"Because." He shrugged. "If you were with someone closer to your own age, things would be simpler."

"For you, or for me?"

He shot her a bland look, but she wasn't about to be put off.

"I don't know how you figure it would be easier," she observed. "Relationships are never easy, regardless what age you are. And in this business…"

"My point exactly," Cash observed. "Relationships are not easy, and this business makes them ten times harder. The difference in our ages isn't going to help." He looked her in the eye. "You can say it's only a number, and it would be true to a certain extent. But you and I are always going to be in different places in our lives. We're going to have different priorities at different times."

"But I think recognizing the issues upfront can only help us," Brit argued. "We can talk those things through. They don't have to be a big elephant in the room."

He studied her. "You seem almost excited about arguing."

A sheepish smile curved her lips, and she ducked her head as warmth crept up her neck and made her cheeks tingle. It was both wonderful and disconcerting to be so transparent to someone. To have someone know her so well, even after so many years apart, she need not try to verbalize things she hadn't yet fully processed. "I am."

Cash shook his head. "Weirdo."

The name-calling upped the wattage on Brittany's smile until she couldn't contain it any longer. She beamed at him. "Why, yes, I am, thank you."

He wagged his head again, this time huffing a chuckle. "You're a mess."

"A hot mess," Brittany corrected, shifting onto her stomach and crawling even closer to him. When he didn't shy away, she wrapped her arms around his torso and snuggled her face into the crook of his neck. She loved the way he smelled. Clean. Simple. Soap and the drugstore aftershave lotion she'd spotted in his medicine cabinet. "And I'm *your* weirdo."

His arms came around her, and he pulled her closer still. As if he could will their bodies to meld together. Twisted and torqued, Brit wriggled until she was able to throw a leg over his thighs and lever herself into a sitting position on his lap.

"Yes, you're my weirdo," he agreed. "But why do I get the feeling you like inviting those elephants into the room?"

Brit shook her head and pecked a soft kiss to his stubbly cheek. "I don't like inviting them in. It's more I don't like having to try to stuff them in the closets so the world won't see them." She sighed and pulled back enough to look him in the eye. "I know it's been a while since you've been to a Sunday supper, but I can tell you they haven't gotten any more congenial."

"I suppose it's too much to hope your mama and Marie had mellowed with age."

Brittany gasped and stared at him in wide-eyed horror. "We don't use three-letter words in our house." She snickered at him. "You should know the only age anyone acknowledges is mine, because it's still acceptable. In a few more years, we'll conveniently forget mine too."

He grinned up at her, a dimple flashing in his cheek. "Yeah, I don't miss worrying about age and stuff." He wrinkled his nose.

"People get het up about the weirdest things."

"You can say that again."

"People get het up about the weirdest things," he delivered dryly.

Brit laughed and then wriggled closer still. "The only thing I get het up about is you."

He paused, then went on as if their conversation hadn't taken a badly comedic turn. "I don't miss the superficiality. I don't miss makeup," he added with a short laugh. "I don't miss the crazy-ass spangly things people would try to get me to wear."

"I'm having a hard time picturing you in spangly anything but enjoying the mental image."

Cash stared at her, his face sober. "Babe, I know you don't expect the age thing to be an issue, and I wish I had your confidence, but I don't. I have a feeling your granddad might be pretty upset when he finds out we're together. Let's not forget, he brought me home as a surprise for your mama."

Brittany guffawed. "Proving how very little Merle knows about his own offspring." She ran a hand down his chest, humming appreciatively as she mapped the planes and valleys.

"Thanks a lot."

"Don't act offended. I know no one was more relieved than you when Wydetta failed to show any interest."

"Might've been because I was already interested in you," he said in a throaty voice.

She laughed him off again. "If that's the case, then you are a pervert. I was way too young for you to even notice me."

"And the conversation comes full circle," he remarked, his tone dry as dust.

"The part you're not registering is it doesn't matter to me whether anyone approves of us, Cash. You're the one hung up on birthdays. You're the one who's always been hung up on them."

He glanced down at her hands, then back up at her. "You aren't the dirty old man in this scenario. You weren't the fella who could've gone to jail if he'd allowed himself to follow his impulses."

Her face brightened. "You had dirty impulses about me?"

He captured one of her hands and pulled it up to his lips for a tender kiss. "Staying away from you was the only good and honorable choice I made in a time filled with bad, bad choices. Let me have this one thing."

Their clasped hands trapped between them, Brittany leaned in and kissed him slow and sweet. "Thank you," she whispered as she pulled away. "If I had a chance, I probably would've found a way to blow it for you. Or at least blow you."

Cash scoffed. "Are you saying you're more mature now?"

"I am," she said without a tinge of sarcasm or rancor. "I had to grow up. I'd had my heart broken."

"Oh, Brit—"

She stopped him with a finger placed gently across his lips. "Made me a better country singer, for sure," she said with a sly smile. "Made me a better singer overall. Lyrics had new meaning for me. Context. A face." She reached up and caressed his face with her free hand. "It seems trite to say you did me a favor, so don't make me say so."

He peeled open the fingers on the hand he still held and pressed a lingering kiss to the center of her palm. "Is it weird if I hate to be the face, and at the same time I love being the face?"

Brit gave him an enigmatic smile. "Proving exactly why you're more than the face. You're everything."

Despite having passed the seventy mark a year before, Merle Owens was as hearty as he was the day he first stepped onto the stage at the Grand Old Opry. His hair was thick and full. Sure, the dirty blond had darkened with age and was now streaked with silver, but the way those platinum strands glinted in the light only helped boost the wattage on his star power.

His daughter and granddaughter had inherited his blue eyes. Marie claimed they were eyes made for staring soulfully off album covers, fan posters, and country music magazines. He was friends with all the greats, and a mentor to many of the not-quite-so-greats. A living legend.

Having stood on this doorstep many times before, Cash knew he shouldn't have been surprised when Merle himself opened the door. Cash had heard him say many, many times he still believed a man was king of his castle, and wasn't about to hide behind some fancy-schmancy butler or maid. Not as long as he had legs to carry him to his own front door, and his daddy's old squirrel hunting rifle close at hand. Seeing him standing there in the foyer always threw him.

Merle wore one of his dozens of hand-tailored Western-cut suits.

His shirt was studded with genuine mother-of-pearl buttons. Cash didn't have to glance down to know he'd be wearing a pair of the Luchese boots custom-made for him. At six-foot-four, Merle towered over most people in stocking feet. The artfully stacked heels of his boots added another two inches to his height without giving the appearance of doing so.

Merle liked to lord his power and strength over people in a discreet sort of way. He wanted the running of his kingdom to seem effortless.

"Cash Dorsett. Well, I'll be damned," he repeated, taking Cash's hand in a firm grip and slapping him on the back with a tad too much force. But Cash held his footing. Barely. "I'd all but given you up for dead, boy."

They all knew Merle was aware Cash was alive, well, and recovering. He was far from being dead, but in Merle's world, Cash ceased to exist the day he'd refused to bend to Merle's will and pick the Owens woman of the king's choosing.

If Cash had to judge by the tension in the man's jaw, he would guess Merle was no more pleased to see him today than he'd been at Brittany's eighteenth birthday party. Lucky for him, Merle was a willful and stubborn man, but he wasn't a vengeful one.

If Cash hadn't done a good enough job of getting out of the way himself, Merle could've easily finished the job with one phone call. But his former mentor hadn't been cruel. While he hadn't been there to offer Cash any help, or a hand up, he hadn't put his booted foot on Cash's throat and held him down, either.

Cash ushered Brit across the threshold with a hand placed gently in the small of her back. His tie was too snug. Brit had teased him about it, and it felt like he might rub his Adam's apple raw with each nervous swallow, but he wasn't about to loosen the knot. He might not be the star he'd once dreamed of becoming, but he didn't show up for Sunday supper at the Owenses' intending to look anything other than the successful businessman he was.

Brittany swooped into the conversation with the sort of force and subtlety of a tsunami. Stretching up to press a smacking kiss to Merle's cheek, she grinned at the older man impishly. "Oh, don't be silly, Granddad. You knew darn well Cash was fine."

"Maybe I didn't expect to be seeing him in my house again," Merle said, tipping his chin up mulishly.

Brittany sank back onto her heels and looped her arm through Cash's possessively. "Cash and I are together."

She said it simply, matter-of-fact, no room for argument or equivocation. Cash couldn't help but smile at her. She might look like spun sugar and gumdrops, but Brittany Owens had a hard candy center. A man could crack his tooth on it if he didn't approach her the right way.

"I'd puzzled the situation out for myself, girlie," the older man grumbled. Switching his gaze back to Cash, he narrowed his eyes and repeated. "More reason you're damn lucky to be alive."

"I don't want to hear any more talk about damnation on a Sunday," Marie Owens announced. The former Bayou Bombshell bustled into the foyer, wiping her hands on a dish towel. "If you keep this up, *y'all* will be damned, and there won't be anything I can do to save you."

She stepped forward, grasped Cash by both arms, and gave him a once-over. "Looks like you saved yourself in time. Maybe you can teach this old fool a thing or two about self-preservation. He keeps running his mouth like he does, and he's gonna meet his maker sooner rather than later."

It was an old refrain, but one Cash didn't mind hearing again. It was good to feel welcome in the Owens household again. "Yes, ma'am. I'll try my best."

Though she was knee-deep in her sixties, Marie Boudreaux Owens was still every bit the great beauty. Her dark hair was dramatically streaked with pewter and silver now, but it flowed over her shoulders like an ink spill. Her even darker eyes were wide and expressive, the faint crinkles at their corner evidence of a woman who spent a good deal of time smiling. The creamy porcelain skin shone like a polished pearl.

Cash shook his head, marveling at the older woman's well-preserved beauty. "I can see by the warmth in your eyes you haven't sold your soul, so I have to wonder, did you get a good price for Merle's?"

Marie's eyes sparked with delight, then narrowed playfully as she swatted his arm. "I swear, I have no idea what you're blathering on about."

"I'm talking about whatever backroom deal you made with the devil to keep you looking so young, Miss Marie," Cash said without missing a beat. "You must have made one. Hell, I look like your grandpappy now."

An awkward silence descended on the jovial quartet. Cash squeezed his eyes shut for a second, wishing them back, but knowing wishes were futile. He'd set himself up like a golf ball on a tee. All he could do now was brace for impact when Merle took a swing.

But Brit jumped into the fray before anyone could line up a shot. "I think it might've been Mama," she suggested with a blinding smile. "Everyone knows managers don't have souls."

"Now, now," Merle cautioned.

Marie gasped and pressed a hand to her mouth. "Brittany Marie, you go on and take those words back. Your mama does they best she can do for you. Bless her heart."

"I take it back," Brit responded dutifully, but Cash doubted her sincerity.

"Good. And the immortal souls of all those I love are intact," Marie said, smoothing a hand over her long, wavy hair. "And if I look young, it's because I never listen to any of the nonsense the ladies at the cosmetics counters are pushing. I stick to the good old Ivory soap and Ponds cold cream, like my grandmother told me." She hooked an arm through Brittany's and started to lead them deeper into the house. "Same as I taught you. Simpler is better. There is no need for all those cell regenerating potions and lotions. It's no better than snake oil. And what's the matter with wearing your years? I say, as long as you've got 'em, flaunt 'em."

"Sing out, Grandma," Brit said with a decisive nod.

"With all the folderol they hawk these days, no one looks like they passed the age of twelve." She straightened her shoulders. "I'm proud of my age. I'm a vibrant, resourceful, exciting woman with a lot of va-va-va-voom left in in the old sassy chassis."

Merle nodded vigorously. "Amen."

Brit wound an arm around her grandmother's waist and gave her a squeeze. "Of course you are, Grandma, but let's not go there. I have a feeling Granddad might steer us into some uncomfortable territory."

Marie's tinkling laugh echoed through the house as they stepped through a set of wide French doors onto the veranda. A pitcher of iced tea and a tray full of tall glass tumblers sat beside a sweating ice bucket. She gestured to the tray. "I made some sun tea," she announced. As always, Cash was amazed to be offered a glass of home-brewed tea by the first lady of country music, but Miss Marie prided herself on keeping things simple.

Cash nodded. "I sure do remember your tea, Miss Marie. I better have my blood sugar tested when I leave here today."

As they took their places in plushily padded patio chairs, Marie passed around glasses of the sugar-laden tea. "We'll be waiting a few minutes for supper. Etta says she's bringing a guest along. I hope it's not another one of her potential clients." She scowled. "I swear, sometimes your granddad and I feel like we're prize ponies being trotted out for show."

Cash smothered a chuckle, but when he met Brit's troubled gaze, it died in his chest. "What?"

"Well, I think we know who it is." She rolled her eyes. "Are they joined at the hip or something? This is so unlike Wydetta."

"They're no more joined at the hip than we are," Cash reminded her gently. "Maybe she likes him."

Marie pounced on the pronoun. "Him? Likes him who? Does your mama have somebody special?" she asked, searching Brittany's face for clues.

Brit kept her expression blank as a slate. Cash watched in wonder as this open, giving woman effectively shut off all emotion. Of course, he'd witnessed her family dynamic in action before, but it never failed to amaze him when somebody so intensely emotional as Brittany played it so cool and close to the vest.

Maybe it was because she never did so when it came to her feelings for him. Brit had a tendency to clobber him over the head with her feelings, wants, and desires.

"I have no idea who Mama is bringing," Brittany lied, her tone comically flat.

As if on cue, a voice rang out from the foyer. "Hello?"

Rather than stirring himself to greet his own daughter, Merle tipped his head back and shouted, "We're in the backyard."

A strangled silence gripped the small knot of people on the patio. Within seconds, the tip-tap of Wydetta's high heels could be heard approaching. Before she reached the doors to the veranda, Wydetta said in a voice loud enough to carry, "Come on out back, we're roastin' a pig and pitching horseshoes."

A low, masculine chuckle drifted out through the open door, but before Merle could fully rise to his feet, Wydetta appeared in the doorway.

"Well, if it isn't Ma and Pa Kettle at home." Wydetta planted a hand high on the doorframe, blocking her guest from view.

"Hush, you," Merle grumbled good-naturedly.

"Really, Daddy? 'We're in the backyard'?" She gestured to the lushly landscaped pool and terraced gardens beyond the wide brick veranda. "You make it sound like you've fired up the grill and we're roastin' weenies for supper."

James appeared in the opening behind Wydetta, wearing the easy smile of a man who knew he was welcome most anywhere in the world. Cash watched as he slid a possessive hand around Wydetta's waist, then gently propelled her through the door.

"Does this mean the horseshoe match is off? I'll be dashed. I throw a mean horseshoe, you know," he said genially. Cash noted James's accent came across clipped and a tad more formal than usual, but his smile never slipped a notch.

Merle and Marie rushed to the patio door.

"Why, Etta, you never said who your guest was." Marie lifted a flustered hand to her hair, then touched the neckline of her dress before smoothing her skirt like a nervous schoolgirl. "Sir James, how lovely. Welcome to our home."

Wydetta rolled her eyes. "I didn't expect you'd shout at us like we should be hauling along a case of Pabst Blue Ribbon to contribute to the beer barrel."

James smiled wide. The man clearly didn't mind being the center of their sparring. A notion Cash found difficult to imagine. Then again, James had a lot more years of bawling and brawling behind him.

"Oh, I do enjoy a beer myself, but I never got used to the way you Americans drink it cold. I like a nice lager, but I prefer my draught to be room temperature. Like any true Englishman," he added with an engaging wink at Marie.

Wydetta rolled her eyes as she scuttled past her parents and guest. "Maybe you can get a nice warm one when you go back to England."

"Oh, indubitably," James retorted. Shifting his attention to Merle, he extended a hand. "We met a while back."

"A long while," Merle said, grimacing as they shook hands.

"Let's not try to pinpoint a year. The 'remember when' game is embarrassing these days."

"It's a deal, mate," James replied congenially. "Perhaps you could show me your Lifetime Achievement awards, though. I want to be sure your collection isn't bigger than mine."

Merle guffawed. "Of course mine's bigger," he boasted, clapping James on the shoulder, then steering him back into the house. "Shinier too."

16

James had expected dinner at the Owens house to be an awkward affair. It was one of the reasons he'd insisted on tagging along. He wasn't by any means a glutton for punishment, but the few comments Wydetta had made about her relationship with her family made it clear things were strained on every front.

He didn't thrive on discord or wish Wydetta's parents any form of ill. On the contrary, he thought he might be able to help. For some reason, people stumbled all over themselves to be polite in his company.

It was a phenomenon his former bandmates would've laughed to discover if they had lived long enough to encounter it. They were rock stars, for Christ's sake. Once upon a time, they'd been known for tearing up hotel rooms and defiling young virgins. Okay, maybe he hadn't been a defiler of virgins, but he certainly had his fair share of pretty girls around. He couldn't for the life of him figure out why people treated him like he was the Pope's twin brother these days. He hadn't changed his behavior as far as he could tell, but something about his age seemed to offset any troublemaking he might get into.

Scanning the impressive array of awards lining Merle's office walls, he asked, "Do you find people are nicer to you now?"

"People have always been nice to me." But the flat expression he wore told James he knew exactly what he was saying. His host rocked back on his heels, a speculative gleam in his eyes. "Now, if you're asking if people treat me like I'm somebody's old granddad, well, yeah, they do. Stands to reason, though. I *am* somebody's old granddad."

Both men glanced in Cash's direction. Truthfully, James saw no reason for Merle to be upset with Cash. When he had finally settled down himself, the age difference between him and his late wife, Lydia, hadn't been a whole lot smaller than the stretch between Cash and Brittany. He didn't even like to calculate the difference between him and Wydetta. Sometimes, even the simplest arithmetic caused too many problems.

The tension was thick in the air. They were going to have some fireworks, and he was looking forward to seeing Wydetta in action. Still, it was best to try to keep things polite, wasn't it?

He twisted his lips into a sad downturn. "My own children don't seem to be interested in having any children. At least so they tell me. I admit I despair of it, because I quite enjoy being a father, and I think I'd be a very good grandfather."

Merle nodded. "I'm sure you would be," he replied politely. "Best job in the world, if you ask me."

"Is it?" James folded his hands and gave the older man his full attention. "How so?"

Merle pursed his lips, then blew out a sigh. "Now, I'm not saying you don't have all the worry, because it passes right on down from generation to generation. You never stop trying to do what's best for them. But you don't have all the responsibility. You know what I mean? Discipline was not my job, and spoiling Brittany was my right as her granddad," he added, lifting his chin in defiance.

Brittany, having walked in at the tail end of his commentary, beamed at Merle. "Darn right. And you were good at it."

Her smile was so filled with warmth and adoration it made James's heart seize. Not because he was jealous, but because he knew Wydetta likely yearned to see the same smile aimed in her direction.

"I just try to steer her in the right direction when I can," Merle said gruffly.

"You're the best granddad in the world," Brittany said pertly. "All the french fries and ice cream a girl could eat. And I had the chubby thighs to prove it." She kissed his cheek. "Supper's ready, and I'm planning to plump them back up with some dumplings. Y'all come on now."

Merle scoffed, but allowed her to herd them into the dining room where the table had been set and was now laden with platters and bowls. There were a couple awkward miscues as they worked out the seating, but Marie took the situation in hand.

Once everyone was settled, Merle picked up the thread of the conversation again. "You were never chubby, sweetheart. You had a smidge of baby fat to grow out of," he asserted as he passed a bowl of green beans to Wydetta. "And now you're as pretty as a picture. Even if you do dress funny."

"Speaking of dressing funny," Brit piped up, sitting straighter in her chair. "We watched an old episode of *HeeHaw* the other night, Granddad. You had this lime-green suit with those big, wide lapels and orange stitching. It was a sight to behold."

"I do wish you would speak to those costume people about making Brittany's wardrobe less revealing," Marie said to Wydetta as she helped herself to a small piece of fried chicken. "Some of those dresses are almost obscene." She looked at Brittany, and her smile softened. "Why, sugar, I was worried about you the whole time you were at the Grammy awards. I thought for sure the police were going to bust on in there and arrest you for indecent exposure."

Brit laughed, but James saw Wydetta's grip constrict on the spoon in her hand. He wondered if he was going to see some good old-fashioned bloodshed here at the Owenses' dinner table.

Before either Wydetta or Brittany could formulate a response, James waded into the fray. "Well, you know, it's mostly stage craft. What we wear up there and what we wear out in the real world are often two very, very different things." He gestured to Brittany's simple, yet perfectly suitable top and blue jeans, then smiled benevolently around the table, playing the reformed-rocker-turned-elder-statesman to the hilt. "When Brittany attends award shows and such gatherings, she's on stage, even if she doesn't have a microphone in her hand. Aren't you, love?"

Brit blinked as if stunned anyone would dare to contradict Marie. "Exactly."

Cash shot him an admiring glance and gave a chortle. "I rarely see her in anything other than jeans and a hoodie."

An awkward silence descended on the table. Everyone seemed to be uncomfortably aware Cash Dorsett often saw Brittany Owens in far less than blue jeans and a hooded sweatshirt. But James wasn't going to let the conversation go there. This meal was dragging on far too long as it was.

"Like that computer fella. The one who invented the chat space everybody's on all the time." He waved his fork at Brittany, his expression questioning but his lips tilting up enough to let her know he wasn't the buffoon he was pretending to be. "MyFace?"

Cash caught on before anyone else at the table. "Oh, yeah. All those tech guys dress casual. No three-piece suits there."

There were the general hums of consensus before the lull descended again. This time the comforting clink of cutlery on china filled the silence. Still, he wasn't about to let it plod on without attempting to fill the void with more innocuous conversation.

"To comfort." James raised his glass in the mock toast. "Funny, there used to be a time when I would agonize for days over what to wear on an airplane." His smile became sly and self-deprecating. "Of course, I'm not photographed in airports nearly as often as I used to be, but back in the day, air travel was quite the smart thing."

Merle nodded. "I remember the first time I wore a pair of blue jeans onto a flight, people stared at me as if I walked into church naked."

Marie treated Merle to a beatific smile. "I remember our first airplane flight together. I wore a pink suit with a pencil skirt and a matching hat. Snow-white gloves with little pearls on the cuffs." She sighed happily. "I loved that outfit."

"And you were lovely in it, darlin'," Merle responded, hitting his cue without missing a beat.

When Marie split a smile between Merle and Brittany, he couldn't help but notice the genuine affection in her expression was noticeably warmer than anything she cast Wydetta's way since they'd walked through the door. Something fierce rose up inside of him. He would protect her. This strong, proud woman who needed no white knight to rescue her and asked for no help from any quarter. He'd make it so she didn't have to ask, he'd simply give.

He'd try, anyway.

Not because she needed him to, but because he needed to give her something. Something no one else seemed willing to give her. Something no one ever imagined she craved. Not even Wydetta herself.

Warmth flooded through him as James realized he alone was keen enough to see the spectacular warrior they had in their midst. Oh, he was sure Brittany was aware, and even appreciative in her own way. But children seldom saw their parents in any kind of role other than parent. The business aspect of their relationship was a complicating factor. Duty seemed to weigh down every interaction between mother and daughter.

"I was thinking of trying to lure Wydetta off to Rome with me for a few days," he announced without any preamble or segue.

Wydetta's head jerked up. She gaped at him for a second before shaking her head emphatically. "I can't go to Rome. We're about to kick off a world tour."

"Right, but you have staff, don't you?" he asked, disingenuously.

Of course she didn't have staff. Wydetta's photograph was in the *Encyclopedia Britannica* next to the entry for control freak.

"No, I don't, and I won't," she answered shortly. "Stop trying to rearrange my life."

James smirked when she shoved a serving dish heaped with green beans into his hands. And so it went, dish after dish passed in silence. Once the last bowl had been passed, the Owens family tucked into their meal as if it might be their last. James couldn't resist giving the pot one more stir.

Zeroing in on Brittany, he asked, "Has your security team been able to glean any more evidence as to who might have thrown the brick through your window?"

All three generations of Owens women stared at him, aghast. Fury sparked in Wydetta's eyes. She'd been keeping him apprised of the security situation by sprinkling tidbits into the conversation here and there, but never painting the full picture. Before his eyes, her features hardened, then settled into an expression of resigned betrayal. He almost regretted tossing the conversational gambit out onto the table.

Almost, but not quite.

There were too many secrets in this family. Too many people acting independently from one another on something of vital interest to them all. If there was one thing his experience over the years had taught him, it was that secrets did no one any good.

Wydetta might think she was protecting Brittany by keeping her in the dark, but by leaving her ignorant, she was also opening her to the very threats being made against her. She needed to be armed with enough information to have her guard up.

James believed if she briefed Cash on the full extent of the threats, the lad would be happy to step up and do his part to protect the woman he so obviously loved. But Wydetta had a bit of a hard-on where Cash was concerned. One James didn't push to know more about. He might be a legend, but his ego still had its soft spots. He didn't want to know if Cash and Wydetta shared a past.

"Brick?" Marie asked as if she'd never heard the word before.

Merle straightened in his chair and harrumphed. James pondered whether Brittany's grandfather knew what was going on, but had also been keeping his lips zipped.

"Actually, I believe it was a rock," James said, correcting his earlier statement. "Was it a rock, love?"

When neither Wydetta or Brittany contributed to his conversational salvo, he set his knife and fork carefully on the edge of his plate, wiped his mouth with his napkin though he hadn't tasted a morsel, then folded his hands on the edge of the table as he focused on Brittany.

"You do realize you've received some threatening letters and notes in the weeks since you performed at the concert in Austin."

Brittany's gaze darted from him to Wydetta and back again before she responded. "I've been told about some threats we've received lately," she said, choosing each word carefully. "It's not unusual, as you know."

James shrugged, then nodded. "No, sadly, it isn't. But whoever's writing these letters seems to know some very specific details about your life."

"Details like what?" Cash demanded. "What kind of threats?"

James lifted one shoulder. "Details like you, Cash," he replied with deceptive equanimity. "Her relationship with you. How she spent the night with you in Austin."

"I did not spend the night with him in Austin," Brittany denied hotly.

Both James and Cash rolled their eyes. She was splitting hairs. "Fine. Since you were with Cash in Austin. In his hotel room. Alone. Presumably having sex," he added as if they couldn't get the clear picture without him painting it for them.

Wydetta kicked him under the table. Hard. James let out a small "Oof!" then grinned appreciatively at her. He loved a woman with fire in her belly.

"Brittany Marie!" Marie gasped.

James's assailant shook her head pityingly at the shocked expression on Marie's face. "Seriously, Mama? That's what you're upset about."

"Well, if you'd pay more attention to what your daughter—"

"Brittany is my child—"

"And I am not a child," Brit cut in, her voice rising above theirs. "Stop talking around me as if I were one," she added hotly. Leveling the full force of her glare on Wydetta, she demanded, "Tell us all everything. Everything from the beginning. I'm tired of being left in the dark. I'm tired of all the secrets."

James's lips curved into a smile and he gave a slow clap. "Finally," he said approvingly. He paused to gaze at each person seated around the table pointedly. "If there's one thing I've learned, it's shutting people out does no one any good. If anything, it jeopardizes more than relationships."

Wydetta did exactly as Brittany asked—slowly, calmly, and in a voice so controlled it didn't ever quaver. She laid out all the details of the mounting threats made against her daughter. She started with the letter written on plain white printer paper in a man's angrily spiky handwriting. Handwriting she admitted seemed vaguely familiar to her at the time, but whose ownership she hadn't been able to confirm. Until recently.

Wydetta stared hard at her father.

James looked around at the occupants of the table, their expressions showing utter confusion. Then he saw the deep red flush creeping up Merle's neck and put two and two together. "You wrote a threatening letter to your granddaughter?"

James truly believed when shocking or bad news was dropped into somebody's life, it was good to have an outsider in the midst. Someone like him. A person with enough distance to remove oneself from hurt and anger and remain calm and rational. He figured he could absorb some of the fear and resentment that filled the room as the story unfolded. But this...

"I did no such thing." But Merle's bluster fell flat, and the blush grew up his neck and fed into his cheeks. "I wrote a letter to my daughter, expressing my concern about the company my granddaughter was keeping," he clarified with exaggerated dignity.

Wydetta's eyes opened wide. "I thought maybe it was a coincidence the handwriting looked like yours. You didn't sign it," she said with preternatural calm.

"I didn't think I had to," Merle shot back. "Who doesn't know their own daddy's handwriting?"

Wydetta's brows arched. "Well, I suppose the answer would be a woman who never received a letter from her daddy in her life. I never expected the first to be one threatening all sorts of mayhem if I allowed my daughter to continue to consort with a man known to have such an unsavory past." She shot a glance at Cash, as if they didn't all know who the man in question was.

"I didn't say he was unsavory. I said he was unsuitable," Merle corrected.

"Thanks for the clarification," Cash said dryly.

"Granddad," Brittany gasped. "How could you? I'm a grown woman."

Merle brushed her argument aside with a dismissive wave. "Pffft! You're barely more than a child. You think age is the number of candles on your birthday cake, and each year you get smarter. But you don't. You are a twenty-three-year-old girl who still has stars in her eyes when it comes to this one." He jabbed a finger in Cash's direction.

"Granddad!" Brit barked, tossing her napkin onto the table.

"Ironic, considering I'm not a star," Cash murmured.

"Brittany wouldn't be the first girl to go gaga over some wannabe. Don't have to be a star to make a girl moony. Ask my daughter," he added in a grumble.

"Moony? I'm about to moon you," Brit sputtered.

"Now, young lady—"

"That was the first letter," Wydetta interrupted, bringing their bickering to an abrupt halt. When she had all their attention again, she shrugged. "I thought it was some jealous man who saw her go up to Cash's hotel room. At least I choose to think it was, because God knows I couldn't imagine my own father writing a letter so filled with gloom and doom about his very own grandchild."

Merle fell back in his chair looking suitably chastened.

"Can we get back to the threats?" Cash asked, not bothering to mask his impatience with what was boiling down to a family squabble.

Wydetta gave a soft cough, and James reached over and placed his hand over hers. The gesture earned him a death glare. James gave her hand a consoling pat, then withdrew before she could stick a fork in him.

He settled back into his chair, and Wydetta began to speak again. She used a low, measured tone he found both arousing and infuriating. He hated seeing her rein in her passion, her anger, her frustration. He liked her better when he had her stripped naked in bed, all raw emotion and physical demands.

"Yes, well, as I said, I've since come to realize who the author was and managed to dismiss any perceived threat I read into the unsigned letter," she said, emphasizing each word carefully.

"I can't believe you don't recognize your own father's handwriting," Merle muttered.

"I must've missed all those picture postcards you sent me from the road, Daddy."

"The threats," Cash repeated, tapping the table hard enough to get their attention.

Wydetta blinked twice, then continued. "We received that one after we'd come back to Nashville." Her forehead puckered, and she paused. "Now that I think about it, we got the second one after you and Cash ran into one another at StarRise."

She looked at James, worry clouding her eyes. If she hadn't looked so vulnerable, he might have bristled with pride. She'd turned to him first. With the whole of her family at the table, she looked to him for confirmation and reassurance.

"The timing is off. Brittany and Cash weren't really together when we first started getting notes."

"But we had been together," Brittany reminded her.

"This is far too much information for a grandmother," Marie announced, rising from the table. "I'll go see to dessert. I don't want to hear any more of this." She shot a meaningful glance at Brittany and Cash, then gave her head a meaningful shake. "Any of it."

Brittany rolled her eyes but waited for grandmother to leave the room before she spoke again. "Cash and I didn't have any contact with one another until the day we finished the album."

Cash nodded. "So somebody who knows I'm connected to StarRise and knows you and I had been together in Austin."

Wydetta dropped an elbow onto the table and let her forehead fall into her palm, massaging her temples lightly as she rolled her head from side to side. "I wish I could remember the timing. We'll check with the security team, but something tells me the timing was way off." She looked up and her eyes locked on her daughter. "I'm pretty sure I got the second letter right after we signed the contracts with StarRise, but before you wrote 'We'll Be We'."

"Sounds to me like we need to work out a timeline," Merle chimed in. "I'll put a call in to Hank, and we'll get this lined out so everybody's clear on what happened when."

Cash frowned as he divided a glance between Wydetta and Merle. "What did you say about a brick?"

James made a point of staring at his plate while the uncomfortable silence filled the room. Brittany hadn't told Cash about the broken window. The omission was obvious now. He wished he'd known a half hour ago. He'd stirred the pot, but he wasn't sure he wanted to drink from it.

"It was a rock," James corrected with quiet calm.

"Fine, a rock. But nothing has happened, right?" Cash asked, enunciating each word with such deliberation Brittany went still.

James leveled a pointed stare in Wydetta's direction. The man was asking a direct question about a situation he was involved in personally. As far as James was concerned, Cash had every right to know what was happening. "Tell him," he prompted.

As expected, Wydetta bristled at being told what to do. "Why don't you mind your own business?" She glared at him. "Why are you even here? I swear, you're like a damn barnacle."

This time, James didn't dare reach for her hand. "I told you, I'm here to lend moral support."

"You have the morals of an alley cat," she grumbled. "This is my family. I don't need your kind of moral support."

"Then why are you so scared to tell them what's happening?"

The implication made Wydetta scoff outright. "Scared? I'm not scared."

"Prove it," he said calmly. When she didn't rise to the bait, he lowered his voice so only she could hear. "Secrets are about as good as closed doors with no locks. You might be able to hold some things in or keep scary monsters at bay for a while, but sooner or later you have to open it up."

Wydetta clamped her mouth shut, a stubborn gleam lighting her eyes. "I'm about to slam the door on you, you meddling limey."

"You can try, love, but I learned to pick locks way back in my misspent youth."

This time Cash slammed his palm flat on the table, making all the china and cutlery jump and jangle. "Oh, for God's sake," he exploded. When all eyes swung to him, he blew out an aggravated breath. "The threats," he prompted through clenched teeth.

James covered Wydetta's hand with his and spoke before she could draw a breath. "In the grand scheme of things, they aren't terribly serious." Both Wydetta and Merle opened their mouths to protest, and he raised his free hand to stop them. "Yes, they are disturbing, and someone was on the property, which is even more so, but what the notes say carry more of an implied threat than a direct one."

Cash looked him square in the eye. "What kind of things do they say?"

James waved his hand in a dismissive gesture. "The usual. Brittany should not be with you, you're too old for her, she's too good for you, etcetera, etcetera." He offered Cash a reassuring smile. To Wydetta, he said, "We both know they could be worse."

"Yes, but—"

"They are troubling, I know." Glaring at Merle, he said, "Perhaps it would be best if you expressed your concerns to your daughter in a more direct manner in the future. A phone call, or in person?"

"I thought I was being direct," Merle grumbled. "And who are you to tell me how to communicate with my own family?"

"I'm no one. No one at all," James said easily. "Simply a concerned, and somewhat unbiased, bystander." Shifting his attention to Brittany, then Cash, he smiled again. "I find solving most family conflict is fairly easy. All you need is open and frank communication, and a referee."

Wydetta jerked her hand out from beneath his. "And you've appointed yourself to the position?"

"I saw a need, and I filled it," he countered. "Now, give everyone the pertinent information so we can finish this lovely meal and move on to dessert. I do believe I heard Marie mention something about a cobbler?"

He glanced around the table as he picked up his fork once more, satisfied he'd kicked the door in well and good.

17

Cash gripped the steering wheel so hard all of the blood rushed from his knuckles. Brit knew what was coming, but she wasn't going to invite the conversation. Particularly when she had so few concrete answers.

Listening to her mother and grandfather discuss the threats to her security so openly threw her. James Paulson seemed to know more about her situation than she did, and that flat-out pissed her off.

But she had no one to blame but herself.

If she wanted to take more control in her career, she needed to stop letting people handle the important stuff for her. She wasn't a fool. Hell, she couldn't have a career at all if she wasn't playing an active role in maintaining her own safety.

"How long have the letters been coming?"

Cash's delivery was terse. Brit couldn't blame him for being upset. He knew she was upset too, but she didn't have the answers he was going to want to hear so the only thing she could do was evade and deflect.

"I get crazy letters all the time, Cash. You know the drill."

"How long have you been getting crazy letters about *me*?"

She could tell by the way he bit off each word his patience was wearing thin, but so was hers. "Check your ego, buster. The letters were about me," she said pointedly.

He shook his head and struck the steering wheel with the heel of his hand, his frustration palpable. "You know what I mean."

"I do know what you mean," she replied with exaggerated calmness. "But you also know what I'm saying about getting questionable letters all the time. I bet you still get some. Didn't you have some woman from Paducah sending you fingernail clippings and locks of hair from places not on her head? You more than anyone should know you can't take every threat to heart."

He cast her a sidelong glance. "Charlene from Paducah never threatened me."

The problem was, she couldn't defend her statement. She hadn't seen the letters Wydetta and Merle had been discussing. She didn't know exactly what threats were made. They only knew they referenced her relationship with Cash.

She wanted to kick herself for being so complacent. But every time she asked questions, her mother told her not to worry. To let her security team handle everything. They were the professionals. She chose to believe that she was better off not knowing. After all, wasn't that what everyone told her?

She pressed her forehead to the cool glass and tugged at the ends of her hair. She took time for three calming breaths, then broke down and admitted the truth. "I don't know, okay? They haven't shown me, I didn't ask, and I don't know."

The tires hummed on asphalt, and the silence stretched between them. At last, Cash reach over and placed his hand on her thigh, giving it a gentle squeeze. "Okay," he said quietly.

His calm acceptance of what was essentially a non-answer surprised her. Lifting her head, she cast a wary glance in his direction. "Okay?"

He shrugged. "They didn't tell you, and you didn't ask. I get it."

"You do?"

"Yeah." He let out a humorless chuckle as he sat up straight in his seat again, but kept his eyes glued to the road ahead of them. "Frankly, I could've gone all my life without ever thinking about Charlene from Paducah again."

"True for all of us."

He gave her leg a pat, then withdrew his hand and returned it to the wheel. "But I think it's time you started asking more questions. You have a good team around you, but no one can take care of you as well as you can take care of yourself." He glanced over at her to gauge her reaction.

Brit smiled and expelled a breath. "I know."

"You'll start asking more questions?"

She nodded. "Yes, and when I do, I'll let you know what I find out."

"You don't have to report back to me."

"Don't you want to know?" she asked, unable to keep the hurt from her tone.

He studied her then, a sad lift to the corner of his lips. "I want to know everything about you, Brit, but I don't want to be your stalker from Paducah. You tell me what you want to tell me, and I'll do my best to help in whatever way I can."

Brittany figured she shouldn't have been so surprised when Roger pulled to a stop at Cash's house, and she found herself staring at the back of an Acme Alarm Systems van. Barely two days had passed since supper at her grandparents' house. When had he set this up?

"What the—" She huffed. Guilt panged in her gut. He didn't want this for himself, he wanted it for her. And didn't that just blow?

Rog nodded approvingly as he put the car in park. "Maybe he's not such a loser after all. He wants to take care of you."

Brit rolled her eyes. "I'm not some helpless damsel in distress, you know."

She snapped her mouth shut, regretting the words almost as much as the bite she put into them. Roger had been looking after her since she was knee-high to a niblet. It wasn't fair for her to get huffy when he expressed concern for her safety.

An alarm system was not an indication Cash doubted her ability to care for herself. She'd been the one who mocked him for not having one, but... Lately it seemed too many decisions were made in her best interest rather than at her request. Like Mark choreographing a brand-new transition in the dance routine to replace the intricate footwork that tripped her up that morning.

He shouldn't have done it. So, she'd twisted her knee in practice. She wasn't used to the shoes, that was all. It wasn't like she couldn't dance. The doctor said it was only a strain. Wasn't like she'd broken her leg or something. She simply needed to rest and let it heal.

"You need help up the porch steps?"

Brittany rolled her eyes again. Grabbing her bag, she reached for the handle and threw her shoulder against the door. "No. Thank you," she added the gratitude as an afterthought. She was tired and crabby, but being sore didn't give her cause to be ugly to Roger. "Have a good night."

She stepped gingerly from the car, making sure to shift most of her weight to her right foot so her left leg wouldn't have to bear the burden. The strain wasn't even bad enough to require crutches. Her doctor's nurse wrapped her knee in an elastic bandage and handed her a neoprene brace and a paper bag with a bottle of painkillers. Then, she bustled out of the private exam room with a reminder to rest, ice, and elevate.

Brit had almost toddled her way to the top step when a workman in an Acme shirt stepped out of the front door. His double take was so exaggerated, it might have made her smile on any other day, but today she was running on anti-inflammatories and impatience. Ducking her head, she averted her eyes as she made her way to the front door with a mumbled "Excuse me."

She was through the door before he could stammer, "Oh. No. Excuse me, uh, miss—"

His reaction and immediate recognition had dashed any hopes she had of talking Cash out of installing an alarm system he did not want on her account. She'd been planning to argue that no one even knew they were dating, but the service technician's rapid recovery after seeing her told her he wasn't entirely shocked.

Their days of anonymity were numbered, if not already gone. They'd been photographed by one of their fellow diners at a barbeque joint, but as far as she knew, the pictures hadn't appeared on anything but a local food blog. Of course, the incident made Cash and his reluctance to be seen together in public more of a sticking point. It didn't matter to her what anybody thought about their relationship. They were together, and nothing was going to change that now.

"Hello?" she called into the house. When she got no immediate response, she dropped her bag onto the couch, then flopped down beside it. Throwing her head back, she sang out, "Hel-looooo?"

Cash emerged from the bedroom with another service technician hot on his heels. "Hey," he said, sounding slightly out of breath as he leaned down to kiss her. "Sorry, hoped I would have this done before you got home."

Got home.

Something about the casual way he said those two words made

whatever irritation she'd been feeling dissipate like smoke. "I see we're getting an alarm," she said, trying for nonchalant but sounding snarky even to her own ears.

"Yeah, well, someone freaked me out when she reminded me of Charlene from Paducah." He shrugged. "For all I know, she still has an altar built somewhere."

Brit couldn't help but smile. "Oh, so this is for you, not for me?"

He pulled a face and guffawed as if the suggestion was the most ridiculous thing he'd ever heard. "Of course it's not for you." He looked over his shoulder as the two technicians gathered their tools while they exchanged surreptitious glances. "I know better."

"Do you?"

One corner of his mouth kicked up. "I should only buy you glittery, sparkly presents, right? No vacuums or kitchen appliances, because those would be sexist and stupid."

Brit smoothed her features into an expression of mock solemnity, then gave a grave nod. "Yes. Yes, they would. And almost as sexist as installing an entire alarm system because the little woman needs to be protected from the big, bad wolf."

"Or maybe not sexist, but practical. Especially since the little woman is about to become even more of a superstar than she already is."

"Keep talking," she prompted, making a lazy circle with her hand.

"And definitely not a present," he hastened to add. "I'm buying this solely for me. And Charlene from Paducah," he said as an afterthought. "But if you happen to, you know, hang out here, you'd be protected too," he said with such studied offhandedness she had to laugh.

"Man, you suck at subtle."

Cash pressed a smacking kiss to her cheek, then pushed away before she could catch him. "Yeah, well, it's not exactly your thing, either." He tipped his head toward the workmen. "Let me go finish up with them, then I'll grill you about this twisted knee and we'll sort out what to do for dinner."

Brit leaned back against the worn-soft leather of the couch cushion with a huff. Crossing her arms over her chest, she swung her left leg up onto the coffee table. She wanted to go out tonight. She wanted to go someplace where she and Cash would be seen and photographed. Documented and presented to the world as fact, not subject to speculation and chickenshit anonymous threats.

But her knee wasn't going to cooperate with anything remotely resembling high heels tonight, and the last thing she needed to do was show up somewhere hobbling and holding on to Cash's arm. Not on their initial outing. Somehow the jackals would twist it into something it wasn't. Something ugly. She'd seen it happen often enough. Stars weren't allowed to have innocent everyday mishaps. They were supposed to be invincible. In some cases, immortal. Perfect. Not human enough to be hobbled by a simple step-ball-change gone wrong.

She'd seen one of her *TeenScreen* co-stars go through public relations hell when the tabloids decided the black eye she'd scored in a car accident was actually a gift from her boyfriend. All it took was one reporter hungry to make a name for themselves to make a mountain out of a molehill. The last thing she needed was a shot of her grimacing in pain as she held Cash's hand. They'd be all too happy to add one plus one and come up with fifty-two.

She straightened when she heard the front door close. Seconds later, Cash's warm hands landed on her shoulders.

"How's the knee?"

"Sprained but nothing serious," she reported, leaning back into his touch. "Rest and ice."

"And elevate," he added, nodding to the foot she'd propped up on his coffee table.

"Right."

"You take anything?" he asked, his tone wary.

Tipping her head back, she shook it. "Ibuprofen."

Cash skirted carefully around the end of the couch. He settled gingerly on the opposite end, taking extra care not to jostle her. Which only made her feel worse. The man should at least be comfortable in his own home.

Brit heaved a heavy sigh. "I'm sorry. This has been a crappy day from beginning to end."

Cash glanced at his watch. "I hate to break this to you, but it's three-fifteen in the afternoon. We're a ways off from the end."

Letting out a fake cry, she let her head fall back against the cushion and rolled it from side to side. "Can't we go to bed now?" She stared at his profile until he met her gaze. "We can start again tomorrow, and maybe everything will be better."

She stretched out a hand. He didn't take it, so she waggled her fingers impatiently. "Don't make me move, just give me your hand."

"You're very bossy."

"So I've been told." She waggled her fingers again, and this time she smiled. "Hold my hand." Cash closed the gap between them. With his fingers woven through hers, Brit squeezed. "I'm sorry. My sense of humor might be a bit skewed, but I'm not completely self-involved."

"I wasn't trying to imply you are self-involved. But let's not forget a stage injury was what got me into trouble to start."

"Was it?"

"I hurt my back."

Recollection dawned. "Oh, yeah. I remember now. Does it still bother you?"

His lips twisted into a grimace. "Every day since I fell off a stage." He let his head fall against the cushion but held her gaze unflinchingly.

"I'm sorry," she whispered.

He nodded, but didn't say anything more.

Brit stared at him. "That's why you like being on your back," she observed.

He gave her fingers a squeeze this time. A wry smile tilted his lips and he shrugged. "I also like the view."

Brit laughed. "You enjoy the show, huh?"

Cash gave his head a slow shake and closed his eyes as if replaying the previous night. "I admit, I like looking at you." Holding her hand, he slid across the cushions, closing the distance between them. "Sadly, I think we're going to have to take the night off."

She blinked, confused by his comment. "Take the night off?"

"From the floorshow. Or bed show, I guess." He freed his hand and reached up to tuck a lock of hair behind her ear. "I don't know why you won't just cuddle sometimes," he said with a self-deprecating smirk. "Why does it always have to be about sex with you?"

Brit grinned at him. "I am a healthy female in the prime of her life. I have needs, Cash," she said with mock solemnity. "If accommodating said needs is too much for you..." She trailed off, letting the joke die. Whatever she said would've led to a round-robin about getting a younger model, and she didn't want to play right into his fears. Reaching up, she captured his hand and pressed it against her cheek. "I wouldn't mind some cuddling."

His smile was tender and heart-stopping. He leaned in and brushed a sweet kiss across her lips. Before she could capture him and hold him there, he drew back and launched himself from the sofa. "I'm going to get you an ice bag, then we're going to settle in and watch more of those *HeeHaw* DVDs I bought one night when I was high as a kite." He started towards the kitchen, calling back over his shoulder, "I found another one with Merle. If he still has the leisure suit, I want to borrow it at Halloween."

Something woke her in the middle of the night. Her eyes popped open, but the rest of her muscles tensed. Her senses were acutely attuned to a soft rattling noise coming somewhere beyond the open bedroom door.

Careful to move only her eyes, she scanned the wall. A framed photo of a honky-tonk. Sash windows trimmed in white paint and covered with plantation shutters. A framed gold album. She narrowed her eyes and waited for the sound to come again. She didn't have to wait long. The rattle was faint but insistent. Sliding her hand under the covers, she found the sheets beside her cool and empty.

"Cash?" she whispered tentatively. Slinking one leg out from under the blankets, she slid soundlessly from the bed. Well, almost soundlessly. In her haste, she'd forgotten about her wrenched knee. "Unpfh," she grunted, biting the insides of her cheeks to keep any further sound from escaping.

Hobbling toward the open doorway, she caught sight of a spill of golden lamplight tapering toward the living room. Brit slid her feet along the smooth hardwood planks, favoring her sore leg and willing the floorboards not to creak as she shuffled cautiously down the hall. When she reached the entrance to the living room, she intended to call out for him again, but his name died on her lips.

The soft rattling sound echoed through the quiet room. She dropped her gaze to his hands and saw he held the orange prescription bottle between his thumb and forefinger. She stared at it uncomprehendingly, then flinched when he gave the bottle an absent shake.

Pills.

She'd brought pills into his house, and apparently Cash had wanted them bad enough to dump her bag out on the sofa and rifle through her personal belongings.

Brit stared at the detritus strewn across the sofa cushions. There were two tampons, one of them slipping out of its wrapper. Her wallet, the puffy keychain with the pepper spray, and nearly a dozen lipsticks lay scattered. Too many lipsticks. How many lipsticks did a woman need? She certainly had to be over the quota.

Her eyes lowered to the soft leather satchel crumpled in a heap on the floor. It was as if the search and seizure had wrung every bit of life from the bag. But rather than feeling angry and hurt by the violation of her privacy, Brit felt only dismay.

How careless she'd been.

How naïve.

He'd told her about his struggles. Told her about his need for support, and how important maintaining his sobriety was to him. What had she done? She brought pills into his house and locked him in with them, armed with the alarm system he'd bought to protect her. As if an alarm would be any good at protecting him from the devil within.

Swallowing hard, she stepped into the room. He sat deep in the folds of the sofa, enfolded in the shadows cast by the lamplight. The darkness etched lines around his mouth and eyes and highlighted the strong planes of his face. She'd never seen him look so haggard. Never seen him look so vulnerable.

"Cash—"

"They gave you the good stuff," he said, his voice so rough it sounded like he'd been swallowing ground glass. His lips curved, but the expression he wore wasn't anything remotely like a smile. "Only the best for our Brit."

His voice caught, and she hobbled toward him as fast as her leg would allow. "Cash, I didn't think. I was so stupid," she said, the words tumbling over one another in her haste to get them out. "I'm sorry. I am so, so sorry…" She lowered herself gingerly in front of him, then shifted her weight from her sore knee to her rump. Placing her hands on his knees and sliding her fingers up under the hem of the gym shorts he wore. "I wasn't thinking about anything but myself. As usual. Are you okay?"

It was an asinine question, she knew, but it was out there and she couldn't wish it back. It hardly mattered. He could lie, and she would never know.

Cash looked up, finally meeting her gaze directly. Then he shook the pill bottle like a maraca. "Am I okay?" He repeated her inane question with a huff of joyless laughter. He eyed the pill bottle as if sizing up an opponent for a fight. "You know, this is the first time I've actually had to face one of these since I left rehab."

Brittany snatched the bottle from his hand, clutching it in her fist. "I'm so sorry. I didn't think."

He ran his hand over his face, then lowered his gaze to the cell phone on the sofa beside him. "I'm okay. I called Jace."

The fact that he had to call someone else to help him get through something she'd brought on him nearly killed her. She might not have had to deal with these problems in her own life, but she'd certainly been in the business long enough to know better than to bring temptation into an addict's home.

The problem was, she never thought of Cash as an addict. Sure, he'd told her he was. He talked about being sober these days. He'd told her about going to meetings, but it never meshed with the image of him she carried in her head. And in her heart. She was clean and sober. Always had been. But his sobriety was something he had to fight for every day in a world rife with enticements.

She gave his knee a gentle squeeze and tamped down an irrational surge of jealousy. "Jace was able to help?"

He jerked his chin toward the bottle in her hand. "Count them."

Brit wagged her head so hard it hurt. "I don't need to count them. I believe you."

"I need you to count them," Cash insisted, his voice taut. "Open the bottle, dump them out, then count them. Make sure they're all there."

Brit thinned her lips into a taut line. "I don't need to count them. I believe you," she repeated.

"I don't believe me," he snapped. "Count the pills."

Without another word of protest, she began to do so, transferring them from one palm to the other and counting out loud. When she was able to confirm she did indeed have every pill present and accounted for, she dumped them all back into the container and locked the lid down. "There. Happy now?"

Cash's head fell back against the sofa, and his entire body went lax. Until she felt his muscles soften, Brit hadn't realized how rigid his hold on his self-control had been.

"What do you want me to do with them? Should I flush them?"

Cash shook his head so slowly it seemed to take Herculean strength to make the simple movement. "No. I just... I need them out of here."

Brittany briefly considered running up and down the alley behind his house spreading pills from dumpster to dumpster, but doing so didn't seem like a good alternative, either. She looked up at him, feeling helpless. "I don't know what to do. I don't know where to take them."

As if she'd summoned a genie, the doorbell chimed. Brit shot Cash a puzzled look. It was the middle of the night. "Who could that possibly be?"

"Jace," Cash said gruffly. "I told him not to come, but it'll be Jace."

Brit stumbled to her feet, her injured knee screeching in protest. Forgetting she wore only Cash's T-shirt and a pair of panties, she padded to the front door and peered through the tiny window. Cash was right. Jace Allen stood on the welcome mat, his hands shoved deep in the pockets of his jeans.

She started to throw the deadbolt but stopped when Cash called out, "Alarm."

Brit yanked her hands back from the door as if she'd been scalded, then glared at the control panel mounted on the wall. "I don't know the code."

Cash chuckled. "I haven't reset it yet. It's still 1-1-1-1-1."

She jabbed the numbers into the keypad, waited until the green light illuminated, then opened the front door to admit Cash's best friend. The second their eyes met, tears began to well in hers. "I fucked up," she said breathlessly. "I fucked up."

Though they didn't know each other as more than passing acquaintances, Jace wrapped an arm around her shoulders and pulled her close for a reassuring squeeze. "How dare you be human, Brittany Owens." She sniffled and he opened his hand. "Now, hand over the goods."

Sagging with relief, she placed the pill bottle in Jace's palm, a wracking sob rising up inside her as his fingers wrapped around the container. It might've escaped, if another thought hadn't occurred to her. "Wait, hold on. Aren't you his sponsor?" she choked out.

Jace nodded once. "I am."

Brit covered his clenched fist with both her hands. "Then you must have a problem too. I can't give these to you, either."

He chuckled, then carefully extracted his hand from hers. "Pills aren't my Kryptonite. I preferred my drugs in powder form."

She shook her head. "Yeah, but isn't it all the same? Aren't you supposed to stay away from all of it?" She glanced over at Cash for confirmation. "Maybe I should take those and toss them somewhere. Like a garbage can on a street corner. No one would look for them there."

Cash gave a raspy bark of laughter. "Once upon a time, you would've been my dream girl."

His flippant words struck her like a fist to the chest. What did he mean? Was he saying she wasn't his dream girl? Or, was he saying people pawed through trash cans in hopes of scoring discarded drugs?

Before she could puzzle it out, Jace spoke up. "I know a place where I can take them. Safer to turn them in than to leave them out on the street somewhere. You never know who goes digging through garbage cans."

The thought had flitted across her mind as an impossibility, but now she shrunk back in horror. The mere idea of someone like Cash pawing through a street corner trash can to get his hands on drugs appalled her so deeply, it must've shown on her face. The two men exchanged wry smiles, then Jace gently propelled her toward the sofa. "Trust us on this one."

This time, Cash opened his arms when she approached. Brit fell into them gratefully, burying her face in the crook of his neck. "I'm so sorry."

18

He held her firm against him, resting his chin atop her head and rubbing her shaking shoulders. She was about to climb up and burrow deeper when he spoke.

"Jace, would you mind giving Brit a ride home?"

She jerked up so fast the top of her head connected with his jaw. Cash groaned, but it was no competition for her vehement protest.

"No!"

"Sure," Jace replied at the same time.

Brit shot him a nasty glare, but Jace didn't budge. Yanking her attention fully back to Cash, she brushed his hands away from his jaw and began to stroke the offended spot herself. "Don't send me home. I'm sorry. I fucked up and I'm sorry."

He silenced her with a quick, hard kiss. "It's okay," he whispered as he pulled back. "I'm not... You didn't... I'm not punishing you, I promise. I need to be alone. I need time to sort out what's in my head." He kissed her again, this time sweet and lingering. "Go on," he murmured. "I'll call you first thing tomorrow."

"But—"

"Please."

His voice broke on the word, and she sighed, knowing she wasn't going to win this one. She climbed off his lap, pulling the hem of the T-shirt down as she straightened. Cash rose too. He let out a groan Brit had always assumed was habit, but now realized was due to the lingering stiffness in his back. She watched in wonder as he pressed a hand to the small curved base of his spine and stretched the muscles. How had she not noticed he lived with daily pain? And would he ever not be hurting? What could she possibly do to help?

"You might want to put some pants on," he said gruffly.

"Oh." She glanced down at her bare legs, then stretched the hem of the shirt down as she darted an embarrassed look at Cash's friend. "Sorry, Jace."

"No need to apologize." His tone was reassuring but his smile so devilish it brought a scowl to Cash's lips. A bubble of nervous laughter escaped her as she limped toward the bedroom.

"Shouldn't she be on crutches?" Jace asked. She heard the low rumble of Cash's gruff reply, but their tone dropped enough so she couldn't make out the rest of the words. Mind whirling and heart pounding with anxiety, she drew on a pair of yoga pants and slipped her feet into the lightweight canvas tennis shoes Wydetta had brought to the doctor's office.

Had this all happened in one day?

Brit sat on the edge of the rumpled bed, gripping the mattress as she tried to regulate her breathing. Cash truly had a problem. A big one. And she hadn't the first idea how to fix it for him. Or, at least, how to make things easier. What good was she going to be to him?

As if conjured, the man himself appeared in the doorway. He still appeared tired and haggard, but he no longer looked like a stranger. This was the man she loved. The man who loved her back, whether he liked it or not. She had no doubt she'd figure it out. They'd figure it out. Together.

Still, she had remorse and apologies piling up inside her. She had to let some of them out, or they'd choke her. "I'm sorry," she whispered.

"I know you are. Sweetheart, it's okay." He crossed to her and took both of her hands in his. "We're okay. I just need…"

"Some space," she finished bleakly.

One side of his mouth quirked. "Yes, but not relationship-space and definitely not a break." When she didn't laugh, he squeezed her hands. "I need a few hours to focus on me. Okay? Jace is going to take you home, then come back here. I won't be alone. There's a sunrise meeting, and we're going."

He said it so casually, he might have been talking about catching a movie. But this wasn't a film, or a play, or even some bad sketch TV. This was his life, and she had to trust Cash to know best how to handle his issues.

"Okay." She tugged his hands until he bent over her. Their lips touched and clung. "Do what you need to do. Call me whenever you need me. Any time at all."

The next morning's rehearsal looked something like a circus. Wydetta was the ringmaster, of course, and Brit her dancing poodle who could barely dance. Though they'd been through the choreography a dozen times, something felt off. The in-ear monitors weren't playing nice with her headset and kept screeching deafening feedback straight into her eardrum.

Her engineer, Gavin, and his team of sound guys scrambled to get the balance right while Brit and her backup dancers sweltered beneath the stage lights. She stood as still as possible while her wardrobe managers fiddled with the modified men's suit jacket she was wearing for the opening number. To take her mind off her discomfort, she hummed a few bars of the chorus, keeping her vocal cords warm without straining her voice.

One of the costume ladies pulled at the hem of the black stretch short shorts currently cutting off circulation in her thighs.

"She has gained weight," Sarita muttered in her heavily accented English.

Brittany sighed. She knew the comment was meant for her ears. If they didn't want her to understand, the two women could have conversed only in Portuguese. But she refused to rise to the bait.

Humming louder, she wiggled the leg Sarita wasn't tugging on to keep time in her head.

"Hold still," Carmen ordered as she tugged the lapels of the suit jacket.

The fabric didn't move, of course. Because Brit wore no shirt beneath the coat, the only thing between her and the ViewTube-worthy wardrobe malfunction was some super-duper double-sided tape. The kind that hurts like hell coming off after a day of sweating through her clothes.

One would think the sweat would make the adhesive break down, she mused. But no, this kind of tape only stuck harder, clinging to her breasts for dear life. Brit gritted her teeth and tipped her head up to look at the ceiling while all the women continued push, pull, and prod her in every direction. She said nothing. She made no complaints. This was their job, and she wasn't about to be the diva who got in the way of them doing it.

When she was finally trussed up to their satisfaction, Mark took her hand and led her back to the center of the stage, positioning her at the front of the wedge of similarly clad, but not quite as sparkly, backup dancers.

"You're good with the new move?" he asked for what had to be the fiftieth time. He eyed the brace on her leg. She'd agreed to wear it only as a precaution. "Knee feeling okay?"

She exhaled loudly. She paid Mark well enough to let her exasperation show. "I'm fine with the new move, if we can ever get to it."

She peered around him to glare at her mother. "They get everything sorted out?" she asked, not bothering to hide the impatience in her tone as she gestured to the mixing board set-up at the center of the auditorium.

Wydetta held up a finger to signal she needed a minute, spoke into her mobile phone, then waved to somebody in from the wings. A nervous-looking young man who looked like he was barely out of high school darted out from the darkness with a new headset and transmitter pack in his hands.

"They'd like us to try a new one, Miss Brittany," he said, his voice low and quavering with nerves.

Brit smiled at him, hoping to put him at ease. "Oh, thank you," she gushed. "What's your name?" she asked as he hooked the pack to the back of her shorts and handed her the new headset to loop around the back of her head. Two hairdressers dashed in at a sprint to assist.

"I'm Jeff, Miss Brittany."

She smiled as he straightened, color rising high in his cheeks.

"I'm just Brittany," she corrected. "And thank you, Jeff. If it screeched at me one more time, I was afraid I might screech back."

He chuckled as if she'd told a joke rather than the absolute truth, then backed away as quickly as he could. Brittany watched him go, and once again, she was reminded of exactly how many people were relying on her to get this right.

She took in the musicians, dancers, choreographer, and even the sadistic wardrobe ladies. She caught a glimpse of her mother as she took her spot again. The sound technicians, the lighting people, hell, even the ticket takers. Everyone. Dozens of people depending on her. And those were only the people involved in her tour production. There were label executives, everyday guys like Heywood, moguls like Leelo, and legends like her granddad counting on her too. She couldn't let a single one of them down.

She adjusted the tiny microphone she wore, took up her first position to start the dance, then glanced over at her mother. "With as much as these thing cost, you'd think they'd make them so they wouldn't pierce your eardrum."

Wydetta glanced into the darkness where Gavin sat. Brit was well aware that they engineer had heard her grousing, but for once she didn't care. For once she wanted to act the star. The diva. But the moment she locked eyes with her mother, the urge subsided.

"Sorry, everyone," she murmured into the mic. "From the top?"

Wydetta nodded once, approving of her professionalism. "From the top," she called out to the musicians, and the drummer started to count off the beat.

The second the run-through ended, her mother drew her aside. They smiled and nodded, exchanging random and innocuous comments as the dancers and crew milled about. Brit jiggled her sore leg, anxious for rehearsal to end so she could head to Cash's place. She closed her eyes and tamped down on her impatience. She'd get there soon enough.

Once the crowd thinned, Wydetta picked at an invisible thread on the lapel of her jacket. "How do you feel?" she asked in a low voice.

"Fine," Brit responded automatically. She caught the twitch of her mother's eyebrow, then blew out a sigh. "I'm good."

"Your knee is okay?"

"Yes," Brit assured her. "Not even a twinge."

"Good." Wydetta paused, then let her hand fall away. "I wanted to let you know we got another note. Same old stuff—Cash isn't good enough, you need someone your own age, your career is going to suffer, you're going to suffer—" she recited the gist of the note almost by rote.

Her mom's deliberately tedious tone gave Brit a measure of reassurance. Sir James had been right. Dishing it all out at the Owens dinner table had somehow managed to make the notes she was receiving sound less ominous. The improved security around the perimeter of the estate also helped put everyone's minds at ease. They didn't discuss the nights spent at Cash's house. Brit assumed his low-key lifestyle and the spanking new alarm system helped take some of the urgency out of those arguments.

"Mama, I screwed up."

The words were out and she couldn't stop them. Wydetta stared at her, her mouth agape. Brit didn't know if she'd stunned her mother with her confession or by addressing her as "Mama." Either way, there was a pause so prolonged, Brittany had no clue how to break the silence.

At last, Wydetta snapped her jaw shut, grasped Brit by the elbow, and steered her away from center stage. "Are you pregnant?" she asked in a rushed whisper. Brit's shock must have shown on her face because her mother surged ahead before she could muster the single word answer. "It's okay if you are. We'll work it out. You'll be okay. We'll be okay."

This time, it was Brit's turn to stare.

"I mean, it's not ideal," Wydetta carried on with an edgy laugh. "But we can work around…anything." She faced her then, her blue eyes blazing with a determination Brittany had previously only seen when Wydetta was deep in negotiation mode. But her lips trembled, and the lines between her brows were etched deep. As if she were using them to dam the floods. Her voice came out choked with emotion, and for the first time in she didn't know how long, Wydetta took her hand and held it firmly. "You won't have to figure this out alone, baby, I promise."

Brit blinked twice when her mother looked away. She watched Wydetta's troubled gaze travel over the bustle on stage as if deciding where she needed to start dismantling their shared dream. A spear of pain lanced through her, and at last, she understood. The tremor. The unshed tears. They weren't for her. Well, they were, but not directly. Not her here and now, but the baby she'd been. The unplanned result of a meticulously planned rebellion. The comeuppance Wydetta's own mother had forced her to face every day.

"I'm not pregnant," she whispered. Wydetta's head whipped around. Their gazes met and held. "I'm not pregnant," Brit repeated carefully.

"You're not?"

"No."

So much tension seeped out of her mother's body, Brit was half afraid Wydetta would flat-out crash to the floor. "Thank God," Wydetta breathed.

"Yes, because we wouldn't want another mistake. I'm a big enough screw-up for everyone," Brit said stiffly.

Her mother straightened, instantly regaining some of her starch. "I didn't mean to imply you were." Always better on offense than defense, Wydetta switched gears as deftly as a Formula One driver. "What do you think you screwed up?"

Brit gave a short, sharp laugh. "Oh, it's not a matter of opinion. It's a fact. I went straight to Cash's house from the doctor's office."

When she didn't elaborate, Wydetta pursed her lips. "I kept telling you seeing him is a mistake, but you wanted to agree to disagree. What changed your mind about him?"

"Nothing. Nothing changed my mind about Cash." She settled a steely glare on her mother, hoping to make it clear her feelings hadn't waned. Unfortunately, her resolve was on shaky footing as it was, and when Wydetta met her glare for glare, she crumbled. "But I wouldn't be surprised if he changes his mind about me."

Her mother let out an unladylike snort. "Not likely."

"I went over there with a bag full of drugs, Mama," Brit confessed in a rush. "Painkillers. I went to his house with a whole purse full of the very thing he says tried to kill him."

Wydetta's soft gasp felt like an indictment. Pressing her lips together to staunch the flow of tears threatening, she nodded miserably.

"What happened? Did he hurt you?"

Mark cast a puzzled look in their direction, but hurriedly fell back into the rhythm of the playback, taking the backup dancers through the routine again.

"No, he didn't *hurt me*," she said, emphasizing the words to show her mother exactly how ridiculous the notion was.

"Did he… Was he okay?"

Brit blew out a breath as at last, Wydetta hit on the right question to ask. "Yeah. Yeah, he was. Eventually. No thanks to me."

"What do you mean?"

Exasperated, Brit snapped. "It means I took a bottle of painkillers into an oxy addict's house. He managed to resist the temptation to gobble them down, no thanks to his idiot girlfriend." Wydetta stared at her blankly, and Brit thought her mother simply wasn't getting it.

"*I'm* the idiot. It's me."

"You are not an idiot," her mother protested with gratifying swiftness.

"I sure felt like one last night."

Wydetta's jaw stiffened. "He brought you home last night because he blames you for his weakness?"

"Cash didn't bring me home. Jace Allen did."

"Jace Allen?" Wydetta repeated, clearly bewildered.

"Yes, Jace Allen. Not only is he Cash's business partner, but he's also his sponsor." Wydetta blinked uncomprehendingly. "For AA or NA or whatever they're in," she explained, irritated. "Jace had to drive me home, because I was stupid enough to bring prescription-grade painkillers into a former addict's house, and Cash was too…I don't know. Upset? Freaked out? Or maybe plain old pissed off at me to—"

"I wasn't pissed off," a gruff voice cut into her rant.

Brit and Wydetta found Cash standing in the shadowed wing of the stage, his arms braced over his chest and his chin tipped high.

"Cash—"

"I wasn't pissed off at you," he reiterated. "If I was pissed at anyone, I was pissed at myself." He jerked a nod in Wydetta's direction, then took a step closer to them. "And I belong to both AA and NA. And we have our own loose group at StarRise." He ran a comforting hand down the length of Brit's arm, then met Wydetta's gaze head-on. "We're all in recovery. We've all hit rock bottom, but we've all managed to rise up again," he added with a note of defiance.

Wydetta gave a stiff nod. "Commendable, but—"

"But you don't want Brit around all of that," he finished for her. "I know. I don't, either." He finally pivoted in her direction and his expression softened. "But she's a strong-minded woman with ideas of her own about what's good for her. I wonder where she gets it from?"

Wydetta gave an appreciative huff, then pivoted on her heel. "I'll give you two a couple minutes, but make it quick. We have people waiting," she reminded Brit.

Brit stiffened, then let it go with a sigh. The refrain was all too familiar. She'd had people waiting for her, depending on her, for as long as she could remember. She knew what her duties to those people were. The problem she was having was figuring out exactly what she owed herself.

Facing Cash, she tipped her head back to hold his gaze. "You haven't been answering my calls."

"I went to more than one meeting this morning," he explained. "I also went for a drive to clear the scent of burnt coffee from my head."

She placed both hands on his shoulders and searched every millimeter of his precious face. Despite the previous night's upset and a lack of sleep, he looked ten times better than the last time she'd seen him. Wetting her lips, she dropped her voice to a husky whisper. "Do I need to apologize again?"

He shook his head. "You don't have to apologize to me ever."

Lifting her hand to his face, she cupped his scruffy cheek in her palm. "You know I would never do anything to hurt you, right?" She smoothed the faint lines at the corners of his eyes with the tips of her fingers. "I'd rather die than hurt you."

"Shh."

He pulled her into a hard embrace, trapping her arm awkwardly between them. She didn't care. He was holding her again, and she was all he needed.

"Shush," he whispered into a kiss he trailed over her temple. He skimmed his hand over the purposefully messy top knot her hairstylist had constructed. "Don't be such a drama queen." His tone was teasing, but the delivery came out rough and rumbly.

"I can't help it." She shrugged as best she could. "I was born this way."

Cash chuckled and forced himself to loosen his hold on her. There were people all around them. Dozens of people. And they were all watching. Of course they were. Brittany was the star they all orbited. There was only so much they could do to keep busy until she took her place.

Pulling back, he glanced down. His eyebrows rose as he took in her stage ensemble. "Wow. I hope they used a lot of tape."

"Tape, crazy glue, Velcro, safety pins, and some kind of spray adhesive, I believe."

He once again thanked the good Lord he'd fallen out of the spotlight. Speaking of falls, he frowned down at the sneakers on her feet. "How's the knee? You're not dancing on it, are you?"

"I'm walking through the steps while everyone else dances around me," she assured him. "And it's fine. Much better. I should be good as new by the end of the week."

He captured both of her hands in his and drew them to his chest. "I want you to know one thing. You are never to blame for any questionable choices I may or may not make. They are my choices—good, bad, and ugly—and they are not on you."

"Oh, Cash—"

"No. That's it. My choices." He gave her hands a squeeze but didn't relinquish them. Glancing back over his shoulder at where the assembled crew waited, he added, "My weaknesses."

"You are not weak," she said through clenched teeth.

Her vehemence made him smile. He inclined his head to hide his pleasure. "I'm not, but I do *have* weaknesses. But knowing what they are allows me to face them from a position of strength."

"I love you so much."

The words tumbled from her glossed lips. His heart clenched and his stomach flipped. Part of him was afraid he'd never hear them again. She'd witnessed the monster inside him, and he'd spent the last twelve hours terrified she'd decide she had seen enough. But he couldn't come to her until he had his head on straight. And now, now she'd reassured him of her love. He could ask her for what he needed. For what they needed.

Pulling her hands to his lips, he brushed kisses of gratitude across her knuckles. "I love you," he said, his voice so low and gruff he almost didn't recognize it himself. "Would you do something for me?"

"Anything."

He smiled at her instant response. "Don't be so quick. You might not like it."

"I'll do anything," she repeated.

"Would you consider attending some Al-Anon or Nar-Anon meetings?"

"Nar-Anon?"

A tiny crease appeared between her brows, and he hated to be the one to put it there. Still, if they were going to be in this for real, she needed to know what she was up against, and know his management of his addictions had absolutely nothing to do with her actions or inaction.

"Nar-Anon is for the loved ones of people battling narcotics addiction," he explained.

The crease deepened. "You want me to go to meetings with you?"

Cash shook his head. "No, sugar. I want you to go to meetings without me. These sessions are so you can talk freely about the impact my issues can and will have on our lives and our relationship. It's a place for you," he said gently.

Brit clutched his fingers. "All I need is to be with you."

He shook his head. "No, sweetheart. You need to be able to talk with other people who understand."

"Understand what?"

Cash blew out a breath and cast about, looking for the answer among the rafters and the pulleys suspended above the stage. "Why we won't ever have wine at a dinner party, or a tub of beer at a cookout," he said, groping for what seemed like natural, easy social situations for most people. "Why approaching a bar at a wedding or whatever to get a glass of water is like swimming in a pool of sharks for me. How there will never be a time when I won't be wondering if I could have one pill to take the edge off the pain," he finished quietly.

Brit stared at him for so long a prickle of sweat tickled his hairline. At last, she nodded and said only, "Okay."

Her single word acquiescence startled a laugh out of him. "Okay?"

She bobbed her head again. "Okay. If that's what you need, okay."

Releasing her hands, he eyed her warily as he took a step back. "Whoa. So much easier than I expected." Squinting at her, he murmured. "Too easy. What's the catch?"

Brit shrugged, then hit him with one of those blinding smiles. "No catch. This is a relationship, right? Give and take. You have needs, I step up. I have needs, you're up to bat," she said a shade too smugly for his comfort.

"Why do I have the feeling I'm about to get *quid pro quo*'ed?"

She grinned and held up a single finger to signal to her mother she was on her way. "I have no idea what you mean."

"Bullcrap," he said as she backed away, her smile widening with each step.

"Look up those meetings for me, will ya?" she said with an airy wave. "Oh, and we need to get your tux cleaned. I'm thinking it's dusty."

"And here it comes," he muttered, planting his hands on his hips. "Why do I need my tux cleaned?"

"The HitMakers Awards are next week, remember?" She grinned, then blew him a kiss. "We all have needs, Cash, and I need an escort."

He shook his head as he watched her disappear into the pack of dancers. He was still shaking it when they spread out into formation with Brittany at the center and the instrumental playback from her hit "Gotcha" burst from the speakers.

"Ha!" He barked the laugh, but it was no match for the music. Crossing his arms again, he widened his stance and counted off the seconds until Wydetta approached.

He made it to thirty-seven.

"I'm fine," he said before she could start.

"Like I care about you," she retorted.

Cash laughed again, but this time it was genuine. Wagging his head in wonder, he glanced over at her. "You never change, do you?"

"Brittany will always be my first concern. Always," she repeated the last with a penetrating glare.

Never one to shrink from a confrontation with Wydetta Owens, he pivoted to square up with her. "Same here."

True to form, Wydetta stood toe-to-toe with him. Her stubborn defiance didn't surprise him, but what came out of her mouth next did.

"Then we're on the same page," she said stiffly.

Taken aback, Cash could only nod. "Yes. The same page."

She compressed her lips into a thin line, then nodded jerkily. "Fine. You'll need a tuxedo. Brit's performing your song at the HitMakers Awards, and I suppose she's going to want you there."

Cash chuckled and ran his hand over his rumpled hair. "We're way ahead of you, Wydetta. And I get the feeling Brittany's way ahead of us both, but I'm not so sure about the awards show. Those things are like quicksand..." he trailed off with a shake of his head.

"You have things you need from Brittany, and she had things she needs from you," Wydetta said without bothering to shift her gaze to him. "She chose you a long time ago. I think it might have been the first time she chose anything all for herself," she said musingly.

Cash stared at her, stunned by the admission. Her jaw tightened and he thought he might have caught a sheen of tears in her eyes, but she still didn't spare him a glance.

"I know you two butt heads a lot, but she still wants what you want, Wydetta." He paused long enough to let his meaning sink in. "And I'll never get in her way," he assured her. "I promise."

"Good." At last, she turned those laser-like blue eyes on him. "Now, you all you need to decide if you have the guts to choose her."

19

The dress rehearsal for the HitMakers Awards broadcast proved to be a total goat fuck. Brit crossed her arms over her chest and shifted her weight from one foot to the other. She'd done enough of these to know they were always chaotic, but today's pandemonium seemed to be particularly tedious.

She smoothed her palms over the gown she and her mother had picked out with the help of her local stylist. Their lunch together had been stilted at first. Between them lay a whole field of emotional landmines neither dared to trigger, so the conversation had been superficial, but cordial. They found themselves in closer accord when they stepped into the private dressing room containing a rainbow of sequined gowns in every style. They'd selected one for her to wear on the red carpet. It was short, and daring, and sure to please the palate of the ever-hungry paparazzi.

But this one… The moment she stepped into the dress she'd wear for her performance she knew it was the one. They both knew. And best of all, the stunningly romantic confection of silk and tulle was sure to tick all the boxes on her grandmother's list of appropriate attire.

Brit watched as the act scheduled to go on her screwed up again and again. Beside her, Dylan thrummed his fingers atop his guitar and grunted impatiently. Every noise he emitted made her more determined to keep the Ms. Congeniality smile she wore splashed across her face. There'd been rumblings about her and Cash in a couple of local gossip columns, but nothing about the rock through her window, proving her security was leakproof, if a bit lax in its coverage of her property. One of the national tabloids had printed a smaller speculative piece about her and Cash, but it was fairly harmless.

Rather than the perky pop hits she'd been cranking out lately, this time, she was singing a song that would stick with everyone listening. Not just because it had a catchy hook, or a memorable tune, but because she would be singing it with all her heart. Cash would be in the audience. He'd promised to attend, as long as he didn't have to walk the red carpet, and she'd jumped on the offer. Even with Dylan the guitarist on stage with her, she'd be singing their song for Cash, and they both knew it.

Dylan let out another huff of breath when the lead singer for Aces raised an apologetic hand in their direction.

Brit smiled back and waved, nudging Dylan with her elbow. "Cut it out," she hissed.

He growled. "They're messing up on purpose."

"What makes you say so? Why would they?"

Dylan shrugged. "Lots of reasons. More stage time, or attention from the producers, upsetting everyone else's game…" He glanced over at her.

"They're not upsetting my game," Brit responded without hesitation. She returned her focus to the band and its flamboyant lead singer. Aces was comprised of seasoned performers, but they'd only recently broken onto the charts. This was one of their first big appearances. "I figured they were nervous."

Dylan's reply was another snort. "Nervous." He gestured to the band hogging the stage. "They've been touring longer than you have."

"Yeah, but this is their first big televised show. It's a lot different than playing to an audience."

"There'll be an audience," Dylan reminded her.

"An audience of industry people, not fans."

"My point exactly." He narrowed his eyes at the man taking a spot behind the microphone stand. "I don't think they appreciate being your warm-up act."

Brittany snorted. "Warm-up act. Only in rehearsal. I'll be on stage before they are."

Dylan unfurled his lady-killer smile. It usually left every woman seated in the front row swooning, but had little effect on Brit.

"Doesn't matter. The way I see it, they're all warm-up acts for ours. Bet they see it the same way too."

Brit snorted herself and nudged him again with her elbow, but this time in a friendlier way. "The ego on you."

He cleared his throat, but said nothing more.

She glanced over and caught him rubbing his palms together nervously. "Stage fright got you too?"

He looked back at her, clearly surprised. "Ha."

"You look nervous," she commented, nodding to his hands.

Dylan immediately balled his fingers into fists and let his hands fall to his sides. "No, not nervous." He paused. "At least not about being on stage."

"What's bugging you?" She shifted to look him square in the eye. "You're usually the one calming me down and telling me to be patient."

Dylan darted a glance at the stage, then met her gaze. "You remember when we were kids and we used to dream about the day we'd get away from our parents' control?"

Brit's laugh was short and brittle. "You mean yesterday?"

He snickered. "Yeah, well, I got away from mine."

She didn't bite. Escaping parental control didn't count for much if you swapped one set of parents for another parent. "Okay, so you switched your momager for my momager. How is that better?" she asked dryly. "You feelin' all that freedom yet? The wind in your hair and all? Close your eyes, maybe if you try real hard."

"I want to talk to you about something," he said, lowering his voice and leaning in close to her ear. "Listen, if my album hits while we're out on this tour, I want to be able to… peel off. Go out on my own."

Brit cocked her head, genuine surprise and confusion furrowing her forehead as she stared at her old friend.

Friend.

What did it say about her, as a friend, if it never occurred to her Dylan's album might be a hit? She never considered he might be ready to strike out on his own? One night, she might look over to her left and not see him standing there. And taking him for granted all these years made her a pretty crappy friend, didn't it?

Brit blinked rapidly, hoping to hold the sudden rush of emotion she felt at bay. "No one will be happier for you than me." And she meant it. He'd been a friend for so long, she couldn't imagine them not being in each other's pockets. "And if it happens—*when* it happens," she corrected herself, "we will deal. Or, I will. And Wydetta." She gave him a wan smile. "I'll miss you like crazy, but I'll deal."

His eyes narrowed slightly as he searched her face. "Do you think you can get Cash to come out on the road with you?"

Brittany barked a laugh. "Oh, no." She wagged her head emphatically. "I've been told in no uncertain terms by the man himself I cannot have Cash Dorsett as my lead guitarist."

Dylan barked a disbelieving laugh. "Are you shitting me?"

Brit gave him a small, sad smile. "I shit thee not."

"Why? Is he nuts? This could be his chance to get back in the game," Dylan pointed out as if neither Brittany nor Cash had thought of the opportunity he was passing up.

"He doesn't want to play the game," Brittany explained with a shrug. "He says he's done chasing the spotlight."

"Is anyone ever done chasing the spotlight?"

Brittany patted Dylan's arm and gave a chuckle. "People like me and you? I doubt it. But guys like Cash have seen the other side of things. He has chosen a different path, and I support him like I support you."

Dylan fell quiet as Aces finally hit the last note of their performance on stage. "There you go," he murmured under his breath. "It's about time." He and Brit smiled and waved as the band exited the stage via the opposite wing and the techs scurried about to switch out equipment. He cast a smirk at Brit as she rolled her shoulders back. "Ready to go blow them off the stage?"

"I was ready thirty minutes ago," she answered, looking straight ahead at the mark she would hit the second the stage manager signaled. She wriggled the rhinestone-studded mic she held in her hand. "Now, I'm going to make them cry."

The production team ushered her straight from the red carpet to a dressing room backstage. Her wardrobe team helped her change from the slinky silver minidress she'd worn to walk the media gauntlet to the sparkling ice-blue ballgown she'd wear for her performance. The show played live on a large-screen television mounted on a wall. Between each award or performance, she'd glance up, hoping to catch a glimpse of Cash seated in the crowd.

She had no doubt he'd still be there. He'd never ditch her. He'd promised he'd be there, and he would be.

Brit only wanted to spot him so she could hold the image of him in her mind. If she knew where he was in the crowd, she could sing to him from the stage. Though, in her heart, she'd be singing *with* him.

"Ten minutes," a production assistant called to her as he rushed past the door.

Brit drew as deep a breath as her constrictive underpinnings would allow and pressed her hand to her hammering heart. It was always like this. Always had been. From the first time she'd shared the stage with her grandfather at the Opry. She'd never been able to step out in front of an audience without breaking out into a cold sweat. Truthfully, she didn't believe anyone did. A person would have to truly not care.

And she cared. Wydetta wasn't wrong about her ambition. This night would be the start of something big, and she wanted it as much as her mother wanted it for her. Cash was right. Sometimes the small things made all the big things happen. One simple shopping trip hadn't magically bridged the ever-growing gap between her and her mother, but the afternoon had been pleasant enough. It was a start. And now, this one performance could divide her entire career into before and after.

The moment the spotlight found her, her pulse slowed. Cash was out there, and that meant everything. He'd dipped the toe of his boot back into her world, even though it was the last place he wanted to be. But he was there. Watching her. Waiting for her. She drew a deep breath as Dylan picked out the opening notes, then parted her lips and spilled her aching heart out onto the stage.

A hush fell over the crowd.

Minutes later, she was engulfed again. The magical tidal wave of admiration and appreciation washed over her. Brittany squinted into the glaring stage lights, trying desperately to see the howling crowd beyond the halo. She knew there were many doubters out there, but they didn't matter. She knew she'd proved something to them tonight.

Brittany Owens wouldn't fade away like any other pop princess.

She was here to slay.

Waving her thanks, she squinted into the glaring lights. She had a vague recollection of where their seats were supposed to be located, but to be safe, she tossed kisses in every direction. She didn't want to miss him.

Curtseying gracefully, she clutched the microphone to her chest and gestured to Dylan, urging the crowd to give her partner his due. He beamed into the wave of applause.

"Thank you. Thank you so much," she said into the microphone. And with one last dip of her head, she glided toward the stagehand gesturing wildly for her to get off the stage.

Ten minutes later, her hair and makeup retouched, she'd been shoehorned back into the silver mini dress. A tuxedo-clad page led her down one of the aisles as the broadcast faded out to a commercial break. The house lights came up, and all around her the crowd hummed and buzzed. Snippets of conversation reached her ears, but they were moving at a brisk clip. Almost brisk enough for her to ignore the occasional snide comment as they bounced off of her back.

"So glad to see she's finally growing up."

"So much better than last time. I was afraid she was going run out here stark naked and screaming like a banshee."

"Well, she hasn't entirely mended her ways. I hear she's chasing after Cash Dorsett. Isn't he too old for a girl her age?"

Brittany scanned the seated crowd as the page slowed to a halt beside a row of stars decked out to the nines. A young woman with hair bleached nearly as white as Brit's sat in the aisle seat talking with her hands. The dirty-blond guitar god seated beside her appeared both trapped and mildly bemused by his seatmate.

As if sensing her presence, Cash looked up and grinned at her with such pleased deviltry, her breath caught in her chest.

Brit beamed at him as the page bent to murmur into the young woman's ear. The girl rose with a treacly sweet smile, showing off thousands of dollars' worth of orthodontia. "I'm such a huge fan," she gushed as she stepped into the aisle.

"Thank you. Thank you so much," Brit gushed right back at her. "And thanks for keeping this guy entertained." She touched Cash's shoulder, then let her hand slide down his arm as she claimed her seat.

Cash snorted as the seat warmer cooed in sympathy. Brit wagged her fingers as the page practically dragged the girl up the aisle. She sighed as she settled into her seat.

Maybe she had gone chasing after Cash Dorsett, but this time she caught him, and this time she was hanging onto him.

"Well? What did you think?" she asked breathlessly. "God, I wish it'd been you up there with me."

Cash took her hand and gave it a squeeze. "I *was* up there with you. You were playing my song."

"You know what I mean."

"I do, and we've been down this road too many times to keep having the same discussion over and over again."

Brit exhaled loudly and pressed her cheek to his shoulder. "I know, I know." She stroked the wool sleeve of his tuxedo jacket and let her fingers trail down the back of his hand until he captured them between his. "But I'm never going to get over wishing we could be together everywhere, all the time, and you can't make me."

Cash chuckled. "Fair enough." He leaned over and pressed a tender kiss to her forehead. "You are magnificent. Your voice... The song... You looked so beautiful standing there. You sang so... my heart about jumped out of my chest."

She started to lift her head, but he kept her in place. She subsided, but only because she could hear the raw emotion in his voice. "I sang every word of it to you."

"I know, darlin'. I know." He pressed another one of those clenched jaw kisses to her temple and squeezed her fingers tight. "We can talk more later. Let's get through this night. I'm feeling a bit like a monkey in the zoo."

Brittany glanced around, taking in the tight smiles and stiff nods from those around them. She saw the lead singer of Aces a couple rows back, a smirk torqueing his lips. Unlike the others around them, he didn't bother averting his gaze when Brit caught him. Instead, he stared back insolently.

Brit shifted in her seat until her ass was square on the cushion and her eyes were dead ahead, locked on the stage. "God, who are these people? Who do they think they are? Why do they think they can judge me or you or anything we do?"

Beside her, Cash let out a mirthless laugh. "I don't know. Most the time, gossip doesn't bother me, but it feels kind of ultra-concentrated tonight, doesn't it?"

Brit huffed. "New and improved disapproval. Now more powerful than ever," she said in a mocking tone.

"Screw them," Cash said decisively. "The song's gonna be a smash and they're all jealous. You're about to go out and take the world by storm, and it's eating them up."

She smiled at him. "I love the way you rationalize things."

"Hey, no one has better rationalization skills than a recovering addict," he said dryly. "I can justify just about anything."

Wanting to lighten the mood, Brit pulled back enough to look him in the eye. "Want to try to justify why Blondie there was sitting so close to you?"

His grin widened by a mile. "You mean Steffi with two Fs?"

Brittany blinked. "Her name is actually Steffi with two Fs?"

He fixed her with a blank stare. "Your name is actually Brittany with two Ts."

She opened her mouth to spout off, but the house lights lowered again, and the cameras came back on. As the host ran through a series of jokes that fell flat, Cash leaned closer to her. "Stephanie is a Delta Sigma whatever at Vanderbilt," he reported. "She's majoring in early childhood education and hopes to be a kindergarten teacher."

Hot flames of jealousy hooked through Brit's body. She hadn't attended a traditional kindergarten, so she had no idea what a kindergarten teacher actually did, but she was pretty sure it involved a lot of crayons and finger painting. Jealousy spiked inside her. She would've loved to color with crayons and fingerprint finger paint all day when she was five or six.

Instead, she'd gotten voice lessons, dance lessons, and tutoring on the side by a dry old woman who seemed to think advancing her reading skills was more important than any form of artistic expression. Clamping her lips together, she swallowed hard as the next set of award presenters walked onto the stage. "Good for her."

Cash squeezed her hand again. "She seemed like a nice girl. If I were into younger women, I might've been interested."

He let out a loud "Oof!" as her elbow connected with his ribs, but it ended on a laugh.

Brit gave him the side eye as he covered his mouth with his hand. His shoulders shook with laughter as the names of the artists nominated for best rock album were read off.

"Stop it," she hissed.

"You started it."

She stifled a laugh of her own and screwed up all of her strength to shoot him a disapproving glare. "Act your age."

The admonishment only made Cash laugh harder.

"She had no clue who I was."

She glanced at him. "Was that good or bad?"

"Good, sweetheart." He lifted her hand to his lips and kissed her knuckles. "Very, very good."

"You're a perverse man."

"And don't you forget it."

On stage the envelope was opened and the name of the winner was almost lost in a roar of approval. Almost, but not quite. An even louder cheer rose up from behind them. Brittany swiveled to see the members of Aces rising from their seats and entering the aisle.

She growled low in her throat but fixed a smile on her face and applauded dutifully as the band made their way to the stage. "Ugh, I hate these guys."

Beside her, Cash's laughter died. He studied her, his face creased with concern. "You do? Why? Do you even know them?"

Brittany shrugged. "No. They were kind of jerks during rehearsal."

Cash sat up straighter. "Jerks to you?"

Warmed by the way he bristled on her behalf, but anxious to quell the surge of machismo obviously rushing through him, Brit reached over and patted his leg. "Jerks in general. You know the type. Stage hogs. Demanding. Disrespectful of other people's time."

She felt the tension seep out of Cash. "Oh, *those* guys."

"Exactly," she replied, tactfully ignoring the fact they both knew Cash had been one of *those* guys once upon a time.

He glanced over at her and heaved a sigh. "How much longer?"

"About an hour." She winced when she saw him grimace in distaste. Grasping his arm, she leaned in close to whisper in his ear. "It means everything to have you here. Thank you."

Cash kissed her gently on the lips while absolutely no one was paying attention to them. "You know I'd do anything for you. I can only hope you don't abuse the power you have over me."

His somber expression and sober words only made her laugh out loud. She pecked another kiss to his lips and sat back in her chair to watch the jackass who'd annoyed her earlier in the day accept his award. "Too late. You know I'm going to every chance I get."

20

He shouldn't be there. He knew he shouldn't be there. But there he was.

The after-party was crowded and hot, and the only thing he wanted to do was go home and peel Brit out of the tinfoil dress she was wearing. Sadly, it didn't look like leaving was going to be an option any time soon. Parked in a dark corner of the swanky penthouse loft the show's producers had secured for the after-party—galaxies away from the bar—Cash watched as Brittany and Wydetta worked the room.

Their gambit was fascinating. They each started from opposite corners but gravitated toward each other like planets in orbit.

"Here you are, mate," James Paulson said with a tad too much jocularity. "I figured you'd be hiding out in some dark corner."

"There was a time when I found dark corners for entirely different reasons," Cash said, pulling a face. He started to wave off the tall tumbler James thrust in his direction, but decided it was easier to acquiesce than to explain. He took the glass, but didn't even give the contents a sniff.

"Didn't we all." Without waiting for an invitation, James took the seat next to him and tugged at the end of his bowtie until it unraveled. "I never could stand these things." He waved a languid hand at the packed room. "You would think after all these years I would, but I never understood why people enjoyed getting trussed up like a Christmas goose."

"Yeah, not exactly my scene, either," Cash commiserated. "I mean, it's nice to see Brittany dressed in something other than jeans and a sweatshirt, but I don't envy her all the prep time it took."

James chuckled. "Oh, I know. I was kicked out of the house at ten o'clock this morning. Can you even imagine needing seven hours to get ready to put on a dress and walk out the door?"

Cash gave him a wry smile. "We both know it's more involved than putting on a dress and walking out the door."

"Makes you glad to be a bloke." He inclined his head in the direction of the crowd. "Look at the two of them. Cut from the exact same cloth, but when they get within two feet of each other, they repel like magnets."

"They've always been touchy about each other," Cash observed. "At least, as long as I've known them."

James nodded to the glass in Cash's hand. "Go ahead, by the way. It's good old-fashioned water dressed up to look like a gin and tonic."

Surprised and relieved, Cash lifted the glass and gave the drink a cautious sniff. All he caught was the scent of fresh lime. James chortled, then lifted his own glass in a toast. "Hardly anyone I know drinks anymore. Rock 'n' roll has become quite boring, at least for my generation." He took a sip of his drink and sighed. "I'm told it doesn't mix with all the supposedly legal medications we're all on."

Cash didn't know what to say, so he gave a knowing "Ah." He didn't feel like pointing out the pain meds he'd been hooked on were also considered legal.

James took another drink, then set the glass on the small table in front of them. "Frankly, it's the illegal drugs I miss more. Sort of. You know. Back in the good days. But those ended too. With far too many lessons learned, you know what I'm saying?"

"I know exactly what you're saying," Cash answered without missing a beat.

"I have to say, it takes some of the fun out of being a rocker." He paused as if a career change was under serious consideration. "I guess there are other compensations. Money. Fame." He rolled his glass between his palms. "Then there are always the pretty girls," he added, nodding to Wydetta.

Cash couldn't resist probing. "The two of you seem pretty…close."

James nodded. "As close as one gets to a porcupine."

Cash laughed. He'd never heard such a succinct, yet dead-on

description of Wydetta Owens. He raised an inquiring eyebrow. "Do you like your women difficult in general?"

The older man brushed the question off with a laugh. "No. Not as a rule. My late wife was a lovely girl. Sweet, understanding…a real pal, a partner in her own way."

"I sense a 'but' in there somewhere."

James gave his head a mystified shake, then shrugged. "I can't begin to explain it, but something about Wydetta's stubbornness, her intransigence, her downright mulish attitude…it gets me all revved up." He leaned back in the chair and draped a nonchalant arm over the empty seat beside him. "I guess I've developed a masochistic streak in my old age."

"Or maybe you've had simple and easy, and now you'd like something more challenging," Cash suggested.

"Possibly," James conceded. "She certainly is a challenge."

James craned his neck and scanned the crowd. His snort caught Cash's attention. Wydetta had a short, paunchy man who looked vaguely familiar trapped against the corner of one of the bars and apparently was giving him a rather large chunk of her mind.

James chuckled, then took a sip of his drink. "Don't envy him."

"No, me neither."

The two of them sat in companionable silence for a short time, but Wydetta's conversation did not appear to be congenial. Cash glanced over at James and saw the older man's forehead crease with worry.

"They don't look too friendly," Cash observed.

"No." James rubbed his hand across his mouth as if pondering what to do.

Cash understood his predicament exactly. The urge to protect Brittany from anyone who might wish her ill surged inside him any time he heard of a perceived threat. Though it was hard for him to imagine Wydetta needing protection from anyone, Cash could appreciate James feeling the same urge.

"Do you think you should—"

James barked a laugh. "Do I think I should mind my own bloody business? Of course I should." He pressed his knuckles against the table and rose from the chair. "But I'm going to go over there and act the fool anyway."

Cash chuckled, then set his drink aside and stood too. When

James dart a confused look at him, he shrugged. "I'll be your wingman."

James looked pleased by the offer. Rubbing his palms together, he nodded. "Good. Right. Excellent." He clapped Cash on the back hard. "I might be taller than him, but I think he's about twenty years younger than me."

Cash nodded his understanding. "We can split the difference between the two of us. The question is, who's going to protect us from Wydetta?"

James guffawed as the two of them stepped away from the table. "Oh, son, I don't think there's any force of nature strong enough to protect us from her wrath."

But the two men got no further. Wydetta peeled off from the conversation she'd been having and stalked across the room. They stood watching as she plowed through the crowd like one of those ice cutters, her jaw set and her eyes locked on her destination.

Cash grabbed James's arm to slow him. "Whoa. Whoa. Course change."

James pivoted in the direction Wydetta was heading and scanned the crowd. "She looks like she's about to blow something or someone to smithereens."

"Best to stay out of the line of fire." Cash lowered his hand to his side, curling his fingers into a loose fist.

The two men looked on as Wydetta approached Dylan Carson.

"Huh," Cash grunted.

"Hmm," James concurred.

She gave the people Dylan had been speaking with a tight smile, then grabbed her client's arm and dragged him away.

Cash glanced over at James. "Think you've been replaced?"

James laughed derisively. "By a yappy pup like him? Not likely." He pursed his lips. "Maybe he's being replaced with you."

Cash couldn't help but chortle. "Not a chance." He admired James for many things, but his healthy ego and unapologetic tenacity were moving up the list. "You know, you're pretty sure of yourself for a man who's not at all sure about his woman."

James pinned him with a knowing glance. "I'm sure enough about her. She's the one who isn't convinced. Yet." He nodded to where Dylan and Wydetta stood speaking in the shadows. "Besides, nothing in the way they're standing screams seduction to me."

"No, I'm pretty sure you're reading things right," Cash agreed. "Should we go stick our noses in where they don't belong?"

James patted his back again, but this time with slightly less force. "Let's hang back for a second and see how the conversation plays out. The kid has to know he's overmatched, and I'd hate to get scolded for no good reason."

The two men reclaimed their seats and their drinks. Cash scanned the crowd until he found the silver sparkle of Brittany. For once, he was glad to be loved by a girl who wore her heart on her sleeve. He worried constantly about doing something to break her beautiful heart, but he never had to worry about whether her love belonged to him. Or whether she belonged *with* him. Not anymore.

He didn't envy James and the work cut out for him with Wydetta. Brittany was independent and stubborn—those traits she came by honestly—but she wasn't hard to read. She believed in their destiny. The realization of what a precious gift her unflagging confidence in them was struck him hard.

"And we're off," James announced, jolting Cash from his thoughts.

Cash looked up to see Dylan storming through the crowd, his face dark and thunderous. "Well, now, everybody seems to be pissed off tonight," he commented, sitting forward in his seat.

The two men followed Dylan's movement into the crowd. Cash knew when the other man spotted Brittany, because he stopped, stiffened, then homed in on her like a guided missile. Cash was on his feet in a flash, every nerve in his body on high alert. The quiver in his gut told him something bad was about to happen. Something involving Brit, and there was no way he was going to let anything bad go down without throwing himself bodily in front of her.

He glanced back to find James hot on his heels. The older man shrugged. "Wingman works both ways."

Cash nodded and continued his pursuit. Unfortunately, the crowd had swallowed them up. He searched and searched for the flash of silver sparkle he used as a beacon but came up empty. Halfway across the room, he gave up his polite excuses and started elbowing people out of the way, earning more than a few disgruntled comments and glares.

His breath came fast and ragged. Behind him, he thought he heard James mention something about an irritable bowel, but the music was too loud, and it was hard to hear over the throb of his pulse in his ears.

When they reached the far end of the room without finding her, he whirled to look at James. "Where could they have gone?"

James shrugged and scanned the room. "Out the exit, or maybe the restrooms," he said, nodding to each of the marked doors. "I'll shout into the loos, you check the exit."

Cash nodded once, then headed for the door with the exit sign suspended above it. He pushed through only to find it led into a concrete stairwell. He glanced up, then down, trying to remember the exterior of the building where the limo had dropped them but coming up blank. All he'd been able to recall was Brittany singing to him, smiling at him, rubbing her long bare leg against his as they sat through the excruciating tedium of an award ceremony.

"Let me go," an agitated female voice drifted up from the bottom of the stairwell. "Dyl, you're hurting me."

The last bit was all Cash needed to get his ass in gear. He flew down the stairs, jumping from landing to landing until he spotted Dylan and Brittany standing toe-to-toe at the bottom of the stairwell.

"Hurting you? Well, you're hurting me," Dylan spat the words at Brittany. He gripped her upper arms tighter and gave her a none-too-gentle shake. "How could you do this to me? You know this is my time."

"What's your problem?" she cried.

"What the fuck?" Cash shouted, rumbling down the steps.

"Cash—" Brittany began, but Dylan cut her off.

"This is none of your business," Dylan shouted. "Mind your own business and stop fucking with my life."

Cash blinked, taken aback by the younger man's harsh tone. "Fucking with your life? How have I fucked with your life?"

Dylan waved a dismissive arm at him. "Get out. Leave us alone. This is between me and Brit."

"The hell I'll leave you alone with her," Cash replied.

"What's between you and me?" Brittany asked at the same time. "I don't understand what's going on. I didn't do anything to you."

"Of course you didn't, you had your mommy do it," he snapped. "You play dumb while she does your dirty work," Dylan shouted, spittle flying from his mouth. "You don't care about anything other than yourself and your career. And this asshole," he added, gesturing to Cash. "You come one step closer, and I'll shove her down the next flight."

"Now, wait a minute—" Cash growled, eyeing the long sweep of the concrete stairwell.

But Brittany cut them off. "What dirty work?" she demanded. "How can you say I've been anything but supportive to you? I've brought you along with me the whole way. You have a new album—"

Dylan released one of her arms and stepped back, a sneer curling his lip. "Brought me along?" His voice rose in anger on the last word. Cash pressed a hand to his own temple in a lame attempt to calm the roaring there. "You can't bring me along, Brittany," Dylan insisted. "We started in the same place."

True, they started in the same place, but Brittany's star rose, and Dylan's faded until he became the man at the edge of the spotlight. For a second, Cash felt bad for the kid. He knew what it was like to watch everybody else get exactly what you'd always dreamed of having. But he wasn't overly sympathetic. If he didn't take his hand off Brittany this very second, Cash was going to break the thing clean off.

Unable to simply stand by, he approached with caution. He stepped down one step, then another, and when Dylan didn't make any more aggressive moves, he felt more confident in pressing his case.

"He started in the same place, but you've outpaced him now." He eyed Dylan, gauging the other man's reaction as he approached. "That's the problem, isn't it?"

Dylan must've tightened his grip because Brittany yelped.

"I don't get why you're doing this," Brit's voice quavered but she held up a hand to stay Cash and kept her gaze steady on Dylan. "We're a team."

He scoffed. "A team. Yeah, we will be from here on out. I've got no chance of stepping out from behind you now, do I?"

"What are you talking about? We agreed. When your album takes off—"

"The album has been shelved," Dylan shouted. His voice echoed off the cinderblock walls of the stairwell. "You had them do it. You couldn't let me have—"

"No, I didn't do anything." The vehemence of her denial made her teeter on her toothpick heels.

Cash could see the man's finger digging into the tender flesh of Brittany's upper arm. "I'm telling you, you'd better let her go right now,"

"And I told you to mind your own business," Dylan said through gritted teeth.

"Brittany *is* my business," Cash snapped back. "And if you don't release her this minute, you're going to be a one-handed guitarist." He paused for emphasis. "Which might be interesting, if not groundbreaking. Maybe the novelty will make you as famous as she is. For about fifteen minutes."

He said the last part with injurious deliberation, hell-bent on capturing Dylan's full attention.

"Because you want to be the famous one, right? You want to be the one in the spotlight. And now, you think you can blame Brit for your inability to become something special."

It worked. Dylan released Brittany so abruptly, she stumbled back on her stiletto heels and fell into the painted concrete block wall.

He whirled on Cash. "What the hell would you know? You blew it all up with booze and pills. I'd never be so stupid."

Cash nodded and tucked his hands into the pockets of his tuxedo pants as if he wasn't currently consumed by the urge to tear this kid limb from limb.

"You're right, I was a complete bonehead," he said in a mocking tone. "The difference is, I learned my lesson. I got better. I chose different goals rather than chasing the old one. I choose what makes me happy." He closed the distance between them, placing his body between Dylan and Brit. "But you don't find me roughing up women in stairwells."

Brittany's head snapped back when she heard Cash's low, taunting words. Roughing up women. Like she was some helpless little girl who couldn't take care of herself. And though she knew it wasn't quite rational, it was easier to be pissed at what he was saying than to make sense of what Dylan was doing to her.

She would have said she wasn't the type of woman who allowed herself to be dragged around and "roughed up," and Cash damn well knew it. But that was exactly what one of her oldest friends had just done. If it had been anyone other than Dylan giving her the strong arm, she would have planted a knee firmly in the guy's groin. But this was Dylan. Her friend. Her lead guitarist. The guy who always stood by her side.

Or was it that he'd been standing in her blind spot all these years and she never realized?

Maybe she had. Perhaps she simply didn't want to have to face the pain of telling a friend she simply didn't think he had what it took to make the leap. There was a big difference between being a success and being a star. People often confused the two. A person with talent, drive, and determination could become a success, but only a few could be a star.

Still, some people would never understand the caprice of fame. They shot for the stars time and again, only to end up burning out too soon. She blinked as it occurred to her Cash had done that very thing. And it would happen to Dylan too. Brit believed the spotlight chose who it wanted, not who wanted it the most.

She didn't want to see another friend, another man she cared about, flame out in the name of stardom.

Cash.

God, she loved him, but she never wanted to clobber any man the way she wanted to brain him right now. He wanted to fly in there on his winged white horse and play the savior? Well, she had news for him. She might not have had the most conventional childhood, she may have been a tad too sheltered as an adult, but she sure as shit wasn't anyone's idea of a damsel in distress.

"Okay, okay," Brit shouted, her equilibrium restored along with her balance. "Stop with the macho posturing." She placed a hand on Cash's arm and tried to push him aside, but he wasn't budging. "Stop," she barked.

He twisted to glare at her, and she took the opening. Stepping to the side, she peered around him at Dylan. "Listen, I don't know what the issue is with your album release, but I can promise you I had nothing to do with the label postponing your launch."

"I trusted you."

Dylan hurled the words at her. Brit could almost see them flying through the tension-thickened air, twirling end over end like knives. But when they hit, they didn't pierce her. They were lies. He was lying to her. She felt it in her bones, and the realization nearly broke her heart. Dylan didn't trust her. He never had. He'd stuck close to her year after year, hoping some of the stardust she'd been born to would rub off on him. He wanted to be able to use her name, her connections, and sneak through the secret portal she'd built from television to recording star.

"No. You didn't."

The words came out in a whisper, but Dylan jerked back as if she'd slapped him. Staring into his blazing eyes stirred a sadness in her. She felt a loss so profound it made every breath she took feel like it was weighted with lead. She stepped back, letting Cash provide the human shield he so desperately wanted to give her. It was too bad he couldn't shield her from the truth.

"You wanted to use me. I was your springboard. You know it, and I know it…"

She trailed off as a clatter of footsteps echoed through the empty chamber. She looked up in time to see Wydetta and James draw to a halt on the landing above, their eyes wide and wary as they took in the tableau. Brit shook her head fast and hard. Then relief flooded through her when she locked eyes with Wydetta. The worry in her eyes was far more mama than manager. And a woman was never too old to need her mama nearby when things got scary.

Emboldened by Wydetta's presence, she turned on Dylan. "Hell, you even hired my mom as your manager." She smacked her forehead with the heel of her hand. "God, why couldn't I see it?"

Cash stared at her, his feet planted wide and his fists raised and ready for any advance Dylan might make. "Hey, don't beat yourself—"

"Stop," she snapped, tired of the men surrounding her trying to tell her who she was, or what shoe should feel. "Stop. You don't get to tell me what to do or how to feel."

"Brittany," Wydetta began, her voice so calm and reasonable, she might have been talking to a stranger. "We've alerted security—"

"Mama, please," Brit shouted.

Wydetta abruptly stopped talking.

Frustrated, Brittany threw her hands up. "Stop. All of you stop." She swiveled from one stunned face to another. "I'm not your prize pony," she said, glaring at her mother. She leveled an icy blue gaze on Dylan. "And I am not your cash cow."

Her voice trembled on the word "cash," but she plowed ahead, needing to be certain all the people in her life heard her loud and clear. When the man she loved simply stared at her, his jaw tight with anticipation, she made certain she didn't disappoint her audience.

"And you," she breathed.

"Me." Cash lifted his chin as if preparing for a blow. "What did I do?"

"I love you, and I know you love me, but I am not some helpless kitten you took in from the cold. Stop trying to coddle me."

"I'm not trying to coddle you. I'm trying to make sure you're safe," he retorted tautly.

There was a loud click and a thunk, then the heavy metal door on the ground level swung open. Brittany saw Roger framed in the doorway, his face creased with concern, but his mouth closed up tight. Thank God. He nodded at the odd assemblage as if he broke up fights in the stairwells of strange buildings every night, then asked, "You ready?"

She darted a glance from Dylan to Cash, then finally looked up at her mother. Wydetta inclined her head in the barest of nods, and Brittany seized the lifeline her mom had thrown her. She needed to get out of there. She didn't want to say something she'd regret. To Dylan. To Cash. To any of them. Because, though she'd found her voice at long last, right now, she could only see herself using it to do some damage.

Pivoting on her heel, she met Rog's steady gaze and nodded. "Yep. I'm ready," she answered.

Before anyone could stop her, she rushed down the steps, followed him through the kitchen access door, then out into the night.

She made it three steps toward the waiting town car when she halted in her tracks. Roger stopped too, his expression questioning as he gestured for her to head toward the car.

"No. I can't do this. I can't walk away and let other people fight my battles for me." She dug in her heels when he continued to pull on her arm.

"Now, Miss Brittany," Roger began.

"No, Rog, this is exactly what I've been talking about. I can't let the so-called grown-ups make all the decisions for me. People tell me what songs I ought to sing, where to play on tour, what I need to wear, who I should love… This is my career, my life. I have to start taking control of it."

Roger caught her by the elbow in a firm grip. "Don't go back in there."

Annoyed, she glanced down at his hand pointedly, then up into his worry-worn face. "Didn't you hear me? I can't leave them to sort out my entire life for me. I get to have some say."

Roger's grip tightened, and he dug in his heels, halting any motion she may have made toward the door. "You're not thinking straight."

This time she whirled to face him head-on. "Not thinking straight?" she asked, incredulous. "How can you say that? You know I've been trying to get more control over what I have going here." She flung a hand toward the car. "What do you hear me talking about every day as we drive home?"

His fingers tightened to the point where she let out a yelp. Roger took advantage of her surprise and yanked her toward the car.

She stumble-stepped after him. "Roger, stop. What the hell are you doing?"

"You want to know what I hear you talk about every day?" he demanded, his voice harsh. "I hear you talk about that no-good Cash Dorsett. You act like the man hung the goddamn moon." Propelling her forward, he yanked on the door handle and made to shove her inside. "He's no good for you. I've told you. Your granddaddy's told you. Your mama told you years ago. Everybody's told you, but you won't listen."

Brit braced her hand on the doorframe, resisting his efforts to shove her bodily into the backseat of the car. "What are you talking about? None of this is Cash's fault. Cash has nothing to do with this," she argued. "Why are you doing this? Stop pushing me!"

The crash bar on the metal exit door went off with a bang, startling them both. Roger and Brit swung around in unison. Two kitchen workers stepping from the bright light, griping loudly as they each hauled stuffed trash bags toward a fenced enclosure behind the club.

Brittany was about to call out to them when the door swung open again, and a shadow so familiar it made her chest ache stood silhouetted by the bright fluorescents beyond. Her heart leapt into her throat. She wanted to call out for Cash's help, but didn't. For all she knew, the kitchen crew were catching this whole thing on their cell phones. Cash had been right to be wary. The last thing he needed was to get pulled deeper into the murky swamp her life was becoming.

The whole night was taking on a surreal quality. First Dylan's hurtful words, now Roger acting like a bully. And everyone blaming everything on Cash, who hadn't done anything but love her. Even though he didn't want to. It seemed everyone around her wanted to push or shove her one direction or another and she was getting fed up.

But she needed to do it on her own. No help from Cash, or her mother, or even James Paulson. No white knights riding to her rescue.

Straightening her arm to provide even more resistance to Roger's efforts, she twisted her body to look up into the face of the man she'd trusted most of her life. "Roger, I'm not a child. You can't just pick me up and haul me off the playground when I do something you don't like."

Roger grappled with the hand braced against the car, trying to break her hold so he could fold her into the seat. "You're acting like a child," he grumbled.

His accusation pissed her off. Jamming her elbow into his ribs as hard as she could, Brittany threw in a couple of the jujitsu-inspired dance moves she'd learned for the new tour. But her resistance efforts only seemed to crank Roger's determination up a notch.

"Stop it," she howled, flailing wildly.

"No," he grunted.

Fed up, she threw a punch. She balled up her fist like her granddad had taught her and socked him good. Pain screeched up her arm when her knuckles connected with Roger's granite jaw. She cried out but held her ground. Roger stumbled backwards, cussing under his breath. "Goddammit, Brittany, I'm tired of playing this game. Now, get in the car."

Brit stumbled back out of the open car door, raising both hands to ward off Cash in one direction and Roger in the other. Out of the corner of her eye, she saw the kitchen workers returning from the dumpsters. Their steps slowed as the scene in the alley caught their attention.

"You come near me again, and I'll scream," she warned Roger in a low voice. When Cash moved from the doorway, she waved him off again. "I'll scream so loud and so long I won't have a voice left for anybody to fight over. This is my life. Mine! I don't know what my granddad told you when he asked you to take care of me, but I'm pretty sure kidnapping wasn't on the list."

Roger rubbed his jaw. "He told me to keep you safe at all costs, and I'm going to do what I have to do."

"Brittany," Cash called.

She twisted to glare at Roger. "I don't need you to keep me safe. And I don't need you to, either," she added, gesturing toward Cash.

Two more figures appeared in the open kitchen doorway. One tall, one small, and both ready to wade in. But there was only one she wanted. Only one she needed. Lifting her chin, she locked eyes with Wydetta as her mother stepped from the kitchen out into the narrow back alley.

"What's going on here?" Wydetta demanded.

"I got a whole lot of rescuers, and they're all sure they know the best way to keep me safe," Brit said, her voice trembling with emotion and exhaustion. "But I don't need them. Do I?" The pause lasted a beat too long, so she asked again. "Do I, Mama?"

Wydetta hesitated briefly, then came forward, her hand outstretched. "No, baby, you don't."

With her mother's hand clasped in hers, Brit took in the rag-tag group of men trying to run her life. "I don't need any of y'all," she said, her voice harsh and raspy.

Her mother murmured an approving "There's my girl." She bumped the back door closed with her hip, then yanked open the passenger door gesturing for Brit to get in. "I know you can take care of yourself, but baby, I'm so tired and these shoes are killing me. What do you say we go home and get in our stretchy pants?"

Brit gave a mute nod, and without another glance at the cluster of men standing nearby, Wydetta trotted to the driver's side and slid behind the wheel as Brit claimed the passenger seat. No sooner had the door closed than the two of them peeled out and sped into the Nashville night.

21

Cash stood and watched as Wydetta hooked a sharp right at the end of the alleyway and floored it. Still stunned by the exploits of the last half hour, he searched the faces of the other men. "What the hell just happened here?"

The question was rhetorical, but, of course, James answered. "We got ditched," he said, sounding impressed. "I can't remember the last time a girl ditched me."

Cash snorted and gestured to the two gentlemen in their white kitchen coats. "Show's over, move it along."

Chattering excitedly to themselves, they walked back into the kitchen gesturing broadly as they recounted the drama of the past few minutes. Cash waited until the kitchen door closed behind them, then faced off with Roger. "What the hell, man?"

Roger had the grace to look sheepish as he shrugged, then he averted his gaze. Seemingly fixated on the fenced-in dumpsters, he said, "We thought it would be a good idea to scare her a little. She's way too casual about her own safety."

"We?" James piped up.

"Scare her?" Cash asked at the same time. "You were trying to shove her into the back of a car."

Roger whirled on him. "I was a damn sight gentler on her than anybody else would've been. I'd never hurt her."

"I don't know if you noticed this, but you just did," Cash replied fiercely.

James nodded and shoved his hands into the pockets of his tuxedo pants. "I'm afraid he's right, mate. You might not have injured her to badly in a physical way, but whenever somebody you think you can trust turns out to be someone you can't, it's a bitter pill to swallow."

"Brittany doesn't need to be afraid of me," Roger spat. "She needs to worry about this one." He jabbed a shaking finger in Cash's direction. "He's the one who's going to hurt her. He's the one who let her down."

"I haven't let her down," Cash said, instantly defensive.

"Lately." Roger crossed his arms over his chest stared in unspoken challenge. "I was there. At the house on her birthday. I saw her run off crying because of you."

Unable to contain it any longer, Cash threw his arms up in frustration. "Oh, for Christ's sake, it was five years ago. She's forgiven me. Why can't the rest of the world?"

"One can't help but be protective of the people one loves," James said primly.

"But I love her too," Cash exploded. "I loved her then, and I love her now. I did what I thought was right at the time. I think we can all agree it was the right thing to do for Brittany. Was I supposed to take her down with me? She was barely more than a girl."

"You were supposed to have sense enough to leave her alone, then and now," Roger insisted. "You were supposed to stay away from her. Why couldn't you have gone for Wydetta? She's closer to your age. Brittany was far too young for you. Still is."

"Now, wait a second—" James tried to interject, but Cash cut his protest off with a wave.

"I know, but she doesn't care. And I love her enough to give her whatever it is she wants." He jabbed a finger into his chest and glared at the two other men. "She says she wants me."

"You'll break her heart again." Roger stood his ground, unmoved by Cash's argument.

A strange silence fell among the men. They stood there, glances bouncing off one another as distant traffic flowed past on the streets behind the building. They were all right. And they were all wrong. Wrong to be making assumptions about what Brittany wanted, or needed, or what was best for her. Brit had plenty of mind of her own and could make this decision as she saw fit.

Running his hand through his hair, Cash muttered, "I'm done talking about this. It's none of your business."

He was about to head for the mouth of the alleyway when he heard James ask, "Did you throw the rock through her window? Was making her feel unsafe in her own home part of the 'let's scare her' plan?"

Something uncertain flickered across Roger's face. He spoke too quickly. "What? No."

The denial fell flat. Cash zoomed in on the older man. "You didn't throw it?" When Roger hesitated, he pressed. "Did you arrange for somebody to throw the rock through the window?" he asked, wording the question carefully.

"We only… She wasn't taking things seriously."

James jumped into the fray. "She wasn't taking it seriously because she didn't know what was happening. Her mother was trying to shield her. But I can assure you Wydetta took those threats seriously." He crossed his arms over his chest and braced his feet wide. "I know this, because I'm the one who got to listen to her worries. I got to feel her fret and toss and turn all night wondering how she was going to keep her child safe."

Roger seemed to crumple in on himself as he realized he had two men who felt they had justification enough to tear him to pieces standing in front of him. Cash might have felt sorry for him if it weren't for the belligerent gleam in the older man's eye and the arrogant lift of his chin.

"We did what we thought was best." Roger offered the tidbit of explanation as if they deserved no more. As if his words, and his thoughts, should be enough for them.

They weren't.

"'We'?" James drawled.

"I don't suppose I need to guess who the other part of 'we' is in this situation," Cash said coolly. James glanced over at him questioningly, and he tossed off a shrug. "Merle. This jackass and Merle have engineered this whole thing to try to control Brittany and, by association, Wydetta too."

James's eyes widened as he absorbed the information. "You're shining me on."

"I shine thee not," Cash responded, swiping one of Brit's favorite catchphrases and modifying it to suit.

James gaped at him, then snapped his jaw shut, his eyes wide with wonder. "It's bloody Shakespearean."

"It's bloody Nashville," Cash mumbled. Refocusing on Roger, he asked, "What's your hard-on with me, anyway? I haven't been down any road you haven't ridden up and down at least twice. How come you're good enough to spend time with her, but I'm not?"

"I'm not looking to spend time with her in a *sexual* way," Roger said derisively. "I'm not a dirty old man. Unlike some people."

"Christ, I'm not even forty yet," Cash complained.

"And she's not even twenty-five," Roger said acidly.

Cash narrowed his eyes, searching Roger's. "I think her age is a convenient excuse for you. Keeps you from being a hypocrite."

Roger immediately bowed up, his spine straightening and his hands curling into fists. "What the hell are you saying?"

"This has nothing to do with my age, or what Brittany wants. It has everything to do with my past, and whether you think it might come back to haunt me." He lifted his chin, meeting Roger's belligerence with some of his own. "It won't."

"You can't know how you'll be," Roger snapped. "One day at a time. That's all you can promise her."

Cash nodded. "But I can offer her all my days, one after another. And if she wants them, they're hers."

James stepped forward, running his hand through his shaggy mop of hair. "You know what, gents? This is getting pretty wearying." He looked at Cash. "You're too old for her, and you have a sordid past. If you and Brittany both think you can get past the difference in your ages, the challenge is yours and no one else's."

Then, he zoomed in on Roger. "And you? You and Merle are two ornery old men with too much time on your hands and too much ego. Now, I know I'm old too, but the difference between you and me is I got old and realized I had no control over life. And I accepted it," he added with a pointed stare. "I hope you and your cohort can do the same one day." He stepped closer to Roger. "But in the meantime, this is for Wydetta."

And then, rock legend Sir James Paulson balled up his fist and planted it squarely in Brittany Owens's chauffeur's face.

A lightning storm of flashbulbs lit up the night. All three men glared at the back of the nightclub. The kitchen door stood wide open, and three paparazzi holding high-powered cameras were firing them at rapid speed.

"Oh, crikey," James muttered, shaking out his hand. "I'm too old for this shit."

Cash yanked his phone from his pocket and thumbed the application for a ride-share service. "I'm getting us a car. We need to get out of here." He grabbed James's elbow and pointed him toward the end of the alley.

"I have a car," James said, huffing as he hurried to keep up with the quick pace Cash set.

"Hey, now, wait up," Roger called after them. Cash saw the other man hustling after them, his jaw cradled in his palm and his steps slightly wobbly. "You can't leave me here."

"Bet me I can't," Cash muttered.

Beside him, James chuckled and pulled out his own phone. He opened the message screen and thumbed three keys. He dropped his mobile back into the inside pocket of his tuxedo jacket and jerked his head toward the end of the alley. "I've signaled the SOS. We're going to have to get around to the front of the building." He glared at Roger. "If you want a ride, you better hurry."

On foot, the three men took the same sharp right Wydetta had and limped off in the same general direction.

"There," Wydetta said with a satisfied nod. She jammed a few more computer keys, then thrust her fist into the air triumphantly. "The access code is changed."

Brit leaned over the back of her mother's leather desk chair and stared at the oversized monitors. One screen was divided into sections showing live footage from video cameras installed in strategic spots around the property. The other was filled with what appeared to be complicated code. Computer code. And her mother, the woman who liked to pretend she couldn't work her mobile phone so she didn't have to return texts and calls, had typed line after line into the script like she'd done it thousands of times.

"Do you redo the code thingy a lot?"

Wydetta glanced up at her, her expression one of smug pride. "What? Oh, on occasion," she replied. "Don't worry, I wouldn't compromise the system if I didn't know what I was doing."

Brit straightened. "I'm not worried." Wydetta swung the chair around to face her. "The computer stuff is impressive," she admitted. "When you said you'd reprogram the alarm code, I figured you meant punching in a new number."

"I did." Wydetta gestured to the keyboard with an elegantly manicured hand.

"You did more than punch in new numbers," Brit replied.

Her mother arched perfectly shaped brows. "Well, it's a complicated system."

Crossing her arms over her chest, Brit rocked back on her heels and stared at her mother in open admiration. "You are a complicated woman, Wydetta Owens."

Wydetta smiled. "And don't you forget it."

Brit glanced down at her sparkly dress and strappy shoes. "I want to go change, but I dread peeling all this double-sided tape off."

Her mother winced sympathetically. "I can help you."

After a beat of consideration, Brit dropped into one of the guest chairs across on the other side of the desk. "In a while."

As she bent down to free her feet from the torturous shoes, she replayed the events of the last hour in her head. Well, the last hour. She didn't want to think about Dylan and Roger yet. It hurt too much. Instead, she focused on the *Thelma and Louise*-like escape she and her mother had made as she kicked free of the sandals. Okay, so they hadn't gone off cackling and kicking up dust as they zoomed across dirt roads, but there'd been some semi-hysterical laughter. And a couple of shared looks. They had to count for something, right?

"So," Brit began as she slumped back in the chair once more, rubbing the aching soles of her bare feet on the smooth pile of the rug. "Interesting night."

"Illuminating," Wydetta agreed as she toed off her shoes as well.

"I can't believe Dylan thought I'd mess up his album release. It's not like I control the world. How could I have messed things up for him?"

"The record company is just rescheduling the release. He's not thinking straight right now." Wydetta huffed. "But you know he's always been jealous of your success. That's not on you, it's on him," she stated firmly.

Brit studied her mother. The light from the desk lamps set the sequins sewn onto her dress and threaded through her hair a-sparkle. She tipped her head to the side, admiring the glow of Wydetta's skin in the soft lamplight.

"You look really pretty tonight, Mama," she said quietly. They'd never been a family given to excessive praise, so even the simplest compliment seemed monumental.

The surprise, then the near-blushing pleasure that suffused Wydetta's face and struck Brit like a slap upside her head. Her mother had always been careful in doling out the praise because she wanted Brit to remain grounded even in the midst of all the hoopla around her. She'd said so time and again. But it never occurred to her no one ever complimented her mother. At least, she hadn't. And she'd wager money neither Merle nor Marie had seen any reason to. Wydetta wasn't the daughter they'd wanted, and they'd made their disappointment abundantly clear over the years.

Wydetta may not have been the warmest mother in the world, but Brit knew she hadn't been the most devoted daughter, either. She vowed then and there to change the pattern. After all, what she'd said earlier was true. She needed her mama. And she wanted her as well.

Her own cheeks flaming with shame and embarrassment, she flashed a tremulous smile and repeated, "Really pretty."

"Thank you," her mother replied in a raspy whisper. "You look real pretty too. And you sang so beautifully."

To Brit's dismay, she thought she saw the shimmer of unshed tears in her mother's eyes. "Thank you," she whispered back.

One of those tears must have made a break for it, because Wydetta lifted her hand and swiveled her chair to the side as she brushed a knuckle under her lashes. The sight of her mother getting emotional raised a lump in Brit's throat.

"We haven't been very nice to each other lately," she commented hoarsely.

"No." Wydetta sniffled softly. "I guess not."

"I'm sorry."

The simple apology seemed to do the trick. Her mother straightened her shoulders and nodded once. "Yes. I'm sorry too."

"I want to change it," Brit said, the words escaping before the thought was fully formed. "This. You and me."

Wydetta stared back at her, her eyes wide and wary. "Change what about you and me?"

Brit shrugged. "Change how we are with each other. Have a more… adult relationship. Friendly," she said, tossing the word out as if it were a live grenade.

Wydetta gave her a sad, lopsided smile. "But we aren't friends."

"I'd like us to be," she answered quickly, cutting off any chance Wydetta had of attaching other labels to their relationship. "Lunch was nice."

"It was nice," Wydetta agreed.

Feeling brave, Brit pressed on. "I'd like us to be able to talk—really talk—about things."

The wariness came back into Wydetta's eyes. "What things?"

"I'm in love with Cash. He loves me too. We're aware of the age gap, but it doesn't matter to us. I would like you to respect my relationship," she said, ending with a decisive nod.

"I *have* been respecting your relationship," Wydetta pointed out. "I haven't interfered with you seeing Cash."

"But you don't approve."

"Do you need my approval?" Wydetta asked, and she seemed honestly bewildered by the notion.

"Need it?" Brit pursed her lips as if giving the idea deep thought. "No, but I'd like to have it."

Wydetta nodded thoughtfully. "Yes, well, it's not like you aren't aware of his past issues, or any of the other shenanigans," she said with a dismissive wave of her hand.

"I forgive you for making a play for him," Brit interjected with a cheeky grin.

Her mother huffed. "Honey, if I really wanted to make a play for him, I would have expended more effort."

"I know." Brit's smile widened. "Thanks for your lack of effort."

This time, Wydetta grinned back, her eyes twinkling with amusement. "You're welcome." The amusement faded as quickly as it appeared. "But I do want you to always be sure to do what's right for you first. People with addiction issues—and this is nothing against Cash in particular—but addicts, they know how to manipulate people and situations. Be careful. There. I won't say any more."

"I will, Mama. I am."

Wydetta nodded, then glanced over at the credenza where she kept a small stock of alcohol for guests or shaky clients. Drawing a deep breath, she moved to the cabinet, opened a door beneath the tray of sparkling crystal decanters, and pulled out what looked to be a quart canning jar.

Holding it up, she offered it to Brit. "But there's nothing saying we can't have a drink, is there? Because I sure could use one. Bet you could too. I swiped some hooch last time we were at Merle and Marie's place. What do you say we have a sip?"

"Wydetta, love, the code isn't working," James said into his cell phone rather than the speaker at the gate. His driver, Sherman, had tried repeatedly but received no answer to his calls. "Buzz us in, will you, darling?"

James glanced over at Cash as he ended the call. His driver wisely kept his gaze straight ahead, giving no indication he knew anything about his employer being locked out of his lover's estate.

Cash shifted uncomfortably. "I get the feeling we're not welcome."

A crackle of static broke from the speaker, and James held up a hand to ward off any objections Cash may have been ready to make.

A female voice came through the intercom. "Welcome to Burger Palace. May I take your order?"

James reared back from the speaker, plainly confused. Cash only smiled. He knew only one woman so fluent in smartassery. He nodded to the speaker encouragingly. "Order a number one, with a side of superstar," he instructed James. James looked at him as if he'd gone off his rocker, but Cash simply pointed to the speaker. "Do it."

Leaning out the open window, James spoke into the tiny speaker in crisp, precise, British-accented English. "I say, yes, we'd like to have a number one combination meal, with a side order of…" He glanced over at Cash who mouthed the word to him. "Superstar," James enunciated with relish.

Delighted laughter erupted from the speaker. James looked at Cash questioningly. "Are they smashed?"

Cash only shrugged. "No idea."

Cash knew from experience there was no moving the Owens women when they were dead set on a course of action, but it was one of those life lessons a man had to learn for himself.

But Sir James wasn't in any mood for games. Cash almost felt sorry for him as he spoke into the speaker, his jaw set with determination.

"Wydetta—"

Though he spoke her name with crisp authority, his accent made it sounds like he'd hung an 'er' on the end of her name. His pronunciation only resulted in another round of feminine laughter. James was about to open his mouth again when Cash put a hand on his arm to stop him.

"Let them get it out," he advised.

"Get it out? Get what out?" James asked, exasperated. "They're acting like children."

The intercom must've been open because Wydetta and Brittany only laughed harder.

"Get it out! Get it out!" Brittany chortled. "Oh, that sounded dirty!"

"For God's sake, Brit," Wydetta said in a rush. "Please don't say things sound dirty. I'm still your mother."

Brittany laughed again, full and throaty. "Sorry, Mama," she cooed dutifully.

But Brit wasn't the least bit remorseful, Cash knew by her tone. If she were in the mood, this could go on for quite a while.

James rubbed a hand over his face. "Wydetta, darling, it's been a very long evening and I'm knackered. Would you please unlatch the gates so we can come in?"

"Pip! Pip! Sir Superstar is knackered," Brit mocked in a high-pitched British accent. "Do be so kind as to—"

"Okay, enough," Wydetta said, cutting her off. There were some indistinct mutterings, then the speaker cut out. The two men in the backseat were left staring at the tiny black box, awaiting some kind of verdict.

The chauffeur kept his eyes trained on the gate. Cash marveled at the man's self-restraint. He would've been gazing into the rearview mirror watching it all unfold and waiting to catch reactions if he'd been the one behind the wheel. This man was a pro, through and through. Unlike Roger, who they'd dumped at the end of Merle's driveway with a warning to get his partner in crime in line, because the Owens women were sure to be coming for them.

Tearing his gaze away from the windshield, he said, "You need to give your driver a raise."

James glanced at the man in the front seat, then back at Cash. "You're likely right." He clapped a hand on the open divider between the driver's seat and the rear and leaned forward. "Would you check around for an available hotel room for me please, Sherman?"

"Yes, sir," Sherman replied, his diction every bit as precise as his employer's.

Cash cocked his head. "Giving up so easily? You know these ladies like to fight."

"I'm afraid I've had enough conflict for one night." James's mouth curled into a rueful smile. "Tomorrow morning will be soon enough for me and Wydetta to work things out."

"You're a strong man," Cash said admiringly. "Brave, even. Still, I think we'd do better if we can get a bit of groveling in. We want them to know we made an effort."

"May not be a bad idea." James leaned out the window and pressed the intercom buzzer again. He gestured for Cash to take over. "Have at it, mate."

An endless minute ticked by, then the speaker crackled to life again. "I'm sorry, we're fresh out of superstars tonight," Brit said in an overly congenial tone. "And I'm afraid there are no boys allowed in this fortress. Please call again tomorrow. Good night, and thank you for stopping by the Owens Oasis."

The speaker cut out and the two men in the backseat heaved heavy sighs.

"Sir, there's a king suite available at the Newcomb," Sherman announced from the front. "Shall I book it?"

Cash lifted a shoulder and let it fall. "I have a guest room at my house, but it isn't anywhere near as swanky as the Newcomb."

James smiled at him, then reached over and clapped a hand on the same shoulder. "You are a mate, but I think it's best I go to a hotel tonight." He pulled a face. "Need to regroup and think about how I'm going to storm this castle tomorrow." He tapped on the lowered partition. "Go ahead and book the room, Sherman, and then let's drop Mr. Dorsett at home."

"I can get a car from here," Cash assured him.

But James waved his protests away. "No, no. I'm making sure all the major players are tucked up tonight. I don't want to miss seeing how this all plays out."

22

Brit awoke groggy and disoriented the next morning. It felt like her skin was being pulled in every direction. Her head thrummed like a stand-up bass. Wetting parched lips, she squeezed her eyes shut, then attempted the waking up thing again.

It didn't go much better the second time.

Blinding white light bisected the room and spotlighted the sofa where she'd slept. She raised one hand, instinctively shading her eyes. Pressing herself into a mostly upright position, she whispered, "Don't go into the light, don't go into the light" under her breath until she felt her equilibrium catching up.

She blinked once and focused on a large dark square looming on the other side of the room. Two more blinks, and she deduced the shape was a desk. A big desk. Wydetta's desk. She'd slept in her mother's office.

No sooner had the thought registered than the door flew open. "Good morning!" Martine sang out as she swung into the room bearing a tray filled with rattling china.

"Oh, God," Brit moaned, massaging her temple. "Take it down a few thousand decibels, please."

Wydetta followed close on Martine's trail, looking fresh and bright-eyed in casual leggings and a tunic top. "She never could handle her corn whiskey," she commented, shooting a superior smirk at Brit.

Martine shuddered when Brittany did. "Ugh. I never could either. How you can drink rotgut, I will never know." Martine set the tray on the desk with a clatter.

Brit yelped and dove for the sofa cushion she'd used as a pillow. "God, stop," she groaned.

"She had a half a glass," Wydetta said in an exaggerated whisper. "It's not like she downed the entire bottle."

"It was in a jar." Pulling her knees up, Brit pressed her throbbing temple into the cushion and lifted her butt into the air. For some reason, the change in position helped.

"All the best hooch comes in a jar," Wydetta answered.

Brit let out a squawk and popped straight up when her mother's hand connected with her bottom. She looked down and found she was still wearing the sequin-studded minidress.

"You were showin' your ass, sugar," Wydetta said with a saucy smile.

But there was no teasing light in her mother's eyes, Brit realized as she reached back and yanked the hem of the dress down. That, of course, made the bodice pull on her boobs, and Brit flopped over onto her bottom with a groan of frustration.

"Oh, man. Why did you let me sleep in this dress?" she whined, plucking at the fabric clinging to her like a second skin.

"We tried to get it off you—" her mother began.

"You bit her," Martine said with a nod toward Wydetta.

"I did?"

Her mother nodded and held out her hand. It was still perfectly manicured. Each nail even and oval-shaped, the polish shiny but not too flashy. She wore no rings. Not long ago, Grandma Marie had told Wydetta she was past the age a woman ought to draw attention to her hands. Wydetta, of course, had silently taken her mother's criticism as gospel. And knowing she did broke Brit's heart.

Taking her mother's hand in hers, she inspected it closely. Yes, she had some veins and more than a few freckles leftover from her suntanning days, but her fingers were still long, slender, and straight. She swallowed hard as she searched for any sign of blemish and came up empty. "Where?" she croaked at last.

"There." Wydetta used her free hand to point to the base of her thumb. "Didn't break the skin."

Brit pressed her lips to the spot, then lowered her gaze as Wydetta's fingers curled around hers. "I'm sorry, Mama," she whispered.

Wydetta smiled down at her, and this time, something thawed in those icy blue eyes. She drew her hand away, hesitated, then placed it on the crown of Brit's head, smoothing her sleep-rumpled hair. "It's okay, baby. No harm done."

No harm done.

The words echoed in Brit's mind as her mother pulled back and headed for the desk. But there had been harm done. Lots of harm. And not only the previous night, but over the past few years. Would they be able to work past it?

Brit wanted to. She wanted things to be like they'd been the previous night. Honest. Open. Fun. She wanted them to have the sort of relationship where they could take care of business, then let off steam together. Did her mother want the same things too?

"You'd better come and eat something," Martine said, interrupting Brit's musings. "I have a feeling we're going to have some visitors very soon." Martine placed a slice of toast on the saucer, picked up a coffee cup, and carried it over to where Brittany sat slumped on the sofa.

"Visitors?" Brit looked up, her gaze shifting from her mother to her cousin and back again. "What kind of visitors?"

Wydetta snorted. "How much do you remember about last night?"

Brit rolled her eyes and found even the small gesture hurt. Hangovers were the worst. What was the point of drinking when it got in the way of one's rebellion?

"Well, obviously I remember everything leading up to the point where my mother had me drink the lighter fluid she keeps in a canning jar."

Martine eyed Wydetta. "I can't believe you tried to poison your own child."

Brit took the coffee and sipped at it tentatively. It was hot and laced with chicory. Normally, Brit didn't like strong coffee, but this morning it was necessary. "Thank you."

Martine shrugged. "I know you don't usually like the chicory, but I thought it might be best. If you can get one down, I'll make you café au lait. It'll set you to rights." She paused. "And eat the toast. You need something in your stomach either way."

Brit closed her eyes and sipped. The last thing she wanted to do was ponder what Martine could have meant with her cryptic 'either way' comment.

"Cash and James came by last night," Wydetta said, nibbling at the crust of a triangle of toast. "I imagine they'll be back fairly early this morning. I have the two things they want most."

Brit took a larger gulp of coffee and allowed herself to sink deeper into the sofa cushion. "What do they want?"

Wydetta laughed. "Well, I imagine Cash wants you, and I'm fairly certain James is going to want his wardrobe back."

"His wardrobe?"

"All of his clothes are here. But we didn't want them here last night, so he had to make do."

Wydetta's offhanded manner did not fool Brit for a minute. She saw the crease between her mother's brows. She sat watching as Wydetta dismantled a piece of toast, nibble and tear by nibble and tear.

"You wouldn't even let the man in to get his clothes?"

Wydetta held up a hand, one finger raised as if the next point she made was critical. "Correction, *you* would not let them in."

Brittany paused to digest the information, then nodded cautiously as she lifted the coffee cup again. "I was pretty sick of guys last night. Might still be."

Martine chuckled as she stirred milk into her own coffee. "I find I have a limited tolerance for them as well."

Brit sighed. "Don't get me wrong, I love Cash, and I can spend days and days with him, but when it comes to Cash mixing with other guys…"

"It turns into a cockfight," Wydetta finished for her.

"Pun intended?" Martine asked with a sly smirk.

"It was testosterone overload last night." Brittany looked up at the two older women. "First Dylan, then Cash, then Roger. I get tired of being treated like I'm helpless. We all know I'm not."

Martine hummed her agreement. "But it makes them feel good to think they're protecting you."

Wydetta scowled. "I don't know when it became our job to make sure all men feel good about themselves."

This time Martine let out an inelegant snort. "Only since the beginning of time." She smirked. "Oh, Brutus, look at the mastodon you slayed for little old me! Aren't you the best and strongest of men? And so clever to be able to bring to me this delightful creature you dragged home by its tusk." She pulled a grimace of distaste and set her own cup aside. "It's like when the cat brings you a bird. You have to praise and admire them and thank them for using their skills for your benefit."

Brittany looked over at her, surprised. "Do we have a cat?"

"You see, this is why relationships don't come naturally for Brit and me," Wydetta said. "We don't even know if we have a cat."

A loud buzzer cut into the conversation. All three heads swiveled toward the foyer, where the intercom system beckoned.

"Oh God." Brittany pressed the heel of her hand to the center of her forehead and rocked back and forth. "It's all coming back to me now. Did I take a fast food order?"

Wydetta laughed, but the sound was brittle. "I'll answer it. I don't think James was too amused with your antics last night."

Brit continued to sip the strong chicory coffee as Wydetta exchange garbled greetings with whoever was at the gate. Moments later, her mother shuffled back in to the office, and Brit realized for the first time Wydetta was barefoot. Had she ever seen her mother hanging around the house barefoot?

"It's James," she announced. Nodding to Martine, she gestured to the door. "Why don't you take Brittany up and help peel her out of her dress?" She shifted her attention to Brit. "You'll feel a hundred times better after you've had a long hot shower and slipped into some comfy clothes." One corner of her mouth kicked up in a wry smile. "It worked for me. Well, a shower, comfy clothes, and about four ibuprofens."

"Mother—" Brit chided.

"Wydetta," Martine admonished at the same time.

"Trust me, if I plan to overdose on anything, it's not going to be ibuprofen." She jerked her chin toward the door, then said, "Go on. James and I have some things to go over, and you need to transform yourself back into a human."

As they left the room, Martine asked, "Hey, what happened to Roger last night?"

Wydetta shrugged. "I have no idea. I guess I'm about to find out if he's still alive. If so, I suppose I'll have to get to the bottom of that mess as well." She heaved a heavy sigh. "Don't trip over the—"

"Oh, crap!" Brit cried.

"Luggage," Wydetta finished.

"Oh, shit! My toe."

Wydetta stepped into the foyer to find Brit hopping around on one foot, glaring at the massive pile of perfectly battered Tumi bags stacked in the foyer. She sucked air between her teeth and exhaled a line of expletives under her breath. "Shit, fuck, shit, shit…"

"Okay, we get the point." Wydetta stepped over to her and grasped Brittany by the elbow.

Brittany stopped hopping and stared at her mother in horror. "I hope it's not broken."

"It's not," Wydetta assured her. "Thankfully, he doesn't have Vuitton traveling trunks."

"I meant my toe." Brit gingerly lowered her foot to the floor. "It's a darn good thing you didn't decide to become a nurse."

"Maybe we can get Martine to make us some tea to go with the sympathy you so desperately need," Wydetta returned.

But the doorbell interrupted their bickering. Both women peered at the eight-paned mahogany door. The first item on their to-do list for the day was waiting.

Brittany glanced down at the luggage. "Are you sure you want to do this?" she asked, raising her gaze to meet Wydetta's once more. "You seem… I mean, lately you've been…"

Wydetta quirked a single brow. "Lately I've been?"

"Happy?"

Her mother was quiet for a beat. "Have I?"

The doorbell rang again, and this time their caller gave the heavy door a few solid thumps with the side of his fist. "I'm really in no mood, Wydetta."

The two women looked at each other, their gazes held for a heartbeat, and then the urge to laugh overtook them.

"Wydetter," Brit mocked. "You really need to buy the man a vowel."

Wydetta smiled. "I kinda like the way he says it."

Sensing her opening, Brit seized her mother by both arms. "Then don't give up the luggage too easily. If he wants to go, there's not much you can do about it, but don't let him know you've packed his bags already."

For the first time in Brittany's memory, Wydetta looked uncertain. And then, she nodded. Looking down at the pile of luggage, she glanced at the double doors to the coat closet beneath the stairs. "Help me hide them?"

"No problem."

Sir James hammered on the door again as Brittany and Martine hurried to help Wydetta stash the bulging duffels and suitcases into the hall closet.

Grasping Martine's hand, Brittany dashed up the stairwell toward her wing of the house. "We'll be right up here if you need us," she called over her shoulder.

"Puh-lease." Rolling her eyes, Wydetta strode to the door. "As if I can't handle one man all on my own."

Wydetta opened the door, and James stalked into the foyer. "I hope you enjoyed your girls' night last night," he said with an imperious wave, "but I didn't appreciate being locked out. Particularly when I had done nothing wrong," he added stiffly, then strode past her into the office.

She stopped inside the threshold, maintaining her silence as a defense against self-incrimination.

Gesturing to the mostly untouched breakfast tray on her desk, James asked, "Do you mind?"

She waved a hand. "Help yourself."

"Thank you." He cast about looking for an unused coffee cup. "Do you have—" Wydetta thrust a cup at him. He peered into the bottom and saw the dregs of coffee residue, then glanced up at her questioningly. "Is there a shortage of crockery?"

"It's mine," she assured him.

James took the cup and saucer from her hand, mainly to stop the rattling, then decided he might as well use it. He didn't like seeing her like this—nervous, uncertain, almost contrite. Those weren't words he associated with Wydetta Owens.

They were words he hoped no one ever associated with her.

Tipping the carafe until it was nearly upside down, he emptied some very, very black coffee into the used cup, then added a generous dollop of cream and two heaping spoonfuls of sugar. He'd spent a long night psyching himself up, rehearsing his lines, planning counter arguments, and plotting possible kidnapping attempts if it came down to drastic actions.

He sincerely hoped the last wasn't necessary. He prided himself on being one of the few of his contemporaries who had never been arrested. How humiliating would it be to have his first time be because he couldn't grovel properly enough to capture a woman's attention?

He took a long draught of the coffee, nearly choking as the stout liquid coursed down his throat. His eyes opened wide with surprise. How could anything he dosed so liberally taste so bitter?

As if reading his mind, Wydetta gestured to the carafe. "It's chicory coffee. A Cajun thing. Martine swears by it for hangovers."

He studied her with interest. "Are you hungover?"

Wydetta nodded. "We had a few drinks last night." When pierced her with a skeptical look, she shrugged. "Okay, one drink, but it was from Daddy's supply of corn whiskey."

James cocked his head, trying to figure out exactly what it was she had told him but coming up empty. "I'm sorry, come again?"

"Moonshine," she clarified. "My daddy's partial to moonshine." She lifted her chin. "And so am I."

"Moonshine," James repeated. "I see."

"It's homemade liq—"

He held up a hand to stop her. "I know what moonshine is. You Yanks didn't invent it, you know."

Wydetta snapped her jaw shut, then averted her gaze. "Anyway, I'm sorry about not letting you in last night. Brittany was... We weren't in the mood for company."

James nodded. "We figured this much."

"What happened after we left?" she asked, bewildered. "I still can't get over how Roger behaved."

"Apparently, he and your father were in cahoots."

"Cahoots?"

"Yes, cahoots," James echoed.

Wydetta raised both hands as if to ward off a blow. "Please stop saying cahoots. It sounds wrong."

"Because it was wrong." James took another sip of the coffee and grimaced as it slid down. "Vile stuff."

"I won't tell Martine you said so."

"The whole business is vile. Your father has some kind of power trip going on."

"Well, that's nothing new," Wydetta said snidely.

"Yes, but this time he and his friend Roger had colluded"—he paused long enough for her to acknowledge he'd chosen a different word—"to attempt to scare young Brittany into staying away from my good friend Cash Dorsett."

"Are you good friends now?" Wydetta smirked. "Talk about your odd couples."

James stood taller. "I'll have you know he is my wingman, and I am his."

"Well, this sounds like an unholy alliance," she commented.

"Yes, unholy indeed. But not me and Cash. It's Merle and Roger who were your troublemakers. Merle started off with the letter, and Roger helped carry out the other mischiefs."

"Like throwing a rock through her window," Wydetta concluded flatly.

"Among other things, apparently."

"What did you do with him?"

"We dropped him at his co-conspirator's place last night, which I think was bloody kind of us, if you ask me." He broke off a corner of a piece of toast and prodded the cold scrambled eggs with the edge of it. "Do you mind?"

"Be my guest," she replied with an amused smile.

James helped himself to a fork off the tray, then shoveled some of the egg onto the toast. "Yes, well, I wanted to speak to you about being your guest." He straightened to his full height, the toast poised to be devoured. "I no longer wish to be your guest."

He watched as the light in her eyes flickered out as surely as if he'd pulled a blackout shade down behind those gorgeous blue irises.

"I assumed as much," Wydetta said with a brief nod. "Your bags are packed and in the hall closet."

She gestured to the foyer with one hand, and his jaw dropped open.

"What do you mean my bags are packed?"

"I packed them for you. Last night." She walked rigidly to the sofa where a cashmere throw lay crumpled into a ball. "I may have been a wee bit drunk," she admitted. She picked up the blanket and began to fold it. "I'm afraid I may not have been as careful with some of your shirts as you might've been."

He tipped his head toward her, uncertain he was hearing correctly. "What do you mean, careful? Did you set them on fire or something?"

"Oh no, no," she said as she tossed the blanket over the arm of the sofa. At last, she faced him, her shoulders back and her chin up. "I meant, I may not have folded them as neatly as you would have. I know you're picky about your shirts."

A warm rush of affection flooded through him as he stared at her. Her blonde hair shone in the morning light peeping through the drawn drapes. She met his gaze squarely, a warrior awaiting the challenge she knew was to come. God, he loved her. And he'd be damned if he'd let her toss him out on his ear.

"I don't want to go," he said flatly, then shoved the toast into his mouth. He refused to beg.

"You said—"

The confusion clouding her face gave him hope. "I said I didn't want to be your guest," he clarified. "I want something more… permanent."

"I… you…" She snapped her jaw shut. "You want what? To move in? Get married? What?"

"Maybe move in," he said with a shrug. "To start," he added. He loaded another piece of toast with the remainder of the eggs. "I'd like us to do some traveling. I wasn't kidding about Rome. I'm meant be picking up some kind of humanitarian thing there next month."

"Brit's tour kicks off the week after next," she reminded him.

He toasted her with the morsel, then popped it into his mouth. "Good. You should have most of the kinks worked out, and then we can go to Italy."

"What if I don't want to go to Italy?"

He chewed. "I think it would be a nice place to start."

"Start what?"

"Start us. No more of this pretending we don't care about one another. It's so tiring, and frankly, I'm not the only one who is too old for these games," he added pointedly.

"Watch yourself," she warned in a low voice.

James laughed and nipped a bit of egg from his thumb. "I think we can negotiate the rest from there."

Wydetta crossed her arms over her chest, then tossed her hair back. "Negotiate, huh?"

For the first time since he arrived, James smiled a genuine smile. "Yes, I thought you might like that." He downed one last swig of the nasty coffee, then set the cup aside. "We'll negotiate. Here, I'll get us started off."

He took a giant step toward her, but she didn't move. Hell, she didn't even flinch. He decided that was a good sign.

Plowing his hand into her hair, he curled his fingers into the silken strands and tipped her head back. She parted her lips in invitation, amusement and arousal burning bright in her blue eyes. He kissed her hard and hot, plunging his tongue into her mouth, reclaiming her.

She only smiled as he drew away, then made a show of touching the corners of her mouth as if his kiss had been sloppy. James was tempted to cheer at her not-so-subtle put-down. This was the ballsy woman he fell for in the blink of an eye. His Wydetta was back, and he couldn't wait to get down to business.

"You and me, Wydetta. I'm proposing a permanent partnership, and I'm willing to give one hundred percent." He peered at her. "Are you in?"

23

Brittany waited until she'd been scrubbed free from the previous night's revelries to call Cash. When he answered, he sounded unconcerned, but she also knew he had a knack for playing it cool.

"How's it going?"

Brit tucked her leg under her and lowered herself onto the edge of her bed. "Oh, you know, it's going. The usual stuff, award shows, double-sided tape, two-faced best friends, and more guitarists than a girl can shake a stick at. Oh! And did I mention the part where a guy who's known me since I was a baby tried to kidnap me?"

Cash's laugh was dry as the desert. "You don't say," he replied mildly. "I hear there's a lot of idiocy going around these days."

"Is there?" Brit settled back onto the bed and gazed up at her ceiling. "I hadn't checked *TMZ* lately."

"You're not on it, if you're worried," Cash assured her. "Apparently, the guy from Aces started punching photographers last night. The media is all up in arms about these bad boy rock 'n' roll people. Good thing they didn't catch James popping Roger in that alley."

"Devil worshippers, one and all." Brit bent her knee, planted her foot on the bed, and propped the opposite ankle over it. Bouncing her foot, she said, "I'm sorry about last night. I had—"

"Enough of the male population?" he finished for her.

"Exactly."

"I get it, and I don't blame you." He paused, considering where to go next. "I tried not to take it too personally, but I can tell you James did."

"He blamed me?"

"He took it personally," Cash clarified.

"Oh. Well, he's here now. Talking to Mama."

Cash gave a short laugh. "It's so strange to hear you call Wydetta 'Mama.' I don't think you have the entire time I've known you, and you were a kid when we met."

"Yeah, well, last night she felt more like a mama than my manager."

"Good. I think you need a mama sometimes."

She bristled. "I'm not a child. And I don't go running off to my mommy every time something goes wrong, so don't try to make it sound like I do."

"I wasn't," Cash replied quickly. "And I wasn't trying to imply anything. It was nice you and your mom could be there for each other last night. You both had some big disappointments, and it was good for both of you to be able to step in for each other."

Brit took a deep breath, then touched the tip of her tongue to the center of her upper lip to keep from tearing up as she stared at the ceiling. "I'm sorry," she said at last. "I might be sensitive about her."

Cash barked a laugh. "You think?"

Feeling defensive, Brit sat up. "You know why."

"I do," he replied with soothing swiftness. "I know better than most people. And I also know you have more to deal with today. I'm sorry about Roger," he said, his voice rough. "I know he hurt you."

"I'm okay," she rushed to assure him.

"That's not the kind of hurt I meant."

There was silence on the line. Nearly a full minute passed. With a jolt, Brit realized she was supposed to be the one to fill it. "Would you..." She paused to swallow the ball of emotion lodged in her throat. "Can you come over?" she asked, her voice scratchy and thin.

She heard Cash exhale. "Baby, I thought you'd never ask."

Brit was pacing the foyer when he rang the buzzer. He only had to mutter "It's Cash" through the intercom to get her to mash on the release button for the gate.

She stood on the front porch, hugging her arms to her as she watched his truck wind its way up the long drive and into the circular in front of the house. As he slowed to a stop in front of the steps, he powered the passenger window down and shouted from the driver seat.

"Somebody call for a taxi?"

Brit smiled. "Some girls dream of white knight on a white horse. All I get is a broken-down guitarist in a dusty black pickup truck."

"You've never been like most girls." Cash put the truck in park and killed the engine. "Still if I was you, I'd be looking for new fairy godmother," he advised, throwing his shoulder against the door to open it.

He came around the cab of the truck, pocketing his keys as he walked. "Is it okay if I leave this here?" He gestured to the truck. "Or should I pull around back or something?"

"Oh, no, leave it there." Brit smiled as she leaned in to peck a kiss to his lips. "It will drive Wydetta crazy."

"I thought you two were thick now."

"We are. Always were," she added with a thoughtful frown. "We forget sometimes."

"I don't want to get any further on her bad side than I already am," Cash began.

"Don't worry about Wydetta's bad side. Stay on my good side and everything will be cool." She slid her hand down his arm and took his in hers, lacing their fingers together as they climbed the steps. "Thanks for coming over."

Cash nodded as they stepped into the shade of the porch. "Thanks for unlocking the gate this time."

Brit's laugh bounced off the walls of the empty foyer as they entered the house, sounding shrill and tense, even to her own ears. She felt Cash lagging and found him pressing on the panels of the dark mahogany front door. He gave the knob a good tug and flicked the deadbolt lock back and forth a couple of times.

"What are you doing?"

Cash stepped back as if he'd been caught with his hand in the cookie jar. "Nothing. Checking things. You know."

"The security team has already been up and at it this morning," Brittany assured him. "Everything's good."

"The security team minus Roger, I hope," Cash said stiffly.

"Minus Roger," she confirmed, though the words felt like bricks on her tongue. "I have no idea where he is."

"We dropped him at Merle's. Figured they could use the time to plot their next move."

She held up both hands. "Ugh. Don't even."

Cash nodded, then shoved his hands in his pockets as if he needed to store them to be sure they wouldn't cause any more trouble. When she hooked his arm and headed for the stairs, he resisted.

Brit looked back at him questioningly. "What's up?"

"Why don't you show me around?" Cash glanced over his shoulder toward the back of the house. "Give me the tour."

"The tour?" Brit sighed. "Cash, you've been here."

"Five years ago," he said with a bitter laugh. "And I don't remember a whole lot about the night of your party. Things are different now." He gave her hand a squeeze. "We're different now. I want to see where you live."

Brittany tilted her head to the side and studied him. Satisfied he was sincere, she squeezed his hand back. "Okay. I'll give you the tour, but you can't be checking for security breaches."

His laugh was sheepish, but he didn't protest. "Deal."

Brit led him through the foyer to the back of the house and into Martine's gorgeous kitchen. Her cousin straightened when they walked in and wiped her hands on the kitchen towel wrapped around her narrow waist.

"Oh, hello, *cher*," she said with a warm smile. Nodding to Cash, she included him in her greeting. "Hello, Cash. It's been a long time."

"Yes, it has." He extended a hand to her, and she took it with both of hers. "How have you been?"

"Oh, you know, I've been busy keeping up with these two," she said in her lilting way. "Otherwise, I find ways to amuse myself."

Brittany snorted. "His name is Mark. You should at least call him by his name. It's only polite."

Martine's smile turned sly as she bent to check the flame under the kettle. "He likes me better when I'm not-so-polite, *cher*."

"Ew, okay, TMI," Brit said, raising a hand to ward off any other insinuations. She pulled Cash toward the terrace doors.

"Don't try to play games with the big girls, Britty. You hear things your delicate ears don't want to hear," Martine called after them. "Nice to see you again, Cash. Don't be a stranger."

"I won't. Nice to see you too," he answered.

His gaze lingered on Martine a bit too long for Brit's liking. She gave his arm a yank, and watched as he stumbled over the threshold and onto the shaded patio.

He scowled as he regained his balance. "That wasn't nice."

"I was only making sure you kept up with the tour," she replied, unruffled by his grumbling. "And this…"—she paused and swept an arm toward the beautifully landscaped terrace—"is the pool."

Cash nodded gravely. "Yes, I see."

Leading him down the wide steps, she gestured to the wild assortment of grasses and flowing shrubs. The profusion of plants made it look as if the black-bottomed pool was nothing more than a pond in the midst of paradise. "These are flowers and stuff," she said offhandedly, but in truth she could name many of the plants edging the pool and patio. She'd spent a lot of time keeping the gardeners company when she wasn't performing. "And over there," she said, pointing to a mound of decorative grass as tall as Cash himself, "is pampas grass."

She smiled sweetly at him. "It wasn't quite as tall then, but I seem to remember being kissed and ditched over by the pampas grass by some pompous ass. I've called it 'pompous' grass ever since. Drives Henry, our head gardener, crazy."

To her surprise, Cash's cheeks went a ruddy red. He wet his lips, then began to speak his piece. "I wasn't good enough for you then. I'm not now, either. But I—"

She clapped a hand over his mouth. "Cut it out." She ground the words out from between clenched teeth. "I don't want to hear any more about what's good for me or not. I'll decide what's good for me. And I choose you. I chose you a long time ago. Loving you was the first decision I ever made for myself, and I don't regret it. I won't let anyone make me regret it."

He grasped her wrist and gently pulled her hand away. "Okay, then I guess it's up to you to decide if I come out on the first leg of this tour, then."

She stared at him, uncomprehending. "What?"

"I was going to say I'm not good for you, but I am a good guitarist, and you seem to be in need of one."

"Come out on tour?" she asked blankly. "I thought…You said you needed to stay away from the spotlight. And if that's what you need, then okay. I'm okay with you hiding yourself away, as long as you aren't hiding from me."

"Never." Looking past her shoulder as if searching for what to say next, he finally gave up with a shrug. "But we need each other. And if what you need is a guitarist for a couple months. I'll be your Neil Giraldo until you get someone permanent lined up."

"Neil Giraldo?"

"Pat Benatar," he said gruffly. "She's been with her guitarist, Neil Giraldo, for forty years."

"Forty years," she whispered.

He nodded, apparently unfazed by her parrot routine. "Married nearly as long too. I'll go with you, but no spotlights on me, Brit. Do you understand? I'll tour with you, but let me stay off to the side. No swanky nights out, no more awards shows—those things are awful. I don't want any extra attention drawn to us. I just want to be with you."

"But…" She blinked rapidly to clear the fog. "You would really come out on tour with me?"

Cash slid a hand around her waist and deepened his drawl as he drew her close. "Lord, girl, there's nothing that I wouldn't do."

"To make you feel my love," she whispered, closing her eyes as she let herself melt into his embrace.

"Exactly."

"I do love you." She breathed the words out in a rush, but she couldn't hold them in anymore.

"I know."

His arrogance made her snort. "Good. I want the world to know it too."

He buried his smile in her hair. "All that matters is we know it."

"But we could be like Faith and Tim," she teased.

"No." He pulled back enough to look her in the eye. "If you love me, you'll want what's best for me. And what I need is to stay in the shadows of your life as much as possible."

"I know, but a girl can dream."

"Not this dream. This is non-negotiable." He fixed her with a penetrating stare. "Do you understand?"

"Yes, of course," she stammered. "But can't—"

"No buts," he chided.

Her forehead puckering, she glared at him. "I was only going to ask why you can't do the whole tour?"

"Because performing is not my life anymore," he said, his voice gentle but firm. "It's not what I want, and I need you to respect my needs. I will respect and support everything you want to do."

She swallowed hard, tears brimming in her eyes, making him swim in and out of focus. "And you love me too," she whispered.

Cash laughed, short but sweet. "Ya think?"

"Say it," she challenged, feeling the first tear slip over the edge and tumble onto her cheek.

He caught the tear with his thumb, then pressed it to his lips. A half-dozen more followed the leader over her lashes as he rubbed his damp thumb over her lips next.

"I love you, Brittany Owens. I love you for you. Forever."

The catch in his voice catapulted her over the edge. "Oh, holy hell," she mumbled, then the dam burst. She clasped a hand to her mouth in a vain attempt the catch the sobs, but it didn't matter. Within seconds, Cash had her caught up hard against him, his hand smoothing her hair, his heart hammering in time with hers.

"Shh. Shh," he crooned into her ear.

"Oh, no," she muttered into the soft cotton of his shirt. "I've waited a heck of a long time for this. You're not going to shush me now."

Cash chuckled, and the vibration ran through her, setting her fingertips and toes abuzz. She let out a howl of happiness so loud it brought Martine scurrying from the kitchen.

"What's wrong?" she cried, stopping short when she spotted them. "Are you okay?"

Peeking around the edge of Cash's shirt, Brit nodded, trying to gather herself enough to reassure her cousin. "I'm fine. Good. Perfect," she yammered, and a fresh wave of wracking sobs caught her up again.

Cash began to laugh in earnest, his arms tightening around her, holding her so close she couldn't have fallen even if she wanted to.

"You don't sound perfect," Martine observed, a smile in her voice.

Brit wiped her wet cheeks on Cash's sleeve. They were his fault, after all. When she looked up, she spotted two more shadowy figures hovering in the doorway. She lifted a hand in a weak wave, and Wydetta stepped onto the terrace with James near at hand.

"What's going on?" her mother asked, a telltale quaver in her voice.

"Nothing. Everything. He loves me. Gonna play guitar," she

managed between hiccups.

Cash cradled her head in his palm. "I told her I'd fill in for Dylan on the first leg of the tour. I also have some suggestions for replacements, if you guys are open to hearing them," he spoke the last looking directly at Wydetta.

Brit's mother took James's hand in hers, then straightened her shoulders. "Yes, we'd be open to hearing them."

Cash nodded, then pressed a kiss to Brit's temple. "Good. I've lined up a bunch of Nashville's finest female guitarists. One of them is bound to suit."

Brit pulled back, laughter bubbling up inside her despite her soggy state. "Female guitarists? I like the sound of that," she mused. "Girl power."

"Good, because if you think I'm sending you out on the road with some guy, you're nuts. I've seen firsthand what you do to guys with guitars. You're worse than a groupie, creeping up to a fella's hotel room, hanging around his recording studio…"

Brit laughed. "You're right. I can't be trusted." She pushed her fingers through his thick hair, her thumb trailing behind to caress the wrinkles fanning from the corner of his eye. "Look what I did to the last guy who let me have my wicked way with him."

The End

ABOUT THE AUTHOR

By day, Margaret Ethridge/Maggie Wells is buried in spreadsheets. At night she pens tales of people tangling the sheets. The product of a charming rogue and a shameless flirt, you only have to scratch the surface of this mild-mannered married lady to find a naughty streak a mile wide.

Find her at:

maggie-wells.com
mkethridge1@gmail.com

Women's Fiction by Margaret Ethridge:

Contentment (Windy City Women #1)
Commitment (Windy City Women #2)
Spring Chickens (Windy City Women #3)

Contemporary Romance by Maggie Wells (High heat!):

Love Games series:
Love Game (Sourcebooks Casablanca)
Playing for Keeps (Sourcebooks Casablanca)
Double Play

Play Dates series:
Play Dates (Kensington/Lyrical Press)
Easy Bake Lovin' (Kensington/Lyrical Press)
A Ring for Rosie (Kensington/Lyrical Press)

Stand Alone titles:
The Last First Date (Harlequin-E)
The Art Lover
Seducing Steve
Long Distance Love
Hot Nights in St. Blaise – The Complete Calendar Collection

Love Letters Anthologies:
Love Letters Volume 1: Obeying Desire (Carina Press)
Love Letters Volume 2: Duty to Please (Carina Press)
Love Letters Volume 3: Wicked Whispers (Carina Press)
Love Letters Volume 4: Travel to Temptation (Carina Press)
Love Letters Volume 5: Exposed (Carina Press)
Love Letters Volume 6: Cowboy's Command (Carina Press)